IN A TOWN CALLED PARADOX

A NOVEL

RICHARD STARKS
AND MIRIAM MURCUTT

Prestwicke Publishing

ISBN: 978-0-9746946-0-3 (print edition)
ISBN: 978-0-9746946-1-0 (ebook)

Prestwicke Publishing
Boulder, CO 80304
303 415 0689

Printed in the United States of America
First printing 2020
Designed by Lorie DeWorken, MindtheMargins.com
Cover design by Damonza

PRAISE FOR OTHER BOOKS BY
RICHARD STARKS AND MIRIAM MURCUTT

Lost in Tibet, published by The Lyons Press, now an imprint of Rowman & Littlefield; translated into five languages, with an option for the film rights sold.

"An entertaining and well-written book..."—*National Geographic Adventure.*

"A well rendered story, with plenty of twists..."—*Kirkus Reviews.*

"Absorbing..."—*Publishers Weekly.*

"The story is marvelous, a page-turner for readers enamored of true-life adventure tales..."—*Climbing magazine.*

"Very well written and an easy read for a rainy day."—*Steve Dietrich, Vine Voice reviewer.*

"The authors tell this engaging tale clearly and skillfully... an incredible story."—*Midwest Book Review.*

"The best book I read this year... This one I will reread."
—*Gisela Hausmann, author and blogger and Goodreads reviewer.*

"Superb... could not put it down... unique and engrossing, with a wealth of detail... Outstanding!"—*The RebeccasReads eZine, which gave Lost in Tibet its 'Best in History' award for 2004.*

"This will keep you reading when you should be asleep."
—*Laurence Murphy, Amazon reviewer.*

"This is a 'must-read'... a true adventure in high and unexplored lands."—*Amanda Daflos, former Director, Special Projects, International Mountain Explorers Connection.*

"A fine story of courage and diplomacy..."—*Booklist.*

"Fascinating..."—*Losang Gyatso, artist and actor in Martin Scorsese's film, Kundun.*

"A well-written and interesting tale... a good story."—*Associated Press.*

"This is a book that will stay in my memory for years to come!" —*Lois G Kemerer, Amazon reviewer.*

"This story drew me in right from the beginning..."—*Tamdin Wangdu, Executive Director, Tibetan Village Project.*

"Well told and easy to read..."—*MyShelf.com.*

"A work of scholarship as well as an excellent read."—*Asian Affairs.*

"Would make a good action film..."—*Daily Camera.*

Along the River that Flows Uphill, published by Haus Publishing, London, England; awarded 'Best of 2009 Non-Fiction' by *January Magazine*.

"Five out of five stars... an unforgettably vivid travelogue." —*Midwest Book Review.*

"What a read! Keeps you turning the pages..."—*Bonnie Neely, Editor, Real Travel Adventures International and Top 1,000 Reviewer on Amazon.com.*

"Wonderfully entertaining... an extremely intelligent book, very well written... a stunning account that's nearly impossible to put down."—*RebeccasReads*

We all shine on, like the moon and the stars and the sun
—JOHN LENNON

There is no death, only a change of worlds
—CHIEF SEATTLE, SUQUAMISH INDIAN

We are all star-stuff
—CARL SAGAN

PART ONE

CHAPTER ONE

Corin Dunbar

I wasn't looking for Marilyn Monroe when I bumped into her, even though I knew she was in town filming *River of No Return* with Robert Mitchum. I wasn't looking for him either—way too old and grumpy—but I did have eyes for bad-boy Rory Calhoun, who played a no-good gambler. I'd seen him in *Adventure Island* when I lived in Yonkers and rated him a real "dish," as we used to say back then.

I'd skipped out of school early and made my way to Main Street, where right away I was swept up in the blast of a Macy's-style parade. The Hollywood people would be around for a few days only, because most of *River* had been filmed elsewhere and was pretty near in the can; but it was the first shoot the town had hosted, so Mayor Carter Williams had pulled out all the stops. Four cheerleaders led the procession, wearing short blue-and-white pinafore dresses and holding aloft a red satin banner that shouted in two-foot-high letters, PARADOX WELCOMES 20th CENTURY FOX.

Next came Leland Jellicoe in his open-top Caddy, with him at the wheel and the mayor beside him, waving like royalty. They were followed by Lula McConackie, our Miss Rodeo Queen, who reined in her skittish chestnut with one hand as she tended to the white Stetson bouncing off her blonde curls with the other. A score of wranglers served as her escort, mounted on noise-spooked cattle-horses. They wore checkered shirts, chaps and spurs, and carried lassoes looped at the ready over the horns of their saddles.

It seemed to me the whole town—and the valley too—had turned out to gawp; or maybe just to snag one of the hot dogs that Gabriela's Bean and Burro was grilling behind a haze of smoke in Pioneer Park. Every lamppost was tagged with colored balloons that bobbed in the breeze like supersized M&Ms. I grabbed one the city clerks were handing out for free, then ducked under a barrier to jog alongside Leland Jellicoe's car. He was a big wheel in town who fancied himself a ladies' man, but behind his back we all called him "Jelly" (for the jiggling belly that protruded from his stick-like frame), and that helped put a pin in his ego.

I reckoned the Juniper Lodge was the best place to spot movie stars, so I fell back and elbowed my way there. The hotel had been bought by Jelly, who'd also purchased the Double-D Diner next door. He'd knocked the two establishments together so movie stars could exit their Juniper rooms and enter the Double-D without the need to step outside. At one time, the Double-D had catered to ranchers who slumped on its shiny metal-stemmed stools, elbows on the Formica counter as they forked down the house special of pecan pie with a curlicue of whipped cream. But Jelly had fitted it out with red leather banquettes and lined the walls with autographed blowups of Alan Ladd, Gregory Peck, and Barbara Stanwyck. He'd gussied up the kitchen too, so in place of the pecan pie, he now served Tournedos Rossini, Tequila Shrimp, and Veal Scaloppini to anyone high enough up the list of credits to be able to pay his prices.

My aunt Jessie had told me to stay away. She feared the "movie crowd," as she called them, would turn Paradox into a Sodom or Gomorrah. "Those people are flashy, immoral, and sinful. And wicked too," she'd added for good measure. That wasn't a view commonly shared in town, but it gained traction in Jessie's mind when she learned that Robert Mitchum was a drinker who'd served time for smoking marijuana and then heard (from the pharmacist in Mason's Drugstore) that Rory Calhoun had once been busted for stealing a gun and while on the run had robbed a string of jewelry stores. When he drove a stolen car across a state line, he was arrested again and sent to jail for three years. None of that affected his budding career, since his criminal past gelled with his on-screen renegade image. But it gave Jessie plenty of ammo to use against actors, producers, directors, and anyone else with even a tenuous Hollywood link.

To me, of course, that made Rory even more appealing. I loitered around the Juniper lobby and peeked into the Double-D, hoping to catch a glimpse. All I could see were anonymous strangers—best boys, technicians, props men, and the like. But as I turned to leave—*boom!*—I bounced off the world's most famous pair of breasts.

Their owner staggered back, and so did I. She was the more winded, since even then, at the age of thirteen, I had the advantage in height. She was much smaller than I would have imagined—no more than five feet five—but then I'd only seen her on the silver screen. There was no doubting who she was, in spite of the dark glasses and the checkered scarf she wore over her bleach-blonde hair. Not with that pout coated in bright red lipstick, the Technicolor makeup, and the cinched-in waist of her dress. I was struck dumb and on the point of running away, when she said, "You okay, honey?"

Her voice was tiny, high, and light as a child's. "It was my fault," she said. "These sunglasses. I swear they see better from your side than they do from mine."

"I'm fine, thanks," I mumbled, my eyes fixed on my feet.

She reached out a manicured hand and used a painted fingernail under my chin to lift my face. "You look so pretty and cute. If I wasn't a natural blonde, I'd like to be dark-haired too. Just like you."

I stood tongue-tied and stiff as a dime-store dummy while she fished around in her sparkly purse and came up with a small golden tube.

"Here you go, honey," she cooed, "a little pressie from Marilyn. It's my favorite shade. *Hot Desire*. And it'll look fabulous against that beautiful pale skin of yours."

She took my hand and dropped the lipstick into my palm, closing my fingers around it.

I was still in shock when I arrived back at the ranch. I didn't stop to say hi to Jessie, but took the stairs two at a time and locked myself in the bathroom. *Hot Desire* was an intense scarlet, deep and lush. I smeared it on, pressed my lips together to cement it in place, then turned my head this way and that in front of the mirror and swished my hair from side to side.

If Marilyn Monroe said I was pretty and cute with beautiful pale skin, then maybe I was. I leaned in and blew a kiss at my reflection.

Even now, more than fifty years on, I remember that moment as a turning point.

It was the first time I felt pleased with the way I looked.

In those days, I still saw myself as a city girl who belonged in Yonkers, a quick train-ride north of New York City. That's where I was born and where I grew up. I liked tall buildings and the feel of concrete under my feet. I had friends and a life that centered around ballet classes (where I made my arms move boneless and rubbery as tentacles) and the Bronx Zoo, where my father worked as a veterinarian.

Gene cared for lions, hippos, elephants, and giraffes; and most days when I wasn't at school, he'd grab my hand and say, "Come on, kiddo, join me on my ward rounds." And together we'd stomp from cage to cage, sloshing through disinfectant in our squelchy rubber boots as we checked the animals for parasites, stomach bugs, eye infections, and rotting teeth. Once I put my hands inside a chimpanzee's mouth to help him finish off a root canal. Another time he let me hold the syringe pole he used to inject a sickly viper. And I'll never forget the day he took me to watch Daru, an Indian elephant, give birth to a two-hundred-pound calf that slid onto the floor of its cage in a deluge of blood and guck.

I felt a wave of panic when the calf refused to breathe. I begged Gene to intervene, but he backed off to let Daru prod her baby with a foot big as a tree stump, then use her trunk to yank her offspring free from the shroud of its amniotic sack. At which point the newborn raised its head and peered around, and not for the first time, I fell in love. We watched the baby stand splay-legged on the slime of its cage before Gene and I gave each other a hug of relief.

No one I knew shared experiences like that. My friends were palmed off with stuffed lions or *Jungle Book* cutouts, but I had the real thing—plus Gene's full attention. I didn't want to eat or sleep; I just wanted to be at the zoo with him. It was our world and I treasured every moment. I learned rhinos like to be scratched behind the ears; giraffes hate to be touched but will happily eat out of your hand; and lions enjoy having their manes stroked and combed.

"But only *some* of them do," Gene told me, with a wag of his finger, "so don't try this at home."

The hardest part of his job, he said, was trying to establish when an animal was sick. "It's not in their nature to show even a whisper of weakness in the wild," he said, "because if they do, they know they're as good as dead."

That was a lesson I've carried all my life: Don't show when you are hurting.

I spent as much time as I could with Gene, but it was Grace, my mother, who did the heavy lifting of bringing me up. She was the one who slipped laundered underwear into my chest of drawers, clean socks onto my feet, and a daily apple into my Snow White lunch-box. She walked me to school, supervised my homework, and made sure I arrived at my dance class with the full complement of leotards, leg warmers, and pink satin pointe shoes. She adored children, even I could see that, so I could not understand why she failed to produce a baby brother or sister for me to play with. There was just the three of us—Gene, Grace, and me—and sometimes only two when Gene was called away to work his magic at another zoo. When that happened, Grace spoiled me sick with hot chocolate floated with marshmallows; or she took me out for a grown-up evening at the movies; or she played the piano while we sang "Somewhere Over the Rainbow" or "How Much Is That Doggie in the Window?"

I was devastated when she died.

Just thirty-eight years old.

She'd been sick for months, the energy sucked right out of her; but death is not something a child anticipates. I'd assumed she would recover and the life I knew would go on as before. I was banned from her bedroom, but the more I was told to stay away, the more curious I was to peek in. And one day I did.

Grace was lost in a restless sleep, her mouth gaped open, her head raking from side to side as if trying to shake away terrifying thoughts. Yellowed strands of saliva stretched between her lips in a dried-up web, like the cat's cradles she'd taught me to make out of string. Her eyes were slits, her lips a purplish blue, and the bare skin of her arms looked cold as winter except for a scattering of button-like bruises left by her injections.

"Mommy," I whispered, "it's me."

I hoped she'd heard, that somewhere behind the blank of her shuttered eyes, she knew I was there; but I was startled when she moved. A cough rattled her body and a rivulet of blood oozed from her mouth, dribbling down her chin. As I moved closer, my shoes nudged against a bottle of dark-gold urine that had been drained out of her through a jungle of tubes to give off a sickly-sweet odor—pungent enough to make me gag. It was a far cry from the crisp, fresh scent of the Grace I remembered, who'd take me in her arms and squeeze me until it almost hurt.

After that, I prayed on my knees every night, pleading with God to make her recover, but she died just two weeks later.

My friends didn't know what to say to me. Some shunned me altogether. But their moms veered the other way. I've never been so cuddled, coddled, hugged, stroked, embraced, patted, or pecked as I was then. They thrust jams and jellies, pies and fairy cakes into my hands as if confectionaries could fill the void Grace had left. All I wanted was for life to return to normal. I knew it wouldn't. But my world collapsed again when a month after Grace's death, Gene told me he was going to send me away.

"You'll be living with your aunt Jessie," he said.

His sister.

A woman I'd never met.

She owned a ranch near a speck of a town called Paradox. Somewhere in red-dirt Utah. I didn't belong *there*.

But Gene didn't ask what *I* thought. Didn't inquire what *I* might want. He just packed me up and put me on a train under the care of a grizzled conductor, and off I went, tossed out like yesterday's paper.

I don't like to recall that day and have tried to purge it from my mind, but I remember staring out of the peephole I wiped in a grimy window as the train trundled west, pulling me further away from everything I knew and loved, toward the terrifying blank that was my future. As the miles rolled by, the rails spooled out like a length of elastic, stretching and stretching until—*snap*, the elastic broke and all ties to my past were severed. I felt worthless as a piece of garbage that needed to be buried before it stank.

Deep down, I knew this was my punishment. Grace's death had been my fault because of the worry I'd caused, the grades I'd failed to get, the time I'd lied about sneaking out to the movies, or the day in Macy's when my best friend Nancy Snyder shoplifted a clutch bag and I made no attempt to stop her.

By the time the doors of a Greyhound bus wheezed open and spat me out into blazing hot Paradox, I had convinced myself that if only I'd prayed harder, behaved better, Grace would still be alive and I'd be home in Yonkers. Instead, I'd been farmed out like an orphan, dumped in unknown territory where I didn't know a soul.

Would anyone—ever again—hold me close and say they loved me?

CHAPTER TWO

Aunt Jessie did her best to welcome me. She'd prepared a room at the back of her jumbled ranch house, a large room with plumped-up pillows on the bed and a red-and-green quilt that she told me had been hand-stitched by one of her friends from church. A bright rag-rug covered a pinewood floor polished to a shine you could see your face in. Two square windows looked out over a pond and red-rock cliffs in the distance, and were hung with cream drapes patterned with flowers.

"Sego lilies," Jessie said. "They're the Utah state flower."

As if I cared.

It was a beautiful room, anyone could see that; and I hated every inch of it. I hated Utah. I hated the ranch. And I hated my aunt Jessie too.

That first day, she said I must be hungry, so could she fix me something to eat?

"No," I told her, although I was starving.

So what would I like to do?

I spat out, "Nothing."

Well, perhaps we could visit the library (Gene must have told her I enjoyed reading), but I turned on her. "No!" I shouted. "I'm *not* going to any stinking library. I *don't* like books. And I *don't* like to damn well read *neither*."

I didn't normally speak like that, and as a rule I never swore. It made me sound like the brat I probably was, but I'd just turned twelve— not a great age to be uprooted and ripped from your home—and had an ache in my heart I can still recall today. I spent the better part of the next two weeks face down on my plumped-up pillows, just hating, until one day, Jessie announced she was heading into town and did I want to tag along. I told her—well, you can guess what I said.

I waited until she'd left, then poked around the kitchen. I scuffed across the dirt to the bunkhouse where, in better days, wranglers had lived. There was no sign of the current hired help—a Mexican called Felipe, who fed and watered the cattle, looked after the dogs, and patched up the fencing—nor of his wife, Dominga. I wandered over to the corral and stroked the horses, pinching my nose against the pungent smell of cow dung that always fouled the air. I even managed a gate-vault over the cattle-pen railings to goose up my spirits, and then I mooched into the barn.

The back wall was mounded with hay, so I furiously took a running jump and crashed face down in a volley of snaps and crackles that raised a cloud of dust, fine as powder. I rolled onto my back and a shimmer of light caught my eye. The severed neck of a broken bottle. It crossed my mind to use the glass to slit my throat, and I even made a few mock passes. But then I drew the jagged edge across my arm to make an angry welt.

I did it again, harder this time. And slower too, so I could see the skin split into a ravine that spewed blood. I watched, fascinated, as it trickled down my arm and dripped onto the hay in ruby-red splotches.

It hurt a lot, but at the same time felt soothing. I was back in control, no longer a pawn to be shuffled around in an adult world. I was in command even if only of my own pain. I chucked the bottle neck away and shrugged out of my blouse, using that to sop up the blood. Then I pulled on my sweater and snuggled into the hay. Next thing I knew, Jessie was leaning over me, a horrified look on her face.

"I tore my arm on a piece of fencing," I told her.

After that, I made several trips to the barn, sometimes with the blade of a pencil sharpener and sometimes with the box-cutter Felipe used to slice off ties from bales of hay. I never cut my arm again as it was too easy for Jessie to spot. But I'd hitch up my dress, roll down my panties, and cut jagged designs into my belly, the scars of which I bear to this day. I knew I shouldn't be hurting myself, but every time

I cut, I felt a surge of relief that dulled the pain of a dead mother and a heartless father who'd cast me aside.

I'm not sure what would have happened if I'd kept on harming myself, but later that summer—the summer of 1954—my world shifted again. Because that's when Hollywood rode into town. And sprinkled our lives with stardust.

It was the mayor of Paradox, Carter Williams, who brought the studios in. He was a shrimpy, balding man with a pencil moustache and sallow cheeks who'd worked as a surveyor for two decades before he was voted into office. Most weekends—and some weekdays too—he could be found on his porch, sitting in his La-Z-Boy with a copy of *The Southeast Utah Gazette* teepee-ed over his head.

The town gossips said his wife, Posie, pushed him into public life since wife-of-the-mayor carried more kudos than wife-of-a-local-surveyor. In contrast to Carter, she was a large-boned woman likened once by the *Gazette* as "a Spanish galleon running before the wind with all sails unfurled." She was bright, forceful, and energetic, and might have made an excellent mayor herself had she not been forced by the prevailing standards to live vicariously through her husband.

Once in office, Carter discovered a taste for power. He'd let Posie sit behind him at town hall meetings and join him on stage whenever speeches were made and she was required to wear a hat; but he made it clear *he* was the one calling the shots. So it was Carter who wooed the studios. He knew other Utah towns—like Kanab and Moab—had pulled in millions of dollars by offering the kind of dramatic scenery Hollywood craved for their backdrops, and had played host to movies like *Stagecoach*, *Fort Apache*, and *Wagon Master*. If they could do it, then Paradox could too.

The wise course of action would have been to test the waters to see if the studios would even consider filming in Paradox. Posie was keen to travel to Hollywood for just that purpose, but Carter had his sights set higher. He was determined to forge ahead and build an entire town—a fake town, a Western town—out in the desert. One that appeared so real, so authentic, the Hollywood studios would *have* to come if they wanted to go on making their blockbuster Westerns.

He hired Rose Watson from the local library to research towns of the 1880s, and appointed Coppley & Son, his former employer, to draw up a site plan. For money, he leaned on Leland Jellicoe, who, at the age of thirty-two, had made a fortune speculating in uranium mine shares on the Salt Lake City stock exchange. Jelly had no interest in sinking money into a fake Western town, but Carter told him that one-third of a movie's budget was typically spent on location, and that brought him partway on board.

He might still have backed out if Posie hadn't shown him photos of voluptuous starlets, spreading their glossies over the mayor's desk. Jelly looked and lingered. He'd recently splurged on an Aztec-red Cadillac Eldorado—a two-door convertible that boasted bumper bullets, wraparound windshield, and power windows—and liked to drive at high speed with the top down even on Utah's primitive roads. The passenger seat, he'd always thought, was all too often empty.

"You think some of these young ladies might come to Paradox?" he asked Posie.

"They would," she said, "if we built them a town. And we built it right."

There's little evidence that Jelly put up much in the way of hard cash, as most of the money to construct the town came from a bond the mayor issued. It plunged Paradox into debt, but the numbers added up if revenue from the studios exceeded the interest on the bond. To make sure it did, Carter prodded Coppley & Son to pull out all the stops. The blueprint they drew up was modeled on the Tombstone set John Ford had constructed in Monument Valley when he shot *My Darling Clementine*.

"But I wanted everything *bigger*," Carter said.

He'd already scouted the ideal location: a five-acre lot that had belonged to Amos Whistler, a grubstaker who'd died intestate the previous year. It was ten miles outside town and, like Paradox itself, on flat ground just beyond the jaws of the twin mesas that enclosed the Waterpocket Valley. It was also adjacent to a railroad track that served the nearby potash mine in Burr Creek. That posed a problem, as filming would have to stop every time a Burr Creek train pulled through; but that negative turned positive when Carter found a railroad track was a "must-have" if Paradox was to lure the big-budget productions. Only they could afford a train. B-movies had to make do with a stagecoach drawn by no more than four horses.

The engine of the train was a Class B-R-R locomotive once owned by the Colorado and Southern Railway. It had an iron plaque affixed to its side that said it had been built by the American Locomotive Company in 1906. That made it the wrong vintage for the 1880s, but it clanked and chuffed and blew out impressive billows of steam. And anyway, as Carter told Posie, no one would care if the train *was* of the wrong era because—

"This is the *movies!*"

Only one issue remained to be settled and that was the name of the fake Western town. Carter favored "Hollywood West," while his wife pushed for "Posieville." The matter was resolved when Carter walked past Jelly's spanking new Cadillac convertible and saw how it gleamed and sparkled and threw off an aura of wealth and extravagance that he was sure would appeal to Hollywood moguls.

It was a no-brainer, he decided.

The new town, like Jelly's Caddy, would henceforth be known as Eldorado.

CHAPTER THREE

I could not understand what anyone in Hollywood could see in Utah, let alone a smudge of a town like Paradox. Growing up in the East, I was accustomed to clouds scudding across my day in weather that changed by the hour, not the constant sear of desert heat that scorched the earth a burner-plate red. In New York, I had treasured the sweet scent of large-petal flowers that blossomed in rainbows of color, not the bone-dry bushes of Utah that picked and scratched at me every time I stepped off a trail. And I'd soon had my fill of Utah dust, which crusted my hair and blocked my nose with scabs of blood-colored muck.

But the Hollywood studios loved it. They loved the way the dirt kicked up from under the boots of their high-riding heroes. They loved the long hours of sunshine that meant they could end each day with "footage in the can." They loved the empty vistas that let them angle in on a scene from a dozen different directions. They even loved the yucca, the prickly pear, and the scrub oak. But most of all, they loved the fiery buttes, the chimney spires and hoodoos, and the slits of canyons that fissured the Waterpocket Valley and cut deep into the surrounding mesas. These were the features that for decades had signaled to moviegoers around the world that here was the real thing—the rootin' tootin', always shootin' Wild American West.

In those early days, Jessie did all she could to make me like the ranch—and Utah. I knew I ought to be grateful, but I still burned from Gene's rejection and had no intention of making her life easy. She took a big step forward when, at the end of that summer, she gave me Popcorn, a chestnut quarter horse that once had been her workhorse but now was semi-retired. As Popcorn and I sized each other up, Jessie showed me how to befriend him.

"Take it slow and easy," she said. "Give him space. Never rush him but let him come to you." An approach, I thought, she was trying with me.

As I'd done so many times at the zoo, I immediately fell in love. And Popcorn fell in love with me. He told me so with every nuzzle and nicker, with ears that pricked up that extra inch whenever he heard my voice, and especially when he rested his head on my shoulder every time I wandered over to pat him and say hello. It meant a lot to me that he did all those things even when I didn't have so much as an apple or a carrot to give him in exchange. He just liked *me*. Gene had always said I was good with animals, and now Popcorn was saying it too. He also told me I wasn't alone. Nor as worthless as I felt.

I'd just started my new school, and most days after class, I'd ride Popcorn across the scrub to watch the carpenters hammer and nail the fake Western town into shape. It was startling to see it rise out of the desert, but when it was finished, I could stroll down the main street—Front, they called it—and make-believe I'd been swept back seventy or eighty years. I'd picture cowboys swinging out of their saddles to tether their mounts to the hitching rails, and swanky ladies gliding along the boardwalks that kept their long-skirted dresses out of the mud.

Most of the buildings were just facades. The haberdashery had strips of lace and bolts of cloth displayed in its window, but when I stepped through the door, I was back in the desert, surrounded by prickly pear and spikes of Mormon tea. Same thing with the apothecary next door. Its windows held jars of blue, green, and yellow liquids that glowed bright as neon. But the building was just an empty shell.

Not so the livery stable or the blacksmith's by the railroad tracks. They were real enough, and so, too, were the general store with its barrels and sacks heaped outside, the hotel, sheriff's office, and the jail. Best of all was the Silver Dollar Saloon with its swinging batwing doors. It was furnished with rickety tables and stick-back chairs where poker-playing actors could sit and cheat and shoot one another under the table. A wooden bar the length of a bowling alley was backed by a mirror set in a glowing mahogany frame carved with bunches of grapes, tall-stemmed flowers, and tiny swooping birds. People said Jelly had paid a bundle to have it shipped in from Chicago. He'd sunk much of his fortune into Paradox, and liked to boast that *he* was the one who'd built Eldorado, all on his own. He fancied himself as a gentleman, always wore expensive suits and tipped his fedora at the ladies. But I just saw him as a potbellied beanpole with greased-down hair that ebbed from his forehead like an outgoing tide.

A lot of the kids from school played in the saloon, drawn by the bottles of liquor—labeled Cactus Wine and Coffin Varnish—that really were filled with tea. I played in the saloon too, but always alone as I didn't have friends. Not then. I was the new girl and the other kids poked fun at me, not just because I was new, but also because I stood out. I was tall for my age and wore skirts and sweaters, not Levi's. Also, I didn't eat meat. I mean, I *ate* meat, but not all the time like the other kids did. I preferred my meat on the hoof as at the zoo, not sliced on a plate or tucked into a bun. I'd pluck carrots and lettuce from Jessie's kitchen garden and take them to school for my lunch, which earned me the nickname Rabbit.

That first term, Everett Talbot, a rat-faced kid in my class, tried to kiss me once in the playground. I'd just turned thirteen and was starting to grow curvy. Boys were beginning to notice and I was noticing a few of them too. But I didn't appreciate Everett shoving his face into mine and trying to lock lips. Jessie had told me never to strike another person, "but if anyone hits you," she said, "be sure to hit 'em back—hard as you possibly can."

Everett and I fell into a tussle. Other kids gathered around, yelling, "Fight! Fight! Fight!" as Everett and I circled each other, jigging from foot to foot like boxers. He closed in and threw a couple of weak punches with his stick-skinny arms. I dodged his fists with the fancy footwork I'd learned at dance class in Yonkers, and when he started to tire, I did as Jessie instructed and swung a haymaker at him hard as I could. It caught him high on the cheek and down he went like a sack

of potatoes. I felt good about that, even though my knuckles hurt and
I knew what I had done was wrong.

Girls weren't supposed to fight. We weren't meant to strike back.
But this one did.

The day after I bumped into Marilyn Monroe, I rode Popcorn over
to Eldorado, but the set was quiet except for a couple of wranglers
digging a fake grave on Boot Hill. I hadn't yet learned that movies are
shot in the mornings when the light is best. There was still heat in the
day, but the sun was slipping toward the horizon and the wranglers
were packing away their picks and shovels. I knew them as the Preston brothers, notorious for once pouring sugar into the gas tank of the
school principal's new Studebaker.

I didn't pay them any mind, because parked next to the cemetery
wall was an ancient flatbed hearse, and spread-eagled over the back
was a girl, not much older than me, with jeans pulled down well south
of her navel. She'd stripped off her T-shirt and lay on her back so her
red lacy bra pointed skyward in twin volcanic cones. Beside her stood
a bottle of Coppertone sun cream that she must have smeared over
her body, because her skin glistened oily as a seal's. I waited until the
wranglers left, then nudged Popcorn toward her.

"Do not disturb," the girl said without moving, when she heard
Popcorn's hooves clip the ground beside her. "You not read the sign?"

"I guess the diggers took it," I said.

"Yeah? Well, that's not all they'd like to take. Did ya see the way
they stared at me?" She lowered the cat's-eye shades she was wearing
and peered at me over the frames. That's when I recognized Dorothy
Wittering, the gum-chewing, hip swiveling, self-styled president of the
in-crowd at school. A juvenile delinquent, Jessie called her—a view
shared by most of the adults in town. I'd seen her around, usually the
focus of a noisy throng, but I'd never seen her half naked. Nor with the
sassy ponytail she'd rigged up and tied with a spotted bandana.

"Well, well, well," she said, "if it's not Rabbit. What brings you and the hay-burner over this way?"

"It's Corin," I said. "Corin Dunbar. Not Rabbit. Okay?"

"So the Rabbit talks," she said, and lay back over the hearse again. "The hay-burner talk too?"

"*His* name is Popcorn," I said. "And he's not a hay-burner. He's a quarter horse."

She propped herself up on one elbow and removed her shades to bat a sooty sweep of eyelashes at me. She also blew Popcorn a kiss.

"Quite the little wonder horse, is he?" she said, swinging her legs around to sit up and face me. She had a fake mole penciled on one cheek, a cocoa brown dot just to the right of her mouth. "I saw you KO Everett Talbot. He's a skinny little kiss-up, but you fight him again, you feint a blow to his snout. Then when he raises his hands, you go in low and kick him in his Squirrel Nutkins. That's the way to fight boys. But you did okay," she added. "You hit him good."

"Thank you," I said.

"You got a cigarette?" she asked.

I shook my head.

"I met Marilyn," I said, blurting it out. I was still pumped by the thrill and was dying to tell someone.

"Yeah? Marilyn who?"

"Why, Monroe, of course. Is there any other?"

Dorothy reared her head back as if I had punched her on the nose, then jumped down from the hearse, clutching her jeans and forcing Popcorn to shuffle several steps to the side.

"You met Marilyn *Monroe*?"

"At the Double-D," I said. "She's only here a day or two, shooting a scene with Robert Mitchum. She gave me this," I said, and held out the *Hot Desire*.

"Oh, wow! Can I see?"

I slid off Popcorn as Dorothy cradled the lipstick in one hand, the other cupped beneath it. She stared at it dumbly, her mouth opened wide as if she'd been given a diamond ring.

"I cannot believe you met Marilyn Monroe," she said, shaking her head. "You have to tell me *exactly* what happened."

I reached up to stroke Popcorn and leaned casually back against his shoulder. "She was small," I said. "And friendly. We chatted a while and she called me 'honey.' Marilyn's much prettier in real life than she is on the screen," I added, using her first name as if we'd been friends for life. "And she smelled nice too. Like flowers after rain. She said *Hot Desire* was my color because it suited my skin. My beautiful pale skin."

"Oh, wow!" Dorothy said again. "Oh, wow, oh, wow, oh, wow!" She carefully handed the lipstick back. "I'd give ten years of my life to meet Marilyn Monroe. See if some of that sexy sparkle would rub off on me."

She buttoned her jeans, then reached into her lacy bra to take a sizeable wodge of Kleenex out of each cup.

"What?" she said, when she caught me staring. "You don't think I need bigger boobs? *Every* girl needs bigger boobs. Look at Jayne Mansfield. Jane Russell. Marilyn too. Which reminds me. Have those gravediggers really gone? They were giving me a hard time."

"Well, what d'you expect, lying around half naked?"

"They loved it," she said. "But show's over once the audience's left."

"You *wanted* them to look?"

"Sure. Why not?"

"But the *Preston* brothers?"

She gave a dismissive wave of her hand as she wriggled into her T-shirt.

"They'll be jacking off tonight with a vision of me dancing in their heads. Don't worry," she added, when she saw the look of horror on my face, "they know I'm underage. They can't come near me. Only look-ee, no touch-ee. It's a tease. Just like the movies."

She pulled a powder compact out of her jeans pocket.

"I can't believe you met Marilyn Monroe," she said again, fussing with her hair in the mirror. "You can call me Dottie," she added. "All my friends do."

"And you can call me Corin."

"Okay. Corin it is."

No one ever called me Rabbit again.

CHAPTER FOUR

I first set eyes on Cal Parker about a month later. With his beach blond hair and Utah tan, he'd have put a race into any teenage girl's heart, so it was a measure of how isolated I was that I hadn't noticed him before.

I still thought of myself as an orphan, especially since I'd not heard a word from Gene. I quizzed Jessie about him and why he'd tossed me out, but all she'd say was "I'm sure it was for your own good"—a phrase, I'd come to realize, that was used by adults when they wanted to sidestep the truth. After a while, I stopped asking. I discovered, too, there's a limit to how long you can cry into a pillow, so I made a conscious decision that I was finished with self-pity and tears.

At the time, I was locked in a fight with Jessie over her plans to turn me into a practicing Christian like her. I wasn't about to follow God—not after he'd let Grace die and allowed Gene to toss me out. I played along with Jessie at first because I didn't want to be kicked out again, but I was determined not to let her win. I wasn't being ornery. I just knew that if I wanted to function in my new life, I either had to hide under a shell or develop a steely spine. And I'd gone for the backbone. I made a point of standing taller, looking people in the eye, and if any sympathy came my way, I'd send it scudding straight back.

Every Sunday morning, Jessie tried to soften me up by cooking me pancakes ringed with sliced banana and letting me wear my back-East skirts and blouses if I joined her in church. She'd earned a family pew in the Roman Catholic Church of the Immaculate Conception, two rows back from the altar, and after leading me down the creaky boards of the aisle, she'd stop to genuflect and cross herself, while I stood with my arms folded. We'd shuffle sideways into her pew and stand shoulder to shoulder, sharing a hymnal as Jessie ran a finger under each line as if teaching me to read. I refused to sing most of the hymns, but I liked to belt out every syllable of "All Things Bright and Beautiful." Except for the word *God*.

Jessie would worry the rosary in her lap and sit enthralled as she listened to Father Thomas, hunched over his lectern as he droned a lesson from the Bible. I'd look around at the plaster walls hung with images of Jesus nailed to his cross or staggering under its weight. Where was the joy in that? I wondered. What was the cause for celebration?

I did find hope in some of Father Thomas' teachings, especially when he spoke of Heaven and the eternal nature of life. I needed to believe that Grace was still *somewhere*, she hadn't just disappeared. But the blunt truth was I couldn't wait to get out of the church and into the warmth of the sun and a clear blue sky. I didn't want to be stuck in a pew with old people praying to a God who seemed as deaf as they were.

Jessie was hurt when I announced one day that I would not be going to church again, but wisely she backed off and gave me room. She knew I was still an angry mix of pain and resentment, which made me up for any fight. She knew, too, we hadn't yet settled our ongoing tussle over my budding friendship with Dottie, and like me she figured one fight at a time was enough.

Dottie had been sure—from the age of twelve—that she was destined to be the next Grace Kelly, Kim Novak, and Natalie Wood all rolled into one. In the meantime, she had cast herself as the school delinquent, the one who stuck bubble gum under the legs of the teacher's chair, spray-painted obscenities onto the blackboard, or walked out of class saying the lessons bored her. Jessie may not have liked it, but Dottie's friendship meant a lot to me. It satisfied my need for acceptance and helped me mold a brand of fearlessness all of my own. My ties to Dottie stamped *me* as a rebel too—an artifice I could carry off because of my height. Big meant bold, which helped toughen me up, because if other kids thought I was strong, then I had to *be* strong. I couldn't curl up with a whimper every time life threw me a curveball.

That day I set eyes on Cal Parker, I'd gone with Dottie to Eldorado to watch the filming of *Taza, Son of Cochise*, starring Rock Hudson. He was one of the most popular actors in the world, and was in all the movie magazines. Sets then were wide open, so even though we were kids, we had the run of the place—as long as we stayed behind the ropes and kept quiet during rehearsals and when the cameras started to roll. Filming attracted scores of gawkers—many from the nearby town of Blanding—as well as members of the Hollywood press who were eager to chase down every snippet of gossip.

Dottie and I had snuck away early from school that day, swigged from a bottle of whiskey she'd lifted from home, and taken several deep puffs from a Camel. I felt sick and light-headed, which is probably why I don't recall much about the filming. But I do know that Cal Parker had been hired to portray a rancher, his first time in front of the cameras. He was eighteen then—five years older than me—so from my perspective he was all wide shoulders and swagger hips. He didn't notice me, but he may have turned his dark green eyes toward Dottie. She was chasing a part in the movie too, and had gussied herself up in a tight red sweater from which her breasts—mostly Sunbeam dinner rolls stuffed into her bra—poked out like the bumper bullets on Jelly's Caddy.

Cal was costumed in baggy pants and an unlikely shirt that was fresh and white as new-fallen snow. He didn't have any lines. He just needed to crouch behind a wagon and jump up when directed and be shot in the chest. On cue, the front of his pristine shirt exploded with blood and Cal staggered back. He was shot a second time and more blood poured out of him in a gusher. Dottie told me the fake blood was squirted out of liquid-filled condoms that were taped to Cal's body and set to detonate at just the right moment.

Back then, I didn't know what a condom was, and certainly I'd never seen one. No one talked about sex, so it was Dottie who showed me how they were used. She brought one into school, locked us in the washroom, and whipped out a corn-on-the-cob she'd pilfered from Father Thomas' garden.

"Now, there's someone *else* who doesn't know what rubbers are for," she said.

She shucked off the leaves and most of the silks. "Now pay attention," she said. "This could be important one day."

She showed me the packet first, square and small, with "Trojan Naturalamb Rolled Lubricated Skin" printed on one side.

"Where'd you get it?" I asked. I kept my hands clasped behind my back as if just touching it might get me pregnant.

"Doctor Feelgood sells them at Mason's. He keeps them hidden in a wooden cabinet. But he won't sell them to kids, and he won't sell them to women. I had to score this one from a makeup girl on set who'd had her feller buy her some so she'd always be ready."

I expected the condom to be long and lank, flabby like an unblown balloon, but it was a tight and tiny ring of rubber. Dottie held her corn cob at the appropriate angle. "Show and tell time," she said, easing the condom over its shaft. "You have to do it slow and easy. You don't want a puncture. Sperm can find their way blindfolded, so it's easy to get knocked up. And remember, it'll likely be dark the first time you use one, so you have to go by feel."

She held up the cob to show me the bubble of rubber at the tip of the condom. "That's where the sperm goes. You don't want it getting inside you."

I felt queasy just at the thought of a man's sperm squiggling inside me like tadpoles in a pond.

"And don't believe a man who says he'll pull out," Dottie said, "because he won't. He might *say* he will, but once the sweet talking's done, he'll want to shoot his load any which way he can. You have to tell him, 'Slip it on before you slip it in.'"

I wondered what it would be like.

And what it would be like with Cal Parker.

CHAPTER FIVE

When I first arrived in Paradox, I'd sometimes sit on the steps of the ranch house and rack my brain to find one thing I liked about Utah. But three years on, I found I was spoiled for choice. It wasn't just Eldorado and the movie people who came to film there. They made me feel I was growing up in Hollywood and not in a rural backwater. But I'd also come to love the state. I reveled in the crisp mornings when the sun spread warmth into the valley, the cool shade of the rust-red canyons, the quiet evenings when I'd stretch out on a rock and watch black-tailed jackrabbits zigzag over the desert, and the rain that would drum down in sudden bursts, tamping the dust and waking up a desert bloom of aster, phlox, and yellow primrose. Brick by brick I was building a new life. No longer a city girl, I was settled in Paradox and called it home. I didn't ever want to leave.

Dottie thought I was crazy. But for the first time, I was scoring grades that made Jessie proud. I wasn't so hot at math (numbers laid traps that I would fall into), but I was good with words, and a few of my teachers were kind enough to praise my judgment. There was even talk of college, although kids from Paradox did not progress much beyond high school—especially if they were mere *girls*. What was the point, when all we were good for was making babies and taking care of a house and a man?

Dottie had taken a different route and dropped out when she turned fifteen. She lied her way into a waitress job at the Double-D. "Resting," she called it, while she plotted her escape by way of the movies. She'd taken to wearing false eyelashes as spikey as toothpicks, colored her hair a metallic blonde with a Miss Clairol home dye kit, and painted her lips a Hot Desire red. She wore wide swing skirts cinched so tight at the waist she could barely breathe, and topped them off with halter-necks that bared more skin than was decent in Utah. The wranglers in the pool hall—where the locals often gathered—would whistle and jeer, say she looked "a fine filly" they'd pay to "break in." But that didn't faze her. If anything, it spurred her on, and she started to wear a Patti Page bullet bra that gave her breasts a "modern missile look."

"No need to stuff these babies with dinner rolls," she told me one evening after she'd finished work. "With this bra, I've got double barrels that are better than any guns on a battleship. Here," she said, "grab a feel. Firm, are they not? You'd never know there was next to nothing hiding inside."

On my sixteenth birthday, Dottie took me along for a casting call in the Silver Dollar saloon. The word "audition" was too grand for these affairs, as the studios hired everyone who bothered to turn up. The movie was *The Dalton Girls*, an unusual Western in that its heroes were all women and all of them bad. I was sent to Costume to be fitted with a vintage gingham dress that buttoned tight to the neck, but fell well shy of my ankles.

"You're too tall for the 1890s," I was told.

A fourth assistant director had me stand outside Eldorado's haberdashery and look as if I was window shopping for ribbon and lace.

"Keep your head down," he instructed. "Don't look at the camera. And don't make any move to steal the scene."

I quickly learned that while movies might exude glamor and glitz, the making of them most decidedly did not. I worked as an extra in several films—*Siege at Red River, Canyon Crossroads, Seven Ways from Sundown*—but most of my time on set was spent standing and waiting. I'd wait for the hairdresser, the makeup girl, the gaffers and actors—even the stars, who would flub their lines more often than not. (We all knew that Rock Hudson had once needed thirty-eight takes to get right a single short line of dialogue.)

At least the stars could retreat to their air-conditioned trailers, but we extras were forced to broil under the raging sun so we'd be on call at a moment's notice. We weren't allowed a bathroom break, and if anyone screwed up—easily done with forty or fifty people on set at any one time—we'd be forced to stand and wait some more until the scene could be shot again. And again and again and again.

Jessie disapproved of "my film work," as I called it, but I told her if I was old enough to shoot the rifle she'd given me for my sixteenth birthday, I was old enough to shoot a scene. She found no comeback for that gem of irrationality, and anyway she knew I'd go ahead on my own, so preferred to get in front of the parade rather than let it run her over. Everyone else in town was feeding off the movies because the money was good and it flowed free as the air. Whenever the studios arrived ("descending like a plague of locusts," Jessie would say), all ranch work would stop. Wranglers offered themselves as drivers, set-builders, grips, gaffers, or location scouts, and they'd take on the grunt work of hauling cameras and dollies from one shoot to another. They'd also coach the dude actors to sit on a horse facing the right way; or teach them how to herd and rope cattle.

Ranchers, meanwhile, would hire out their entire spreads, horses and cattle included. Jelly's Juniper Lodge would double its prices, as would his Double-D. And the DreamKatcher Motel would charge by the person, not the room. Homeowners also got into the act, renting out spare rooms, beds, and couches. The shelves of Kemp's Grocery would be picked clean. We locals would be crowded out of restaurants and bars—even the Bean and Burro. And several times Sharkey Gilman ran out of beer in the pool hall.

We put up with all the disruption (including the temporary city of army-surplus tents that often sprang up in Settlers Park), because as Mayor Williams liked to say, "The studios take only pictures—and leave only money."

Even his wife, Posie, muscled into the action when Roger Corman cast her as a comely schoolmarm in *Apache Woman*. She was meant to appear in a scene with Dennis Hopper and Jack Nicholson— two hell-raisers who'd not yet made names for themselves—and sat for hours in wardrobe and makeup. "Buff and puff," we called it. She was directed to sashay along Eldorado's raised boardwalk, turn to a couple of leering cowhands (Hopper and Nicholson), and say, "Don't you boys have something *better* to do?" But Corman left most of the scene on the cutting room floor, so when the movie came out, all we could see of Posie was the back of her head and her bustle-skirted rear end exiting stage left.

I was as keen as anyone to work in the movies and auditioned as an extra whenever I could. After one particularly tedious day, I was about to head home when Jelly Jellicoe beckoned me out of the crowd. It had been five years since he'd helped get Eldorado off the ground, during which time he'd set himself up as a small-time producer, making science-fiction groaners like *Creature from the Black Lagoon* and *Space Devils Target Earth*. He spent most of his time in Hollywood, talking up his film credentials, but he showed up in Paradox whenever one of his movies was being shot around town, drawn by our desert landscape, which could easily pass for another planet.

He took me aside and told me what a pretty face I had, and how much he liked my long, slim legs and the way I'd "filled out up top." I'd be perfect, he said as the wide-eyed ingénue he was about to cast in an upcoming feature, *Revenge of the Martians*. He showed me the script and the part he hoped I would play of a terrified, kidnapped girl.

I'd just turned seventeen and was flattered as well as naïve. Or maybe I was no more fooled than I wanted to be. When he asked if I'd help him scout locations, I slid into his Caddy and let him drive me into the desert. I showed him canyons and buttes and some worked-out mineshafts I thought he would like, as well as a rocky outcrop that had weathered into the shape of a six-gun pointed straight up the sky. These were features he said he was keen to see, and I was enjoying myself riding around in his Caddy with its plush red seats and a bump-free ride that felt as good as floating. With the air-conditioning switched on high, we could keep the windows up and enjoy the rich

tones that played from his radio without so much a crackle of inter-
ference, even out in the wilds of Yellow Cat Flats.

When it began to grow dark, I said we should get back, but instead
of heading for town he drove in a loop that took us out to Castle Rock
with a view across the desert all the way to Tower Arch. The outlook, he
said, would be ideal for the opening credits with my name up there in
lights. He talked more about his movie and the long-legged role he saw
in it for me, then said if he did something for me, then I should do something for him. Even then I wasn't sure what he meant, so I was shocked
when his hand moved sideways and settled onto my thigh. I froze. But
his hand didn't. He eased it higher and slipped it between my legs, making my light summer dress ride up to show the pink lace of my panties.

I didn't know how to react. The boys I'd been out with had
planted plenty of kisses and would squeeze my breasts if I let them,
but nothing had occurred in that no-go area "below the waist." I was
relieved when Jelly removed his hand—but it was only to take one of
mine and place it square on his groin where I could feel his erection. I
was still not sure what I was expected to do, but for some reason that
might have been nerves, I burst out laughing. And right away Jelly's
erection melted away like a Popsicle left in the sun.

He recovered quickly, fired up the engine, and drove us back to
Paradox as if nothing had happened. But there was no more talk of
the promised role.

Something similar happened a few months later when another
producer offered to sponsor me for the Screen Actors Guild. It was
clear from the start what he was after, but he still caught me off guard
when he pinned my arms and used the full weight of his body to thud
me against the wall of his trailer. He'd managed to force his mouth
onto mine and had started to tear at my blouse before I was able to
fight him off.

I didn't report him, as I knew I'd likely be blamed.

And anyway, who was I to report him *to*?

I didn't dare tell Jessie, but I did confide in Dottie, who rolled
her eyes.

"Tell me about it," she said. "Most girls put out, because they know if they don't, there's always another waiting in line who will."

If that's what it took to get into the movies, I figured, then I didn't want to play.

CHAPTER SIX

Jessie was quietly thrilled when I turned my back on the movies and focused more on the ranch. I swept dirt and hay out of the saddle room and imposed order on the threadbare horse blankets we kept there along with a jumble of unused harnesses and tack. I also helped Felipe erect a cross bar by the valley road to show the entrance to our spread wasn't just a gap in our fence, and I hung a sign, forged in iron, from the boom pole, that said, *The Dun-Bar Ranch*—a play on our surname and our cattle brand too.

I even resurrected an antique dump rake that had been left to rust in a clutter of abandoned machinery and dragged it down to the entrance where, along with a sulky plough, it served as decorative marker that said the owners of this ranch have a sense of history. The Dunbars didn't have savings or jewelry to hand down from one generation to the next. But they could, and did, leave a legacy of hard work along with the land. A legacy that now had registered with me.

Each morning when I walked down the stairs of the ranch house, I'd pass rows of people staring sightlessly out of the photographs Jessie had hung on the walls. These were her forebears, the people who'd homesteaded her land at the end of the previous century. I started to respect the effort they'd made, the work they'd put in, and the lives they'd invested, not for themselves but for future generations. I saw it in the chutes and corrals, the barn and bunkhouse, and in the core of the ranch house they'd built from timbers sawn by hand. And I began to understand what Jessie meant when she told me, "You don't work the land if you're a Dunbar. Nor do you live off the land. Instead, you become *part* of the land, just as it becomes a vital part of you."

Wisely, she let me get on with my minor improvements, but one day when she was at the kitchen table, working through a stack of bills, she opened the ranch's books and walked me through the numbers. I still hated math, but I didn't need a Harvard degree to see how deep in the red we were. Jessie worked the ranch as best she knew how, but nothing could hide the fact that we'd struggled all the years that I'd lived there, and many more before that.

"Raising cattle was never meant for the faint of heart," she told me. "You can't just sit on your porch and watch your cows eat grass. It's a constant battle, because the plain truth is, no matter how bad things are today, you know they're going to be worse tomorrow."

Jessie uttered this nugget of wisdom without rancor. She expected life to be tough, yet never once did she think about giving in.

"You have to let hope beat out experience," she said. "Like the dive people make into a second marriage."

We hit bottom in the summer of 1963 after an extended drought that reminded old timers of 1934. We'd exhausted our credit at the Farmers Co-op, so when we needed to buy a new batch of cracked corn, Jessie sent me into town to persuade Old Man Ullrich to keep our tab open.

"Use your charm," Jessie said, "because right now that's all we've got in the bank."

I figured Old Man Ullrich had heard more than his share of hard-luck yarns, so rather than spin him another, I wriggled into a black skirt I'd bought mail order from Sears and a white peasant blouse with a scoop neck low enough to show promise. Then I drove into town.

Ranchers may have been struggling that year, but the movie business was on a tear. We had two studios filming in Eldorado—Columbia Pictures and Universal—so the streets of Paradox were gridlocked, a situation made worse by the temporary failure of our one traffic light at First and Grant. A cop was struggling with the chaos, and when I drew near I saw it was Cal Parker. He was a deputy sheriff now, part of the family who'd supplied Paradox with law officers for three generations. I'd seen him around, behind the wheel of his cruiser or in the pool hall where most of us hung out. He'd bulked up since that day I first set eyes on him, but he still ranked as the best-looking guy in Paradox, even next to the Hollywood stars when they were in town.

I ducked down Adams and took a back-alley route to the Farmers Co-op at the south end of Fourth. I double-parked by the Seed and Feed sign and an empty cattle truck that stank of manure, then ducked inside the warehouse. Old Man Ullrich looked fragile as a ghost as he shuffled around, shrouded in the drifting motes of dust that rose from the bins and bags of feed. His wife had died of farmer's lung, contracted after a lifetime of inhaling those same swirls of dust, and it looked as if Ullrich was heading the same way. "That's the price of earning a living," Jessie had said.

Ullrich put up no resistance as I used the currency of my low-cut blouse to stretch our line of credit. Mission accomplished, I walked up Grant to the Five and Dime on Main and the Chocklik Scoops ice-cream parlor, where I rewarded myself with a cherry float.

When I arrived back at my Plymouth, I found Cal Parker in his deputy's uniform writing out a ticket. I stomped up to him, slammed my half-empty float cup onto the hood—and pouted. It's what we girls did back then when we needed to dig ourselves out of a hole. It had worked with Ullrich, so maybe now it would work with Cal.

"Haven't you got any outlaws to chase, Officer?" I said, in a breathy Marilyn voice.

He kept writing my ticket and didn't look up. "You're Corin Dunbar, aren't you?" he said.

His hat was pushed back to let loose a shock of blond hair. His sleeves were rolled up, and a gun belt hung low on his hips. Sunglasses hid the full blast of his flecked green eyes.

I tilted my head. "That's not a crime, is it?"

"Being double-parked is."

"Well, who wouldn't be today?"

"Still double-parked, no matter what day of the week it is."

He looked up and used a finger to slide his sunglasses down his nose. "Now how about you turn around. Real slow," he said.

"Do what?"

He circled a raised finger. "Twirl," he said.

I hesitated, then did as I was told. I spread out my arms and spun in a circle. I twirled. Real slow, just as he said.

He made a show of looking me up and down. "So no concealed weapons then."

I still had my arms out, palms up. I curved out a hip and may also have batted my eyelashes.

"I could make this ticket disappear," he said.

"And how would you do that, Officer?"

"Depends on whether you're free Friday night."

"I'd have to check my dance card."

"I can see why it might be full."

"Is this how you get the girls?"

"Hasn't failed yet," he said.

We dated regularly after that, hanging out in the pool hall or tooling up and down Main Street shouting trash talk at other couples doing much the same. A few times we fished for trout in the San Juan, and once we drove to St. George so Cal could try his hand at saddle bronc riding in the Dixie Round-Up rodeo. He didn't stick the eight seconds, but was bucked off in five, and when one of his spurs hooked in a stirrup, he was dragged like a ragdoll across the arena before a pickup man could pry him loose.

Cal didn't mind. He was fun, always ready with a laugh—although he once told me he worried that people didn't take him seriously as a cop. He'd been made deputy the day he turned eighteen when his dad, Dale, the Blade County sheriff, gave him a beige shirt, high-waisted military-style pants he called "pinks" (even though they were dark brown), and a pair of shiny black shoes. Dale strapped a gun on his son's hip, pinned a silver star onto his chest, and told him, "You're now a deputy sheriff, duly sworn in and appointed. So don't slouch, don't stink, and don't accept free smokes, food, drink, or tips. You may be my boy, but screw up and you're on your own, so don't come whining to me if you dig yourself into a hole you can't claw yourself out of."

Cal moonlighted as a stuntman—I once watched him tumble head-first out of a second-story window to land on a mattress and a stack of cardboard boxes—until Dale told him movies and police work didn't mix. "All that muck and makeup on your face?" he said. "I don't think so. It's not manly."

And being manly mattered.

Cal's mother had left home when he was five, so Cal grew up in an all-male household of Dale and *his* dad, Tommas, the first of the three generations of Paradox lawmen. There was nothing rounded in that household; it was all flat planes and rough edges. Dale and Tommas were hard-nosed, and would brook no weakness, not even in a child. Both were gun nuts with an arsenal of Colts, Remingtons, Spencers, and Berettas they kept in a gun rack in their house on the corner of Sixth and Adams. (Pride of place went to a Civil War lever-action rifle that Tommas had "liberated" before a trial.)

Both men had killed in the line of duty—Dale when he shot a couple of Indians from the nearby Navajo Nation ("scalpers off the reservation," he called them) who'd been selling blankets on the sidewalk outside City Hall; and Tommas when he fired at a wrangler, Riley What's-His-Face (Tommas could never remember the man's name), who'd failed to obey an order to raise his hands. Both men dated other events in their lives from those shootings ("That was before I took down Riley What's-His-Face," Tommas would say). And both were proud of what they had done.

It put a swagger into their step and showed they had paid their dues.

CHAPTER SEVEN

I knew none of this when I started going out with Cal. I just knew he was the guy all the girls wanted and he had picked me. That boosted my ego and set it purring like a cat. I wasn't too tall, my shoulders not too broad, my breasts not too small, and my hair, dark and wavy, was more than passable at a time when poker-straight blonde bangs were all the rage.

He often took me to the drive-in after it opened the following year—the "passion pit," we called it—where we'd see the latest Westerns and play "spot the blooper." Of which there were a surprising number. A cowboy wearing an Omega watch. A jet-engine vapor trail marring an 1890s sky. Even a cameraman we once spied, framed within a band of Indians and sporting a Boston Bruins baseball cap. If the movie had been filmed in Eldorado, the whole town would turn out; and if one of our own appeared on the screen, we'd blast our horns, bang on our doors, and wolf-whistle our wild approval. That ruined the movie for anyone hoping to follow the action, but that didn't bother us. Long before the movie ended, we'd be busy making out in the backseat.

One night, after we'd seen *A Fistful of Dollars*, we were on our way home when Cal pulled off the road, doused the lights, and we picked up where we'd left off in the passion pit.

"What's holding you back?" Cal asked at one point.

Well, quite a lot, to be honest. In those days, girls were either fast and did it, or they were nice and didn't. None of us wanted to be seen as damaged goods, so nice girls like me, with sex drives every bit as rampant as the guys we were dating, were forced to abstain. Boys could have a one-night stand at the DreamKatcher Motel and be rewarded in the morning with a nod and a wink and a slap on the back from their friends.

Nice girls could not.

But I didn't complain when Cal slipped off my shorts and dipped his hand into my panties. We'd done that before. I could feel him hard against me, so I figured we'd carry on until he came on my stomach. We'd done that before too. With his hand moving the way I liked, I was on the way myself, pressed close against him and letting my body do as it wanted. Before I knew it, he'd raked my panties aside and was deep inside me. I hadn't agreed to let him in, and although I didn't put up much resistance, it was my body, my life, and I should have had the right to choose my own moment.

When our second Thanksgiving rolled around, I agreed, with Jessie's blessing, to cook Cal dinner—and Dale and Tommas too. I arrived early at their house at Sixth and Adams with a turkey, raw and stuffed, ready for the oven. Riding beside me was a pumpkin pie Jessie had baked and that I only had to reheat, as well as a bag of potatoes and carrots that Dominga had helped me pull from our kitchen garden. Two cruisers, a Bronco, and a trailer were slanted across the Parker front yard, which was little more than a scratch-patch of sun-browned grass. The house was a scab of sun-blistered paint, single story with an asphalt-shingle roof; and like its neighbors it had been built from a ready-cut kit bought by mail order during the 1930s, then shipped to Paradox in boxcars and erected on a simple concrete slab.

Dale opened the door. I'd met him before, of course, but only on the street when he was on duty. Cal had never invited me into his home.

"Oven's hot," Dale said.

Cal emerged from the darkness behind him and helped me lug the turkey down the stub of a hallway into the kitchen. The walls there were cream, tinged with nicotine brown. The floor was linoleum and covered by a couple of deer hides, scuffed and worn, that served as rugs.

"Tommas got one," Dale said, prodding a hide with his boot. "I dropped the other. Same day, same herd. One shot each. Bang. Cal's kill's in the back. He'll want to show you later, won't you, Cal?"

Tommas was on the back porch, swathed in a blanket and the acrid fumes of a paraffin stove. As with Dale, I'd only ever seen him in town, sticking his way along Main. He was slumped in a wicker chair, his back curved like a crescent moon. His hair was a thick wodge that stood out startlingly white against the leathery brown of his face. His palm felt rough when I shook it, his fingers spindles as dry as kindling. His eyes—flecked with gray like Cal's under a pair of caterpillar brows—were alert and alive, and only mildly skimmed with cataracts.

"Fetch your girl a beer, Cal," Dale said. "Don't just stand there like a dummy. Show her some manners, won't you?"

Dale sank into a chair amid cumulus clouds of stuffing that billowed out of its cushions. He didn't have Cal's physique. He was tall and straight, but lacked his son's bulk of muscle. And his face was etched with deep lines carved into his cheeks. His nails were better manicured than mine, and his gray pants had a military crease I'd have expected to see only in his uniform pinks.

Cal had told me his father had once been a drinker, and after a day's work he'd force his then-ten-year-old son to stand on the back porch, stiff as a soldier—arms at his sides, back straight, head up—while Dale settled into a chair and worked his way through a couple of six-packs of Ballantine. He would do that silently and methodically, as if it were a chore he had to complete. There was no pleasure in it. He never seemed to get drunk, Cal said, but the strong beer would bring out a mean streak that Cal had learned to fear. When he was done, he'd tell his son to set up the empties on the back fence, then hand him his .38 Special and with a lift of his head give the signal to shoot. To avoid a whipping, Cal had to hit every one of those cans, reloading as he went. "I was good," he told me once. "But never quite good enough."

"I'd best get to work in the kitchen," I said.

Cal followed me through. He was dressed in Levi's and boots, with a crisp new red-checked shirt. He gave my shoulder a squeeze in place of a kiss, showed me the crate in the larder that held the pots and pans, then left me to it.

I thought the turkey would never cook, and it took me an age to peel the potatoes and carrots. The men stayed on the porch, but twice Tommas shuffled into the kitchen to use the bathroom next door. I tried to block out the tinkle of pee that came in sudden stops and long hold-your-breath starts. My plan was to eat at the dining room table, so after removing a bowl of sand with cigarette butts poking out of it like worms coming up for air, I set up everything there. But Dale called through from the porch—"We eat in the kitchen"—so I schlepped everything back again.

Dale carved while I handed round the trimmings—cranberry sauce, gravy and stuffing, and a sweet-potato pie I'd topped with marshmallows—and then we dug in. Tommas sank several cans of Miller from a cooler he kept on the floor beside him. Cal kept pace. But Dale confined himself to a few sips of Dr. Pepper. No one spoke beyond a grunt. They attacked their plates with heads down, elbows out.

We'd finished the pumpkin pie Jessie had baked when Dale scraped back his chair, rose to his feet, and raised his can of Dr. Pepper.

"Corin," he said, "that's as fine a meal as I've ever tasted, and I want to thank you for it. It makes it a pleasure to welcome you into the Parker family."

I looked across at Cal, wondering what he'd been saying about me. He kept his head down and dolloped a scoop of ice cream onto another slice of pie.

"I have just one request," Dale said. "Make sure my first grand-kid's a boy. We don't breed girls, do we, Tommas?"

"Only boys," Tommas agreed. "Parkers don't shoot blanks." He leaned to one side and squirted a gob of tobacco and mucus into an empty paint can next to his cooler.

"We need boys," Dale went on, "to grow into lawmen who'll wear the star. Just like his daddy does. His granddaddy—and his great-granddaddy too. Ain't that right, Tommas?"

"Fourth generation sheriff," Tommas said. "I'm holding on for that."

I waited for Cal to speak, to tell Dale he was out of line, running way ahead of the pack. We'd never spoken of marriage, and I wasn't just a baby-making machine. Cal's color did rise, but he kept his head down and spooned up more ice cream and pie.

I realized then his view of the future didn't sync with mine.

I didn't yet know what I wanted from life. But I did know I wanted more.

CHAPTER EIGHT

It was Rose Watson who set me off in a new direction. She ran the Paradox Library, and true to type she was a quiet woman born with a shushing finger pressed to her lips. As I browsed her shelves one day, she took me aside to recommend a book called *The Feminine Mystique* by Betty Friedan, which I duly checked out and read. The book must have done the rounds of most of the women in Paradox, since its text was a riot of red, blue, and yellow marker-inks with one highlighted sentence that caught my attention. It said the only way for a woman to find herself was through creative work of her own.

That simple notion started me thinking, because it gave me permission to wriggle out of the pigeonhole society wanted to slot me into. I'm not sure Friedan's book told me anything life hadn't already revealed, but the written words transcended talk and vague ideas. Just as Jessie maintained that God lives deep within us, if only we'd listen for his voice, so Friedan's book roused a belief that had long been lying latent inside me. I didn't have to go along to get along. I could, if I wished, set my own course. I may have come into this world as a blank slate, but I wasn't obliged to accept the story society had written. I could, instead, create my own.

Friedan's book also cast a new light on Jessie. I'd always considered her old for her years, but had put that down to the way she let her religion sap all joy out of her life and to the way she dressed in voluminous shirts and baggy pants. That, I knew, coupled with her close-cropped hair and clean-scrubbed face, titillated the gossipmongers in town. They disparaged Jessie as a man-hater, even a lesbian. Or worse than that, they said Jessie was a *spinster*. A woman who'd never been able to find a man.

I came to realize that some of their disdain had rubbed off on me, but after reading Friedan's book, I started to see Jessie as a woman who had no *need* of a man. She lived and died by her own decisions. She wasn't someone to pity, but someone to admire.

And, I thought, to emulate.

My chance to progress came in the summer of 1965 when we heard that Lyle and Connie Griffin—long-time ranchers with a six-thousand-acre spread further up the Waterpocket Valley—were selling off all their stock. Or rather, Connie was. Lyle had died of a heart attack five months before when he overdid it stacking bales of hay. A few months shy of sixty, Connie was getting on in years herself. She couldn't manage the ranch on her own so planned to move to Arizona where she'd be close to a daughter who'd married a car salesman in Phoenix. It was a big move for Connie, and a sad one too. Connie was a rancher's wife through and through, and a two-story box on a housing estate was never going to be her style. She knew it too, but put on the same brave face she'd worn when staring down the feast-and-famine of ranching over the past forty years and the shock of Lyle's sudden passing.

I waited for Jessie to be receptive, then sat her down one morning after we'd cleared away the breakfast dishes. I poured us both a second cup of coffee and laid out my five-year vision for the ranch.

Jessie heard me out in bemused silence.

"We need to graze more and feed less," I told her, "and we need to up our return per acre."

"It was like hearing Moses deliver the Ten Commandments," she later told me. "And where did you get that 'return per acre' from?"

When I had finished, she leaned back in her chair and took a thoughtful sip of coffee.

"My, my, Corin," she said, "you've surely given this a lot of thought. Don't think I'm unappreciative. But where would we even *start*?"

It was the opening I needed.

"With Connie Griffin," I said. "Everyone knows that she and Lyle raised a superior herd. And for the most part, their cattle have been sired by just two prize-winning Herefords. Connie's put them up for sale, and I think it's a good time for us to buy."

Jessie's eyes widened. "You want me to buy her herd?"

I shook my head. "I want to buy one of her bulls. A two-year-old twelve-hundred-pounder named Sherman. He has a long pedigree."

Jessie set her coffee cup on the table and took a moment to arrange it just so. "You serious about this?" she said.

I nodded.

"We've never had a pedigree bull," she said.

"Which means it's time we did."

"We could buy five cows for the price of one bull."

"Maybe. But think of it as an investment. Not an expense."

"Bulls eat too much. Not just forage, but corn, barley. Oats too. They chomp their way through a mountain of feedstuff every day, dawn to dusk. And there'd be extra vet bills to pay, a new corral we'd need, tougher fencing, a winter shelter. And that's just for openers."

"We could extend our line of credit," I said.

She snorted. "At the Agribank? I don't think so."

"Well, we do have *some* cash on hand," I said. We'd recently sold ten of our herd at auction.

"But that was to *cut* our debt, not to raise it." She pursed her lips and I could guess at her thinking. Once a child, always a child. She couldn't see me as an adult.

But in my favor, I'd earlier drawn up a roster that moved our herd around to give each of our pastures a rest; and that had saved us a bundle on feed, as well as boosting our milk production.

"The right bull," I said, "could sire offspring that every rancher around here would covet. Sherman's up for that. He's a rock star. Three times Grand Champion at the Utah State Fair."

Jessie drummed her fingers on the table.

"Well, I suppose it wouldn't do any harm," she said, "if we swung by the Griffin place and took ourselves a look."

CHAPTER NINE

In the summer of '52, when I was ten years old, I was still living with Gene and Grace in Yonkers. It was August, close to the end of a month when I'd swam and biked and stuffed myself sick with strawberry ice cream and too many hot dogs, when I wasn't going bug-eyed in front of the new television Mark Johnson's parents, two streets over, had bought. Temperatures were high, the air muggy, and the animals at the zoo were twitchy and fretful. When the weekend rolled by, we understood why. Animals are smarter than people, and they knew the long hot spell was about to end with a bang.

Grace was out of town visiting friends, so I dogged Gene's footsteps more closely than usual. When the blue skies turned black, I helped him coax a family of nervy lemurs and the zoo's four koalas out of their open cages and into the safety of covered sheds where we made sure they were watered and fed. As we drove home that day, hail the size of rocks battered and dimpled our car, and a howling wind tried to buffet us off the road.

Gene told me to stay with him in the house, where I'd be safe from the forks of lightning that were splitting the sky and bringing crashes of thunder so loud I clapped my hands over my ears. But I couldn't resist sneaking onto our back porch so I could feel the unleashed forces raging around me. The hail that had rattled down hard as nails soon melted into sheets of rain, while the wind whipped the leaves from our maples and sent them whirling into the sky like flocks of startled birds. The willow at the back of our yard flexed its limbs better than any dancer I'd ever seen; then a branch snapped off with a crack and blew away as light as a kite. I was scared, but at the same time riveted by the violence. I sheltered under the roof of the porch, and although the driving rain soon soaked me through, I stayed where I was until the kitchen light blinked twice and then shut off completely. I groped my way indoors in the dark.

Gene was mad at me for getting so drenched, and maybe he'd have ripped a piece out of my hide, but at that moment the phone rang to tell him there'd been an accident involving an animal of some kind—a *big* animal—and could he help. He struggled into his waterproof leggings, fastened the side studs, and grabbed his heavy-duty rain jacket. He didn't want to leave me on my own, so he hustled me into raingear too, making me wear his rubber overshoes even though they were several sizes too big.

The roads were rivers and the wind pummeled and battered us so hard it made the car shudder. I had to grip the sides of my seat to stop myself from jouncing around. Fallen branches littered the highways, and when one thudded onto the road in front of us, Gene had to stomp on the brakes and slalom around it.

We saw the accident before we arrived, lit by a watery haze of flashing lights that cut through the blear of our windshield. Gene came to a stop in the lee of a fallen beech where the fresh sod of its root-base gave us shelter. Rain hammered onto our roof, and even with the wipers slapping double-time, it was like sitting inside a car-wash. Gene grabbed his medical bag, ordered me to stay put, and ran toward a couple of state troopers who were hunched with a pair of paramedics at the rear of an ambulance. A man was stretched out on a gurney there. I could see his contorted face, bathed in the queasy citrine light that washed out from the back of the ambulance. The paramedics were holding him down, but he struggled to rise, gesturing at a trailer that was tipped against a tree in a concertinaed mass of fractured metal.

Gene joined the huddle, then ran with one of the troopers to the back of the trailer. Over the howl of the wind, I heard a visceral bellow as well as a thrashing and snorting that came from the trailer. Its rear door had flapped open and now hung by a single hinge so it was half submerged in a torrent of water that pumped around it like an incoming tide. I scooted sideways into the driver's seat and inched down the window. The inside of the trailer was black as the sky, but the cherry light on the troopers' patrol car pitched a beam into the darkness each time it spun around. I could make out an eye, rolling with fear. A foaming mouth. A flash of metal. And then the sweep of a massive forehead.

It was a bull, tethered through a nose ring, trapped and collapsed onto its knees. It shook and twisted its head and shed lather that spewed from its mouth, but it couldn't find its footing. I watched, holding my breath, as the animal rocked the trailer with its haunches and flailed its feet in a slop of urine, dung, and water that surged in and out with each heave of the trailer's open rear door.

The trooper with Gene stabbed a finger into his chest. "You got two minutes, Doc," he yelled. "Then I'm putting a bullet into that bull's head. Water's rising and we got trees coming down. We can't hang around here any longer."

I couldn't hear Gene's reply, but the trooper leaned in toward him, rain sluicing off his hat like water down a drain, and shouted again.

"No way, mister. I can't risk an animal *that* size cutting loose and running wild."

The trooper kept his hand on his holster as Gene opened his bag and edged into the trailer. Thunder rolled in the distance and the rain continued to slash down, so I was sure the trailer would be swept away. A branch the size of a canoe slammed into its side like a battering ram.

I stayed where I was, a lot longer than the trooper's promised two minutes, while Gene used his tranquilizer gun to shoot a syringe of Rompun into the bull's neck. Within minutes, the animal stopped its frantic thrashing but was not so dozy it couldn't struggle onto its feet. Gene eased the pressure on its nose ring and coaxed the dazed animal out of the trailer, then roped it best as he could between a couple of sturdy oaks.

I scurried back to my seat so he could slide into the car beside me. He was drenched through as if he'd been doused by a hose, and had a stench of blood, gore, and manure about him. But he grinned, laughed, and gave me a victor's thumbs-up.

"Animal's a bastard," he said. "If you'll pardon my French."

"I didn't hear any gunshots," I told him.

"No, Corin, and you won't. Because I saved it. Shooting an animal like that would be worse than taking a knife to the *Mona Lisa*. You see the state the owner was in?"

The troopers had called in a fresh trailer, which appeared just as a tow truck rattled up. Gene backed us out of there and we headed for home. The rain picked up, washing over our windshield and blurring our vision worse than peeling onions, but as he swerved around an abandoned car trapped by fallen wires, he again thumped the wheel in elation.

"I saved it, Corin!" he said. "Held off that trooper, and saved it!"

I matched his grin with one of my own. I felt proud. Proud that he was my dad. Proud that I was his daughter.

"No one in his right mind shoots a bull like that," he said. "I mean *no one*."

"Is that because it's a stud?" I asked.

He looked at me sideways. "What would you know about studs?"

I rolled my eyes. "Da-aa-ad. I know what animals do. I know how they do it too. They *hump*. One on top of the other."

He gave me another sideways glance.

"Don't let Grace hear you talking like that. But yes, that bull's a stud. And not just any stud either. He's a Black Angus. A bull like that—they call him a rock star—can sire as many as fifty thousand offspring, every one of them top grade. The fact is, Corin," he added, "that bull's worth millions."

"Mill-yuns?" I said, deliberately aping the way he'd said it.

He cracked another smile at that. "Yup, mill-yuns," he said, and his smile grew wider until it morphed into a belly-shaking laugh that threatened to engulf us both.

"Mill-yuns," we chorused, "mill-yuns and mill-yuns and mill-yuns!"

CHAPTER TEN

"One ejaculation," Connie told us, "from a bull, that is,"—and she gave Jessie a theatrical wink—"can yield up to five hundred straws. A lot more'n any man I've ever met, I can tell you. So do the math and you see the potential. But—and I don't want to fool you here—the yield might be less than fifty or sixty, so not so good then, is it? It all depends on how often you get your bull to shoot his juice. Some of them have a high old time, drop their load as soon as they get a sniff of a cow, so for them it's Christmas twice a week. But for others—well, there can be problems.

"You have to coax them to mount and then it can be tough to get them to come. If that happens, you might think, whoa, you got yourself a shirker, but you can't just zero in on quantity. Quality counts too. You may get less semen, but if the quality's high, you can charge way more per straw, just like they do for Kentucky barrel-aged bourbon and not that watered-down gnat's-piss beer that's all we're allowed to drink here in the good state of Utah. I think I might like Arizona after all," she added, and let out a cackle.

Connie sat back in her chair and took a long pull from the fruit jar of sour-mash whiskey she was nursing in her lap. She was kitted out in a pair of baggy jeans that had so many roll-ups they must once have belonged to her husband. Never one to let anything go to waste, she could have been wearing his checked shirt too. Her shoulders slumped like a fighter who was tired of throwing punches, but her conversation flowed as pithy as ever and her voice rang with all the traces of her former spirit. A harsh light streamed in through her kitchen windows to highlight the veneer of dust that decorated every surface, as well as the deep furrows that time and worry had ploughed into her face. Her skin stretched over her bony arms, dry as leather, and her hands shook as she raised the fruit jar to her lips. Her knuckles bulged, swollen and bent with arthritis.

She slid a caramel-colored folder across the table toward me, but I tilted my head to indicate she should show it to Jessie first. Jessie plucked at the knot of string that tied it together and took out Sherman's papers, but not before she threw me a glance that said she knew this wasn't the first time I'd spoken to Connie about the bull. I waited as Jessie skimmed through the numbers on Sherman's progeny. Birth weight. Weaning weight. Yearling weight. Mature weight. Ease of calving. Total body fat. The papers showed that Sherman had been sired by a Utah State Champion named Marshall, while the dam, an Angus called Cleo, was described as "good uddered, a superior milker, and productive."

"You want to meet him?" Connie asked, when Jessie had finished reading.

"Well, since we're here," Jessie said.

My time with Gene at the zoo had left me at ease around large animals. But Sherman was in a class of his own. He stood solidly in his pen, feet planted. His hide glowed the color of a ripe conker, save for a wash of white hair that curled against his forehead and flowed like a river down his dewlap and along the underside of his belly. The white brush of his tail swished like a metronome at the flies that buzzed around his hindquarters. He appeared composed, but when he turned his attention our way, his muscles tensed as he brazenly assessed us out of deep-set eyes the size of bullet holes.

Jessie and I took a moment to study him. His massive head needed all the strength of his thick neck and chest to hold its weight, while his short, stumpy legs were braced to support his boxcar of a body. His muzzle, threaded with a metal nose ring, shone slippery pink and dripped slobber, and when we edged closer, he emitted a throaty *rrrruuumph, rrrruuumph, rrrruuumph* like the revs of a powerful engine. He stared balefully at us, but as I took another step forward, he lowered his head and pawed the ground, gouging out salvos of dirt. His ruby-red eyes, protected by the overhang of his brow and the sharp curve of his horns, flashed a warning like taillights as he blinked.

"Sherm's saying he doesn't like to be stared at," Connie said from behind me. "He thinks it's rude. He also doesn't like trespassers pushing into his space, and he's warning you about that too. It pays to mind what he says, because Sherm's the boss. You work for him, not the other way around, and you'd best not forget it."

She shuffled into the space in front of me. "If you need to get this close," she said, "let him know where you are, so always come at him from the front. He can see more'n three hundred degrees, which is nearly full circle, but he doesn't have eyes in the back of his head. Sneak up behind him and he won't be happy, and nor will you. Sherman doesn't like surprises, do you, Sherm? He don't celebrate Christmas, nor birthdays and saints days neither."

Connie had stopped a few feet shy of the fence and the dried mire of the bull's pen. She eased into a stiff-kneed crouch and beckoned Jessie to join her.

"We're not talking rocket science here," she said. "You want to know if a bull's a good breeder? You look at the size of his balls. Big balls, good breeder. Small balls, bad breeder. You with me so far?"

Jessie nodded.

"Sherman's package is thirty-six centimeters around," Connie told her. "Find a man like that and you hang onto him tight. I'm still looking," she added, "though Lyle was man enough, God rest his soul. We had a life here, we did. A *life*. One we built up over the years, brick by solid brick. It wasn't easy, I can tell you."

Jessie rested a hand on her shoulder. "We'll only take the bull if it'll help," she said. "At fair market price too. What you'd get at auction. We're not after favors here. Or to take advantage."

"I know you're not," Connie said, covering Jessie's hand with hers. "And yes, it would help to have him off my hands. I may hate what I'm doing, selling everything that Lyle and me put together, but time marches on and I'm just trying to stay one step ahead."

She leaned on Jessie's arm and pulled herself upright.

"I'll give you Sherm's customer list for references," she said, "'cause the proof of the pudding's in the eating, as my granddaddy used to say. You'll want to ask around and make sure the cows Sherm's serviced got bred, calved early and easy, and their offspring produced a whole lot of milk. You get what you pay for in this world, and Sherm's top of the line, though I say it myself. But you'll still want to check."

"Your word's good enough for us," Jessie told her.

Connie grunted acknowledgment.

"Now if you take him," she said, "you gotta look after him good. Sherm may seem tough, and I have to tell you he's a mean son of a bitch, although I don't like him to hear me say that. But to keep him as a breeder, you have to mollycoddle him some. He don't like the heat, and he don't like the cold. Either one can lower the quality of his semen, and if he doesn't have good protection from the wind in winter, frost can bite his scrotum and he won't be a happy camper then, either. So he needs a windbreak and a lot of bedding.

"He's not cheap to feed," she went on. "Ol' Sherm'll work his way through thirty pounds of grass hay a day, in addition to the grain he likes, corn and barley. He enjoys his dinner, does Sherm, but treat him right and over time he'll more'n earn his keep."

Jessie pulled a long face at the list of expenses. We were used to cows that grazed year round on the open range with maybe some extra silage thrown down to help them through the winter.

"But a word of advice," Connie said. "Never think of a bull as your friend. And never give him a second chance. If he turns nasty, it's one strike and he's out. He may be sweet as a fresh-baked pecan pie, always showing his best side. But bulls are nasty as they come, believe you me. They'll put a hoof through your skull and a horn in your gut and think nothing of it. All in a day's work for them. Zeb Franklin got his ribs crushed one time when his Angus shimmied a two-step sideways and jammed him against a wall. And Preston Farley, he bled out when his Simmental gored him in the guts. Blood everywhere," she said. "Punctured his lung too. And even with Lyle knowing more'n there is to know about bulls, we had a wrangler here get his leg broke when an Angus stomped on him for no good reason we could see. Made a crack louder than a gunshot. I never did like that wrangler, but he didn't deserve to get his leg broke. Snapped clean as a candy stick. Which is why you need to keep a hot shot handy. To give him a prod, just in case."

She tilted her head at Sherman. "You want to see him perform?"

CHAPTER ELEVEN

"It's a three-man job," Connie told us when we'd followed her into the barn. "Not one for us girls, I'm afraid. It can get dirty." She let out a short bark of a laugh. "The motivation's easy enough," she continued. "I mean, you've gotten sperm out of a man, haven't you? Don't answer that, Corin. But it works much the same way with a bull. Just give ol' Sherm the sniff of a cow in heat, and Nature will take its course."

She reached for a length of tubing on the workbench behind her. About three inches in diameter and some eighteen inches long.

"You need this," she said. "For the artificial vagina. It's the outer casing. Not much to look at, but Sherman's not picky. He's none too bright either, so he's easily fooled. More brawn than brains, in my view. But you can say that about any male, and not just the four-footed kind."

She threaded the tubing with a thinner rubber sleeve that hung out at both ends.

"You fold each end of the sleeve back on itself like so, stretching it over the casing; then you fasten each one with a couple of rubber bands. This hole here," she said, pointing to a valve about halfway along the casing, "is where you pour your warm water in. That heats everything up so Sherm gets the feel of a nice hot vagina just before he ejaculates. It helps keep the temperature of his sperm up too. You need to test the sleeve for leaks every time you use the vag, because you don't want any sperm to be wasted. Makes no difference to him, of course. He's happy either way. But it's bad for you, when a bull's only got so many ejaculations in him. It's money down the...well, down the tube," she finished, giving a fresh airing to what must have been an old gag.

She picked up a cone-shaped piece of rubber that was wrapped around the neck of a plastic test tube and attached it to one end of the outer casing, again using a rubber band. "This here's the collection bottle," she said, "which I'm going to wrap in cotton wool, so when the semen's in there, its temperature stays near as dammit the same as Sherman's. That helps maintain the quality. Last thing," she said, "is the Vaseline." She grabbed a big pot from the workbench and used what looked like an old pastry brush to smear a mess of it around the open end of the casing and inside the neck of the sleeve. "You could use K-Y jelly, if you've a mind. Anything that lets Sherm slip his penis in smooth and easy. You don't want to damage his shaft. He won't thank you for that, I can tell you. He likes it smooth and easy."

She paused to see if we had any questions.

"In my limited experience," she said, "any male'll jump to attention and shoot out sperm like it's the Fourth of July, if you give him the right incentive. Happy as clams they are, as long as they have a tube they can get themselves off into. Keeps a smile on their faces, the poor fools, so come on, let's see if we can make Sherman's day."

We followed her out to the cattle pens, where a couple of wranglers flanked Sherman as if he was under arrest. Each one held tight to a thick rope tied to a makeshift halter around the bull's head and then passed through the metal ring in his nose. Sherman stood stock-still, but I could see his power in the wide plant of his legs and the thick musculature of his body. When he shuffled a hoof, both wranglers jumped back to keep their feet clear of his crushing tonnage.

"You know these two?" Connie said, and inclined her head at the wranglers.

Bose Manly was a grizzled old hand with a sun-pruned face and legs shaped to the curve of a horse's belly. I'd met him in town a few times, but mostly I'd seen him on the big screen as he had the look that movie directors adored. Grizzled, rheumy eyes. Nicotine teeth.

And a shock of unruly hair as stiff and wiry as steel wool. His side-kick, Chance Butterfield, was Bose a decade younger. He, too, had been in the movies, but mainly when his bull-riding skills were in demand. Chance had twice been a PRCA champion and had broken more bones than he knew he had in his body, some of them twice.

A third wrangler I knew only as Hal led a Hereford cow into a short, dead-end chute that had been set up on one side of the pen. The chute flanked half the cow's body but stopped short of its haunches. Hal stood in front of the animal and roped its head to the chute's railings on either side. He hung onto the ends of the ropes to steady it further, then let it munch through a pile of hay stacked in a manger by its head.

"Like I said, a three-man job," Connie told us. She waved the artificial vagina in Hal's direction. "That there cow he's holding is the teaser. You gotta be sure she don't see Sherm coming at her and you gotta be sure she can't shimmy around. Out in the pastures she'd lead a bull a fine dance before he'd be able to service her, but we don't have time for foreplay here. Mind you hold her steady!" she shouted.

"I got her, ma'am."

"Okay. Shall we do it?" Connie said.

As if he'd been waiting for a starter's gun, Sherman swung his huge head in the cow's direction. That jolted Chance off-balance, and he had to fight to stop himself from falling face down in the dirt. An earthquake-like rumble came from deep within Sherman's throat, and he lumbered across the pen toward the cow, dragging Bose and Chance with him.

"Hold him!" Connie yelled, and the two wranglers tightened their leather-gloved grip on their halter ropes.

"He's got a whiff of the cow, Connie," Chance shouted. "We gotta go with him, so gimme the vag."

"Make his nose feel us!" Bose shouted, and pulled hard on his rope.

"Sherm's not that excited yet," Connie said to Jessie and me. "He's caught a whiff. But wait 'til he really starts to sniff around."

She tossed the vag over the rail to Chance as the bull shambled forward, thwarting the wranglers who did their best to hold him back.

He stopped a nose-length from the cow that was still placidly chewing, then reared his muzzle high and flared his nostrils. He took another step forward, nosed the cow's tail out of the way, and slathered his pale pink tongue over her vulva, wetting his muzzle and mouth and spreading a trail of her mucus, whipped frothy as egg-white, over her flanks.

"Now we're talking," Connie said as Sherman's penis emerged long, slender, and pink as cherry blossom out of the protection of its sheath. "Hotter than a fired-up poker, he is."

She crouched low and pulled us down beside her. "Tough to see," she said, "but Chance has trimmed the hairs off Sherman's sheath, and off his balls too. Remember, you gotta keep everything clean as a whistle, not easy to do when there's all this shit and flies and piss around. But he's good and ready now."

The bull had backed off to give himself space for a run-up. As he moved forward, Bose and Chance tightened the halter ropes, dug their heels deep in the dirt, and leaned their full body weight against him, pulling hard on Sherman's nose ring and bringing him to a halt. The bull let out a furious bellow and thrashed his tail against his flanks, then lowered his haunches into a crouch. The two wranglers bent with him, their bodies braced in a tug-of-war to stop the bull mounting. Their biceps bulged with the effort until the veins and sinews in their arms popped. Sherman released another strangled bawl of frustration.

"You get more semen out of him," Connie said, "if you hold him back a couple of times. But wait too long and you'll have semen squirting every which way, and that'll get you nothing more'n a load of laundry."

Sherman lunged for the cow again.

"Third time lucky," Connie said. But again the wranglers yanked on his nose ring and kept him back. "Spoke too soon," she said.

"Ready!" Bose shouted, and this time he and Chance loosened their grip.

Sherman felt the freedom and staggered forward, snorting with effort and arousal. He shifted his weight onto his haunches and bent his stubby hind legs into a crouch, looking for leverage in the dirt. He lunged forward and heaved the bulk of his body to land full weight onto the cow's hindquarters. His massive head rose over her back, proud as a figurehead cresting a wave, and his eyes rolled back into their sockets as he thrust his penis toward her.

At that moment, in a smooth, practiced motion, Chance slipped the bull's penis into the greasy neck of the artificial vagina. Sherman buffeted him off to one side, but Chance regained his balance and moved in sync with the bull. Sherman gave one massive thrust, then frantically rolled his torso from side to side, panicked by the need to get his slab of a body back on four stable hooves. He thundered onto the ground, slipped once in the squelch of the cow's fresh dung, then stood panting and snorting with effort.

"With Sherm it's always a quickie," Connie said. "No sweet talk. No dinner. Not even a cocktail. Just right to it."

The cow, contained by the sides of the chute, had barely moved, although she'd stiffened when she sensed Sherman about to mount, then buckled at the hocks and teetered when the massive weight of his body crashed on top of her. There were bloody scuff marks along her flanks where Sherman had clamped his forefeet tight to her haunches, but already she'd resumed her placid chewing. Hal dragged the manger out of the way and led her out of the front of the chute so she could rejoin the herd.

"That's the sissy job," Connie said. "Holding the head of the teaser and staying away from the business end. I've done it myself a few times, but I wouldn't recommend it."

Chance and Bose grabbed Sherman's halter ropes and tightened the slack, but the bull was in no mood to resist. He was spent, not by the ejaculation, but by the sheer physical effort of heaving his tonnage off the ground. His great maw hung slack, and I could smell his steamy breath mingled with the wranglers' sweat and, I think, some of my own.

Connie clamped a hand onto my arm as the wranglers led Sherman back to his pen.

"Chance is pretty good at this now," she said, "but I saw him once take a load straight in the face. You get christened like that and you soon learn to master the vag, I can tell you." And she released another one of her cackles.

She turned to Jessie. "So what do you think? You want to take him home?"

She saw Jessie hesitate.

"Tell you what," she said. "You take Sherman off my hands and I'll throw in the five straws of semen I've got in storage, plus three nitrogen canisters for freezing them and a water bath for thawing. Can't do fairer than that. And I'll make sure Chance and Bose are around to help you collect, at least for the first few months. They can do the grunt work, and you can get that Mexican of yours—what's his name? Manuel?—to do the sissy job with the teaser."

"Felipe," Jessie said.

"Whatever."

Jessie turned to face me. "What d'you say, Corin. This is your idea. You sure you want to do this?"

"I'm sure," I said.

In the back of my head I could hear Gene's voice as clear as if he were standing there beside me.

"That bull's worth mill-yuns. Mill-yuns and mill-yuns and mill-yuns!"

It was a refrain that would haunt me the rest of my life.

PART TWO

PART TWO

CHAPTER TWELVE

Noah (Ark) Stevenson

If, on a clear night, you gaze up at the sky, you can see as many as five thousand stars. Beyond them are billions of galaxies, none of which can be seen by the human eye—with the sole exception of Andromeda. Its stars are the closest to those in our own galaxy, but they are still about 2.5 million light-years away. Which means light from those stars, racing along at the Universe's maximum speed of 186,000 miles per second, takes 2.5 million years to reach us. So if you can find the smear of light that is Andromeda, tucked between the constellations of Pegasus and Cassiopeia, you would not see its stars as they are now. You would see them as they were two and a half million years ago. You would be looking back in time. This is true of all galaxies and all stars. There is no present in the heavens, only a past. And the further out into space you look, the further back in time you see.

Noah Stevenson was nine years old when he realized this. And he was entranced. He knew that the stars—like everything else in the Universe—had been made by God in a violent burst of energy over a period of just seven days. He knew this because his parents had told him, and because it was a truth revealed in the Bible ("the only book you'll ever need," his father had said). Noah understood that if he looked *far* enough into space, he'd be able to see right back to the *beginning* of time. To those seven days of creation. He'd be able to see God at work. He'd be able to see God himself.

So every night for a week, Noah slipped out of his hammock in the *shabono* where he slept and stared up at the sky. But he didn't see God. Only stars. And not many of those. Maybe he needed a telescope, he thought. Or be able to glimpse more sky. Because the world he lived in was a shadowy one, even at noon. Hemmed in as it was by plumes of emerald ferns and a towering canopy of *wimba* and *kapok* trees.

He would never find God here, he decided.

Not in the heart of the Amazon jungle.

Where he'd been born.

Noah's parents, Martin and Joyce, had been raised in mud-caked farming villages equidistant from the Roman city of Bath in south-west England. They met as youngsters when they pored over the Gospels at the Sunday school run by the vicar of the Protestant Church of St. Mary, a stone structure so damp that swatches of sphagnum moss sprouted from its interior walls in spongy hummocks of green. But then they drifted apart. Until Martin, determined to spread the good news of Christ, graduated with a Bachelor of Divinity degree from the One World Missionary Society's theological college in Oxford. Other students in his year hoped to serve "the benign parishes of the Home Counties," as one of them put it, but Martin vowed to be a "proper" missionary who would "dwell among savages, rude and illiterate."

But first he needed a wife, as it was Society policy that its apostles be married "so as not to fornicate or in any other way interfere with native women." He rekindled his friendship with Joyce, now a "pretty, curly-haired woman" who worked in a sweet shop on Weston High Street, dispensing licorice allsorts, sherbet fountains, and creamy whirls, and married her six months later in the Church of St. Mary, where they'd first met.

Within a week, the couple set sail for the New World. Missionaries from Britain were normally sent to the colonies in Africa, but One World focused on South America, where it hoped its creationist teachings would find fertile ground and challenge the resurgent

Jesuits who were winning most of the converts. After six weeks in a harbor-side hostel in New York, Martin and Joyce found passage on a Booth Steamship freighter that took them to Belem, at the mouth of the Amazon. They transferred to a tramp steamer that made slow progress upriver. The air on deck changed from damp to humid to muggy until it wrapped them in a miasma of heat from which there was no escape. A tinny fan did little to scare up a breeze or to disturb the glossy-backed roaches that plagued them nightly in their bunks. But at least, Martin wrote in a letter to the One World Society in Oxford, "we were able during the day to stand in the bow ahead of the choking fumes that belched thunderclouds of smoke out of the steamer's funnel..."

After a stopover at Santarem, they arrived at the floating docks of Manaus, where, to Martin's frustration, they were forced to wait three months until they could buy hammock-space on a riverboat piloted by a half-naked mestizo traveling up the Rio Negro as far as San Carlos. With frequent stops, the journey took nearly six weeks, by which time Joyce had become heartily sick of the mosquitoes and pepper-like *jejenes* that feasted on the tiniest patch of her exposed alabaster skin. Martin tried to distract her by combing the riverbanks for a sighting of the piggish capybara or the organ-grinder capuchin monkeys he'd been told were endemic; but he could not gloss over the hardships imposed by the close, open-deck quarters shared with a squabbling mix of miners, soldiers, Dessana Indians, and thieves.

San Carlos proved to be little more than a clearing burned out of the jungle. "Blackened stumps of trees poke out of the charred earth like the battlefields of Verdun," Martin wrote. Another five weeks passed before he and Joyce could bundle their scant possessions into a dugout and head farther upstream. "We are now reduced to two military-style canvas bags that fit into our canoe," Martin reported, "but at least we have retained our Bibles, a jumbo packet of digestive biscuits, and a three-month supply of Tetley tea which Joyce swears she would be quite unable to manage without."

After two days of strong paddling by a pair of Indians hired for the task, they left the Rio Negro and turned east into the much narrower Casiquiare, a natural canal that linked the Amazon river system to that of the Orinoco. A week later, they passed Culimacare Rock, the only significant physical feature they'd seen since Belem, until finally they disembarked by a hump on the riverbank that marked the trail to the Yanomami Indian village of Viriunave. "The boats we boarded on our journey from England," Martin recorded in his journal, "became increasingly smaller until I feared we'd be obliged to *swim* the last few miles... The two Indians who paddled us upriver were both members of the Yanomami tribe we had come to convert. The men spoke little in the way of English—just functional words like *food* and *sleep*—so we mostly communicated with smiles and gestures on our part, and shoves and grunts and globular spitting on theirs. Both men had wodges of tobacco stuffed into their mouths, which greatly stretched their lower lips and gave their few remaining teeth the fungal stippling of rotten wood. To Joyce's discomfort (and I have to say mine too), both Indians were entirely naked, but had tied their flaccid penises flat against their stomachs with what appeared to be an uncomfortable arrangement of string, looped first around their drawn-out foreskins and then around their waists. The older of the two men had three large and bulbous growths emerging from the black of his hair like the rocky tors one sees on Dartmoor, and for reasons I have not yet been able to fathom had dyed them an angry red as if he deliberately sought to draw our attention to them..."

For a long moment, he and Joyce stood in silence—"alone on the bank of an unknown river, encircled by jungle and the peril of a hostile tribe of Stone Age savages"—as they watched the two naked paddlers propel the canoe back to San Carlos. Then, with a glance at a sky that again threatened rain, Martin pointed his chin toward the trail and with a resolute "Well, shall we?" marched into the jungle.

Joyce hated life in Viriunave. She'd known the Yanomami were members of a tribe that only recently had come into contact with the outside world. Life among them was never going to be easy, but she'd imagined that she and Martin would be dealing with people like the Maasai of Kenya or the Polynesian islanders that Captain Cook had encountered on Tahiti. Savages, yes; but *noble* savages who might worship the wrong gods, but who nonetheless were imbued with an innate humanity. The Yanomami were nothing like that.

Among the men, disputes were common—usually beginning with ritual chest-thumping that quickly escalated as the opponents took to pounding each other with rocks or staves. Nearly every one of the men was seriously disfigured, either by open wounds or scars they proudly displayed. When not fighting, they would blow a strong hallucinogenic drug called *yopo* up one another's nostrils; it produced a splitting headache as well as a glob of dark green mucus that hung from the user's nose. The women, like the men, mostly went naked, but they painted their bodies and decorated their faces with sharp sticks that pierced their noses, lips, and cheeks. All had children when they were little more than children themselves; all bore the scars of frequent beatings; and all had been the victims of rape.

Martin's journal gives a hint of his feelings. "God forgive me, but these people are uncouth... Their guttural language is simply impossible... There's no water, no toilet... And most of our Bibles have been stolen and shredded for kindling..." Joyce, he was sure, would have given up and returned to England, especially after their son, Noah, was born. But Martin saw every setback as a sign from God that he was not trying hard enough and so redoubled his commitment.

It was a different experience for Noah. He took in stride the sapping heat, the humidity, the dirt and disease, and saw nothing wrong with the smoke-filled hut where he'd been born or the communal palm-thatched *shabono* where he now lived. He found no fault in the culture and standards of the children with whom he played and was more than content to walk single-file into the jungle, foraging for roots, grubs, and edible shoots. He couldn't compare the overgrown trails with the Royal Crescent in Bath, so accepted the heavy air, the filtered sunlight, and the fierce bursts of sudden rain. He didn't complain about the insects, the enforced hunger, or the grieving families who drank a soup concocted from the ashes and bones of their recently dead.

By the time he was nine years old, Noah could catch the *boto*, or dolphin, that swam in the Casiquiare as well as the wiry-whiskered catfish that sometimes grew to six feet long. He could net a basket of thrashing piranha from the relative safety of a canoe, and he knew where to find *maracuja* fruit and the ripe berries of the *manaca* tree, which the Yanomami women crushed into a thick and nutritious mush. His favorite pastime was exploring the jungle on his own. He'd paddle off in a dugout, supposedly hunting for turtle or iguana, then steer for a break in the wall of green and plunge into the darkness, daring himself to go deeper and deeper into the gloom. He could not cut a path through the stockades of lianas and vines, but with Martin's machete he was able to slash a tunnel through which he could crawl. Bent double, he'd stumble over tripwires of roots that crisscrossed the ground, sink ankle-deep into the spongy earth, and feel drops of cool water splatter down from the canopy above. He ignored the scrapes and scratches from the stickle-backed spines that clawed at his face and eyes, as well as the halo of insects that fussed and buzzed around his head. The jungle was a world of mystery and adventure— one he was always keen to explore.

Noah's childhood came to an end when his parents decided he should be schooled in England. Joyce had taught him to read and write, to do his sums, and to study the Bible until he knew it chapter and verse. Against Martin's wishes, she had shipped in from Manaus as many of the classics as she could find—*Black Beauty, A Tale of Two Cities, Vanity Fair, The White Company*—as well as a copy of *The Night Sky*, an astronomy book for children, that at least won Martin's approval. "There's no better way," he told his son, "to honor our Maker than to gaze at his greatest works, the stars and the planets he made for our enjoyment. 'The Heavens declare the glory of God; and the Firmament sheweth his handiwork:' Psalm 19." But both parents knew that a home-school in the jungle was no substitute for a proper education.

"You'll find a different world in England," Martin told his son. "But I'm relying on you to stick out your chin and push on through. That's the ticket. And remember, God will be watching us all, so we'll be in touch through him."

When the fateful day came, Noah looked back from the canoe that carried him on the first leg of his journey. A few of the Yanomami boys who'd come to see him off whooped and hollered and splashed in the shallows, then quickly melted into the jungle. Noah kept his eyes locked on his parents, his hollow-cheeked father and his weeping mother. Martin had said in the service of God a sacrifice must always be made, and "since God had surrendered his only son for us, so it is fitting that we should relinquish ours for him."

In San Carlos, Noah was put on a boat to Manaus, then shipped like a parcel to Belem, where he boarded the *MV Marlin*, a Hamburg-Sud cargo-liner that sailed a convoluted route—via Trinidad, Vera Cruz, and Havana—to Southampton on the south coast of England. At the quay, he was met by Miss Thora MacDonald, Matron of St. Dunstan's Academy, who waited with the school's chauffeur in a beige Rover parked outside the customs shed. Noah was easy to spot as he was a child alone and his skin was many shades darker than his features suggested.

Two hours later, the Rover scrunched along a gravel driveway that ran for half a mile between sturdy oaks before it swept to a halt outside the iron-studded doors that marked the school's main entrance. Noah remained seated—he did not know how to open a car door—until Matron came around to let him out. By the time she had him washed and fed (a slice of corned beef and a generous mound of baked beans), it was after nine o'clock and long since dark. She led him past a fireplace flanked by snarling stone lions, up a creaking staircase, and along a corridor to a wooden door with DORM 8 stenciled on its panel. From the other side came a noise like the roar of crashing waves, then a thump and a thud as something hit a wall and precipitated a muffled cheer.

Matron flung open the door and the noise snapped to silence. Nine rosy-cheeked boys, dressed like a team in identical blue-striped pajamas, spun around to face her. She pushed Noah forward. "This is Noah Stevenson," she said, "the new boy I told you about. I trust that you will make him welcome as we discussed. He's traveled a long way and so will be tired. I want you to let him sleep, and I want you to get some sleep too. Tired boys are wicked boys, so come on now." She clapped her hands briskly. "Get into bed where you belong. And. No. More. Noise. Do you hear me?"

"Yes, Matron," they chorused.

She waited while Noah fumbled into the blue-striped pajamas she gave him before she swept out, extinguishing the lights as she went. He lay in bed and stared at the starless void of a strange ceiling, his hands tugging the heavy blankets under his chin. He had never been so scared in his life.

CHAPTER THIRTEEN

The other boys had prepared well for the new arrival. Aware that he had come "from the jungle" (as Matron said), they'd secreted in his locker a warty-skinned toad from the school pond as well as a half-eaten jam sandwich they knew would attract ants. They also whooped monkey noises at him while scratching their armpits and shouting "Tarzan! Tarzan!" until the House Master—a heavy smoker named Froggy Thornton—pointed out, somewhat pedantically, that Tarzan was not an acceptable name as that fictional character hailed from Africa, not South America. That technical hitch was overcome when Christopher Arpley, a tow-haired boy in Noah's form, tipped a bucket of bathwater over Noah's head and demanded to know, "So where's your ark *now*, Noah?" At which point, a bigger crowd of boys gathered to chant, "Ark! Ark! Ark! Ark!"—giving Noah the nickname that would stay with him for the rest of his life.

Ark quite liked his new name. He saw it as a sign of acceptance. Which was greatly enhanced when, in revenge for his dousing, he hid the warty-skinned toad under the sheets at the foot of Arpley's bed, and that same night in the dorm ate not just the jam sandwich but most of the ants too. (Much larger bugs had been a Yanomami delicacy.) His integration took another step forward when Matron refashioned his pudding-basin haircut and issued him with the looka-like uniform that all boys were required to wear: long gray flannel trousers, a navy-blue serge blazer with the school's motto (*Servire regnare est*: To Serve Is to Reign) emblazoned on the breast pocket, and a gray school cap decorated with blue-cord stripes that split the crown into segments like an orange. The cap had to be doffed at the sight of a master and removed entirely in the presence of a lady, Matron included.

Ark squirmed under the burden of his new clothes, and he kicked against the school's strict regimentation. He was often put in defaulters and forced as a punishment to bunny-hop the length of the rugby pitch or write out one hundred lines (*I must not run in the quadrangle, I must not run in the quadrangle...*). And twice he received "six of the best" from Headmaster Austell Winsor—once when a prefect caught him smoking a Wills Whiff in the outdoor bog, and a second time when, on Guy Fawkes' night, he was seen (in a game of Knock up Ginger) dropping penny bangers through Froggy Thornton's front-door letter box.

Slowly, though, Ark settled into his new way of life. He disliked the meals of tripe and onions, tinned spam, frog-spawn tapioca, Spotted Dick, and treacle-sponge stodge. And he continued to reject the pettiness of the school rules (trousers must have turn-ups, shoes needed toe-caps, and eating in the street was strictly prohibited even if it involved only the wine gums, pear drops, and gobstoppers that his ration coupons allowed him to buy in the tuck shop). But he was good at games—he played fly-half in rugby and silly mid-off in cricket—and he did well in class, often achieving straight A's as well as the occasional star.

He learned that Gaul was divided into three parts, and the Romans enjoyed central heating (notably absent from St. Dunstan's). He also learned how to divide £2-6sh-4d into £10-8sh-8d; read Napier's log tables; measure angles with a protractor; and calculate sines and cosines by manipulating the stock and indicator of a slide rule.

Ark's best subject, however, was religious instruction. The long hours he'd spent in the jungle memorizing passages from the Bible meant he regularly won the Edmond White Prize for Christian Studies presented on Founder's Day. But that deep knowledge could also land him in trouble, as he found out one day when his teacher, Anthony Strickland, built a lesson around the expression "Gospel truth."

"I am sure you are all familiar with this term," he told his class, "as I've heard many of you deploy it when you attempt to convince a master of your angelic innocence. 'It wasn't me, sir,' you say, and to drive the point home that it really *wasn't* you, you declare that you are not just telling the truth but are telling the *Gospel* truth. A higher level of truth that we know is—well, *indisputably* true."

At the back of the class, Ark raised his hand.

"Yes, Stevenson, what is it?"

"Please, sir, if the Gospels are indisputably true, why is it that they say one thing in one place and something else in another?"

"What do you mean, boy?" Strickland was an elderly master who liked to pace up and down in front of the class, mortarboard balanced on the dome of his balding head, black gown billowing in his wake like Dracula's cape.

"Well, Matthew says there were twenty-seven generations between King David and Jesus, but Luke says there were forty-two. They can't both be true, can they, sir? And Mark says Jesus came from Nazareth, but Matthew and Luke both say he was born in Bethlehem. He can't have been born in two places at once, sir, can he? Not even Jesus could manage that."

A titter of laughter spread around the class, which Strickland silenced with a look. "Of course, he wasn't born in two places at once, Stevenson."

"But if one Gospel says he was born in one place, sir, and another says in another, then at least one of the Gospels must be wrong, mustn't it, sir? It can't be telling the Gospel truth."

"The Gospels aren't intended to be taken literally, Stevenson. And nor should they be subjected to your searing logic." Another snicker of laughter, this one allowed. "They need to be given a certain *leeway*, some poetic license, if you will."

"But when we read the Gospels, sir, how are we to know which bits are true and which bits are—well, leeway?"

Another round of sniggering laughter.

Strickland stopped pacing. "Quiet, boys! Stevenson, no one likes a smart-aleck. If you wish to pursue this line of discussion, I suggest you see me in my study. I can't waste the class's time with your...*pedantics*."

"No, sir. I mean, yes, sir."

Ark would have let the matter drop, but later that day, as he headed out to the cricket nets, dressed in his whites with a bat shiny with linseed oil clutched under one arm, Strickland called him into his study and sat him down on an overstuffed chair.

"Did one of the older boys put you up to this, Stevenson? This business about the Gospels?"

"No, sir."

"Then where did your questions come from? Have you *read* the Gospels?"

"Oh, yes, sir. Many times. My parents—"

"Ah, yes, the missionaries. Well, your questions are sensible ones. But you need to understand that the Gospels are best seen as an allegory. You know what an allegory is, do you not?"

"Yes, sir, it's a story, sir."

"A story with *meaning*. And the meaning here, Stevenson, is God, and faith, and religion, and a set of beliefs that all of us share. They help determine how we live, how we behave, how we treat others, especially those less fortunate than we are in England. We're not *meant* to ask questions, because there are some things in life that are better just accepted. People have believed in the Gospels for two thousand years. They've shared the same story, followed the same lessons, and have as a result helped to build a vast civilized society that would have been impossible without that common agreement and mutual understanding. We can't cast all that aside merely because Noah Stevenson of the Lower Fourth questions the Gospel's literal truth. All those people over all those years cannot all have been wrong, now can they?"

"But people have been wrong before, sir. I mean, for thousands of years people believed the sun went around the earth. But it doesn't, sir, does it?"

"No, but that's a different matter. A factual error that Copernicus—with a certain amount of assistance from Galileo, I believe—was able to correct."

"And Kepler too, sir."

"Yes, yes, and Kepler too, I'm sure. But we're not discussing science here, Stevenson. We're talking religion, and religion is all about *faith*. It's about believing in something bigger than we are, which gives shape and meaning to our lives. The Christian faith has been the bedrock of civilized society for so long that without it we'd be at one another's throats in no time at all. It's what binds us together. It's what helped us build an Empire that covers a quarter of the globe. It wasn't a shared language, a shared culture, or a shared history that allowed us to do that. It was a shared religion that tells us where we come from, why we are here, and what our purpose is. We need a shared *story* to hold us all together, and religion gives us one. That's why it's so important that we believe."

He laced his nicotine-stained fingers together. "It doesn't matter what the story is. It doesn't even matter if the story is true. All that matters is that there *is* a story and that all of us accept it. *All* of us, Stevenson. Which includes you. We need a common narrative and that's why we need faith, a faith that tells us there is a God, there is order in the Universe, and we're not just here by chance. That's where your parents are helping, is it not? They're bringing savages into the fold so they can share in the story?"

"Yes, sir."

"Very well, then. We'll leave it there." He leaned back and reached for a cigarette. "I see you have cricket. Is it practice? Or are you playing a match?"

"A match, sir. Against Commons."

"Well, I won't delay you further. Keep your eye on the ball and keep a straight bat. We don't want you out for a duck, now do we?"

"No, sir."

"And whatever you do, Stevenson, don't let the side down."

When Ark moved from the Prep School to the Upper School, he immediately joined the Astronomical Society so he could look through its six-inch reflector telescope. He wanted to know how and where he fit in, not just in this world, but in the Universe as a whole. His childhood copy of *The Night Sky* had included a fold-out map that showed the constellations; but the stars on the map had never matched those he'd seen from the jungle. Now, with the help of a planisphere, they did. He could find Polaris, the small cluster that made up the Plough, and the three bright stars of Orion's Belt.

He'd hoped the stars would help him connect with Martin and Joyce since they, too, might be peering up at the night sky. But six years had passed since he'd last seen them, and they were fast becoming strangers. His knew his jungle life was slipping away as he became more English. And it all but disappeared when Austell Winsor called him into his study one day to give him the sad news that both his parents had been killed.

"Some kind of skirmish with the natives, I'm afraid," Winsor said. "I know it's a bit of a googly, coming at you like that. But your parents died in the service of Christ. Remember that, Stevenson. They're in heaven now, and from there they'll be able to keep an eye on you and watch your progress through life. So remember that too, there's a good chap. You'll always have them, and you'll always have God."

"Yes, sir," Ark said.

A year later when he turned sixteen, he was allowed into the senior boys' common room, where he could put his hands in his pockets, loosen his tie, and slip off his blazer. He was also permitted to watch the common room's bulbous black-and-white television, one of three authorized by Winsor so the whole school could watch Queen Elizabeth II trundle up the Mall in a gilded coach for her coronation. Until then, Ark had relied solely on books for entertainment, so had adventured on Kirrin Island with the Famous Five, accompanied Gimlet to the Gobi Desert, and flown alongside Biggles on numerous sorties over wartime Germany.

Television revealed a different world. Broadcast hours were restricted, so the screen was often filled by a flickering test card; but Ark watched popular comedies (*Hancock's Half Hour, Whack-O!*) as well as police procedurals (*Fabian of the Yard, Dixon of Dock Green*). He also tuned in every month to *The Sky at Night*, hosted by Patrick Moore. There, alongside discussions on comets, asteroids, and UFOs, he heard from astronomers like Harlow Shapley and Fred Hoyle. They made life in the stars seem much more exciting than life here on Earth.

But Ark's favorite programs were the Westerns imported from America—*Boots and Saddles, Rawhide, Maverick,* and *Bronco Layne,* starring a 220-pound granite block of a man named Ty Hardin. One evening, sitting glued to the set in the common room, Ark noticed in the credits that many of these Westerns were filmed on location. Near a town called Paradox. In the American state of Utah.

That meant nothing to him, until one afternoon he snuck out of school to take a local girl to the pictures at the Gaumont Theatre in Tunbridge Wells. The film they saw was *Taza, Son of Cochise,* starring Rock Hudson in the title role. Ark's date swooned over the actor's good looks, his on-screen charisma and macho physique, but to Ark the real hero of the movie was the awe-inspiring landscape in which it was set. Big, wide, open, and full of vibrant reds and oranges of an intensity he'd never known Nature could display. As the credits rolled, he lingered in the back row, one arm around his date's shoulders, and saw that this movie had also been filmed on location. Near Paradox. In Utah.

He wondered what this Paradox was like.

And if he'd ever go there.

CHAPTER FOURTEEN

Corin Dunbar

My Plymouth had broken down again, so I hitched a ride into town with Jessie, who was headed there for a church social. I planned to meet up with girlfriends in the pool hall for a mix of music, burgers, and the low-alcohol beer that Sharkey Gilman served on tap. More than a year had passed since my Thanksgiving dinner with Cal, and I was now twenty-five years old. We were still going out together, but our relationship had cooled. I hadn't broken it off completely as I knew that would be awkward. Paradox might swell like a blowfish when the movie crowd arrived, but the rest of the time it was a close-knit community where everyone knew everyone else's business.

We hadn't planned to meet that night, but it was a Saturday and I noticed Cal through a fug of smoke as soon as I walked in, elbow-leaned against the bar, slim-hipped and muscled in a pale gray T-shirt I'd once told him enhanced the flecks of gray in his green eyes. He'd let his hair grow to a length Dale might not have liked, so it fell over his ears and down the back of his neck to form an ash-blond frame to his sun-tanned face. A bevy of girls clustered around him, with one, the zaftig Kay Short, caressing the back of his neck the way you'd stroke the family cat. As soon as he saw me, Cal shook her off, ground out his cigarette, and started toward me—arousing again the satisfaction that came from knowing I could have what other girls so clearly desired.

I let him join us in the booth the girls had snared away from the action around the tables, and it began to feel like a date—an impression that grew when word spread that Columbia Pictures was throwing a party and we were all invited. The studios often held bashes before a shoot to create goodwill, or after a wrap to say thanks to the town; and that week, Columbia had started to film *A Time for Killing*, starring Glenn Ford, George Hamilton, and Inger Stevens.

Cal was keen to go, which made me think I should give it a miss. But then Dottie flounced in, dressed like a starlet up for an Oscar. More than ten years had passed since she'd left school and started her waitress job at the Double-D, but her movie career had still to gain traction. She'd surrendered none of her Hollywood ambitions, but had managed only to land non-speaking roles—one as an onlooker in a crowd and another as a passenger who alights from a stagecoach in a flurry of petticoats and garters. No one gave her a chance of hitting the big time. They said she was trying too hard (she'd recently changed her name from Dorothy Wittering to Dottie DeVine). But the doubters didn't faze Dottie, who'd always disdained the approval that I'd so often sought.

Like most of my girlfriends squished into the booth, I was dressed in rolled-up 501s. I'd also slipped on a jeans jacket over a blue T-shirt—no makeup except for pink lipstick I'd applied after waving goodbye to Jessie, and hair that was drip-dried, hanging long and loose from the shower. But Dottie had opted for Hollywood "tight and bright." She spilled out of a silver-sequined, V-necked top, and had wriggled into a purple miniskirt that plastered to her thighs like paint. Rhinestone jewelry dangled around her neck and nestled into her cleavage. Her lips and nails were slicked crimson. And when she notched her sunglasses down her nose so she could see in the dim of the pool hall, she batted false eyelashes that were long enough to fan my face.

I followed her into the washroom so she could freshen up. She still favored *Hot Desire* in the hope its Marilyn link would work its magic.

"There's a party tonight," I told her, pleased that for once I knew the scene better than she did. "It's up on Dolores Mesa. A 'star party,' they're calling it, so George Hamilton should be there. Also Inger Stevens. And some new guy named Harrison Ford."

Dottie caught my eye in the mirror. "Harrison Ford? He was in *Dead Heat on a Merry-go-round*. Terrible movie. A total flop."

I didn't argue. Dottie's knowledge of movies was as up-to-date as the latest issue of *Confidential.*

She dabbed perfume behind her ears and into the flesh of her cleavage.

"What do you think of these babies?" she said, cupping her hands under her breasts. "I've got a new enhancer cream called Bust Up, but I'm not sure it's coming through for me."

She slotted an L&M into a holder and directed a plume of smoke at her image, testing a smile and pursing her lips into a pout.

"Harrison's kind of cute," she said, hoicking up her breasts again. "And I'm sure he'd love to meet *these* leading ladies."

She turned to face me. "So what are we waiting for? Let's party!"

I let Cal drive. I sat beside him in his Bronco with a decent space between us, but he reached over to rest his hand on my knee, then wiggled it higher before I pointedly scooted away. We made a detour to pick up Bridger Milan, a buddy of Cal's, who brought along a couple of six-packs of Schlitz, which he ripped open as soon as we were moving again.

"You're off duty, ain't you, Cal?" he said, tapping him on the shoulder and handing over a "brewski."

Dottie wasn't pleased to have company in the back, and made a show of pulling down the hem of her purple skirt. But she happily accepted a beer as other cars swung in behind us. By the time we left the gravel road and hit dirt, we'd formed a convoy, our headlights cutting swathes through the dark and spooking deer that grazed in the ditches beside the road. I could tell from the way Cal threw his Bronco into the bends that he'd put more than a few beers under his belt. But he was the law. No cops were going to pull over one of their own.

I spooled down the window while he fiddled with the radio. He raised only static until he locked onto KBEZ, which was pumping out "Ballad of the Green Berets." He cranked up the volume and belted out the song full voice, with Bridger joining in from the rear. He didn't kid glove the Bronco, but it still took us the better part of an hour to get to Dolores Mesa. At first, the dirt road was flat but with a rippled surface that would have put us in a ditch if we'd jiggered too far to one side; but then it began to twist and turn as it climbed the side of the mesa. It seemed an odd spot for Columbia to choose for a party, but the movie crowd often behaved in strange and unpredictable ways.

When the road petered out, we ground to a halt on the flat top of the mesa with Nancy Sinatra thumping out "These boots are made for walkin'." Cal killed the engine and the radio died with it. We piled out and looked around. He'd left the Bronco's high-beams on, sending a double cone of light over the only other vehicle we could see: a rust-bucket Olds parked to one side. Within minutes, half a dozen other cars and pickups pulled to a stop around us, including a canary-yellow Barracuda that had no place on Utah's washed-out roads. It was a muscle car driven by Everett Talbot, the rat-faced kid from school who'd grown up into a rat-faced man. Car doors slammed. Someone passed around a forty-ouncer of Wild Turkey, and I caught the skunky drift of marijuana. Jessie would have been horrified. The sheriff too. But Cal snapped open another Schlitz, handed me a can, and we all stood around as silly as beer and a Saturday night could make us.

As my eyes adjusted to the night, I made out hunches of rock that rose above the stunted outlines of sage and rubber rabbit brush. About twenty yards away, a tall figure stood alone in the dark with a peculiar shaped object planted on the ground beside him. Its black cannon of a barrel rested on legs that were long and spindly like a heron's. The figure beside it raised a hand.

"Over here!"

Cal and I started toward him, a tall, rangy guy with hands on his hips and hair long and straight and so inky it melted into the night.

"Would you mind turning off those headlights?" he said as we drew near. He spoke with a clipped accent. Not prissy. But unmistakably English.

"Why would I want to do that?" Cal said.

"Because they're spoiling the darkness."

Dottie had joined us, along with Bridger Milan and Everett Talbot, who'd brought along his kid brother, Chad.

"That a telescope?" Everett said, waving a half-pint of Old Forester.

"It is indeed," the Englishman said. "We'll need it if we want to see Vega. And Sirius."

There followed a long moment of silence. Then behind me I heard Dottie mutter, "Oh, boy," as it dawned on her—as it dawned on us all—that we were not about to meet anyone famous from Hollywood.

This might have been a party.

But if so, it was for the wrong kind of stars.

CHAPTER FIFTEEN

Cal wanted to leave. So did Dottie, who spoke for a lot of people when she said, "This is a waste. We need to split."

"For once, Dottie's right," Cal said, "C'mon." He put his arm around my shoulders and tried to draw me away.

"No," I said. "I think I'll stay."

I resented Cal's possessive arm, and something about the stranger seemed to deserve my attention. Even white teeth in the dark. The relaxed way he stood. He wasn't at all perturbed to see his audience melting away. If anything, it seemed to amuse him.

"Suit yourself," Cal said. He gave my shoulder a harder squeeze than needed, and moved off. "Let me know when you're ready to leave, and if I'm still here I'll maybe give you a ride home."

Kay Short fell in beside him before they were swallowed by the dark. Car doors slammed and Cal's high beams were doused. The stranger smiled in his untroubled way and held out his hand. It felt warm and supple when I shook it. Definitely not a rancher's hand.

"I'm Noah," he said. "But my friends call me Ark."

"I'm Corin," I told him. "And *my* friends call me Corin."

His smiled widened. "I'm sorry if I've disappointed them."

"They were expecting movie stars."

"Not my specialty, I'm afraid. But I can show you stars that are every bit as intriguing. Or possibly not," he added, tipping his head to give me a quizzical look.

"Let's find out," I said. "We might both be surprised."

❖

"The telescope's aimed at the North Star," Ark told me. "That's Polaris, and it's the only star in the heavens that doesn't appear to move. That's because it lies on the earth's axis of rotation, which also means you can always see it. Doesn't matter what time of year it is; if you want to find it, you just follow the pointer stars, Merak and Dubhe, that form the bowl of the Big Dipper, and there it is. For centuries, navigators have used Polaris to find true north. You can too. So if you're ever lost in the desert, all you need to do is locate Polaris, and you'll be home before you know it."

I bent to look through the eyepiece.

"Don't touch it," he told me. "You'll bump it off target."

I tried to make sense of what I was seeing. A fuzzy smear of polka dots with blackness all around.

"That fuzziness comes from turbulence in the atmosphere. It messes with the image. Sometimes you have to wait for the air to settle down."

It was better when he tilted the telescope left so I could see Orion's Belt, low in the west, and a bright orange star just to the right of it.

"If you saw its name written down," Ark told me, "you'd think that orange star was called Beetle Juice. Which makes it sound like a squashed bug. In fact, it's called Bet-el-geuse, an Arabic name, and it's likely to be the largest object you'll ever see. It's about a thousand times bigger than our sun. It's also going to explode one day as a supernova, but—fingers-crossed—not tonight. Even if it did blow up, we wouldn't know it, because Betelgeuse is more than five hundred light-years away. Which means you're seeing it now as it was before Columbus arrived in America.

"If you look the other side of Orion's Belt, just above the horizon," moving the telescope again, "you can see a star called Rigel. It could be as bright as a hundred thousand suns, maybe more, which makes it brighter than Betelgeuse even though it's farther away. What we're seeing is how it looked when the Normans invaded England or when the first Crusade set off for the Holy Land. Then if you follow the tilt of Orion's Belt to the south," he continued, "you come to a star called Sirius, or the Dog Star. And *that's* the brightest star in the night sky. Not because it's bigger or *really* brighter, but because it's so close—only about eight and a half light-years away."

I'd admired the stars before, of course. You couldn't live in Utah and not be impressed by them. But they were up there, and we were down here. Two different worlds.

Ark fiddled again with his telescope, aiming it low to the east.

"I've pointed it now at Vega," he said. "Brighter than Rigel or Betelgeuse. It'll be visible much of the night as it follows the sun west, but you'll still have to be quick if you want to see it. You might think we're standing still here on this mesa, but this part of the earth is spinning at a rate of about seven hundred and fifty miles per hour. That's more than twelve miles a minute. At the same time, we're hurtling around the sun at about sixty-seven thousand miles per hour, which is more than eighteen miles a *second*. And of course Vega is also charging through space, so it won't be long before it moves out of the telescope's line of sight."

When I looked, Vega must have done just that, so Ark fiddled again with the eyepiece. When I still couldn't spot his star, he took my elbow and guided me into position with one hand on my shoulder and the other in the small of my back. It was the lightest of touches. Like slow dancing. But it bumped my heart rate up a notch.

It was Dottie who brought me down to earth. A car door opened, light streamed out, and I heard her shout, "Get off me, you sod-ass!"

She stumbled into view with her purple skirt a hula hoop around her waist and her sequined top yanked down and twisted so it hung half off one shoulder. A moment later one of her spike-heeled shoes came flying toward her, followed a moment later by the other.

"Cock-teasing bitch!" Everett Talbot shouted. "You put out for the Hollywood crowd. What's the matter with us?"

He stood by the open door of his Barracuda, his shirt flapping open, then stepped toward Dottie and might have swung a fist at her if Cal hadn't loomed out of the dark and grabbed his arm.

"Get outta here," Cal told him roughly. "You and your brother both."

He strode toward me, holding Dottie as if she were under arrest.

"I'm taking her home," he said. "And you're coming too." He took my hand. "Come on. Party's over. So get in the car."

I shook him off. "I'm staying, Cal," I said, and planted my feet.

He pulled me closer. "I'm the one that brung you, Corin, so I'm the one taking you home. That's the way it works, remember?"

"You were my ride," I told him. "Not my date."

He glared at me, hands clenched by his sides.

Ark said quietly, "I can offer a lift should anyone want one. If that would help," he added.

Cal ignored him.

"Come on, Dottie," he said, turning away. "Let her do what she wants."

Ark folded the tripod of his telescope into the trunk of his car like a foal might tuck in its legs, then drove me into Paradox and out to the ranch. His car was the rust bucket I'd seen parked on the mesa top—an Oldsmobile 88 convertible that was more rattle than steel. He'd known he'd need his own set of wheels, he told me, and there was only one make of car he was willing to drive.

"We had a television at school," he said as he drove me through the valley, "so we could watch the Queen being crowned. But my friends and I much preferred a program called the *Six-Five Special* with Don Lang and his Frantic Five. 'Time to jive on the old six-five.' It introduced me to Eddie Cochran, Little Richard, Buddy Holly, and Chuck Berry. I spent most of my pocket money on their records, once we acquired a Dansette player. We loved American music, American blues, American rock. And it all began with a song called "Rocket 88." Written by one Ike Turner. Now married to a lady named Tina. It's all about an Olds 88, and it's reckoned to be the first rock n' roll song ever recorded: '*A V8 motor, baby, it's a modern design; black convertible top, and the girls don't mind.*' You remember that song?" he asked.

I shook my head.

"Too bad," he said. "You must have had a misspent youth."

I had to smile at the zest he showed, not just for American music, but for *all* things American. His enthusiasm far outshone mine. But then he hadn't been exposed to the divisions that then were threatening to tear our society apart. The Vietnam War, the race riots and shootings, and the ongoing war between flag-waving conservatives on one side and the druggies and hippies on the other. To Ark, Americans were one big happy family in the land of the free and the Great Outdoors. He was in love with the image, and his Eighty-Eight fit right in. He didn't see the rips and tears in its seats, nor the soggy slump of its springs. Just its aura.

At the ranch, I told him to drive around to the bunkhouse, where he could bed down for the night. The building was all but abandoned with a floor littered with mud, but it was a step up from the backseat of his Eighty-Eight.

We stoked up the belly of the stove and lit a couple of half-burned candles we found in the kitchen, then dragged a bench in front of the fire to sit shoulder to shoulder as flames licked over the wood and shot out fountains of firefly sparks. The stove had lost its door, but its pipe-cleaner chimney was still attached, and the blaze warmed our outstretched hands. I was no romantic and thought love-at-first-sight was a Hollywood myth the studios invented to hurry along the plot. But I was acutely aware of an invisible thread reeling Ark and me together.

We sat for a while in easy silence, but then raced through the years of our lives like a couple of kids swapping toys, picking one up and dropping it again, because our attention had been caught by something else that was even more new and exciting.

CHAPTER SIXTEEN

Ark Stevenson

The day Ark left school he took an overnight sleeper to Scotland, where he'd been accepted by the University of Glasgow's School of Physics and Astronomy. He'd never had doubts about the subject he would study, but his interest in the stars had been kicked into a higher gear when, on October 4, 1957, the Soviet Union launched the world's first artificial satellite. Through the eyepiece of his school's reflector telescope, Ark watched Sputnik curve across the night sky, 143 miles up at its perigee. The satellite appeared as a white dot with no intrinsic interest, but Ark knew that science fiction had just become science fact. The Space Age had started, and he was determined to play a part.

He moved into the attic room of a seedy bed-and-breakfast on Botanic Crescent, one of the University's approved lodgings, and unpacked his worldly possessions from a small suitcase while his landlady, a sagging redhead with a taste for blue eyeshadow, read him the house rules. No noise. No music. No alcohol. No cooking in the room. And no visitors of the opposite sex. Ever. For electricity he could slot a shilling in the meter; and for heat he could rely either on the cast-iron radiator that hissed steam at unpredictable times or on the two-bar electric fire that he soon discovered worked best when flat on its back, grilling toast. The toilet was two floors down, next to the communal bathroom. Rent of four pounds a week was due on Monday. Breakfast, usually a pungent kipper or a soft-boiled egg, was served at 7:00 a.m.; and high tea—macaroni cheese or haggis and swede—was at 6:00 p.m. sharp.

After the mild climate of southeast England, Glasgow seemed a dank and dour city where the rare sighting of a watery sun was cause for celebration. With clouds blowing in from the shipyards that even then were struggling to stay alive, it was a strange place to study stars that were almost never visible; but the University, founded in 1451, was world class, counting among its graduates Lord Kelvin, Joseph Lister, James Watt, and Adam Smith. The city itself held few attractions. Poverty was rife in the tenement slums of the Gorbals, and "rammies" and knife fights were commonplace after "last call," when sozzled patrons tipped out of the pubs.

Ark spent his free time in the student union, playing snooker or darts while nursing a pint or two of McEwan's. It was there that he learned he need never lack for female company. Women, or "quines," arrived at his side and as often as not in his bed.

He studied planetary systems, instrumentation, and particle physics, and took a short course on the history of astronomy, the oldest science of all. That module was taught by a German Jew named Reinhard Moser, who, as a student, had been forced to flee the Nazis before he could earn a PhD.

"The Ancients," Moser told his class, "had very different views of the Universe than the one we have today."

Early Egyptians believed it to be shaped like an open-ended box with the Nile flowing along the bottom. The Chinese thought it was a living organism that moved with the force of the wind. And early Greeks pictured it as an endless sea with the earth as a disk floating on top.

"We laugh at these ideas now," Moser said, in his clipped accent, "but the people who devised them were among the cleverest the world has seen."

Two thousand years ago, Eratosthenes had used two sticks and Euclidean geometry to measure the circumference of the earth; while one thousand years ago, al-Jayyani employed the angle of the sun and its evening speed of descent to determine the height of the atmosphere.

"Who among us could perform such feats today?" Moser said. "And get the calculations *right*?"

His course ran the gamut from the Babylonians, who first realized that motion in the Heavens is periodic, through the Egyptians, who used their astral knowledge to align their pyramids, and then to the Greeks, who deployed a complex arrangement of epicycles and eccentrics. By the time Moser had worked his way through the heliocentric ideas of Copernicus, Brahe, Kepler, Galileo, Huygens, Newton, and Kant, Ark was convinced that the PhD *manqué* was following his own agenda. A seditious agenda, aimed at undermining the certainty with which other, better qualified teachers dispensed their science.

"As far as we know, the Universe was formed only once," Moser said. "No one was there to observe its creation, so the best we can do is *deduce* what happened. We cannot really know, not with the sureness with which we can state the molecular structure of, say, water or methane. It's possible that there is an objective reality, something that's fixed forever in time and space, but we should never presume that we know what it is, far less that we understand it. Furthermore, we have to accept that we may *never* be able to understand it.

"We flatter ourselves into thinking that we are the smartest creatures in the Universe, but even if that were true—a highly speculative assumption, given the way we behave towards one another and the planet we live on—our abilities would still be finite. It's more than likely that the Universe operates on a level that's beyond our ability to comprehend. A blind beetle, crawling over a curved branch, will think the Universe is flat. A fish, swimming in the deepest ocean, knows the beetle is wrong, but *its* universe, while three-dimensional, would consist only of water. Who is to say that we are not trapped in the same situation? Able to interpret only what we see or otherwise detect around us?

"Quantum mechanics tells us that the way we see the Universe is not the way it really is—because the act of measurement changes whatever it is we are trying to establish. We live in a non-deterministic world—one in which there are no certainties, only probabilities. We can construct models that *replicate* the reality we observe. But our models are *not* the reality itself, and we should never be fooled into thinking they are. Even the Roman Catholic Church—not known for its love of science—understood this basic fact. It didn't object when Galileo began to teach, counter to the Scriptures, that it was the earth that revolved around the sun and not the sun that revolved around the earth—but only as long as he stressed that this novel idea was merely a *model*. Only when he taught that his idea was *real* did the Church haul him before the Inquisition and place him under arrest.

"The basic fact is," Moser said, "every model we've ever devised has either been modified or abandoned for the simple reason that something about it has been shown to be wrong. That will happen to every idea that we hold today. Which is another way of saying that everything you now believe to be true will one day be shown to be false. We don't understand the reality around us, and most likely we never will. We just have our models. Which work. Until they don't."

Ark never spoke of his parents during his years in Glasgow. If anyone asked, he said they'd been killed in a car crash. It was simpler that way. In truth, he was ashamed of them. Angry too. And hurt. He resented the fact that they'd sent him away—and then lost their lives in a futile attempt to convert a tribe of Indians who'd developed their own set of beliefs.

The Yanomami were sure the Universe consisted of four disks stacked on top of one another like the layers of a cake. They lived on the third layer, where they'd been placed by a god who'd created them either from the blood of the moon (the men) or from the fruit of the *wabu* (the women). Ark's parents believed in a *three*-layer cake—heaven above the earth and a hell below, and the people who lived there had been created by a god who'd made them either from dust (Adam) or from one of Adam's ribs (Eve).

Both sets of beliefs were models. Which worked. Until they didn't.

When Ark graduated, in the spring of '63, he found himself at a loss. He had no family to return to, and no place to call home. At a friend's suggestion, he found work in a pea-canning factor in Norfolk where the money was good. The job was supposed to be short term, but he met a girl and stayed six months. He then moved on to a Gripper Rod factory in Wales, where he packed brushed-nickel stair rods into boxes of ten. When summer came, he relocated to Perranporth, a seaside resort in Cornwall, where he was employed as a lifeguard on its surfers' beach.

The following year, he signed on as a "deckie learner" on a Lowestoft trawler fishing for cod in the North Sea. After that came a series of jobs—delivering the post at Christmas, waiting tables in an Egon Ronay restaurant in Cheltenham, and serving behind the cheese counter of Harrod's Food Hall in London. In the cathedral city of Exeter, he worked briefly as a Quicksilver courier until one day, in the fall of 1965, when he was delivering a crate of Chablis Grand Cru to the oenophile Dean of the University's Science Department, he saw an advertisement in *Sky & Telescope*, an American magazine for astronomers.

The University of Utah—in Salt Lake City—was seeking a graduate student who could further its astronomy department's mission to teach the public the mysteries of the stars...

CHAPTER SEVENTEEN

Corin Dunbar

"**...S**o you applied?" I asked him.

"I did."

It was past three o'clock in the morning and the logs in the stove had burned to cinders. We could both feel the chill seeping into the bunkhouse.

"I don't think the University of Utah expected to hear from someone in England, but I wrote them a long letter to say that the public today is woefully ignorant about the stars. A hundred years ago, the average person could identify any number of objects in the night sky, but today most can find only the moon. I blamed Thomas Edison. He may have switched on the lights in our cities, but he also switched off the light from the stars. We needed to change that, I said. We needed to bring back some of the knowledge we'd lost, and I pointed out that the ancient Egyptians knew enough about stars to determine when to plant their crops. The Phoenicians used stars to find their way around the Mediterranean, and the Polynesians did the same to navigate from one side of the Pacific to the other. Even God made use of a star when he hovered one over a stable in Bethlehem. I think the university liked that idea."

"So star parties? That was your answer?"

Ark nodded. "To show the beauty of the stars."

"But in *Paradox*?"

He looked at me sideways and grinned.

"Stars are a passion of mine, I admit. But they've been around a long time—ever since the Big Bang—so I don't feel the need to rush.

No, the real reason I came to Paradox was to see where Westerns are made. I've seen *Taza, Son of Cochise*. I've seen *The Searchers, Shane, High Noon, The Big Country, Last Train from Gun Hill*. And I've watched every episode of *Wagon Train, Gunsmoke, Boots and Saddles,* and *Have Gun Will Travel*. I've wanted to come to Paradox since I was a child. To experience the scenery, the red rocks, the mesas and canyons. I want to explore the real American West."

"And you will," I said, laughing. "But not tonight."

It was an effort to tear myself away, but I left him to sleep on one of the bunks the wranglers had used and made my way to the ranch house. A slice of a moon cast a patina of silver over the land, turning it ice-cool and magical. I tiptoed upstairs, careful not to wake Jessie. I knew I wouldn't sleep but lay in bed, willing the dawn.

The next morning, I'd fetched Ark over from the bunkhouse and brewed coffee for his breakfast when Jessie came into the kitchen from the back porch. She'd been up since first light and was rosy-cheeked from an early ride to check on the cattle. When she let the screen door slam behind her, she gave a twitch of surprise to see a stranger at the table.

"This is Ark," I said as he stood and extended his hand.

Jessie took her own sweet time shaking it, first shucking off her gloves and settling them just so on the dresser.

"I slept in the bunkhouse," Ark said. "I hope you don't mind."

Jessie looked at me, then back at Ark. "This is Corin's house as much as it's mine," she said archly. "She's free to do as she pleases."

"Coffee's hot," I told her. "Want a cup?"

She nodded slowly, still assessing. I'd never brought a man home for breakfast, not even Cal, and she found it hard to accept. At the best of times, Jessie didn't warm to strangers, as she tended to suspect their motives. Sometimes she was right.

"That's my chair," she told Ark.

"Oh, I'm sorry," he said, and shifted one place over. "I'm not familiar with the seating arrangements."

I had to suppress a smile. He sounded so English. We didn't have seating arrangements. Not in Utah, where we just sat.

"No reason why you should be," Jessie said, "you not being here before. You haven't been here before, have you?"

He shook his head. "First time."

I was serving him eggs over-easy with hash browns when I heard the familiar clatter of Cal's patrol car draw up outside, followed by the double-toot of his horn that he usually gave to announce his arrival. Jessie raised an eyebrow and I gave her a shrug in reply.

The door pushed open and Cal strode in, dressed in full cop uniform, hat in hand. He, too, checked himself when he saw Ark at the table.

He folded his arms across his chest. "What's *he* doing here?"

"I believe we met last night," Ark said, standing for a second time.

Cal ignored him. His eyes were puffy, his skin blotched and dry, and I noticed he'd picked up a scratch on his neck that ran from behind one ear down to his collar.

"We're having breakfast," I said, as if that supplied an explanation.

Cal stepped further into the room. Jessie, at least, seemed pleased to see him for she offered him a slice of her homemade banana bread.

He shook his head and turned again to me.

"I wanna talk to you," he said.

"Okay."

"Outside."

I followed him onto the back porch, then moved a few steps away from the door so we were clear of the windows and couldn't be overheard.

"So what *is* he doing here?"

"Like I said. Having breakfast. Eggs over-easy with hash browns."

Cal thrust his face close, so I had to make an effort not to step back. "Don't get cute with me, Corin. A man has breakfast, it means he spent the night."

His neck had flushed an angry red that even his tan couldn't hide.

"Which he did," I said. "Spend the night." I knew that would provoke him, but I was angry myself now.

He grabbed my chin and yanked up my face. "You telling me he slept over?"

I jerked myself free of his grip. "You've got no say over me," I told him.

He grabbed my shoulders in both his hands and pushed me back against the porch rail. "You take him into your *bed*, Corin? Is that what you're saying? You turning into some kind of *tramp* now?"

"He slept in the bunkhouse, if it's any business of yours."

Cal said nothing for a moment, then nodded slowly as he clenched and unclenched his fists.

"Last night I should have waited," he said. "Given you a ride home. I came here to apologize. But seems I shouldn't have bothered."

He took a step back, the muscles in his jaw still working.

"I don't want to see that Limey again," he said, his eyes hard as stones. "He shouldn't be here. Shouldn't even be in this country. And I don't want *you* seeing him again, neither."

He didn't wait for a reply but turned and stomped off the porch. I stayed where I was until the rattle of his patrol car faded away, then went back into the kitchen.

"You two done out there?" Jessie asked.

I nodded.

"Good. Because we got a day's work to do and not the time to do it in."

CHAPTER EIGHTEEN

Jessie didn't take to Ark. Not at first. She preferred local boys, because good or bad, she understood them. Cal had won a place in her heart because she knew if we married, he'd keep me close and rooted at the ranch. Ark was a threat. An outsider. A foreigner. There was no telling where he might take me.

"What that man doesn't know about ranching would fill an encyclopedia ten times over," Jessie told me once, as we watched Ark drive off in his Eighty-Eight. "And he couldn't tell a coyote from a chipmunk if one snuck up and bit him on the *bee*-hind."

Ark, she said, was "highfalutin'," when in reality he was just different. It was true he could sound ridiculously English. "Pleased to meet you," he'd say; or "How do you do?" when I introduced him to people around town, so they didn't know if they should take him seriously or if he was having fun at their expense. Sometimes, when he joined us for dinner at the ranch, he'd ask Jessie, "May I have the butter please?" Or "Could you please pass the water?" She told me on more than one occasion she didn't know if she should get out of her chair to serve him or "drop him some kind of royal curtsy."

What won her over—other than his manners—was his knowledge of the Bible, which he revealed—strategically, I think—one evening when he came for supper. Jessie had slow-cooked a beef brisket smothered in sweet onions, which she took out of the oven using a pair of well-singed pot holders.

"Careful," she said, carrying the dish to the table. "It's hot."

As we pulled up our chairs, she took one of my hands and reached over to clasp one of Ark's.

"Bless us, O Lord," she said, "and these thy gifts, which we are about to receive from thy bounty. Through Christ, our Lord. Amen."

She just had time to cross herself before Ark said, "'I am the bread of life; he who comes to me will not hunger, and he who believes in me will not thirst.'"

Jessie looked at him in surprise.

"John 6:35," he said.

"'My food is to do the will of him who sent me, and to accomplish his work,'" Jessie responded. "John 4:34."

"'Go then,'" Ark said, "'Eat your bread in happiness and drink your wine with a cheerful heart, for God has approved your works.' Ecclesiastes 9:7."

"You surely know your Bible," Jessie told him.

"'Heaven and Earth will pass away, but my words will not pass away.'"

"Luke?"

Ark shook his head. "Matthew 24:35."

"You sure about that?" She squinted at him sideways.

"I'm sure."

"I'll check," she said. "Later. Now get on and eat your brisket. Before it gets cold."

For a month I managed to juggle Ark and Cal and keep the two of them apart. But then Columbia Pictures announced a wrap party for *A Time for Killing*—a *real* star party this time, not one of Ark's sound-alikes—and the whole town prepared to celebrate. The locals who'd worked as extras had all been paid; settlements for damages to land, property, animals, and people had been agreed; and the residents who'd rented out their houses to cast and crew had banked their fist-fuls of dollars.

I'd arranged to meet Ark outside the pool hall, and we planned to go to the party from there. But when I drove into town I found

Main Street hung with fairy lights and my way blocked by a parade of candy-striped floats, a brass band, and bunch of whooping cowboys on horseback. The delay made me late—so I didn't see the start of the fight.

I caught my breath when I saw Ark face down in the dirt with Cal towering above him, his legs splayed, fists up, elbows tucked into his sides. A sizeable crowd had gathered, mostly Cal's friends, but already they were starting to drift away, so I hoped the fight was over. I elbowed my way forward and squeezed into a gap behind Hal Jenkins, a drinking buddy of Cal's, and a wrangler named Rob Wishart, a mountain of a man who often worked as an extra.

Ark pushed himself to his feet and slowly raised his fists. Cal shuffled sideways as Ark moved toward him. Ark's fists were still up, but he'd adopted a strangely upright posture, back straight, head high, one foot square to the other. Cal spat on the ground and threw a right that caught Ark on the side of the head and knocked him off-balance. He punched Ark again, not as hard as before, but hard enough to put him down again.

"Doesn't have a prayer," Hal Jenkins said. He'd been faking jabs in tandem with Cal's.

Wishart put out an arm to hold me back.

"Okay," he said. "That's enough. Show's over, folks."

Cal backed off, sucking in air. More onlookers turned to leave, but Ark rolled onto his stomach, then onto all fours. He rested a moment, then forced himself to stand. Blood welled from his nose and a split in his upper lip. He swiped an arm across his mouth.

"You done?" he said to Cal, his voice thick and nasal. "Because I'm just warming up."

Wishart said, "Better you'd stayed at home, amigo."

Ark swung, but Cal stepped out of the way. Ark tried again, and Cal moved his head. The punch sailed harmlessly by. Another punch missed, but when Ark hit out a fourth time, Cal moved in and put Ark down a third time.

"Fight's over," Cal told him. "We're done here. Okay?"

But Ark wasn't through. Again, he pushed himself up, the front of his shirt a bib of red. I shoved hard against Wishart, but he laughed and again held me back.

"Someone oughta stop this," Cal said, looking around at the crowd.

"Ark," I shouted. "Stay down!"

I batted at Wishart until he lowered his arm and let me through. I got between the fighters, my back toward Ark, my hands jammed against Cal's heaving chest.

"You won, Cal. Okay?" I said. "You trounced him fair and square. But it's over. Time to quit."

"He should've stayed down," Cal said as he allowed me to pull him away. "Damn Limey. He should've stayed down. On the ground where he belongs."

"I know, Cal. You're right. But it's over now. It's finished."

I yanked him toward the pool hall and almost had him inside when we both heard Ark shout, "You stopping already, Cal? I didn't take you for a sissy."

Cal tensed and his fists bunched.

"Come on, Cal," I said. "It's just talk. It doesn't mean anything."

"I oughta go back and put him down so he *really* stays down."

"I know, Cal. But you're a better man if you don't."

His jaw tightened and the muscles in his arms bulged. But he let me walk him into the pool hall.

He wiped his hands on his shirt.

"Loser!" we heard Ark shout.

But with his swollen lip, it came out as "Loosher."

An hour passed before I could join Ark in the attic room he'd rented month-to-month in Pattie Grosvenor's boardinghouse on Seventh. He lay on the bed, his clothes in a shucked-off heap on the floor, replaced now by a clean T-shirt and baggy cotton pants. His feet were bare and his hair was damp from the shower. His bottom lip had puffed up into a monstrous pout, and his right eye had narrowed to a slit that was swirled by a kaleidoscope of colors.

"What got into you?" I said.

He groaned as he propped himself up.

"Your friend's been spoiling for a fight from the day I arrived. And unfortunately, he's the kind of person who settles disputes with his fists. I'm not. But with Cal, it was never a question of whether we'd come to blows, but where and when. I didn't want *him* to decide. That would've given him too much of an edge."

I frowned. "You mean *you* started it?"

He nodded, flinched, and pressed a hand against his ribs. "I thought it best to have the fight out in the open. In daylight, not up some back alley after dark. And best, too, if there were people around. Not that I wanted witnesses, but I was betting someone would stop the fight before anyone—me, that is—got hurt. I may have misjudged things," he added.

"You're saying you *knew* you would lose?"

"The thought had occurred to me."

"Then why didn't you quit? Stay on the ground and save yourself the pain?"

He clutched at his ribs again. "There's more than one way to win. Even when you lose. I guess I came in second," he added, trying out a smile that turned into a grimace.

"You didn't let *Cal* win, if that's what you mean. You didn't give him the satisfaction."

"The last time I hit anyone was when I was twelve years old. I punched a boy named Scruffy Sanders. It worked then, but I'm out of practice. Did I really do so badly out there?"

I brushed wayward strands of hair from his forehead, then gingerly curled up beside him and rested my head on his shoulder.

"You did just fine," I told him.

CHAPTER NINETEEN

That summer—the summer of '66—I was kept busy with my chores, managing the water troughs and setting out the salt blocks in the pastures. I also ran the grazing program I'd devised; tended the kitchen garden to keep us supplied with squash, carrots, beets, and potatoes; and I watered and foddered Sherman and made sure he was well looked after. My main task was to care for the aluminum tanks where the straws of his semen were frozen in liquid nitrogen. I'd deliver the straws to ranchers in the valley, or they'd drive their cattle to our ranch so we could inseminate them here. Felipe had constructed a new pen, and when we wanted to collect from Sherman, we'd call in Bose Manly, who worked freelance now that Connie Griffin had sold her spread. Bose would bring his sidekick, Chance, and with Felipe handling the teaser cow, we had the three-man team we needed.

Connie had been true to her word and passed on her customers to us. I was careful to build on her reputation, and pretty soon the numbers in Jessie's books started to turn from a blood-letting red to a healthy black. I was thrilled with the progress we were making. But my mind was always on Ark.

We soon found we needed somewhere to be alone. The attic he'd rented wouldn't serve: Pattie Grosvenor would never have allowed it. There were secluded places at the ranch, but I didn't want Jessie to catch us, not even exchanging a chaste kiss on the cheek. As it was, we were already tiptoeing around her, dainty as a couple of cats stalking a bird.

For a while, we settled for a blanket out in the desert, where there was little or no chance of discovery. And it was there that I first showed him my scars—the thin white stripes that scored my belly where I'd cut myself as a child. I'd never let Cal see them, always managed to keep them covered, as I hadn't wanted to expose myself to quite that degree. With Ark it was different. The scars had faded with time but still stood out in sharp relief against my flat belly. He traced his finger along them, one after the other. "Another part of you to love," he said, and I came to see them that way too. I hadn't been ashamed of them, not really, but had kept them hidden so I didn't have to explain or excuse them. But now I could view them as another part of my history, a small part of my story.

Our desert blanket served us well, but it lost its appeal when we were stretched out one day and heard a hiss as loud as static. Ark didn't know what it was; but I did. Even before I saw the wedge-shaped head. We both leapt up as a rattler, hidden in the lee of a rock, slithered toward us, its horny tail erect and shivering in angry vibrations. Behind it, in a roiling den, half a dozen young writhed together like slippery strands of spaghetti. Ark and I needed a better retreat, and after racking my brain, I thought I had the perfect answer.

About six months after I arrived in Paradox, Jessie had bundled me into the passenger seat of her pickup and driven me up the valley. I sat still as a statue as she followed the whisper of track that cut off left from the valley road. She jarred the pickup across slick rock, and gunned it through drifts of sand until finally we came to the scattered ruins of a wood-and-wattle cabin that—decades before—had sheltered cowboys working the open range. Three of the cabin's walls were buttressed together like drunks in a bar, while the fourth (and front) one lay face down on the ground with spikey pads of prickly pear thrusting through the empty frames of its windows and door. Crumpled beer cans were scattered around, and a tangle of barbed-wire fencing lay dumped on a heap of campfire ashes.

Jessie didn't stop, but swung us onto another track in the bed of a wash. We snaked over sand through gooseneck curves and dodged stumps of juniper that had been snapped off like breadsticks by the force of flash floods. Jessie drove in a concentrated silence I didn't have the courage to break. The wash narrowed and walls of rock closed in on either side until we were brought to a halt by a boulder the size of a house with a pool of water at its base. Jessie switched off the engine, grabbed me by the hand, and tugged me around the boulder, then up and over a shallow bench of rock until we were halted again at a pour-off where the rocky wall of the canyon rose sheer above us, worn smooth by eons of wind and water.

She pointed to the wall on our left where a long line of markings—stick figures, stick animals, and stick birds—had been etched into the black patina of desert varnish, alongside a gallery of strange shapes and symbols.

"Petroglyphs," she said, the first word she'd spoken since we'd left the ranch.

She stared at the figures, saying nothing, but squeezing my hand so tight it began to hurt.

"And over there," she said, pointing to three letters and a date carved into the rock farther along the wall on our left—

AKW
1942

"*—graffiti.*"
All but spitting the word out.

She stared at the letters, then, without saying more, pulled me back to the pickup, and off we drove, down the wash and back to the ranch. She never spoke of the place again, and we never returned. But I was sure I could find it again, because the cabin we'd passed was one that Vernon Tucker had been restoring. He was editor of *The Southeast Utah Gazette* and, like Ark, an avid fan of the American West.

I drove Ark there in the Dodge, as his Eighty-Eight would never have made it off road. We paused for a moment at the cabin. Its four walls had been rebuilt—they were upright and notched into place, their planks chinked with mud and grass—and a freshly sanded front door now hung from a pair of sturdy hinges. I drove on, following the wash Jessie had taken and seeking out benches of sandstone that might give the Dodge traction. Several times Ark was forced to jump out and flag me around a particularly intrusive outcrop of rock; and once we crashed through a swath of flattened brush and snapped-off branches that poked out of the dirt like stakes.

I stopped by the house-sized boulder and the pool of water shiny as engine oil at its base and guided Ark around it, much as Jessie had done with me. Right away, we entered a magical world of sheer rock walls that rose all around us in swirls of orange streaked with the yellows and reds of a sunset. Tufts of green showed through a sandy floor wherever cattail, bluestem, and Indian grass had been able to find water. A trio of cottonwoods flickered with color and offered dappled shade—we later christened them "the Three Wise Men," after they'd witnessed all our secrets—and further on we found a water-pocket pool and a bench of rock that was weather-buffed smooth as a hand-laid floor.

We sat there that first time just shy of the pour-off and the petroglyph wall, listening to a silence broken only by the muffled echo of our voices.

"It's perfect," Ark said. "Our Eden."

Over that long, hot summer, on too many days to count, we spread our blanket on the bench of rock while Ark covered me with the warmth of his body. We dangled our feet in the cool of the water-pocket pool, or lay on our backs "sunny side up," as Ark would say, or "over easy" when I lay on my front. We'd wonder at the petroglyphs cut into the varnish. There were scores of glyphs like these all over southeast Utah, left behind by the Anasazi who'd lived in the area in prehistoric times. I'd often come across them, but these were the first Ark had seen, and he was instantly enthralled by their primitive beauty.

There were carvings of deer and sheep and a horned bull; meandering snakes and big-beaked apterous birds. Also, a smattering of skeletal people with boxy bodies and ovals for heads. There were imprints of hands and feet. Catherine-wheel whirls and spirals. And a chorus line of dancing figures standing shoulder to shoulder with triangular bodies and lozenge-shaped heads. A favorite of Ark's was a crude circle with squiggly lines like tentacles that fanned out from its core. It looked to me like an exploding star.

"Which," Ark said, "is probably what it is."

As a newly minted member of his school's Astronomical Society, he told me, he'd been allowed to swivel its telescope onto any target he liked.

"I chose a supernova. A smear of gas and dust called the Crab Nebula that's all that remains of a massive star that exploded nearly a thousand years ago on the Fourth of July in the year 1054. The explosion was one of the brightest in history—so glaring it was seen by observers on Earth even during the day. The Chinese recorded it, and so did astronomers in Japan and the Middle East. And now, it seems, these Anasazi recorded it too. As a petroglyph, carved here into a rock in our canyon.

"So you have all these people," he said, "separated by the curve of the earth and the width of oceans. They didn't know the others existed, yet all of them saw the same explosion of a star, which tied them together in ways they couldn't imagine, because every time a star explodes, it spews its contents into space. And the elements that have formed deep in its core join those that have been around since the beginning of time. Together they make *new* stars. And planets. And moons. And everything else you see around you. Not just these rocks and trees, but the birds, flowers, plants—and people too. People like us. People like them. That's how we're all connected.

"The atoms we're made of—the ones we think of as ours— were all formed during the Big Bang or in the center of stars that later exploded. They've been roaming the Universe for billions of years, and before they reached us, they passed through other people—through every historical figure who's ever lived. Every caveman. Every slave, farmhand, and worker. As well as every famous person you've ever heard of. Archimedes, Julius Caesar, Isaac Newton, Beethoven, Bach...anyone you care to choose. They've been inside Genghis Khan, Attila the Hun, Hitler, and Stalin. And yes, they've been in Jesus, Muhammed, and Buddha too.

"If your aunt Jessie wants to share a breath of air with Jesus," Ark went on, "all she need do is inhale. Because some of the atoms that *he* breathed in are in *your* lungs right now. Same thing with the water he drank. If you want to share that water, just duck your head under a tap. Because some of the atoms you swallow will be ones that once passed *his* lips too.

"We are all related," Ark said, "because we're all made of the same material. Stardust. That's all we are. We share the same atoms, not just with the people who've already lived, but with all those people who've yet to be born. We'll become them, live on through them. Because none of us truly dies."

Jessie often said that Ark's head was in the clouds, but it was much further away than that. He had a way of seeing what others did not. When he looked at the buttes and spires that towered above the sandy washes, he didn't just see desert; he also saw ghosts of the men who'd ridden there, tall in the saddle, sheathed in dust and squinting toward a far horizon. When he gazed at the moon, he didn't just see a big pizza pie or a sliver like an eyebrow; he also imagined standing on its surface and looking back at a blue Earth as it ploughed through an ocean of space.

Many times, we'd lie side by side in our canyon hideout, watching day turn into night and the stars seed the bell jar above us, and he'd spin me stories. About the past, the future—about where we'd come from and where we were headed. He pictured himself as a traveler on spaceship Earth, twirling in circles around the sun like a carousel rider at a county fair.

"We have a ringside view of the Universe," he said, "if only we'd open our eyes. I can't understand why some people take no interest in the stars. They're like passengers in a car who drive cross-country yet can't be bothered to raise their heads and look out the window."

He wanted to understand the Universe, to reach back in time and witness its beginning, then leap ahead and know how it would end. He comforted me with the thought that we didn't just come from the stars, but we'd one day return there. And then live on forever. When he first broached this idea—that there was some kind of eternal life in the stars—I was happy to embrace it, because try as I might, I'd never come to terms with Grace's death. It had been so sudden, so final. I wanted to think she was still *somewhere*. That she hadn't just ceased to exist. Father Thomas' belief in an afterlife had given me solace once. But Ark's ideas were founded on facts that were not tempered by myth or illusion.

"My world crumbled when Grace died," I told him one evening as we lay on our favorite slab of rock. "And it was just as bad when Gene threw me out. It seemed I wasn't good enough to be loved."

Ark raised himself onto one elbow. "I felt the same way when my parents sent me to England. I'm not sure I've properly forgiven them."

He stood up and lobbed a stone at the canyon wall opposite, where it set off a riff of echoes.

"They were so certain that *their* view of the world was right," he said. "That's what I found so hard to accept. Never once did they show even a shadow of doubt."

"Jessie's like that," I told him. "She's convinced that Heaven and Hell really exist."

"That's to mistake belief for knowledge."

He slumped onto the blanket beside me. The shadow of a crow skimmed across our bodies and climbed the rock face opposite, and we both watched it perch high on a crag and cut the silence with its rasps.

"I was fifteen years old," Ark said, "when my headmaster told me my parents had been killed. 'An unfortunate mishap,' he called it, as if they'd tripped over a root and sprained an ankle. He wasn't good on the emotional front. But then he *was* English."

"I'm sorry," I said.

He waved the sentiment away. "In many ways he was right. My life continued much as before, so perhaps it *was* just a mishap. But it still left a gap."

"I once asked Jessie to adopt me," I said. "But the suggestion threw her into a panic."

"Perhaps it was enough to have you with her." He reached out to take my hand. "Sometimes, that's all that's needed."

Near the end of that long, hot summer, I brought a camera into our canyon—an Instamatic I'd ordered from Sears. Ark banged off a couple of snapshots of the Three Wise Men, and would have taken more if I hadn't stopped him. Film was expensive in those days. He propped the camera on the flat of a rock, then dashed over to stand beside me so we could both be in the picture. We held our breath—and our smiles—until we heard the click of the shutter.

I remember that moment as the time I fell in love. I was drawn to Ark physically, by his dark good looks and his lean, sinewy body. I thought him poetic, although he laughed when I told him that. I was also attracted by his cool self-sufficiency—and his inquisitive mind that daily tested the boundaries of my pragmatic thinking. We developed a bond that encompassed body, mind, and spirit, but it wasn't always easy. I had to work at our relationship—because Ark always kept a certain distance. He didn't chase me the way Cal had done. I had to wait for him to open up much like a bud in springtime.

At heart, he was a dreamer. But he could shape his dreams into plans and then into action. He liked to have options, independence of thought, and he constantly kicked against rules that confined him. That's one reason he was so entranced by the American West, by its empty spaces and endless horizons. They spoke to him of liberty and freedom. And boundless opportunity.

When our canyon photo came back from Kodak, my hair could be seen hanging long over my shoulders in a dark muss of waves that had escaped from behind my ears. My hands are clasped in front of me, and I'm smiling up at Ark with a look on my face that's an open declaration of love. Ark is mugging for the camera, one hand raised behind me and the other across his chest, fingers spread in a *ta-da* gesture that says, "Here she is—am I not the luckiest man in the world?" His shoulders fill out a faded T-shirt that hangs roomy over his hips. His eyes shine big and dark within the contours of cheekbones I loved to trace with my fingers. Like reading Braille. His smile instantly grabs your attention—the broadest, happiest smile you're ever likely to see. It permeates the photo and fills your heart with such joy, you just *have* to smile back.

In the top left of the photo, the camera captured the chorus line of petroglyph dancers, and above them the crude circle with the shafts of light that radiated from it: Ark's exploding star. Many a time he would clamber over fallen boulders to study it more closely, while I, sated by our lovemaking, would drowse on the blanket beside the rock pool. He'd kick off his sandals and squirm his toes into the sand, then hover his palm a few inches from a handprint that someone had etched into the rock beside the star.

"How long do you think it's been here?" he asked me once.

"The handprint? Centuries," I said, although in truth I had no idea. "Longer than that over there," I added, and nodded my head at the three initials chiseled nearby.

He wrinkled his face. "I don't know how anyone could disfigure a rock face like that."

"Given enough time, it might be valued."

"You think?"

"Somewhere near Mesa Verde," I told him, "Richard Wetherill's name is carved into the stone. He's the man who discovered the site back in the 1880s. His name's preserved now. A treasured artifact with historical worth."

"Well, at least it has meaning. But these initials here are just... initials. A miner's perhaps. Or maybe a cowboy's."

He came back to lie beside me.

"The first man to walk on the moon," he said, "will leave footprints in the dust. They'll stay there forever, because there's no atmosphere on the moon, so no wind. Nor any water, so nothing to wipe them away. It would be good to leave a mark like that. One that can never be erased."

CHAPTER TWENTY

I was elated when Ark found a niche in Paradox, since that gave him a reason to stay other than me. His star-party work for the University of Utah had come to an end. But he found a way to carry the program forward on his own. Paradox had always been off the beaten track, but tourists quickly discovered it once they realized they could watch a movie being made in the morning and then rub shoulders with their favorite stars in the Juniper Lodge or the Double-D at night.

Even when the studios *weren't* in town, the tourists still came, because Mayor Williams let them play cowboy in Eldorado. He'd opened the town so they could wander along Front Street, peering into the windows of the haberdashery and the general store; or tie up a horse in the livery stable, then watch them being re-shoed at the blacksmith's. The tourists could also sit in the wooden-backed pews of the church, lock each other into the cells of the jail, or pretend they were checking in for a night at the Eldorado Hotel. It wasn't long before we started to see meaningful numbers of sunburned strangers ambling along the elevated boardwalks, drawing make-believe guns from fantasy holsters, then barging through the batwing doors of the Silver Dollar saloon to slide "Howdy, pardner" out of the corners of their mouths.

A tourist detour to Eldorado meant an overnight stay in Paradox. So Ark offered trips into the desert where, for a nominal fee, visiting urbanites could gaze up at a sky they'd never see in their cities.

"You don't mind working at night?" I asked him, when the first of his earnings began to trickle in.

He shook his head. "If you like stars, dusk is really your dawn."

Like everyone else in town, he also found work in the movies. Standing in for the actors or watching a stagecoach arrive as an extra, or sitting in the background in the saloon, knocking back shots of whiskey that were really tea.

"It's easy work," he said. "But tedious."

Most evenings, he'd stop by the ranch house for supper, which Jessie was happy to offer.

"That Ark of yours," she once told me, "needs to put some meat on his bones, and he won't be getting it at Pattie Grosvenor's. Not the way that woman cooks with one eye on the price of butter."

I was secretly pleased, as food and friendship were one and the same to Jessie.

These mealtimes were quiet, convivial affairs, but one day—late in September that year—Ark was in the kitchen, cleaning and polishing his telescope and taking it apart to sight along each piece the way I'd seen Jessie clean and polish her rifles. Ark was getting under Jessie's feet, but she didn't seem to mind. She'd spent the better part of the morning baking a chocolate layer cake that, though she wouldn't come out and say it, she'd made with him in mind.

When the cake was cut, we sat with a pot of tea (another concession to Ark) and watched Jessie flour a pastry board to roll out a pie crust. The two of them started another one of their Bible duels, batting quotations back and forth with me piggy-in-the-middle.

"'I am the resurrection and the life,'" Jessie said at one point.

"'The one who believes in me will live, even though they die,'" Ark responded.

"Is that John?"

"John 11:25-26," Ark said.

It was harmless fun until Ark suddenly stopped and shook his head.

"What?" Jessie said.

"Nothing."

"You run out of Bible?"

"No," he said, and I could see him retreat into his shell.

"What then?"

"Nothing."

But then he said, "Do you really believe what Jesus said?"

"About the resurrection? Of course I do."

"You really think Jesus ascended into Heaven in a chorus of singing angels?"

"It's what the Bible tells us. And that's good enough for me." She wiped flour off her hands with a dish towel. "Why?" she said. "You got a problem with that?"

"No. It's just—"

"Just what?" she said, and took a step away from her pastry board.

"It's just that you *have* to believe," Ark told her. "Don't you? Otherwise, the whole temple of your faith comes crashing down. 'If Christ has not been risen, then our preaching is empty and your faith is in vain.' That's Paul writing in Corinthians. He knows that without the resurrection, Jesus would be just another Jewish rabble-rouser, one more failed messiah who was put to death along with any number of petty criminals. There were plenty more like him in those days, tramping through the Holy Land and proclaiming God's kingdom on Earth. Some of them even said they were King of the Jews, before they, too, were crucified by the Romans."

Jessie plonked down her rolling pin and leaned across the table toward him. "I believe in the resurrection," she said, counting out her words, "for the simple reason it's true. It says so, right there in the Bible. Right there in John."

"You think?"

"I know."

"Maybe," Ark said, in a skeptical voice even I found annoying.

"Exactly what do you mean—'maybe'?" she said, with more than a hint of aggression.

Ark toyed with the crumbs of chocolate cake that littered his plate. "There's a well-known principle in science," he said, "that goes back hundreds of years. It's called Occam's razor, and it basically says the most likely explanation for any event is the one that's the simplest."

"So?"

Ark edged forward on his chair. "So suppose you wake up one morning and see a puddle of water on your front porch. You probably think it rained during the night. But there could be another explanation. Maybe a flying saucer arrived from Mars, with little green men who've never seen water before. They've come to Earth to collect a sample, so one of them slides under your door, tiptoes into the kitchen, and fills a jam jar with water. But on the way out, he slips and spills the water, leaving the puddle on your front porch. Which of these explanations is the more likely? Did it rain during the night? Or did the Martians arrive?"

An uncomfortable silence stretched between them.

"I'm with the Martians," I said. "My money's on them."

Ark ignored me.

"That's the story you might *want* to believe," he said to Jessie. "But Jesus was crucified just before Passover and taken down from the cross late in the day, too late to be given a proper burial before the holiday began. We know this from the Gospels, which also say it was Joseph of Arimathea who arranged the burial. He was much too rich to have a tomb anywhere near Calvary, which was an execution site for common criminals. So Jesus was given a *temporary* burial in a cave. A cave-tomb that was sealed with a rock and, as the Bible says, close at hand. Then, come Sunday morning—after Passover has ended—three women arrive at the tomb, the *temporary* tomb, and find it empty. That's Mary, the mother of Jesus, Mary Magdalene, and Salome, who was probably Jesus' sister."

"Let's clear the cups away," I said, pushing back from the table.

Ark didn't move.

"The fact that Mark, the earliest Gospel writer, has mere *women* serve as witnesses," he said, "implies that he thinks the empty tomb is of no importance. Women had no standing in those days. They were not allowed to testify at trials as their word was considered unreliable. The women themselves are a little surprised to discover the tomb is empty, but they don't seem to think much of it either. Even John, the last of the Gospels to be written, has Mary Magdalene tell Simon Peter, 'They have taken the Lord out of the tomb, and we do not know where they have laid him.' Meaning—simply—that Jesus' body has been moved. From the *temporary* tomb to the permanent one that Joseph of Arimathea had promised. So did Jesus rise from the dead and ascend into Heaven in a chorus of angels? Or was his body merely moved? Did the Martians arrive that day? Or did it simply rain?"

Jessie leaned forward. Both her fists were pressed into her pastry board. "You done yet?" she said.

Ark nodded.

"I'm glad of that," Jessie said, "because let me tell *you* something, mister. The resurrection is real. It's true. It happened. Just like the Bible says. The Bible *also* says there's a Heaven up above and a Hell down below and God keeps a ledger. When the time comes, *he* decides which way you go, so you might like to keep that in mind before you go running off at the mouth. In the meantime, I'll thank you to remember this is *my* house and you're eating *my* food. So keep your blasphemous opinions to yourself, because this is *God's* house too. You got that?"

She didn't wait for an answer, but stormed out of the kitchen, slamming the door behind her so hard her rolling pin trundled onto the floor to send a stack of skillets flying off like ten pins.

Ark and I sat in a silence that was broken only by the *tick, tick, tick* of the kitchen clock. He focused on his hands, clasped in his lap.

"Sorry," he said.

"You ought to be," I told him. "I don't care how much you resent your parents and the views they held. Nor do I care how much you resent the certainty with which they held them. Jessie's beliefs are every bit as important to her as yours are to you. And they're every bit as valid too. In fact, the Bible's 'let there be light' sounds a lot like your Big Bang. And just as credible too. So don't do this again. Don't take your hurt and anger out on Jessie."

"I won't," he said.

And he didn't.

CHAPTER TWENTY-ONE

W e were married the following month, in a simple ceremony to save money. Also, Ark had no family to invite, and since he didn't know as many people in Paradox as I did, we agreed we should hold down the numbers on my side too.

"You're not pregnant, are you?" Jessie asked, when I told her our plans.

"Not yet."

She pushed for a ceremony in her church, but graciously accepted a City Hall setting once she realized our guest list extended to two. She also made an effort, arriving at the courthouse in a navy blue pant suit, matching striped blouse that was buttoned to the neck, and a pair of shiny dress flats. She must have scavenged the pants suit from somewhere near the back of her closet since—outside Sundays—I'd rarely seen her in anything other than Levi's, checkered shirt, and boots.

I'd asked Dottie to serve as my bridesmaid, because I felt guilty over the way I'd neglected her since I'd taken up with Ark. Also, I knew this was an event—simple though it might be—that she would relish. A chance to dress up and outshine the bride. Dottie did not disappoint. I wore a pale blue cotton shift dress and no hat, but Dottie arrived—an attention-getting twenty minutes late—in an outlandish outfit she'd sewn herself.

"I got the idea from that new TV series, *Star Trek*," she said as she struck a pose in front of me, "and thought it would do on account of Ark's interest in astrology."

"Astronomy," I said.

"Well, it's all stars, isn't it?"

The top half of her outfit bared one shoulder and arm, then hugged her body in a fire-engine-red material that ended low on her hips in a fringe of "crotch tassels," as she called them. The bottom half was a pair of shiny black PVC tights that disappeared into white vinyl, knee-high go-go boots.

"Are you doing okay?" I asked, as she seemed pumped with a frazzled energy.

"Never better," she said.

After Ark and I exchanged vows and simple gold bands, the four of us processioned arm-in-arm along Main Street—to the applause and whistles of friends and neighbors we met along the way. In the lounge bar of the Juniper Lodge, Ark popped the cork on a bottle of champagne and we drank to our future health and happiness and everyone's success. Dottie presented me with a pink feather duster ("a symbol of your coming servitude"), while Jessie gave us a tree-of-life blanket she'd inherited from her mother. In exchange, Ark and I gave *her* a present when we told her I planned to keep my maiden name. Ark had no objection, and we both knew Jessie was upset by the thought that the Dunbar name might disappear.

Ark said a few words while I admired him in his black pants and tuxedo T-shirt under a black cotton jacket. Then he ordered a second bottle of champagne. Jessie, who'd raised only an eyebrow at Dottie's attire, downed enough of the wine to grow as tipsy as the rest of us.

At one point she leaned across to me. "At least now," she said, chinking her glass against mine, "you won't have to sneak around in that canyon of yours."

"You knew about that?" I said.

"I may be single, Corin. But I'm not stupid. That photo of you and Ark by your bedside? I recognize the glyphs in the background. And I'm quite sure you weren't there to admire *them*."

She took another sip of champagne and placed a hand over mine.

"Corin," she began, then stopped, and shook her head.

"What?" I said.

She sat back. "Nothing. I was just going to say... I hope you'll be happy. You deserve to be. Both of you do."

I grinned across the table at Ark and sent him a hammy kiss. "Happily ever after," I said, and raised my glass.

"Happily ever after," the others chorused, and we clinked glasses again.

But, of course, that only happens in fairy tales.

Or in the movies.

CHAPTER TWENTY-TWO

It was one of those beautiful Utah days that does its utmost to tug you outdoors. Five months had passed since we'd married. Five months of newly wedded bliss—a description that once would have raised a cynical eyebrow from me, but which I now embraced whole-heartedly. Five months filled with lovemaking and planning for a future that we both agreed would include a thriving ranch for me, star parties and research for Ark, and a couple of babies to please us both. I idled in bed with a breeze from the open window passing crisp and cool over my face and pictured the show of poppies and verbena that would soon brighten the desert with swathes of confetti colors.

Ark slipped out of bed beside me. It had been Jessie's idea to convert the bunkhouse into our home.

"Three's a crowd," she'd said. "You can't stay in the ranch house or I'll always be looking over your shoulder."

"You'll be okay on your own?" I asked.

She poked me in the ribs. "I learned a long time ago to look after myself. And it's not like you're moving to England, is it?"

The bunkhouse, with rooms strung out like railroad cars, had once housed as many as a dozen itinerant wranglers. Ark stripped out the cots from the main dorm and used the wood to put up dividers that reached to the ceiling; while Felipe installed a metal chimney for the stove as well as a secondhand electric range we picked up cheap from the Scratch and Dent in Blanding. We still planned to add a dresser that would stand next to the sink—an old stone one Ark had insisted we keep ("we don't want to wipe away history in a blitz of home improvements," he'd said)—but he'd fixed up all the chairs, repairing their wobbly legs and broken stretchers, while Jessie sewed yellow and blue cushions to take the hardness out of the seats. In the bathroom, we kept the three shower cubicles and row of washbasins, but laid down new strips of red linoleum to cheer the place up. The fodder room next to the kitchen became our bedroom, with a large double bed, a five-tier chest of drawers, wardrobe, and my old dressing table from the ranch house (which, with its ruffled and flowered skirt, looked a little girly).

I heard Ark rattle cups in the kitchen, then the drumming of water on metal as he filled the kettle. The radio came on with The Monkees singing "I'm a Believer," followed by The Rolling Stones and "Ruby Tuesday." Ark warbled along. He liked to start his day with a couple of biscuits (by which he meant cookies) and a cup of strong but milky tea. Then he'd patrol the ranch.

I was pleased by the interest he'd shown. But Jessie wasn't impressed.

"He's a dude," she said.

"Give him a chance," I told her, as we watched him struggle to thread the hand baler. Already, he'd gotten to know the horses and dogs, and had a good grasp of the way we managed the stock on the range.

"He's still a dude," Jessie said.

Ark was up early that morning to get better acquainted with Walnut, the black quarter horse Jessie had loaned him. She figured Walnut for a wise old stallion who wouldn't land Ark in trouble no matter how hard he tried, but at that stage of their relationship, horse and rider were in dispute over who was the boss.

Warm in bed, I stretched lazily. I heard the back door creak open. *Hinges need oiling*, I thought.

Ark's boots clomped across the back porch, thumped down the wooden steps, then softened their tread as he stepped onto dirt.

At noon, I met up with Jessie and together we wandered over to the corrals. Sherman was due to donate another dose of his semen. Ark was there, sitting atop the fence like a cowboy; and so, too, were

Bose and Chance. A wrangler named Judd Newton had not yet shown. He was filling in for Felipe, who was off for the day to visit a sick aunt.

The new bull pen Felipe had constructed was solid as a rock. Its sides were two-by-ten planks of cedar, six feet high and anchored in place by railroad ties buried deep in dirt that Felipe had tamped down hard as cement. Near the back of the pen, an open-fronted shelter with a tarpaulin roof gave Sherman shelter from the wind and cold. A five-bar gate near where Ark now sat led to a maze of metal chutes, which linked the bull pen to the collection area.

The teaser cow, a sturdy red and white Hereford, was already tied up in the collection area and was quietly munching her way through a crib of hay. Sherman stood in his pen, tethered by a halter rope that Bose had looped around the bull's horns and fed through the nose ring. His nostrils flared as he scented the cow, impatient to get at her.

"Where's Judd Newton?" I asked. "We said noon, didn't we?"

Bose jumped down from the fence. "Bastard's late," he said.

"Well, we can't keep Sherman waiting."

"Nope. That we can't. He's good and ready to go."

"So, what do we do?"

"I can help," Ark said, and climbed down to join us. He wore the white Stetson I'd given him and looked slim-hipped and fit in novice-bright Levi's he was still breaking in.

I looked at Jessie, who gave a quick shake of her head.

"Thanks," I said. "But we'd better wait."

"No, really," he said. "I can hold the teaser."

Bose looked him up and down. "You sure you can handle that?"

"It's the sissy job, isn't it?"

Bose said nothing. Let his silence speak for itself.

"His hat ain't even dirty," Chance said, still perched on the fence.

Ark looked up at him. "I could scuff it through the dirt," he said, "if you think that would make me smarter."

Bose turned to face me. "What d'you say, Corin? It's your call."

I hesitated a moment, then nodded once.

I didn't want Ark to lose face.

Bose and Chance took Sherman's halter ropes, one on each side. They marshalled him through the chutes and into the collection pen, where they held him in check as he dragged them toward the cow. Ark positioned himself at the head of the teaser, reeling in its tether ropes—as he'd seen Felipe do—to keep the cow still and facing front. The two wranglers dug in their heels and hauled back on their ropes while Sherman snorted and sniffed the cow's flanks. Chance grabbed the artificial vagina he'd hung over a rail, and when Sherman mounted the teaser, he moved in and slipped it over the shaft of the bull's erect penis.

After one urgent thrust Sherman was done. As he heaved himself off the cow and thundered down onto all four hooves, he staggered under his own weight and sideswiped Chance with his haunches. The wrangler lost his footing, dropped the vagina, and as he scrambled out of range of the bull's crushing hooves, let go of his halter rope. Sherman lowered his head and bellowed—and Ark, seeing the wrangler in trouble, vaulted over the teaser's feed crib into the pen. He grabbed for the loose halter rope, but missed. Sherman turned on him, and with a dip and toss of his massive head, hurled Ark against the railings, which collapsed in a clang of tangled metal. The bull backed away, lowered his head again, and shunted Ark's limp body across the pen like rolling out a carpet, dragging Bose, still on his rope, spread-eagled through the dirt behind him.

Ark lay still.

It had happened so fast I was too stunned to move. But Bose was quick to his feet. He jumped sideways to draw Sherman's eyes away from Ark, grabbed the cattle prod hooked to his belt, and drove the animal through the chutes into its pen.

I felt a cold rush of dread. Ark still hadn't moved. I ran toward him. The right sleeve of his shirt, wrapped around his arm, lay hooked above his head like a dancer's. The left leg of his Levi's was twisted as though someone had tried to wring it dry. His foot faced in, pigeon-toed, and his head was turned to one side as if he was trying to look over his shoulder.

I crouched beside him, stroking his cheek. "It'll be all right," I said. "It'll be all right." Over and over, like a mantra.

But, of course, it wasn't.

CHAPTER TWENTY-THREE

Ark was in a Salt Lake City hospital for nearly two months, attached to more tubes and wires than any astronaut he'd ever admired. I sat with him every day but one, renting a room in nearby Glendale. In June, he was transferred to the Severill, a long-term "care institution" southwest of the city, but still a five- or six-hour drive from Paradox. I took another room—this time above a discount furniture emporium—and again determined to sit with Ark for as long as I was needed. My daily presence helped, but the Severill was still hard to take.

A squat block of crumbly brick, it had once served as a state-run asylum for the (often criminally) insane, and was still fenced in with barbed wire six feet high that sagged in places where the wind and snow had worked it free of its rusted moorings. A long driveway led to double iron doors that were almost always bolted shut. A smaller entrance had been cut into the right-hand door to allow staff, patients, and visitors with the right credentials to enter. Above it, a single tier of narrow windows failed to allow even a ray of the dazzling Utah sun to sneak in.

The first time I visited I had trouble tracking Ark down. No one manned the reception, so I followed a labyrinth of unmarked corridors—full of the sulphury smell of boiled cabbage—that ran between brown distempered walls. I climbed a flight of stairs and eventually found him in a long ward that had all the charm of a Civil War barracks. He lay on a narrow iron-framed cot, one of thirty or so that stood barely three feet apart with not so much as a curtain between them for privacy.

I soon discovered he was receiving little in the way of treatment, as the Severill served mainly as a human warehouse. The old, frail, sick—and the incurably insane too—were packed in with no regard for age, health, sanity, or outlook. Like most of the other inmates, Ark was often sedated—for his pain, the nurses told me, but I think that, overworked and underpaid, they just wanted to keep him docile. A physio once showed me how to manipulate Ark's limbs, to keep them loose and as flexible as possible, but after ten minutes she turned that job over to me and I never saw her again.

Sometimes when I'd visit, I'd find Ark had been moved to another ward without explanation or warning. That worked in his favor when he was placed at the end of a room with three casualties of the Vietnam War. Each was disabled, but they passed the time tossing a football back and forth, along with crude and raunchy remarks that at least gave Ark a semblance of company. But after another unheralded move, he found himself trapped between a cross-eyed man on one side (who sat still as a statue and glared at him, only to explode in a windmill of limbs whenever a nurse tried to wash or feed him) and a whimpering fetal ball of a man on the other. And for three long weeks, he was forced to endure a windowless cell that was dark and cold as a dungeon. He'd stare at the patches of damp that spotted the ceiling and distract himself by trying to see patterns that mirrored those of the constellations. I complained to the matron whenever I saw her, but I worried that if I made too big a fuss, she and the nurses would take revenge on Ark.

We made an effort to be positive (and I made certain I cried only at night), but we both fell into a morass of gloom. At least I could leave at the end of each day, but Ark was entombed. I have an image of him now, when I looked back at him through the swinging doors of the ward he was in. He lay on his back, hands shuttering his ears, his eyes screwed tightly shut. We both breathed a huge sigh of relief when I was finally able to spring him loose and take him home to the ranch.

As he was wheeled on a gurney into the sunlight, his face white as the pillow he lay on and his cheekbones sharp under his tightly drawn skin, he reached out to grab my hand.

"Promise me," he said, "that I'll never be sent back to that place again."

His spirits rose as soon as we settled him into the bunkhouse. I'd given Dominga the double bed that Ark and I had so briefly shared, and replaced it with an old hospital one that had a hand crank I could turn to raise the upper third of the mattress and the frame. I set up a chair beside it to show Ark he wasn't going to be lying there alone; and I put a reading lamp on his bedside table along with a stack of his favorite magazines. Felipe rigged up a trapeze and pulley that hung from the ceiling so when Ark was strong enough, he'd be able to pull himself into a sitting position. And without telling Ark, I ordered an Invacare wheelchair—but when it arrived I thought it looked so depressing, I hid it from view in my old bedroom in the ranch house. The crutches we'd brought with us from the Severill stayed propped in the corner, unused.

Doc Mullins regularly stopped by to see him. He was not an easy man to like. He wore black suits, a black string tie, and a black Wyatt Earp hat that he would doff when he saw me and press against his chest like a shield. He also carried a black bag and walked with the lugubrious stoop of a pallbearer. But he was the only doctor in Paradox, and—just as important—he was willing to make house calls.

"Your husband," he told me, during his first home visit, "has suffered not just broken limbs, but also a traumatic blow to the head. To the brain. Specifically, to the cerebellum. An injury of that kind would normally have a mortality rate of some thirty percent, which might not sound encouraging, but a decade ago, a patient in his state would have been lucky to live for more than a few years. With modern medicines and techniques, his life expectancy could now be as much as a decade. Maybe more."

When I failed to be sufficiently consoled, he added, "Your husband is still a young man, Corin. So in many ways he could be considered quite healthy."

"Except he can't walk," I said.

"Well, yes, except for that." As if I'd caught him out on a technicality.

"Will there be pain?" I asked. It was a question I was scared to pose, but no one at the Severill had been willing to say.

Doc Mullins tugged at the wings of his droopy moustache.

"Nerve pain, yes. And he'll have prolonged migraines, almost certainly. You can also expect numbness in the limbs. Tingling, burning, muscular weakness. And unpredictable spasticity or seizures. But at least his thinking will be clear. You can be grateful for that.

"An ongoing threat," he said, "will come from bedsores, although you can manage those by making sure he's regularly turned." As if Ark were a chicken roasting on a spit. "It won't be easy, Corin," he said, "keeping him here on the ranch. I can't pretend that it will be."

On the one day I left Ark's bedside, I drove back to Paradox and headed farther up the Waterpocket Valley to borrow a twenty-gauge shotgun from Tanner Lacasse. Armed with that, I stopped by the ranch and asked Felipe to tether Sherman tight to the railings of the bull pen. I waited until he'd gone, then climbed onto the third bar of the six-foot-high fence he'd constructed, leaned over, and lined up the barrel of the shotgun an inch from the bull's right-hand horn bed. Sherman was so close I could see his torso expand and contract with his every breath, and smell the earthy odor that rose from his hide. He stared up at me, his tiny bloodshot eyes unblinking.

I took a few deep breaths of my own and squeezed the trigger. Sherman's legs buckled and he instantly collapsed, showering us both in a haze of dust and a corona of flies as his massive body thundered to the ground. He lay there lifeless as a beached whale.

A bull worth mill-yuns and mill-yuns and mill-yuns.

But not anymore.

With Sherman gone, the ranch's finances nose-dived into the red, so in October, I started to work part time at *The Southeast Utah Gazette*. Jessie helped me get a job writing copy by playing on the editor's affections for her as I had no qualifications other than a lifelong liking for words.

That same month—on the day Ark and I should have been celebrating our first wedding anniversary—he took a turn for the worse and fell into a deep and prolonged sleep. I sat by his bed with my cheek close to his face so I could feel the warmth of his breath. The sky outside was a flawless blue, and crackling, crisp air flowed in from the window with a zest that once had filled me with life. The photo by Ark's bedside showed the two of us in our canyon, but already it had started to fade under the bleach of the Utah sun. As I held it in my hands, tears rolled down my face as I thought of all that might have been. I felt old and bowed and drained of hope—the same worthless person who hadn't been able to save Grace, and who hadn't deserved the love of her father.

That evening, Dottie dropped by with a bottle of California Chardonnay she'd pilfered from the Double-D.

"Jelly can afford it," she said as she struggled with the cork.

She wore a mini-shift, high boots, and a pair of oversized sunglasses that gave her the look of a bug-eyed insect. She plonked herself down at the kitchen table and took off the glasses with a theatrical flourish. I told her Ark had been asleep and although now awake was too tired to see her. But she insisted on saying hello.

When I showed her into his room, she stopped short in the doorway, eyeing the trapeze and pulley Felipe had set up. She glanced at the pile of diapers stacked in the corner, and I knew she could smell the sickly sweet odor of urine that came from the catheter's drainage bag—a smell that carried me back to Grace on her deathbed. Three months had passed since Dottie had visited, and I could tell from the look that flashed across her face that she was shocked by how pale and shrunken Ark had become, with dark eyes huge in a hollowed face.

She stayed in the doorway and for once could find nothing to say. Until she began to babble. About movies she'd seen, friends she had met, a nail polish she'd tried, and the meanness of tips at the Double-D. I had to hurry her back to the kitchen.

"You can't live like this," she said in a hoarse whisper. "You can't waste your life looking after someone like *that*."

"I love him, Dottie."

"But you knew him only six months before you were married."

"I still love him."

"You might think that now," Dottie said, "but in a few years' time? You'll start to hate him. Start to hate what your life has become. Corin, I have to tell you this as your friend. You cannot throw your life away. Not like *this*."

CHAPTER TWENTY-FOUR

Ark Stevenson

When Ark was at school in England, he learned to decline Latin verbs (*amo, amas, amat...*), solve quadratic equations ((x+2)(x-3)=0), and regurgitate important dates in British history (1066, 1688, 1707). Only later did he come to understand that his education had really been aimed at developing *character*.

That goal was reflected in the books he read (the *Biggles* books, *Gimlet* books, even the *Jennings* and *Just William* books) and in the British films he saw on school trips to the Gaumont (*The Wooden Horse, Above Us the Waves, Reach for the Sky*). It was mirrored, too, in the heroes he was expected to emulate. Horatio on the bridge, turning back the Etruscans. Nelson at Trafalgar, defeating the French and Spanish. Baden-Powell at Mafeking, fighting off the Boers. And Guy Gibson, leading 617 squadron to bomb the dams in the Ruhr.

Above all was Titus Oates, the English cavalry officer who traveled with Scott on his doomed attempt to be first to reach the South Pole. The race to the Pole had been a story that was drubbed into Ark—as it was into every English schoolboy—until he knew it by heart.

In January 1912, five Englishmen arrived at the Pole after an epic struggle across the ice—only to find they'd been beaten to the prize by Roald Amundsen, a Norwegian, who'd planted his country's flag there just five weeks before. On the return journey, Scott's team missed a supply point that left them desperately short of food. Fatally weakened, they could travel a mere three miles a day instead of the required nine. Titus Oates, suffering from frostbite as well as gangrene, knew he was holding his companions back, so on the night of March 17, he stepped out of his tent into a blizzard and his certain death.

"I am just going outside," he told his companions, "and may be some time."

He was never seen again.

That story resonated with Ark because among the Yanomami he'd grown up with in the Amazon jungle, a similar philosophy prevailed. The Indians were largely nomadic and when they moved on, they took with them only what they could carry. Anyone too old or sick would be left at the edge of the jungle to die.

They did not complain, did not resist. Because the ethos was the same. You did not let the side down.

You stepped off the trail—and got out of the way.

CHAPTER TWENTY-FIVE

Corin Dunbar

It was Ark who kept us going. His body constantly failed him, but its frailty was countered by his mental strength (far greater than mine), so it often seemed that I was the suffering patient and he the cheerful nurse. His optimism impressed me. While I was overwhelmed with worry and doubt, Ark triumphed as a master of his concerns. He never wallowed in self-pity or doubt, but was able—still—to laugh at the idiocies of life and appreciate the tidbits of gossip I brought home from the *Gazette*. He stayed engaged with the outside world, especially the mission to land a man on the moon, which was then gathering pace. That had become an obsession with him. So he caught me off guard when—out of nowhere—he said, "Corin, I want to die."

I'd lowered the rails that guarded each side of his mattress and was remaking his bed, rolling him this way and that as I checked for pressure sores. I brushed off his words in a flurry of tucking in sheets and plumping up pillows. But my heart raced as if he'd held a knife to my throat.

"You've had a bad night," I told him. "You'll feel better tomorrow."

But in the following days and weeks, he repeated his wish so often, I had to accept he meant it. I knew depressed people sometimes found comfort in death. It was their way out. A Plan B. But Ark wasn't depressed. He spoke with the verve and energy of someone looking ahead to a bright future, not someone seeking a way of escape.

"You can't give up," I told him, painfully aware how trite I sounded. "You've so much to live for."

"I'm not giving up," he said. "Quite the opposite. I want to move on. I've been lying here thinking, trying to decide the best way for me to proceed."

I was fussing again with his bed, and tidying up laundry that was already neatly folded.

"Life is a process," he said. "It's not a result. And death is too. It's not something we need to fear."

"Well, it frightens *me*," I told him. "I want you here. With me."

"Not like this."

"*Yes*, like this. I want you any way I can have you."

"I'm too much hard work."

"What I do for you," I told him, "I really do for me."

He shook his head. "I wanted you as my wife. Not my nurse."

I sat beside him in the reading chair by his bed and brushed his arm with my fingers. I wanted to feel his skin warm against my own.

He shifted awkwardly, using the pulley, so he could face me.

"These bodies of ours," he said, "are no more than bundles of atoms, and borrowed ones at that. They've traveled through a thousand galaxies and a million stars to get to us, and through a billion people too. They stay inside us only a moment, and then they move on—because they're needed to form future generations, the people not yet born. They're part of an endless cycle, Corin, that one day will take them back to the stars. I'm not afraid of death, because none of us ever dies. The material we're made of—it's indestructible. It'll live on as far as we can see into the future, right to the end of time."

I'd heard these arguments before, but valued them only as reassurance. They were like Jessie's stories from the Bible. Spiritual. Magical. Intended to make us feel a part of something bigger. But Ark's story was turning dark. I'd failed to appreciate just how much he'd invested in his beliefs.

My heart sank further when he put his hand over mine, and said, "We're so much more than mere human beings. We're citizens of the universe, not just this earth. And now I want to move forward. I want to continue the journey that'll take me back to the stars. I want to leave, Corin. I want to be free. And I need you to help me."

I was terrified by all his talk of death, no matter how liberating he made it sound. Also frustrated. And hurt, because it meant I had so little impact on his thinking. It made me feel I'd failed him.

"Promise me you won't do anything rash," I said one day, after he again broached the subject.

At the back of my mind was Sally Griffiths, a friend of Jessie's who ran the fabric store in town. Two years ago, she'd come home to find her husband hanging from a beam in their attic, and two years on, she still couldn't sleep without seeing his swaying body, the rope cutting into his neck, and his face spiked with purple blotches, eyes bulging as big as marbles.

"I can't hang myself from a beam," Ark said, when I told him the story, "so I promise I won't do anything 'rash,' as you put it. Not unless we both agree. Not until *you* say it's the right thing for me to do."

For a while, we left it at that. I thought I'd blocked the danger. Only later did I come to realize the burden had shifted to me.

Ark had made *his* decision. All he needed now was me to give my blessing.

I kept my fears and concerns to myself, until one day I could no longer contain them. It was the following February. A day when a blustery wind roiled the dust outside into whirling dervishes that found every chink in the ranch house walls. Jessie and I were sitting in front of the kitchen fire, my hands wrapped around a steaming mug of soup as I watched her darn the heels of a pair of socks.

"The accident," she'd earlier said. "It wasn't your fault. You can't keep blaming yourself, Corin. You can't keep beating yourself up."

It was a conversation we'd had many times before as I couldn't shake the image of Ark's body lying in the bull pen, limp as a heap of discarded clothes.

"I could have stopped it," I told her. "I could have told Bose to wait for the wrangler."

"You could have, yes. But Ark might not have listened. And *he* didn't have to volunteer. Men are such idiots," she said. "Always having something to prove. They can't resist butting heads."

"He just wanted to help."

"Which he could have done best by staying put and doing nothing."

We sat in silence a moment. I took a sip of my soup and watched Jessie put away the socks to pick up a sweater she had been knitting. The wind howled outside, rattling the windows, and sent a shiver running up my spine.

"Ark wants to die," I said quietly.

Jessie's needles picked up a beat.

"I'm not surprised, the state he's in. It's a wonder the way he's managed to hold up."

"No," I said. "I mean, he *really* wants to die. He's not depressed. It's something he genuinely wants to do."

For months, I'd listened to Ark expound his beliefs as I struggled to find a counter to his set way of thinking. I'd resisted confiding in Jessie because I had a good idea of how she'd react. But now I could no longer carry the burden on my own.

"He says we're all made of atoms," I said, blurting out the words out in a rush, "which of course we are, if you want to see things that way, and these atoms were created either in this Big Bang of his or when a star blew up. So these atoms have been around since the beginning of time and they live on forever. Indestructible. They sit inside us, Ark says, but not for long, because they're constantly being replaced. So we're not the same person we used to be, not even the same person we were last week, last year. We're always renewing ourselves, picking up atoms to replace the ones that move on. Even the atoms that make up our brains aren't with us for long. They may be as old as time itself, but as far as our minds are concerned, they're younger than the memories they hold. And when we die, our atoms live on in other people and in rocks and trees and birds and rainbows and...and, well, in *everything*. They reappear in the 'unborn,' as Ark calls them, the people who'll live here on Earth after we're gone. So we'll one day be part of them, until finally we go back to the stars, where we'll live on forever. That's what he calls eternal life. Do you think he's crazy?" I said.

Jessie had frozen during my outburst, her knitting untouched. Now she stared at me open-mouthed.

"Eternal life?" she said. "In the stars?"

I nodded. "Yes. Because the stuff we're made of—the *atoms*— they'll always be with us, because we're all connected, all related. We're all part of the same...*stuff*."

Jessie pulled a face. "Nonsense," she said firmly.

"Ark says his ideas are based on fact. On *scientific* fact, not on dogma or any religious convictions."

Jessie bit her lip at that and shifted in her seat.

"We won't go there again," she said, "but I will tell you, there *is* eternal life. One that waits for us all. There's a Heaven and there's a Hell, like I told Ark. We're all headed for one or the other. And I have to say," she added tartly, "that more than once I've been worried about him and where he'll end up. I admire him, I do. I'm amazed at the way he's handled himself after the accident. He didn't give in to pity, he never complains, at least not to me. But he does have some wild ideas."

"But that's just it," I said. "It's his ideas that are holding him up. He really does want to die, not because his life here is so terrible, although God knows it is, but because he can see a way ahead. He has *hope*, Jessie. He can see a *future*. I've watched him become positively *excited* by the prospect of death. By the journey he's sure is coming next."

Jessie's needles started again to clack.

"You checking his pills?" she said.

"I ration them, yes, if that's what you mean. So he never has too many at any one time. He knows I'm doing it, but he's promised he won't try to take his own life. He knows it would destroy me. But if I truly love him, am I right to hold him back?"

"He thinks you're the one holding him back?"

"I am. He knows what he wants to do. And when he wants to do it. He's just waiting for me to agree."

Jessie sat upright and with a gesture of finality thrust her knitting needles into the ball of wool.

"You can't do that," she said.

"I don't want to. But what *should* I do?"

She tossed the half-finished sweater to one side and leaned toward me.

"I'll tell you one thing, my girl," she said firmly. "I don't want to hear any more talk of Ark dying. And nothing more about you helping him, either."

"He's told me his plan," I said.

"His plan?"

I nodded. "The one thing that really engages him is this race to put a man on the moon. I've read him articles about it, about how it's heating up. The flights that are scheduled, the people who might land there. He wants to get there first."

"He wants *what*?"

"Before he ends up in the stars, he wants to go to the moon."

"Then he *is* crazy," Jessie said. "If he really wants eternal life and the kind of existence we'll have after we pass, then all he needs to do is read his Bible, not follow some cockamamie ideas that some lab-coat scientist has dreamed up."

"I still have to decide," I said.

She wagged a finger in my face.

"You *cannot* let him die," she said. "And nor can you *help* him to die. It's a sin against God. Life is sacred. It's a gift from him. You can't throw it away, and you can't throw it back in his face. Ark will go to Hell with this talk of dying, and if you help him, Corin, you will too. And that is something I'll fight tooth and nail to prevent."

I gloss over this period now—the weeks and months after the accident—because it's still too painful for me to recall. But the truth is Ark was grinding me down with his logic. He never wavered in his resolve, never once expressed any doubts. I remained perched on a seesaw, first tipping one way, then the other. Weeks would pass when we avoided the subject, but it was always there, the elephant in the room that stood between us. My mood would shift with his condition, and both took a turn for the worse when the following summer he suffered a spate of thundering migraines that brought on vomiting and head-spinning bouts of dizziness.

I'd just started to work full time at the *Gazette*, since Ark's bills were piling up and I needed to bring in more money. From the day Ark came home from the Severill, Dominga had helped me bathe and dress him. Now, she agreed to sit with him during the hours I was away.

This new routine worked well enough until one weekend soon after Ark suffered another one of his migraines. I'd spent the day with him, drapes closed, laying cold compresses onto his forehead. His eyes were shut because, he said, if he kept them open, my face would dance in front of him with the shimmer of a heat haze. I wanted him to take a dose of his pills, but he always resisted any medication that dulled the sharpness of his mind.

When he finally managed to sleep, I lifted the rail on the side of his bed and left him to prepare his next meal. I hadn't been gone ten minutes, and when I tiptoed back he was still dead to the world, much as the doc had predicted.

"Sleep is a healthy sign," he'd told me. "It's an indication your husband's brain is trying to heal."

I straightened Ark's bedclothes and pulled the covers around him. As I did so, his sheet slid to one side to reveal four small triangular punctures on the outside of his leg. On his calf, low down near the ankle. The marks were ringed with blood and were swollen into angry hillocks, livid against his ashen skin. They had not been that morning, and the more I studied them, the more alarmed I became.

I called Doc Mullins, who arrived within the hour. He bent low to study the marks just as I had done, then slowly straightened.

"This bunkhouse," he said, looking around and tugging at the loose ends of his moustache. "Has it ever been neglected?"

"Some," I said, remembering what it had been like before we moved in.

"Hay stored here perhaps?"

"Maybe," I said. "I wouldn't really know."

He pinched his nose and looked back at the puncture marks.

"Rats," he said.

"Excuse me?"

"You ever see them?"

"Rats?"

"Yes. Rats."

"Well, this is a ranch."

"No. I mean *here*. In this room."

I shook my head. "Never," I said.

"I wouldn't be too sure," he told me. "These marks—they have the look of rat bites."

I reeled back in horror. "*Rat* bites?"

Mullins nodded. "Rat bites," he said, with finality.

Just the thought of it repulsed me. Ark lying asleep while a rat scratched its way onto his bed to gnaw at his leg as if he were already a corpse.

For the first time, I began to question whether I could keep him safe with me on the ranch. Perhaps he was right. Perhaps he *would* be better off in the stars.

PART THREE

PART THREE

CHAPTER TWENTY-SIX

Yiska Begay
(aka Lowell Smith)

Two days later—on the morning of Tuesday October 8, 1968—a work party of twenty-two prisoners huddled by the side of a dirt road that ran straight as a zipper across the flat top of Kicking Horse Mesa. The mesa, about a dozen miles northwest of Paradox, ringed the Waterpocket Valley and its thirty or so ranches. Dawn had yet to break, so the air was cold, the sun not even a promise. The prisoners huddled around the engine warmth of the vehicle that had brought them there—an old school bus painted army green that was parked on the desert scrub of the mesa, tail end in. The men stomped their feet and blew hot breath onto their hands. As they nudged and shuffled against one another, they formed a single body like an amoeba. They were not allowed to talk.

Two guards stood nearby. Prison Officer Earl Hill had positioned himself in front of the men, while Prison Officer Chester Willis stood off to one side. Both officers were armed with Winchester Model 70 bolt-action rifles, backed by orders to shoot if any of their charges tried to escape. Their relative positions meant they could pump slugs into the prisoners without hitting each other. The two guards wore long-sleeved work shirts, hip-length brown wool serge jackets, and thick tan slacks; but their prisoners were dressed only in dark denim pants, light-blue chambray shirts, and thin jackets with PROPERTY OF UTAH STATE PRISON DRAPER stamped across their backs in orange.

Over the summer, lightning storms had swept across the mesa, bringing fierce bouts of torrential rain that had filled the culverts with sand, gravel, and grit. The men were there to clear the culverts in what they viewed as a make-work project. The dirt road dead-ended in a spire of chiseled rock called the Devil's Corkscrew and had been constructed two years before because United Artists wanted to feature the spire in *Duel at Diablo*, a second-rate oater starring James Garner and Bibi Andersson. The town of Paradox—with help from Utah's Department of Publicity and Industrial Development—had financed the road for a single scene, then neglected it. The prisoners were nonetheless happy to be there as otherwise they would have been locked in six-by-nine cells at Draper, the Utah state jail twenty miles southwest of Salt Lake City.

One man among them had been convicted of murder: a full-blooded Navajo Indian named Yiska Begay, aka Lowell Smith, the hated name the nuns had given him at his school. Incarcerated for another offense, he had broken a fellow inmate's neck to earn a sentence of life without parole. Now, twelve years into this term, he'd qualified as a trusty, which meant he could wear his black hair long over his shoulders and work outside the prison's walls.

As the sun cast its first rays over the horizon, a dented panel truck bounced and swayed along the road toward the men and stopped parallel to the camo-green bus. The truck had come from a temporary camp of three trailers that housed the men while they cleared the culverts. Its driver, Prison Officer Seth Fowler, eased out from behind the wheel and tracked around to the rear. He opened the double doors and crabbed inside, careful to stay low so as not to bump his head. A pile of shovels and picks lay scattered about like so many jackstraw sticks. He handed them out to the prisoners as they stepped forward in turn.

As each man took a pick or shovel, he moved to the rear of the group so the amoeba retained its essential shape. When his turn came, Yiska Begay grabbed a long-handled shovel with a heart-shaped blade and shuffled to the back. At that moment, Officer Hill felt a call of nature and stepped out of position, moving to the far side of the bus, while Officer Willis cupped his hand around a match as he tried to light a Camel. The wind intervened, so he dropped into a crouch behind the hood of the truck. Seth Fowler, still in the truck, was crouched low, handing out the picks and shovels.

Without a word, Yiska Begay leaned his shovel against one of the open rear doors. He did this carefully, as if to avoid scratching the paintwork, then stepped into the dirt road and took off at a run. The mesa was flat and devoid of cover save for saltbush and a few stunted shrubs of sage, so Yiska ran straight at the sun, now balanced like a ball on the horizon. He knew he'd be a silhouette, but hoped the sun's glare would make him disappear.

He ran steadily, lifting his feet high. He had no real plan. It just felt good to be out in the open and running free with a breeze in his face and the sky high and wide and open above him. The other prisoners saw him go, but none watched him run. They shuffled their feet and switched positions to preserve the shape of their amoeba. The guards only noticed one of their charges was missing when they marched the prisoners away from the truck and saw a shovel leaning against the open door. That delay was enough to give Yiska the time he needed to reach the edge of the mesa.

A steep cliff fell away beneath him, so he turned right and loped south along the rim with the Waterpocket Valley deep in shadow on his left. He heard a shout and the crack of a rifle, but didn't stop to look back.

The three guards needed half an hour (twenty-seven minutes, according to their later report) to hustle the prisoners into the bus and drive them back to camp. There, Officer Willis used his car radio to alert the warden at Draper, who phoned the sheriff's office in Paradox. Sheriff Dale Parker was out stumping for re-election, so his long-time secretary, Erma Belnap, fielded the call. She reached the sheriff only when he returned to his house at the corner of Sixth and Adams.

Dale's knuckles whitened around the phone as he listened. He grunted once, then hung up. The runaway Injun was not someone Dale wanted to see, especially now, right before an election.

He banged on the back bedroom door for his son, Cal, who at that moment was stripped to his briefs, halfway through his daily quota of push-ups.

"It's a 10-98!" Dale yelled. "A 10-80 too! So get a manhunt started. I'm calling Sims. We need to get this Injun caught!"

Running south along the rim of the mesa, Yiska Begay spotted a possible way down. A wash, scooped by rain, had eroded the rock and sent large boulders tumbling onto a mound of scree that was heaped against the base of the cliff below. He hesitated a moment and then jumped, arms windmilling as he dropped through the void to land on a slab of rock. A scrawny pinyon pine had found a home in the gritty soil, its roots probing the cracks and crannies for water. He grabbed its trunk and swung himself lower. The rock face below was broken and jagged, but he was able to slide down to the scree, loose rocks scooting out from under his feet. His right boot caught in a fissure, and when he tried to free it, the boot remained trapped in the rock.

He paused a moment to catch his breath. The sun had rolled back the inky shadow in the valley so he could look down on ranch houses and barns surrounded by pickups, tractors, and balers, and the sliver of road that linked them. The road followed the curve of a river fringed by yellow-leafed cottonwoods now on the turn. The wall of the mesa stretched sheer to his left, curving around to meet a line of cliffs on the other side of the valley. The valley looked like a trap, but there was no cover on top of the mesa, so for the next twenty minutes, he picked his way over the scree, then scrambled down a talus slope to a bench of rock at the bottom.

He stripped off his jacket with its orange insignia and stuffed it into a crevice, then set off at a jog across the valley floor. After a few minutes of running, he shucked off his remaining boot, then resumed his pace, his powerful legs carrying him east and a little south.

At that moment, Sheriff Dale Parker was driving west on Highway 164 in his county-issued Ford Galaxie. He drove fast, and when he reached the KBEZ radio station, he slewed to a stop beside the only car there—a rusted Buick Skylark with four near-bald tires. The radio station, the only one to serve Paradox, was a concrete bunker with no windows, hunkered down at the foot of the stubby butte that supported its antenna.

Dale shouldered open the metal door and marched into the cave-like reception area. No one was at the desk, so he barreled down a cement-block corridor and banged on the glass wall of the broadcast booth. Inside, Danny Valence, a nineteen-year-old kid he'd once arrested for D&D (drunk and disorderly) was in sole control of the radio board. Danny modeled himself on Wolfman Jack, an exuberant DJ who broadcast from Mexico with a signal powerful enough to reach every corner of North America as well as parts of Europe and, at times, the Soviet Union. The Wolfman howled and growled at his listeners, urging them to "lay your hands on your radio and squeeze my knobs"; but Danny—a skinny kid with acne to rival the rust on his Buick Skylark—lacked both the howl and the growl, so he relied instead on a string of rapid-fire inanities: "I spin the platters that matters." "We're the firstest with the mostest." "They may hate us but we're the greatest."

Dale hammered on the glass again. Danny, with his back to the sheriff, dropped needle to vinyl, then raised a hand, forefinger pointing upward. The finger said, "Wait," then curved behind Danny's ear to point at the red "On Air." Dale cursed and banged again, and the kid, with the record now in play, shimmied to the door and cracked it open.

"You couldn't see I was live?" he said.

Dale barged past him. "I don't give a rat's ass," he growled.

"You can't just come in here—"

"Can't I though?"

"I'll have to call the manager—"

"Call whoever you like," Dale said.

He slumped into the DJ's chair, pulling the microphone toward him.

CHAPTER TWENTY-SEVEN

Corin Dunbar

I first heard of the Indian from the radio. I'd slept badly the night before as I'd twice needed to turn Ark and give him water from the jug he kept on his bedside table; and in the early hours a storm had blown through, rattling the windows louder than a percussion band. When you live in the desert, you savor rain. So at first light I tip-toed onto the front porch to watch the deluge mire the dust before I stepped into the downpour to let it plaster my nightdress tight against my skin.

I was in a down mood that morning, still shaken by the horror of a rat biting Ark's defenseless body and by another seizure he'd suf-fered during the night; it had disrupted his brain and set his arms and legs twitching like someone possessed.

"All part of his healing," Doc Draper had reassured me.

But I had my doubts about that.

I was also low because the day before I'd been to see Jay Lam-bert—a friend from school (we sat in the same class for the better part of six years) who'd matured into Paradox's only independent lawyer as well as someone I could trust. Jessie had asked him to check on her insurance to find out if it would continue to cover Ark's ever-mounting medical bills.

"Good news and bad," Jay had told me, as I faced him across his desk. It was high noon and the October sun still held a hint of sum-mer heat, but Jay, as ever, had imprisoned himself in a three-piece navy-blue suit and a white pressed shirt he'd livened up with a vintage silk tie imprinted with art deco motifs. On the office wall behind him were a dozen sepia prints he'd rescued from libraries and attics in Bicknell, Moab, and Cedar City, where they'd been left to curl and molder. He'd framed the photos himself. Miners with heavy moustaches and wooden-handled picks. Rivers of sheep flowing down Wasatch Street on the way to the dip. Paiute Indians with braided hair and striped blankets. And respectable ladies in crinolettes, standing poker-straight under lace-fringed parasols.

"Those are times we won't see again," he told me, when he noticed me looking at the prints, "but they represent our history. They show us who we were. Most people don't care. They throw out the past like it's yesterday's news, but if we don't know where we've come from, how are we ever to know where we're going?"

"Give me the bad news first," I said.

He dipped his head and spread his hands in a gesture of defeat. "The insurance company won't pay for the kind of round-the-clock care your husband needs—if it's provided 'in home.'" Finger quotes in the air. "You've got a month before the money stops, since in the eyes of the insurance company, Ark isn't sick enough."

I had to close my eyes, clench my jaw, and slowly count to ten.

"Not sick enough?" I said. "Jay, Ark can't walk. He's bedridden. He can't even sit up without a trapeze and pulley to help him. And they say he's not *sick* enough?"

"I know, I know, but I'm just the messenger here." He carefully adjusted the wire frame of his glasses. "The statistics show he could live five, maybe ten years. And the insurance company won't cover him, not for that length of time. It'll take your premiums, no questions asked. But when it comes to paying out on a claim—well, the insurance companies write the policies. They seed them with any number of small-print opt-outs and loopholes. And in Ark's case, they say they won't pay past November."

I must have looked as distraught as I felt.

"You said there was good news," I finally managed.

He clasped his hands and leaned toward me. "The company *will* pay for Ark if he is cared for with 'the similarly afflicted'"—more finger quotes in the air—"or with 'those in the same ratings class.' It has no choice. It's in the contract, and they can wriggle and jiggle all they like, but they can't weasel out of that."

"So what's that mean in English?"

"It means they'll pay if Ark goes back to the Severill."

I shook my head. "Not going to happen," I said. "He hated it there. He was often in a ward with the mentally ill. He'd go crazy himself."

"It's an option, Corin."

"Not one I'm going to take," I said with finality. "I promised Ark."

Jay sat back and swiveled his chair from side to side. He pinched the bridge of his nose and looked at me over the top of his glasses.

"There is one other piece of good news," he said carefully.

"Oh?"

"The Fairchilds have improved their offer."

I frowned. "What offer?"

"Ah," he said, and toyed with a pencil on his desk. "I thought you knew."

"Knew what, Jay?"

"About the offer."

I shook my head.

"For the ranch?"

"The Fairchilds want to buy the ranch?" I said incredulously, my heart suddenly thumping against my chest.

"I've spoken out of turn," he said. "Haven't I?"

But I didn't think so. Jay never spoke out of turn. Jessie, I thought, must have put him up to it.

When I arrived home that evening, I confronted her in the kitchen.

"It's just an offer," she said. "Doesn't mean I have to accept it. It's another iron in the fire, that's all."

But I didn't believe that either.

❖

When the rain stopped, I dressed and went into the kitchen to make Ark his breakfast. Looking toward the saddle shed, I saw Felipe—a shadow in the thin light—mount Walnut, Ark's old quarter horse, and with the dogs yapping beside him, ride off to mend a gap in our fence by the valley road. "'Open range' means 'drivers beware,'" Jessie often said, but that nugget didn't stop cars and trucks crashing into our cattle if they wandered onto the road.

I prepared Ark his usual stewed apples from our few fruit trees, then cracked a couple of eggs into a bowl and seasoned them with chives and a sprinkle of pepper. I flipped on the radio and listened with half an ear to the Top Twenty countdown. I didn't like the DJ with his endless, mindless patter, but Ark appreciated some of the groups in "the British invasion"—the Animals, the Kinks, and the Rolling Stones. When the Beatles' "Hey Jude" started to play, I cranked the volume up a notch, but halfway through the track, the song died and the gruff voice of Dale Parker boomed over the air.

"This is your sheriff speaking," he said. "I'm cutting in 'cause early this morning we had a Draper state prisoner by name of Lowell Smith escape from a work party up on Kicking Horse Mesa. He's an Injun and a killer. Been convicted of murder and he's on the loose somewheres in the valley. Keep a lookout for him, but don't approach. He's not armed best we know, but he is dangerous, so if you see him, get to a phone and call my office. It's my job to get him caught, and get him caught I will. And this ain't no election stunt neither. This is for real."

His voice dropped to a hoarse whisper as I heard him say, "Now turn this damn thing off, jackass."

For a moment, the radio went dead. Then the music started again.

I didn't pay the sheriff much heed—the Waterpocket was a big valley—but I did glance over at the Marlin that Jessie had given me for my sixteenth birthday. We kept the rifle stashed in a rack behind the kitchen door. Ark hadn't wanted a gun in the bunkhouse, but Jessie said every ranch in the valley had at least one, so he'd better get used to it. She herself owned a Savage 99 as well as a Winchester 77, and was a better shot than I was—although the previous summer, the town's optician, Larkin Phillips, had diagnosed astigmatism in her right eye (her "shooting eye" she called it) and said she needed glasses.

"At your prices?" Jessie told him. "I don't think so."

CHAPTER TWENTY-EIGHT

Cal Parker

At just past 9:15 that morning, Deputy Cal Parker pulled his Bronco to a stop a mile shy of the entrance to the Jensen ranch, as close as possible to the base of the chute where the Injun had last been seen. Luke Sims, a retired deputy, sat beside him, cradling a Remington 870 that he kept pointed out the open window in case a sudden bounce caused it to fire. Sims had been put out to pasture several years before but could be called back if a "situation developed," ("and we do have a situation here," Dale Parker had said), mainly because he owned a dog, a German shepherd that was now crouched in the seat behind them, shedding hair. Cal didn't like the dog. He could hear it panting, and when it stuck its inquisitive nose over his shoulder, he could smell its breath, rank and rancid against his neck, and he knew from experience he'd later find his backseat slick with ropes of drool.

Sims was a lean, leathery man with close-cropped hair and a sprinkle of gray in his stubble. Not the sharpest knife in the cutlery drawer, Cal often thought. On the drive from Paradox, Sims had barely uttered a word—except to insist that his German shepherd be given the call sign, K9. A play on the word "canine."

"This the LKP?" he said now.

Cal nodded. The last known position. "Injun needed to get off the mesa, and this here's his only way down."

He slipped out of his seat and strode around to the trailer he'd hitched behind his Bronco, dropped the ramp door with a thud, and led out a skittish chestnut stallion already saddled up. He walked the animal away from the trailer, pulled a stirrup toward him, grabbed the cantle, and swung himself into the saddle, feeling rather than hearing the creak of leather as it settled under his weight. With a squeeze of his legs he urged the horse between the green stands of Mormon tea toward the chute. Sims and his dog were already there.

Cal looked around. Anyone coming down from the mesa would have had to cross the stone bench at the base of the scree.

"Start the nosework here," he said.

Sims held a blanket to the dog's muzzle—the scent article that had covered the cot the Injun had slept on the past few nights. He ran out the dog's leash, and K9 hunted, his nostrils grazing the ground. But soon he began to move in circles.

"Problem?" Cal said.

"Dead space," Sims told him as he leashed the dog in. "No scent."

"You think the Injun went for the river?"

Sims shrugged. "Maybe."

Cal walked his horse east, then led Sims and the dog south. It was the obvious way to go. Away from the mesa wall, he cocked his head to feel for the wind against his cheek. Dogs could track a scent on the ground, but as often as not they'd trail a raft that lingered in the air. K9 was again following his nose, when suddenly he stopped, body tense, and looked back at Sims.

Cal rode his horse over, sliding to the ground beside an old boot that he toed upright.

"The Injun's?" he said.

"Gotta be," Sims said.

Cal lifted his hat to scratch at his head.

"Well, that'll slow him down some," he said.

CHAPTER TWENTY-NINE

Corin Dunbar

The Bee Gees were halfway through "Gotta Get a Message to You" when I heard Sheriff Dale Parker's voice come over the radio a second time.

"This is your sheriff speaking. We just got word the Injun's been sighted on the Fairchild spread by the water tower there. He's limping, which means he's hurt. But like I said before, do not approach. This Injun's a murderer. Killed a man in cold blood, and he's likely out to kill again."

I froze when I heard that. The Fairchilds were our closest neighbors—one reason I figured they wanted to buy the ranch—and their water tower was less than a mile away across a strip of grazed-out open range. Jessie and I had helped them dig it in not more than a year ago. Without thinking further, I shouted through to Ark in the next room—"Gotta go"—and I tore out of there, pausing only to grab the Marlin from its rack behind the kitchen door.

I scrambled into the Dodge, bounced it over the washboard of our driveway, and swung hard left onto the valley's dirt road. At the first rise, I skidded to a stop. It was just a hump in the land (Ark had once said it was a sleeping bear that one day would wake up and scare us all to death), but from the top I had a beeline view of the water tower on the Fairchilds' ranch.

I sat for a moment—no sign of the Indian—but then he broke cover, heading for the river. He was doubled over and dragging his left foot as if it was weighted down by a stone. I slammed the truck into gear and floored the accelerator, shooting out a fountain of grit. Fifty yards on, I veered cross-country along a rough track that led to the ford—the only way to cross the river before the county put in a bridge.

The Dodge straddled a center ribbon of grass as its wheels churned through deep ruts. The Marlin danced a jig in the footwell beside me, and the windows shook so hard I thought they'd pop right out. Brittlebush raked the sides of the cab, and when I hit a rock, the steering wheel shuddered out of my grip and all four wheels left the ground. My butt left the seat too, and the Marlin thumped over and bruised me on the leg.

I eased to a stop thirty yards short of the tangle of bushes that lined the river, then grabbed the rifle and slid out of the truck, leaving the engine ticking over. With my back pressed against the cab, I scanned the brush with the barrel of the Marlin, sweeping it this way and that, hoping the landscape would give me a clue. When a tamarisk bush twitched more than it should have done, I dropped low and ran toward it, slowing only when I spotted daubs of blood that glistened bright as paint on its leaves. I poked the rifle into the tamarisk and almost fired when a flycatcher broke cover to flap past me and swoop low over the river. I wiggled the gun barrel around to part the branches that had interlaced into a tunnel.

The Indian was hunkered down a dozen feet away. His dark eyes glared at me. Long, ink-black tendrils of hair plastered his forehead, and rivulets of sweat coursed down a face that was streaked with dirt and runnels of blood. His torn shirt flapped open, so I could see coiled muscles and bulging arms. His feet were bare and bloody, a mess of oozing cuts; and his hands, clenched into fists, were pressed into the ground so he was crouched like a cougar ready to spring. I could smell him too. Rank, pungent, and ripe.

When I raised the rifle, he didn't shrink back. I hoped the gun gave me control, so I gripped it harder and sighted along the barrel.

We stared at each other until he swept hair out of his eyes with a quick motion that made me jerk the rifle higher.

"Get to the ford," I said, and flicked the gun to show him the way. My heart was racing and my insides churning, but I forced my voice out flat and firm.

He didn't move.

"Go on," I told him. "Get!" And I flicked the rifle again. "I'll pick you up there."

I didn't wait for an answer, but backed out of the thicket and sprinted to the Dodge. I jumped in and dumped the rifle beside me. At the ford, I threw the truck into a tight turn and backed into the water. I could hear the Indian thrashing through the underbrush, then splashing toward me through the water.

"On the back!" I yelled. "And hold on tight!"

He lunged for the truck and sprawled onto the flatbed. I gunned the engine, found traction on the river stones, and jetted water out of the wheel wells. I had no real plan. Just a harebrained idea I already knew was cracked. But at least I felt I was taking action that Ark might actually want.

CHAPTER THIRTY

Cal Parker

Cal Parker arrived at the water tower an hour after the Injun. He was in no real hurry. Dale might have been desperate to see the runaway back behind bars, but Cal knew the Injun wasn't going anywhere fast. A fugitive could hole up in one of the side canyons that bit into the sheer cliffs of the mesas; and after last night's storm, which had sent rain sluicing over the mesa tops like water tipped from the lip of a jug, he could survive by drinking from the pools that were saucered into the sandstone—the water pockets that gave the valley its name. But the Injun had gone for the river, where there were only a few places to hide.

Cal walked his horse and let Sims and the dog take the lead. Last night's rain had softened the sandy loam into a squelch, so there were footprints to follow as well as a breadcrumb trail of red-splotched blood. K9 bypassed the water tower and set off for the snake of vegetation that marked the river. The dog paused, then dove into a clump of tamarisk. Cal dismounted and bent down to examine a dollop of blood that lay slicked on one of the leaves. He rubbed it between his forefinger and thumb. It didn't smear, so the Injun was still a fair ways ahead.

K9 left the thicket and yanked Sims downstream before he plunged into the water, forcing his handler to wade in too. At the ford, the dog sniffed the air, then settled onto a patch of sand and gazed up at Sims, his jaws open, tongue lolled.

"What?" Cal asked when he rode up.

"Trail's end, looks like."

Cal looked around. "So where'd the Injun go?"

Sims shrugged.

"Well, he didn't take off and fly," Cal said.

"Nope. That he didn't."

Cal studied the ground. Fresh tire marks stood out bold as a woodcut where someone had made a three-point turn. He dropped beside them. Coopers, he thought, with a lot of miles on them. Or maybe Kelly's. Two brands that offered traction on sand. He caught the sweet smell of sage from bushes the tires had crushed; and nearby, a small rock had been flipped onto its back like a turtle, its underside muddied from the rain.

Definitely Coopers, Cal decided.

But Coopers were fitted on almost every set of wheels in the valley.

He waded into the river and sloshed across to the other side. The track there was choked with a neglect of grass and bushes. Stands of prickly pear that grew in the ruts had not been disturbed, and the drop-seed grass that thrived on the center hump stood tall with the stems unbent and unbroken.

"What do you think?" he asked Sims when he'd splashed back through the river.

"Wind's dropped is what I think. And it's getting hot. That means the scent plume's rising so K9 can't get to it."

"You reckon the Injun stuck to the river?"

Sims peered around as if the answer might be hiding nearby.

"Could be," he said.

Cal teased a Lucky Strike out of a paper pack in his breast pocket and bent his head to flare a match. He spat out a fleck of tobacco.

"We'll follow the river," he said. "The Injun's barefoot and bleeding. He can't get far."

CHAPTER THIRTY-ONE

Corin Dunbar

I backed the Dodge up to the barn and gestured with the rifle for the Indian to climb down. He did so stiffly with his hands half raised as if under arrest. I nudged him inside and pointed the way to the loft.

"Up there," I said.

He did as he was told and hauled himself up the ladder. At the top, he turned to look at me. Wide, flat face, high cheekbones, eyes dark as a raven's. A feral animal, cornered and trapped. And stinking worse than a day-old corpse.

"Move back," I told him. "And stay out of sight."

I stepped back into the sunshine, dragged the barn doors shut, and snapped the heavy padlock into place, slipping the key into my pocket. Then I drove the Dodge the few yards to the bunkhouse and parked it next to the Plymouth. It occurred to me the Marlin might not have been loaded, but I didn't have the nerve to check. I stashed it behind the kitchen door and tiptoed into the bedroom to check on Ark. He was fast asleep, so I closed the door behind me and leaned back against it, eyes screwed closed.

My hands trembled as I reheated coffee in the kitchen and carried a cup onto the front porch. Cattle grazed on the open range, and on the horizon the red scratch of the mesa cliffs stood livid against an azure sky. Just as they always did. But down by the river I saw Cal on horseback with Luke Sims and his dog on a leash. I knew Cal would come to the ranch, and sure enough, a few minutes later, he kicked his horse into a canter and rode across the range toward me.

❖

His boots clunked on the wooden boards of the rear porch, but I didn't move to let him in. Only when I heard the screen door creak and his rat-a-tat-tat on the wooden frame did I move through to the kitchen.

"Cal," I said flatly when I opened the door. Not a welcome, but not a rejection either.

"Corin," he said. "How ya been?"

"Oh, so-so. Not much changes, you know?"

He nodded slowly, as if weighing his options, then took off his hat to run fingers through blond hair that was slicked with sweat.

"You hear about the Injun?" he said.

I nodded. "On the radio."

"He can't have gotten far."

He waited for a response, but when I didn't reply he poked his head further into the kitchen.

"Coffee smells good," he said.

I cracked the door wider and he brushed past, closer than needed.

"Y'know he killed a man, don't you?" he said. "Snapped his neck with his bare hands."

"Dale said something like that."

"Well, we'll get him soon enough."

I turned away to fuss with the coffeepot, and Cal moved behind me.

"Me and Luke tracked him to the river," he said.

I poured coffee into a mug, added cream and two spoonfuls of sugar. Cal had a sweet tooth. I could feel his eyes roaming across my back. He'd recently tried to kiss me here, with Ark lying in the next room. With a rush of shame, I realized a small part of me hoped he'd do so again. It had been a long time since I'd been with Ark. I worried that some of my thoughts might show on my face, so I fussed some more over the stove before I turned around.

"We lost him at the ford," Cal said. He stood with his feet apart, thumbs hooked into his gun belt, filling the space between us.

I circled my way to the sink and leaned against it to put distance between us. Cal lifted a chair and flipped it round to straddle it. It had once been Ark's, back when we still ate meals at a table.

Cal said, "I don't see you around much."

"I'm in town every day at the paper," I said. "Let's go outside," worried that Ark might hear his voice.

Cal picked up his hat and followed me onto the back porch. He set his mug on the rail and turned to give me the full force of his flecked green eyes. A mingled tang of leather, tobacco, and sweat wafted toward me, and I felt another stab of guilt. It wasn't just the morning's rain I'd wanted to feel plastered against my skin.

"So how you really been?" he said.

"We do okay," I told him.

"Him too?" Cal angled his head toward the bunkhouse. "How's *he* doing, locked up in there all on his lonesome?"

My guilt instantly turned to anger.

"He has a name," I said sharply. "It's Ark. Remember? He's still got that."

Cal shrugged and bent to light a cigarette. He blew out smoke, tucked the pack back into his shirt pocket.

"Fence down by the road needs fixing, I see."

"Felipe's on to it."

"The Mexican?" He spat a loose flake of tobacco off his tongue. "That's not all that needs fixing around here, and you know it. Porch on the main house wants painting, I can see that from here. And when was the last time someone checked the shingles on the roof? Fact is, Corin," he said, bearing in on me, "you can't manage a place like this. Not just you and Jessie. Two women on your own. You need a man you can rely on."

"I've got one, Cal."

"Part man, if you ask me." He drew on his cigarette. "You could do better."

"I already *did* better. That's why Ark's here and you're not."

He looked at me squarely through the tendrils of smoke that hung between us. "You need a man to run this place," he said. "And you need a man in your bed too."

I should have slapped him, hit him as hard as I could. But I felt myself flush. Scared he might have been reading my mind.

"Get out of here," I said. "Go on. Now!"

He dropped his cigarette and ground it out under his boot. "Well, I do have a redskin to catch. So maybe I should be on my way." He settled his hat and moved off the porch. "You take good care now, you hear?"

"Don't worry about me. We're both doing fine."

As he walked to the tree where he'd tethered his horse, he passed the Dodge next to the Plymouth. He paused, rested his hand on the hood.

I knew he could feel the warmth of its engine.

"You take the truck out this morning?" he said.

"Out?"

"Yeah. The truck. You take it out?"

"It needed water," I said.

I'd always been a stuttering liar. But the truck *did* need water. It was old, it always needed water, which I'd draw from the hand-pump next to the barn.

He bent down and scratched sand off one of the tires, then straightened and wiped his hands down his Levi's.

"Well, hope to see you in town, Corin," he said. "I'll buy you a shake."

"I'll tell Jessie you stopped by," I told him. "She'll be pleased to know you did."

He nodded again before he mounted up.

I stayed where I was and watched him ride away.

CHAPTER THIRTY-TWO

Dominga turned up a few minutes later in a swirl of black hair and garrulous Spanish and shooed me out of the kitchen. She was there to take care of Ark's "personal needs"—his *cosas personales*, she called them—which he refused to let me handle. Since the age of twelve, Dominga had cared for every member of her extended family, from newborn babies to dying *abuelos*, so she was unfazed by any human condition.

I finished making Ark his breakfast, waited until he was properly settled, then drove the short distance to the ranch house, kicking up a haze of dust as I swung round to line up with the front steps of Jessie's porch. She'd heard the clunk and clatter of the Plymouth's engine and was waiting at the top of the steps.

"You want to give me a hand?" she said.

Tuesday mornings were set aside for a "bake-out," when she cooked a week's worth of pies and cakes for The Good Shepherd Shelter for the Homeless, as well as half a dozen biscuits for Mildred Curtis, a widowed octogenarian who lived alone on the fringes of Paradox and was past cooking for herself.

I let down the tailgate and used the emergency blanket I always carried to wedge three trays of her output into the trunk, surprised by the normal way I could function after stashing a murdering Indian in the barn.

"These look good," I said. "Smell good too."

"Well, don't drop them," Jessie said. "I spent too much time with my head in the oven to see them go face down in the dirt. I've put in half a dozen biscuits for Tuck, but tell him not to eat them all at once.

He's fat enough as it is. But don't tell him I said that," she added.

I dropped into the leather sinkhole that served as the Plymouth's driver's seat and lifted the hinges of the door so it would close. Jessie slipped in beside me and shoved the fleece she'd been holding into the small of her back for support.

"You know there's a runaway Injun on the loose?" she asked, as we rattled down the driveway, bouncing over the rock-hard dirt that years of rain and drought had sculpted into braids. "Bea Fairchild called to warn me, which I thought was a bit ripe, seeing as how she and Virgil have their eyes set on our ranch—and it's still just an offer, Corin," she added—"but that Injun, he killed someone. With his bare hands."

"I heard," I said. "Cal told me. When he stopped by. Said to say hi."

Jessie grunted. She still harbored a soft spot for Cal and would have seen more of him at the ranch if I'd agreed.

"I phoned to warn *you*," she said. "But there was no answer."

"No?"

"The Dodge was gone," she said, and glanced sideways at me.

"I was up early. Couldn't sleep because of the rain." Another weasel truth, to avoid telling a lie.

I cracked open the window. The cakes and pies filled the Plymouth with a homely aroma of cinnamon, cloves, and wild onion, but I needed air.

Jessie braced a hand against the dashboard as we turned onto the road into town, and when we hit a bump we rose in our seats with the perfect unison of synchronized swimmers.

"Mind my pies!" she said.

Then a moment later: "So how is he?"

Even with Jessie, it was often just "he."

"Ark's fine," I said. "I had to wake him a couple of times to turn him. But other than that, we were okay. He's still sleeping a lot. After his seizure."

"Has he changed his thinking? About wanting to die?"

I shook my head. "I don't think he will."

"You can't help him," she said. "You can't help him end his life."

"I know. You've said."

"It's a sin. A sin against God."

"You've said that too."

I swung wide to overtake a grip truck that was belching fumes and forcing us to ride in its smother of dust.

"Life is a gift from God," she added.

"Not now, Jessie. Okay? I'm not in the mood."

But she wouldn't be deterred.

"He has a plan, Corin. You have to believe that. Even if we can't always see what it is. What happened to Ark? There's a reason for that too."

"Oh, really? You think so?"

"I *know* so."

"Well, it seems to me this god of yours is either cruel to have let it happen. Or helpless because he couldn't stop it. Either way, I don't see he's much use."

I felt the Plymouth slew sideways as I took a bend too sharply. A hare dashed out of the brush and made a run for the other side of the road. Halfway across, it turned and darted back.

"I know it's hard for you, Corin," Jessie said. "And for Ark too. But you need to have faith. God *does* know what he's doing."

"Well, if he knows what he's doing," I said, my voice rising, "why don't we sit back and let *him* drive?"

And I took my hands off the wheel and flung them high above my head so they rapped against the roof of the car. At the same time, I screwed my eyes shut and stamped the accelerator flat to the floor. The Plymouth surged forward, and the ivory steering wheel danced and spun free. I heard the scrape of bushes along the side panels, and the back end slithered again before we bounced onto the verge and all four tires caught in a rut.

"Corin, look out!" Jessie yelled. "You'll get us both killed!"

"No, no, no," I shouted, as the car veered back onto the road. "He'll save us, won't he? You just need to have faith!"

"Corin! For Heaven's sake!"

She leaned over and grabbed the wheel, and I opened my eyes in time to see a cattle truck bearing down toward us. The driver's mouth gaped in horror as he blasted his horn. Jessie yanked the wheel and the cattle truck thundered past in a blur, the driver's face a contorted mask of anger and fear.

"Brake, Corin! Brake! And pull over—now!"

My anger drained away as quickly as it had flared, and for a moment it was all I could do to fight back a flood of tears I hadn't realized were building inside me.

I took the wheel back and eased up the accelerator.

"It's okay," I said more calmly. "It's okay."

"Corin, you need to let me drive."

I shook my head. "No. Really. I'm fine."

The incident had scared me as much as it had Jessie. I was losing touch with my feelings, a blurred confusion of jumbled emotions. I slowed some more until I was driving at a matronly speed.

"I'm all right," I said again, more to reassure myself than Jessie. "It's just that sometimes everything gets too much."

"I know," she said, and patted my knee. "But just promise me you won't do anything foolish."

I didn't want to tell her I already had.

The roadblock had been set up on the neck of land where the pincer claws of the surrounding mesas came together to enclose the valley. The pickup I was following—crammed with a tangle of tripods, light stands, and reflectors—ground to a halt and I stopped a few feet behind. Up ahead, a patrol car with "Blade County Sheriff" blazoned on its side was slewed sideways across the road. A hot and flustered Wayne Coleman stood beside it. One of the deputy sheriffs who worked with Cal.

"Gotta be the Injun," Jessie said.

I grunted in reply, and we settled into silence.

We edged forward as Wayne ordered the driver of the pickup out of his cab, checked inside, then mounted the running board to peer into the back. When our turn came, I cranked my window down to let Wayne lean in, his elbow resting on the sill. He was a veteran who'd been on the force as long as I could remember. The sweet scent of Jessie's cakes and pies wafted around us, but it had to fight the sour smell of Wayne's sweat floating in from the oval patches under his arms. Wayne was known to kick-start his day at the Bean and Burro, where he'd take on lashings of onions, garlic, and peppers, and I could detect the rancid backwash from that too.

"Ladies," he said, and tipped his hat. "Apologies for the delay, but we got an Injun on the loose, you might have heard?" He took a cursory glance into the back of the Plymouth, then sniffed the air like a bloodhound. "Got pies back there?"

"None for you, Wayne," Jessie said, leaning across me. "Looks like you packed away a few too many as it is."

He grinned and patted his stomach. "All bought and paid for," he said, and rapped his knuckles twice on our roof. I took this as a sign that we should move on and slid the Plymouth into gear.

"Is everyone in this valley overweight?" Jessie asked as we drove away.

"Must be your home cooking," I told her, by way of a peace offering. "No one can resist that."

She harrumphed and turned away, but not before I caught a glimpse of a smile.

At Balanced Rock, I left the main road to take the cutoff into Paradox that went through Eldorado. It was a shorter route, but when we arrived at the fake Western town, we found Front Street had been blocked off by a rope slung loosely across the road.

A man approached, wearing maroon bell-bottoms, a pink paisley shirt, and a leather band that was tied around his head to hold back shoulder-length hair.

"My, my," Jessie breathed, "what kind of get-up is *that*?"

"Your timing's good," the man said, bending down to speak through my open window. "We're just about to wrap. If you don't mind waiting?"

Off to one side an idle film crew stood around smoking and chatting.

Jessie and I sat in another silence until suddenly the batwing doors of the Silver Dollar saloon blew open and two cowboys rushed out. The one in the lead, outfitted in black, wore a flat-top Stetson that he'd tipped back to show a mop of long blond hair. The one behind was dressed head to toe in brown, with a narrow-brimmed, off-white hat.

Jessie jerked forward as if someone had stabbed a knife into her back.

"Is that Paul Newman?" she said. "That *is* Paul Newman. Well, as I live and breathe. Corin. That's Paul *Newman*! In the flesh!"

Jessie may have disliked the movies and have nothing good to say about the people who made them, but she drew an exception with Paul Newman, with his chiseled features and famously blue eyes. Whenever one of *his* movies came into town, she'd sneak into the drive-in and bring me along as her excuse. We'd seen pool shark Newman take on Minnesota Fats in *The Hustler*; half-Apache Newman fight ingrained prejudice in *Hombre*; and inmate Newman stuff back fifty hard-boiled eggs in *Cool Hand Luke*. We'd even seen a Roman Newman in *The Silver Chalice*, where he'd been costumed in a toga that looked more like a cocktail dress. The two of us had sat straight as stalks in the front seat of Jessie's Chevy, a couple of old maids, the only people there to see the film, surrounded by the steamed-up cars of necking teenagers.

She leaned out of her window and beckoned toward the paisley shirt with the bell-bottom pants.

"Is that Paul Newman?" she asked in awe.

"Yes, ma'am. He's Butch Cassidy. The other feller's a new guy named Robert Redford. He plays the Sundance Kid."

CHAPTER THIRTY-THREE

I dropped Jessie off at the Good Shepherd homeless shelter before I drove across town to the offices of *The Southeast Utah Gazette* at Main and Lincoln. I parked outside, next to a junction box that had a "Re-elect Dale Parker" poster plastered on its front. The sheriff's unsmiling image stared back at me and did little to ease the disquiet I felt over the way I was thwarting his hunt for the Indian.

As I entered the newsroom, the familiar sounds of the paper's business day washed over me, and I heard Willard Standish on the phone, shamelessly plucking readership figures out of the air as he pitched an advertiser for a tabloid spread. Willard was blessed with a foghorn voice that he never moderated, even when the clattering of our linotype machine fell silent and he had no need to shout. I hurried past him to the desk I had snared by the window. It gave me a view along Lincoln and across the street to the buckets and bins stacked outside Wyman's General Store.

I was supposed to be working on a color piece about a Marlboro commercial being shot in Cottonwood Canyon, but I had too much on my mind to focus. I still felt a fraud at the paper since I'd no experience as either a writer or a reporter when Vernon Tucker—or Tuck, as everyone called him—had taken me on. He'd only done so as a way of cozying up to Jessie. He'd long had a crush on her (which he tried to hide), and had caught on at once that when she said I wanted work, that really meant I needed money.

When I first started work on the *Gazette*, Tuck gave me easy assignments producing copy for the back of the paper. Write-ups about John Deere cutters and shredders. Notices of Jaycees meetings.

Upcoming ball games and church bazaars for the Calendar section; and fifteen-line obituaries that ran next to the Classifieds.

"Keep it short and sweet," he'd told me. "I'm not looking for *War and Peace*."

I soon found I enjoyed the work. I was good at it. I had a way with words that Tuck seemed to like. He soon put me on bigger pieces. A feature about Eldorado and the way the mayor had made it his baby. Then a series of profiles of Paradox residents who'd successfully made it into the movies. While all of us worked for the studios as pin-money extras, a few had managed to forge lasting careers. Like Cactus Greenaway, who'd turn up whenever a star needed a wizened partner to sit beside him astride a horse or crouch over a campfire, brewing coffee. Or Merle "Duke" Addison, whose oil-dark looks and slicked-back pompadour had graced dozens of barroom scenes, tossing back slugs of cold-tea whiskey or dealing High-Dice or Faro from the bottom of the pack. Writing about these people had given me a chance to escape. A way to enter another person's life and take a break from my own.

I'd recently profiled Cash Moseby—Paradox's answer to Ben Johnson—who'd been given prominent roles in *Fort Yuma, Bad Day at Black Rock,* and *The Man from Laramie*. And one day I hoped to write about Dottie, and how *she* had made it big in the movies.

I'd barely settled behind my desk when I saw Tuck emerge from the editor's office, clutching a doughnut he'd bitten through to the jelly. He lumbered toward me, his sleeves rolled up and an egg-stained tie circled loosely around his neck like a noose. Normally, he sported a Roy-Rogers-style kerchief that he knotted at a jaunty angle under one ear, as he was an avid fan of the American West and had built up an extensive collection of spurs, saddles, hats, and holsters. He displayed them in the cabin he'd restored near the mouth of the canyon I'd favored with Ark.

His most prized possession was a frock coat once worn by Doc Holliday. "Allegedly," Tuck always added. Ever the newspaper man. "Provenance is so hard to establish."

He waved the remnant of his doughnut at the bag of biscuits I'd set on my desk.

"For me?"

Tuck could spot a biscuit at more than a hundred paces.

"Jessie told me to say you shouldn't eat them all at once, because you're already big enough as it is. She also told me not to say that."

"And she was right. You shouldn't have said that."

The first of the biscuits disappeared as if he'd inhaled it, and his fingers moved toward another. Tuck's full name was Vernon Mortimer Tucker, and he'd been editor of the *Gazette* for more than a decade. Paradox born and bred, he'd lived in town most of his life save for a cluster of years in the 1950s when he worked on the desk of the *Chicago Sun-Times* and in the 1940s when he'd been drafted into the American Office of War Information to spiel out propaganda that showed doubtful Americans why their country had gone to war. Jessie once told me Tuck viewed this latter assignment as "a noble effort in support of a noble cause," but felt he'd written "the worst kind of horse manure anyone could ever imagine."

When I asked why he hadn't been sent overseas to kill Germans or Japs, Jessie told me Tuck was color blind. Which, if nothing else, helped explain the curious palette of pants, shirts, and ties he usually wore.

"Your aunt Jessie's a saint," he said, licking the last vestige of biscuit from his lips.

He was eighteen years older than she was—an old man, by my standards—but he didn't see that as a hurdle to asking Jessie out ("only means I'm more experienced," he'd say). But from her side, Jessie always made sure to keep him at bay. "Romance might suit some," she'd confided to me, "but it's a sure-fire way to kill a friendship."

Tuck perched himself on the corner of my desk. I could tell he was bursting with news, excited as a kid at Christmas.

"I tied down my interview with George Roy Hill," he said. "He's in town directing the Butch Cassidy movie they're shooting in Eldorado. Great guy. Used to be a newspaper man like me, so he understands the need to schmooze the press. He tells me Brando was offered the part of Butch but turned it down. Too upset to work on account of Martin Luther King being shot. Warren Beatty was a possible for Sundance because of *Bonnie and Clyde*. And Dustin Hoffman, too, can you believe? I mean, Dustin *Hoffman*? The guy's no more than five-foot-zilch in his boots. He'll always be *The Graduate*, far as I'm concerned."

He reached for another biscuit, ignoring my warning look.

"Warren Beatty thought he could play Butch, but he didn't want to ride a horse. Jack Lemmon was in the running; and so was Steve McQueen. He's coasting on *The Magnificent Seven* and *The Great Escape*, so he could have had his pick of the parts. He'd have been great too—Angela pinked up when I just mentioned his name—but he couldn't decide, Butch or Sundance, which should it be? Plus, McQueen wouldn't work with Paul Newman. He's jealous, feels he's lagged a few steps behind him in his career. And Newman had the role sewn up, because Goldman—that's William Goldman, who wrote the script—had him in mind from the start. He wasn't about to walk, so that ruled out McQueen."

Tuck plucked a half-sucked lollipop out of his pocket and picked at the sticky wrapper. He had a stomach big enough to possess a mind of its own, and although he held it back with a belt with a bucking bronc buckle, it still hung over his pants like a water-filled balloon.

"Newman was down to play Sundance at first," he went on, "so Goldman called his movie *The Sundance Kid and Butch Cassidy*. But that's like Hammerstein and Rodgers, Sullivan and Gilbert, McCartney and Lennon. It doesn't have the right ring to it, does it? Finally they settled on Newman for Butch and this guy Robert Redford for Sundance. I saw him in *Barefoot in the Park* and he was so-so, because the guy he played was a flat tire, an establishment bore. But as Sundance, he's rugged and craggy and tanned and blond, so Hill's got high hopes. It's another oater, I know. But the script zings and there's buddy love between Newman and Redford.

"Only one problem," Tuck continued. "Hill's planning a shoot over by the San Raphael Swell. It's a long sequence of scenes where Butch and Sundance are on the run, pursued by a posse of hard-nosed lawmen who track them for days. Redford barely utters a word, and all Newman says is, 'Who *are* those guys?' But Hill told me he wants to make the scenes a central part of his movie and give it plenty of screen time. The posse's guided by an Indian tracker named Lord Baltimore, but as luck would have it, the actor playing Baltimore fell off his horse and broke a leg, so Hill's short one Indian. He's going to have to bus in a bunch of Navajo from the Nation and hold an audition."

He paused for breath, and his attention shifted to something over my shoulder. When I turned to look, Sheriff Dale Parker was striding toward us, all gussied up in a pristine tan shirt, a glinting silver star on his chest, and a knife edge crease down both legs of his pants.

"Speak of the devil," Tuck said, levering himself off my desk and turning to face him. "Here's someone else who's short one Indian."

I shrank in my chair, thinking that Dale might have come with handcuffs for me. But he made straight for Tuck.

"What's on your mind, Sheriff?" Tuck said.

"You heard about the Injun?"

"The one that got away? Sure, I know about him. We're a newspaper; it's our job to know these things."

"I don't want you saying we can't catch him."

"I wasn't planning to," Tuck said. "But *can* you catch him?"

"Damn right we can. And by sundown too. Have him back in Draper before you can spin around."

"So what's the problem?"

"No problem. I just don't want you tilting the election away from me in one of your editorials, saying I can't get my man."

"This paper supports your opponent, Sheriff, if that's what you're getting at, because he represents change, and we sure need that as far as your office is concerned. Jay Lambert may not have a snowball's chance in hell, but a Parker backside's been warming the sheriff's chair for far too long. Dynasties are un-American. That's why we kicked the British out. And anyway, we've got the Kennedys for that."

"I'm not breaking sweat over some scraggy-assed lawyer," Dale said. "I just don't want you telling your readers there's something amiss with the law and order I've been giving them all these years. I'm the one that put that Injun away, so I'm the one he'll be gunning for. I'm the one in the firing line here, so I'd thank you—and your readers—to keep that in mind."

Tuck frowned and tilted his head. "This Indian *is* a problem for you, isn't he?"

Dale didn't answer. Just stood there glowering, his chin out. His color was high and the veins in his neck bulged. He took a step back and forced out a smile.

"You were always the fat boy, Vernon," he said. "Even at school, you were the one who couldn't catch a ball. The last pick for a team. They'd rather have a traffic cone than choose you."

"My editorials *are* getting to you," Tuck said. "That's really why you're here, isn't it?"

"No one reads the crap you write."

"Seems maybe you do."

The two of them stood, eyes locked, until Dale said, "I got an Injun to catch and an election to fight. I need to shake me some hands, kiss me some babies.

"Well, maybe you can start," Tuck said, "by trying to kiss my ass."

"Now, now, boys," Willard Standish boomed from the other side of the room. "School's out and your mamas'll be here soon."

Dale stood still a moment longer, then as he turned seemed to notice me for the first time. A flicker of meanness tightened his mouth.

"Corin," he said, "how's that cripple husband of yours? You got him committed yet?"

Before I could answer, Tuck stepped in and used the bulk of his belly to shove Dale back.

"We don't go in for that kind of talk," he said. "Not here."

"I'm just asking."

"You're just asking nothing, Sheriff. You want to talk like that, you take it outside."

Dale glared at him before he wheeled and stomped away.

"Thanks, Tuck," I said, and could have hugged him.

He waved a hand in the air. "Better get back to work," he said gruffly. "We've got a deadline to meet and a paper that won't write itself."

CHAPTER THIRTY-FOUR

Jessie Dunbar

When Jessie left the homeless shelter that day, she turned left onto Pierce and then onto Seventh. Walking past the small wooden houses that lined the street, she set off the dogs that were kenneled behind them, barking and rattling at their chains. At Jackson, she turned right and picked up her pace as she passed the pool hall, head bent against the din of a jukebox hammering out "Born to be Wild." When the music died, she heard the click of cue balls and the raucous noise of laughter. But by the time she reached Third, the sounds of carousing had faded to an almost eerie silence.

Jessie relished the quiet. She liked the small-town feel of Paradox, with its dusty blocks housing friendly neighbors who swapped baby clothes and toys and sometimes sizeable loans to tide each other over until payday. That was the *old* Paradox, the one that existed before the movie crowd arrived, and the one Jessie still hankered after. Most towns in the southeast part of the state had been founded by Mormons, but this one was proper Christian. The Latter Day Saints had ignored the Waterpocket Valley in favor of better land to the west. Pretty much everyone else had too, until a homesteader found he could tap water under the ground and not just draw it out of the river. That had brought in a straggle of ranchers, as well as a few enterprising traders who set up shop outside the valley where the railroad was mooted to run. By the time Jessie was born, the town was big enough to boast a bank, a courthouse, and its own weekly paper, but small enough to still feel like home.

Jessie had been distraught when Mayor Carter Williams—and that "awful man" Leland Jellicoe—had pushed for the construction of Eldorado. She saw the fake town as a metaphor. A false front that hid shameful secrets.

On the corner of Lincoln, she unlocked the door of her church and stepped inside. Other than Father Thomas, she was the only key-holder, an honor that meant little before the coming of the studios, because in those days the door could always be left open. But a spate of recent thefts (unsolved by Sheriff Dale Parker) had seen the disappearance of a golden chalice, an ambry, and most recently a silver-plated ciborium.

Jessie crossed herself, genuflected, and with hands clasped and head bowed, approached the altar. Apart from the sanctuary where the thefts had taken place, the church was unadorned. It had been built in the 1930s to compete with the First Baptist church the other side of town on Fifth. Catholics and Baptists had little in common, but their congregations had briefly united in outrage when, in the early 1960s, they learned that the fake church in Eldorado would be given a makeover, while their real ones would continue to be neglected.

She clunked a nickel into the wooden box and lit a votive candle, then crossed herself again and went to kneel in the family pew. She'd prayed the rosary that morning, but reached for her beads again to summon Mary to intercede on her behalf and to bring those she loved the gift of faith. There were so many people in need of God's help—far too many to single out—but she said a prayer for Ark ("I ask you, Lord, to provide the strength he needs to carry on in his time of troubles and find the hope and light he lacks"). And she said one for Cal. She prayed, too, for Tuck. For Dominga and Felipe and their children in California. And then she prayed for her ranch ("so it stays in the Dunbar family and I don't have to sell"). But most of all, she prayed for Corin. Because of all the people Jessie knew, Corin was the one who most needed the kind of guidance only God could provide.

Jessie often thought back to the day Corin had stepped off that Greyhound bus in the center of Paradox. She'd looked so frail, so scared and vulnerable, a waif-like figure lost in the stream of rumpled travelers who jostled her aside as they fought to reclaim their luggage, until finally the driver handed out a suitcase that, like Corin, was clearly on its first journey away from home. Corin had gripped the case in one hand, clutched her ticket with the other, and hung on to both in white-knuckled fear. Watching from a distance, Jessie had experienced a surge of emotion of a kind she'd never known. She could not help but love this child with all her heart and being.

As the years passed, she'd watched Corin grow from a child into a teenager and then into a resolute, sometimes stubborn, woman who was gifted with an innate intelligence as well as a natural beauty. Jessie had tried to steer her along a path toward God, but Corin had resisted and then flat-out refused. Jessie had told her that God lived within us all, so if you wanted to find him, all you need do was listen. But with Corin, there had been too much noise. Too much background static.

Jessie had found God at the age of sixteen and attended church ever since. She wanted to feel closer to him.

And to atone.

"But what are you atoning *for*?" Tuck had once asked her. "What could you possibly have done that you feel such a need for forgiveness?"

She could never tell him, of course. She could never tell anyone other than her confessor. And even that was not enough to spare her from Hell. A real place, not a figment of medieval imagination, but a genuine realm of licking flames, thrashing bodies, and screams of agony and remorse.

She bowed her head and prayed again for Corin's soul. "Please Mary, Mother of Jesus, do not let Corin, in her love for Ark, fall into the ways of the Devil and commit a mortal sin. I beg you to turn her away from the path I fear she has chosen, for surely otherwise she'll burn forever in Hell."

CHAPTER THIRTY-FIVE

Corin Dunbar

I was anxious to leave work early that day as Dominga had asked for the afternoon off to visit a cousin in Blanding and I needed to get back to Ark. Then, too, I was starting to panic at the thought of the Indian I'd locked away in our barn. But as I shoved my papers away, Tuck emerged from his office and puffed toward me.

"Corin," he said, "I've been thinking about this Indian of Dale's. He *does* seem to be a problem for our good sheriff. So I want you to check the archives. See if we published anything about him. Then check the court records. If nothing else, a short piece on the Indian's escape will put a burr up the sheriff's ass, and that's never such a bad thing; it'll help to keep him on his toes."

Tuck's "archives," I knew, were old clippings stuffed into a three-drawer wooden filing cabinet that his secretary, Angela Morton, was supposed to sift and sort and keep up to date. But Angela was a well-meaning dreamer who tottered around the office on killer heels. Tuck had inherited her from Lick Gardner, the previous occupant of the editor's chair, who'd supplied a reference so glowing "you could toast marshmallows on it," as Tuck had phrased it. When he found out he'd been duped, he was too soft-hearted to fire Angela, but consoled himself with the thought that she liked the same iced oatmeal cookies he did, and proved to be a reliable supplier.

I figured Angela would have dumped most of the clippings under "Miscellaneous," so was pleasantly surprised to find a file labeled "Indians." Not a big file. No more than a dozen or so articles over a period of fifteen or twenty years. The *Gazette* didn't publish much about Indians, even though the Navajo Nation was little more than forty miles away, and tribal members were often camped outside town when a movie was being made, and they were in high demand as extras. Rarely were Indians seen on the streets of Paradox, as too often the town folk brushed them off as "savages" or "redskins." Even Jessie had once told me, "They're not like regular Americans; they don't have our values."

I found a 1955 clipping—complete with mug shot of "Lowell Smith"—that was yellowed and curled and nibbled at the edges.

Indian convicted in reckless driving

Written when Lick Gardner was editor, I thought. Tuck would never have allowed that wrong use of a preposition.

I leafed through the other clippings, looking for one that would tell me about the Indian's conviction for murder, but came up blank. I took the one clipping I'd been able to find and made my way along a crowded Main Street to City Hall.

Tuck must have phoned ahead because the zaftig Kay Short, who worked as the town clerk, had Lowell Smith's arrest report ready.

"This is it?" I asked her, looking at the single page.

"That's it," Kay said.

"But he's serving time for murder. This just covers reckless driving."

"If you say so."

Kay had long had her sights on Cal, and as far as I was concerned, she was welcome to him; but she still saw me as a rival. She was blonde as well as buxom, a combination that had earned her a walk-on part as a dancehall girl in *How the West Was Won*. Another disappointment for Posie, the mayor's wife, who'd been angling for the same role. But all *her* curves, the director had said, lay south of her equator, not north.

"You sure this is all you've got," I said. It wasn't much to look at. Mostly a bunch of boxes, some of which had been ticked.

"I'm sure," Kay said. "And you can't take it with you. That's the original."

"Can I get a copy?"

"I suppose."

Like pulling teeth.

"Better make it two," I said.

I waited for her to fire up the Xerox machine, then headed back to the office. Tuck didn't raise his head when I slapped the clipping on his desk along with a copy of the arrest report. He was busy stabbing two-fingered at his Olivetti, banging out an editorial that would tell his readers which way to vote in the upcoming election. The local level was easy, he'd told me—Carter Williams for mayor (again); Jay Lambert for sheriff (as a change)—but the national level was not. Nixon had "too much of the dark about him"; Humphrey was "too close to Johnson and the failure of Vietnam"; while the third candidate, the unabashed segregationist, George Wallace, was simply out of the question. "It'll be a sad day for America," Tuck had said, "if we ever let a white supremacist sit in the Oval Office."

He was hitting the keys with such ferocity, the crumbs around him—all that remained of Jessie's biscuits—jittered about like Mexican beans. I could never understand how someone so blind to his surroundings and his personal appearance could be so fastidious with words and ideas and the placement of commas, hyphens, and periods.

"Accuracy and precision," he'd told me when he first took me on, "are the hallmarks of a good paper. And a good journalist. We have to *earn* the trust of our readers, and that means we tell them the truth, the whole truth, and nothing but the truth, and we always strive to get our facts *right*."

I started to make my excuses so I could leave, but Tuck waved me away.

"Go," he said. "Take all the time you need. Tell Ark I said 'hi' and that we're still thinking of him."

"Thanks," I said.

And left, taking with me the second copy of the arrest report.

I made good time on the drive to the ranch. Filming had finished for the day in Eldorado, and the roadblock didn't delay me as I was heading into the valley, not out. I snuck into the kitchen and listened at the door of Ark's room. Dominga had not yet left—I could hear her voice quiet as the murmur of bees as she gamely read him one of his books. I grabbed the rifle from behind the door, checked it was loaded, and snuck out to the barn, where I snapped open the padlock and dragged the double doors ajar so I could slip in. I was worried about the Indian, about the state he was in, and whether he'd be willing to help.

Sunlight filtered through the gaps in the siding, just enough for me to see. I edged over to the base of the ladder and craned up at the loft, the Marlin in front of me as I'd seen it done in the movies. I listened, but heard only the rhythm of my own breathing and the *thump, thump, thump* of my heart.

I called out.

No answer.

I tried again. "Hey, you! Up there!"

I hauled myself up the first couple of rungs of the ladder, rifle in one hand, tight against my chest.

Five rungs higher, I stopped. A rustling came from the back of the loft. I called out a third time.

The ladder creaked as I shifted my weight and moved up another rung. The rustling grew louder and a black shape loomed above me. It tipped forward, over the edge of the loft, then hurtled into my face. I screamed, ducked, and cowered as a panicked rooster swooped by me screeching like a banshee, then cackled and flapped its way through the open door to freedom.

When my heart slowed, I pulled myself higher until my head poked above the floor of the loft. I swept the rifle left and right. But there was no longer any doubt.

The Indian had gone.

PART FOUR

CHAPTER THIRTY-SIX

Yiska Begay
(aka Lowell Smith)

For almost four hundred years—from 1500 to 1900—European settlers in North America attempted to solve "the Indian problem" by genocide and apartheid. By the time the Indian Wars officially ended in 1924, more than two hundred tribes had been exterminated; and those that survived had been herded onto land that no one else wanted. Once numbering as many as seven or eight million, the American Indian population sank to a low of about two hundred and fifty thousand before it slowly began to recover.

The Navajo were among the more fortunate. In the 1860s, they endured the Long Walk, when US government agents forced them to march three hundred miles from their homelands in New Mexico and Arizona to an internment camp at Bosque Redondo, a desolate wasteland near the brackish Pecos River; but in later years they were allowed to return to a tract of land in northeast Arizona and parts of neighboring Utah and New Mexico that's now known as the Navajo Nation. About the size of West Virginia, it is the largest reservation in America.

It was there, in 1928, that Yiska Begay was born.

His home—in Canyon de Chelly—was a simple hut, or *hogan*, made from pine logs, cedar bark, and mud. It had a dirt floor, a door that faced east, and an opening in the roof to let out the curled smoke of a damp juniper fire that constantly burned in the hearth. There was no electricity, no running water, and the outhouse was thirty yards away, just inside a perimeter fence of spiny *ocotillo* sticks. Like his brothers and sisters, Yiska slept on a sheepskin rug under a blanket his grandmother had woven. He was often hungry, sometimes going days without food; and when he and his family finally ate, it was often a basic diet of corn, beans, and squash. He had no toys other than a truck his uncle made with a block of wood for the body and four discarded cotton spools for the wheels. Yiska would play with this truck for hours, dragging it behind him as he ran barefoot with the other boys through the rust-red dirt of the canyon.

For the first few years of his life, Yiska helped supplement his family's meager diet by gathering fruits, nuts, and herbs, and he tended its small herds of sheep and goats. When a slinking coyote threatened the animals, he'd scare it away with deftly aimed stones that he fired from his father's handed-down catapult. Coyotes were bad, his mother had told him. They were the reincarnation of evil people. She'd also said there were two classes of beings in this world: the spirit ones, who were supernatural, and the Earth ones, who were human. It was vital, his mother said, for *hozoji*, or harmony, to prevail between these two classes; but if it did not, it could be restored by singers, or priests, using a combination of song, dance, ritual, and prayer.

When Yiska was five, his father Bidziil (meaning "he is strong") fell ill with a heart condition that even the singers couldn't cure. On the point of death, he was carried out of the hogan by two of his brothers—he could not be allowed to die at home, since tradition dictated the hogan would then have to be destroyed—and taken to a cleft in a rock a mile away. Yiska was not allowed to join them—nor to shed tears, as that would have slowed his father's journey into the underworld—but he was consoled by the knowledge that his uncles would remain with Bidziil until his final breath.

A year later, a second calamity struck the family when a gang of white men—all of them armed—rode up to his hogan in an uproar of shouts and a thunder of hooves. They were followed a few minutes later by a tanker truck that lumbered over the desert, spawning a funnel of dust as big as a tornado. The armed men rounded up as many of the family's sheep and goats as they could find and herded them into a ditch, poured gasoline over their backs, and burned them alive. Stragglers were shot and the carcasses left to rot in the sun. The men then turned their guns on the family's few cattle and horses and shot those animals where they stood. The slaughter went on for what seemed like hours. But it was all done for the family's good.

At least, that's what the armed men said. They were agents of the US government's Department of Agriculture and Bureau of Indian Affairs, and they said the Indians were overgrazing their land. For the soil to recover, all the animals had to be destroyed.

Yiska's mother Johona (meaning "sunny") did not agree. A small wiry woman hardened by life, she viewed the carnage as a deliberate attempt by the United States government to destroy the family's sources of milk, cheese, and meat, and to deprive it of the low-grease Churro wool the women wove into blankets and rugs. An Indian's home was supposed to be sovereign, she told her son, because it was built on land that was not subject to the white man's rule.

"That is the law," she said. "But the government has no respect for the law, even though they write everything down. Indian people have no need for such writing, because if the words are true, they sink into an Indian's heart and stay there. White people must write everything down, because then they can lose the paper. And with the paper they can also lose the truth, because there's no truth in the white man's heart."

Over the years, she told her son, the United States government had signed hundreds of treaties with the Indians, and broken every one.

"The way to survive injustice," she said, "is not to fight. Life is unfair, and no Indian should expect it to be different. You must meet every challenge with dignity and strength. That way you show you are a better man than those who seek to cheat and destroy you."

As Yiska grew older, he missed his father and often wondered where the two of them would have hunted. But Navajo society was matriarchal, so he continued to be raised by his mother—and his grandmother too.

One day, when Yiska was eleven, the two women took him to the trading post at Oljato in Monument Valley, where the movie director John Ford was shooting scenes for his Western, *Stagecoach*. After making their purchases, the two women stood with Yiska and watched from behind the mounted cameras as a driver rattled a six-horse stagecoach across the floor of the valley with a troop of cavalry riding escort. The stagecoach followed a trail that had been roughly marked out in the shadow of Merrick Butte, then wound between the East and West Mittens—at which point, a marauding band of whooping Indians charged into the scene, firing a broadside of arrows.

"Hollywood Indians," Johona scornfully called them.

On the long journey back to their hogan, his grandmother Nizoni (meaning "beautiful") told Yiska, "White people make Westerns to further their lies. They want to believe our land was empty before they came, so they can claim it as their own, given to them by their God. That's the lie they like to tell—and the one they teach their children."

For the next three years, Yiska lived a simple life, eking out an impoverished existence in a sunbaked land that was harsh and demanding. But he was happy—loved and secure in his home—until early one morning the government men returned, driving up to his hogan in a battered truck. This time, they hadn't come for the sheep and the goats.

This time, they had come for him.

When the Indian Wars were brought to an end, the United States government switched tactics and set out to destroy the Indians' culture. Its policy was summarized as "Kill the Indian, but save the man," and it used re-education to force out Native beliefs and instill superior white ones in their place. The government men who came for Yiska dragged him from his mother's embrace and dumped him into the back of their truck. He wiped grime from its rear window and, as he was driven away, watched his mother recede into the distance, tears streaming down her cheeks, his younger brother squirming against her leg with his face buried into the folds of her dress. His turn would come soon enough.

Yiska had never left the Navajo Nation and had little idea of the white man's world. His journey lasted the better part of a day and long into the night, and only ended when the truck stopped at the Sonoran School for Indians a hundred miles north of Phoenix. He was stripped of his warm wrap of a blanket, as well as his breeches, leggings, and deerskin moccasins, and issued with a military-style, five-button jacket and a pair of full-length woolen pants. His long hair was forcibly chopped and shaved above the ears by two of the Catholic nuns. And then he was given a new name.

"From now on," Sister Catherine told him on that first day, "you will be known as Lowell Smith. You will not answer to any other name. You will not speak without permission, and then only in English. If you utter a single word of Navajo, you will be severely beaten and have your mouth washed out with lye soap."

At the school, his life followed a strict regime. In the day, he was drilled like a soldier and made to learn the white man's version of American history, as well as selected passages from their Bible. At night, he was confined to a cold dormitory with a roof that leaked. He was punished for minor offenses—an untied shoelace or an unpolished toecap—so he was always afraid. He was also hungry, forced to scavenge for scraps in the garbage cans outside the kitchen doors. Malnutrition was rife in the school, and so were contagious diseases like tuberculosis and trachoma. The Catholic nuns said the Indians' sickness was caused by their inherited inferior strength.

Yiska couldn't wait for his schooldays to end. When he turned sixteen, he was released like a prisoner with a brown paper bag containing the few possessions not on his back. No longer was he a Navajo. But nor was he white. On paper he was an American citizen, but as an Indian he knew he wouldn't be able to vote. He was trapped in a no-man's land between two opposing cultures.

For several years Yiska drifted, sleeping rough and taking odd jobs when he could find them. He worked in the darkness of a coal mine. Washed dishes in dives and diners that would have refused him service. And cleaned the stalls of public washrooms he was banned from using because of his race. He swept factory floors and heaved sacks of grain into boxcars, and during one long, hot summer picked apples with illegal immigrants from Guatemala, who welcomed him as one of their own.

Then one January day in Chicago, with snow thick on the ground and a frigid wind gusting off the lake, he huddled at a desk in the city library, searching the want ads in the *Tribune*. The work he'd found in the past had come from bulletin boards in homeless shelters, handwritten cards in shop windows, or word-of-mouth recommendations from people he met under bridges where he slept at night. He was looking for something better, and found it in a classified ad for a warehouse stacker.

He phoned the number.

"You saw our ad?"

"I did," Yiska said.

"Can you lift seventy-five pounds?"

"I can."

"Work a twelve-hour shift?"

"I can do that."

"When can you start?"

"Today, if you want."

"Okay. What's your name?"

"Yiska Begay."

There was a pause.

"You a featherhead?"

"I'm a Navajo," Yiska said.

The phone went dead.

The next day, he walked into a recruiting office on Western Avenue and enlisted in the U.S. Army. Six months later, as a dogface in the 7th Infantry Division, he was battling communists, fighting his way north on the Korean peninsula.

Five years later, on July 31, 1955, Yiska Begay waited in the wings of an elevated stage that had been set up in the exact center of the 7th Infantry Division's parade ground at Fort Ord near Monterey Bay, a hundred miles south of San Francisco. Thirty-two rows of metal chairs faced the stage and the Division's flag that swished and swirled above it. The chairs were filled with proud parents sitting next to soldiers who had recently returned from the Far East. The Korean War had ended nearly two years before, but the 7th Infantry Division had been deployed to Japan and only now were its soldiers returning home to the States.

Standing with Yiska were two other soldiers who, like him, wore full parade-dress Class A uniforms. At a signal from their staff sergeant, the three men marched in unison onto the stage and took their seats next to the podium. When Yiska's name was called, he rose from his chair, took one step forward, and stood smartly to attention. With his heart beating faster than normal, he stared fixedly at the cloudless blue sky above and beyond the rows of upturned faces as his commanding officer read out his citation.

"On February 19th, 1952, Corporal Yiska Begay advanced at great personal risk towards a machine-gun nest near the village of Taerni-dong, where the enemy was dug in and inflicting severe casualties on the regiment. Ignoring intense cross-fire, Corporal Begay advanced close enough to throw two grenades into the machine-gun nest, killing its crew and risking almost certain personal injury or death. Wounded and bleeding, but without hesitation, he led a second assault on a camouflaged enemy pillbox—again under heavy fire— and once more ran close enough to sweep the emplacement with his carbine, before hurling a grenade through its opening and killing the five enemy inside. Corporal Begay's unhesitating courage and resilience undoubtedly saved the lives of many of his comrades. His actions reflect utmost credit upon himself and are in keeping with the honored traditions of the United States military."

In the silence that followed, his commanding officer pinned a Distinguished Service Cross onto Yiska's chest. The two men shook hands and exchanged brisk salutes. At that moment, the spectators rose to their feet to holler and cheer. It was the first time Yiska had heard white people applaud him. He wished his mother could see him now, and resolved there and then to place the bronze cross in her hands before she died.

The next day, he stripped off his uniform for the last time, dressed in civilian clothes, and hoisted a kit bag onto his shoulder. He carefully pushed his medal (with its red, white, and blue ribbon) into the side pocket of his new Levi's, said goodbye to other members of his platoon, then boarded the military bus that took him the twelve miles into Salinas. With two hours to kill before his Greyhound left to take him home to the Nation, he sauntered into the station bar.

The conversation died as the drinkers turned from their beers to face him.

"No Injuns allowed," the barman said. "Beat it."

"I have every right," Yiska said.

"Not in here you don't. No Injun's going to set his backside down on any stool in my bar. So beat it while you can still walk."

Yiska fingered the medal in his pocket. "For valor," it said. He stared at the barman, then turned and walked out.

Twenty hours later, the doors of a Greyhound bus creaked open, and he stepped down into the center of Paradox, the closest town of any size to the Nation.

It was 1955 and almost a year to the day since the doors of a similar bus had wheezed open and spat out Corin Dunbar onto the same spot.

CHAPTER THIRTY-SEVEN

Dale Parker

Across the road from the bus stop, Sheriff Dale Parker sat behind the wheel of his cruiser and used the back of his tie to spit-polish his sheriff's badge to a mirror-like shine. His uniform shirt was starched and his pants held a crease that was sharp enough to slice bread.

He straightened when he saw the Injun. For the past couple of days, he'd been kept busy while Paradox overflowed with movie people newly arrived in town—notably Rock Hudson and Barbara Rush, here to film *Taza, Son of Cochise*. The two actors had been chauffeured along Main Street in an open-top Chrysler Imperial, waving grandly at the cheering crowds. They'd been followed by co-stars Rex Reason and Ian MacDonald in a Buick Riviera, both cars shipped in by trailer for this, their only appearance.

The crowds were here to see Rock Hudson, recently named *Photoplay Magazine*'s Most Popular Male Star for the second year running. Main Street had been strung with a blaze of bunting, balloons, and banners (WELCOME UNIVERSAL—OUR TOWN IS YOUR TOWN), and both of its sidewalks were filled with stalls selling hot dogs, sodas, and fries. The ChokLik Scoops ice-cream parlor was doling out free samples and cut-price cones, while the school's marching band had belted out a rickety version of "In the Mood" from the stage in Settlers Park. Mayor Carter Williams seemed everywhere at once, shaking hands and slapping backs; and so, too, was Leland Jellicoe, inviting all and sundry to stop by his refurbished Juniper Lodge and the adjacent Double-D.

"Just look for my shiny red convertible parked outside," he told anyone who'd listen. "It's a brand-new Eldorado, the Cadillac model that Eldorado was named for."

After two days of hype and hysteria, the celebrations were winding down, but Dale could hear the megaphoned voice of Mayor Carter Williams on the granite steps of City Hall as he addressed a crowd that already was starting to turn away.

"With the Hollywood money we'll be bringing in," the mayor was saying, "we'll be able to fund the farmers' ditch at the top of the valley and bring forward the expansion of the Fourth Street Medical Clinic I know you've all been waiting for."

His wife Posie stood behind him—one step back (and one step higher, *The Southeast Utah Gazette* snidely reported). She was powdered and packaged in a boucle lavender suit and matching cloche hat.

Dale cranked up his window to silence the mayor and turned his attention to the new arrival. He didn't like Injuns in his town and resented the fact that the *Taza* director—with not so much as a by-your-leave—had hired a bunch of them for his movie. They'd set up teepees in the park, and while most of them kept to themselves, Dale sometimes caught one scuffing along "sly as a fox on the prowl," as he told his son, Cal, with beads "rolling off them like so many shucked peas."

But this Injun was different.

Dale watched him drag a military kit bag from under the bus and heft it onto his shoulder. The Injun looked around, then strode along Main, carrying himself straight and tall.

Way too cocky, Dale thought.

For a fleeting moment before he quashed it, he felt a flicker of envy for the Injun's physique. The man was honed, with the solid, muscled body that Dale had aspired to in his youth; and he moved with a supple grace. He was bare-headed with midnight-black hair that hung straight as a plumb line onto his shoulders. It was tucked behind his ears to reveal the broad-bridged nose and almond eyes of a Navajo, the bronze skin taut over sculpted cheekbones.

"Get a haircut, you blanket-assed Yazzie," Dale muttered.

He eased his cruiser away from the curb to keep pace with the Injun, trailing about fifty paces back. The Injun ducked into Wyman's General Store to emerge a few minutes later with a frosted bottle of Coca-Cola. He used a dime to flip the cap, then tipped the bottle back and drank deeply. When he finished, he took the bottle back inside, then resumed his walk along Main. A woman pushing a stroller came toward him. The Injun stepped into the gutter to let her pass on the crowded sidewalk, and she nodded her thanks, said something to him that Dale couldn't hear. Graced him with a smile too. And a backward look that showed she shared Dale's opinion of his physique.

"Getting fresh with our women now, are we?" Dale said.

When the Injun paused to window shop at JJ's Western Wear, Dale gunned the engine of his cruiser to close the gap between them. He slowed again and leaned across to reel down the passenger window.

"Hey, Geronimo!"

The Injun ignored him.

Dale touched the gas again and spurted ahead.

"I'm talking to you, Yazzie," he said.

He pulled to the curb and stepped out of his cruiser to block the Injun's path.

"Is there a problem, Sheriff?"

"Damn right," Dale said, poking the Injun hard in the chest. "And you're looking at it."

He took a step back to make a show of looking the Injun up and down. Crisp, black Western shirt with an embroidered pattern on its bib. New Levi's that were stiff enough to stand up on their own. Only the boots showed a history.

"When I talk, you listen," he said. "You got that?"

The Injun nodded.

"But when I question, you answer. We clear?"

The Injun nodded again.

"Good," Dale said. "So let's start by me finding out what you're doing here, walking along Main like you owned it."

"Is that a question?" the Injun said. "Or should I treat it as talk?"

Dale felt his face darken. He crinkled it into a smile that played only around his mouth.

"Well, well, well," he said. "I like a smartass. Gives me something to work with."

"I'm just passing through, Sheriff."

"You got ID?"

"I do."

Dale waggled his fingers. "Then gimme."

"I don't need to show it. Not to walk down a public street in daylight."

"You a lawyer now?"

"A citizen."

"Not in this state, you're not. You're an Injun. Got no rights here unless you're resident. So show me your ID. Nice and slow."

The Indian didn't move for a moment, but then he carefully slid a card loose from his wallet. Dale examined it, both sides.

"Says here your name's Lowell Smith. Don't sound Injun to me."

"My birth name is Yiska Begay. And I'm not an Indian, I'm a Navajo."

Dale's eyes narrowed. "So where you live, Mister Navajo?"

"Like I said, Sheriff, I'm just passing through."

Dale took another step back, his hand resting on his gun. He shook his head in mock despair.

"We're not understanding ourselves here, are we?" he said. "I didn't ask where you're going. I asked where you live."

"And I told you. I'm passing through. On my way home."

"To the Nation?"

"Yes, to the Nation."

"You got a place there?"

"I will have."

Dale turned his head to spit on the sidewalk.

"You will have," he repeated. "But right now you don't have. Makes you a vagrant in my book."

The Indian said nothing. And he didn't resist when Dale forced his head down and shoved him into the back of his cruiser.

In 1955, the sheriff's office in Paradox was a no-frills, cement-block building on Third, one story high, square as a soda cracker, with no windows save for two narrow panes at the front. Outside, it was painted the camouflage gray of a battleship; inside, the walls had not been painted at all. When he was in the office and not on patrol, Deputy Sheriff Wayne Coleman sat at a metal desk right-angled to an identical desk occupied by Erma Belnap, Dale's secretary. She faced the windows and the black iron bars defending the main door. Next to her, at a right angle facing Wayne, was a third metal desk recently taken by Cal Parker.

Of the three of them, Erma was the smartest, Dale figured, but a woman. She'd been his support for all eleven years he'd been sheriff. Wayne was reliable if dull—able to see the next move, but not a chess player. He'd been on the force six years and was now twenty-five years old. As for Cal, he looked the part in his uniform, and always made a point of squealing his tires whenever he took off in his patrol car; but Dale knew that beneath the gloss and bravado, his son felt the weight of inexperience and a lack of training.

Well, let him grow into it.

Against one wall of the office, behind Wayne Coleman's desk, a low wooden table was furnished with a kettle, a jar of Folger's instant coffee, a cardboard packet of powdered milk, a five-pound bag of cane sugar, and a selection of chipped and cracked coffee mugs embossed with the NRA's golden logo. On the opposite wall, next to the door of a cramped washroom, a gun rack held enough Remingtons, Winchesters, and Marlins locked into its ports to arm a posse of twenty.

Dale's office was in the back. Natural light could stream in through a barred rear door that, when open, gave him a view over the lot where the cruisers were parked. For decoration, he'd hung behind his desk a government-issued photograph of President Dwight D. Eisenhower dressed in a mud-brown suit with the Stars and Stripes drooping listlessly behind him. Alongside it was a portrait of Dale's father, Tommas, in full sheriff's regalia with a stiff white Stetson, bootlace tie, and shiny six-point badge on his chest. Across the bottom of the portrait, scrawled in black crayon, was a quote from Robert Heinlein: "An armed society is a polite society."

A hat stand made of elk horns took up one corner, and opposite that was a large filing cabinet that housed witness statements and incident and arrest reports before they were sent for storage in City Hall.

To stir the air in his office, Dale liked to keep all three of his doors open—the rear door to the parking lot, the inside door to the front office, and a third door that let him see into the short row of windowless cells that made up the final corner of the building.

Each of the cells was furnished with a pair of drop-down bunks, one above the other, and a metal bucket with lid that served as a toilet. Most of the time the cells were empty, but now the nearest held the Injun. Dale had searched his prisoner and found a Distinguished Service Cross in the left-hand pocket of his jeans.

"Must have ponied it up," he'd said to Erma. "No way an Injun could have earned it legit."

He leaned back in his swivel chair, swung his feet onto his desk. He'd recently bought himself a new pair of boots. Alligator skin with pointed metal tips and decorative stitching on the shafts. He looked through the open door at the Injun, lying on his back on a lower bunk, eyes closed, fingers laced across a broad chest that rose and fell with each quiet breath.

Do him good, Dale thought, to spend a few days in jail. Show him just how much he wasn't wanted.

CHAPTER THIRTY-EIGHT

Corin Dunbar

It bothered me that the Indian had no arrest report linking him to the charge of murder—only the one covering his arrest for reckless driving. I phoned Tuck early the next morning and found he'd been doing some thinking of his own. Along much the same lines.

"Find out more about this murder," he told me. "And why there's no report on file."

I phoned the prison and finally got through to the warden. Then I called the Fort Ord army base in California and spoke to the desk sergeant there. I'd just hung up when I heard the familiar clatter of Cal's patrol car circle the bunkhouse and come to a stop next to my Plymouth.

I met him on the back porch.

"Morning, Corin," he said.

He was all business that day. Newly showered and shaved, military-sharp like his dad in his brown pants and tan uniform shirt. He lifted his hat and ran fingers through his hair, then looked around as if he'd never seen the ranch before.

"We're still hunting the Injun," he said. "Figure he must have gone to ground someplace 'cause we can't find so much as a whiff of him in the valley."

He waited for me to respond, but when I didn't, he said, "Thing is, there's not many places for him to hide, except maybe down by the river, and I've had Luke Sims and his K9 cover that. The two of them been up and down the valley twice, and both times come up empty. I reckon the Injun's got to be holed up on one of the ranches, maybe in an outbuilding or someplace like that."

He paused again.

"Mind if I look around?" he said.

"Be my guest," I told him.

"We're checking all the spreads. Started with the Fairchilds', since that's where the Injun was last seen, and now we're fanning out, widening the circle."

"Well, look around all you want."

He hung back as if hoping I might say more, then put his hat back on and strode around the side of the bunkhouse. I returned to the kitchen to watch him out the back window. He poked into the storage shed where we kept our muck boots and Felipe's fencing tools, then moved to the barn. He rattled the padlock on the double doors, and when it didn't yield he bent down to check under the rock where he knew we kept the key. It was still in my jean's pocket, so he yanked the padlock again and stepped back to crane up at the cross-buck doors that led into the hayloft. Then he tracked along the front of the barn and around the corner out of sight.

He was gone long enough for me to reheat my coffee—and to fret. A knot tightened my stomach as I went onto the back porch again to wait for him to reappear. When he finally did—coming full circle around the barn—he was stooped in a crouch, his gun gripped in both hands, arms outstretched as he swept it side to side. Once more in front of the double doors, he slowly straightened, holstered his weapon, and gazed up at the cross-buck doors as if planning to shinny up and get in that way. He stayed like that a moment, then marched toward me, moving fast.

"He's been here, Corin," he said, striding past me to his cruiser. He leaned through the open window for the licorice-spiral radio cord, spoke into the mic, and said "Over" several times, then "Out."

He chucked the mic onto the seat and turned to face me.

"He's been in your barn," he said. "The Injun. Up in the hayloft. You got boards at the back that've been kicked out. I went in that way, and found a bloody rag up there that he must have ripped from his prison shirt. And I could smell him too, worse'n a roadkill skunk. You know about the boards?"

I shook my head.

"How come the doors are locked?" he said. "You keep them open, right?" He teased out a Lucky Strike from the pack in his breast pocket, but didn't wait for me to answer. "I don't see how he could've gotten in. Could maybe have been where the boards are out. But looks like they were kicked from the inside, the way they're splintered."

He took a deep drag on his cigarette, then ground it out in the dirt.

"He was in your barn," he said again, before climbing into his cruiser. "In your *barn*, Corin!" he shouted at me through the open window. "Not a hundred paces from where you sleep!"

Wayne Coleman all but waved me through the roadblock when I drove up a half hour later. I was stuck behind a limousine with the number plate OSCAR2 and watched as he hauled out the chauffeur and the three suits inside. He forced them to stand in the rising heat as he searched the interior and then the trunk, so when my turn came, I expected similar treatment. But Wayne said he was under instructions from Dale to search only those vehicles he hadn't seen before.

"Sheriff don't want me upsetting the voters. Not this close to an election. As it is, I'm run ragged. All of us are. So 'busy' ain't the word for it. Sheriff wants this redskin caught more'n I want a six-pack in July, but if you ask me, the Injun's long gone. But then Dale don't pay me for my opinions, does he?"

He rapped on the roof of the Plymouth and I drove on. At Balanced Rock, I swung on to the cutoff to Eldorado to pick up some stills Tuck wanted. Photos to run alongside his interview with George Roy Hill and his Butch Cassidy movie.

I parked behind a couple of camera dollies that had been left near Boot Hill and picked my way along the creaky boardwalk of

Front Street. Two horses were saddled up and tied to the hitching rail outside the haberdashery, but I didn't stop to stroke them. I pushed open the swing doors of the Silver Dollar saloon to find George Roy Hill leaning against the long bar surrounded by arc lights, reflectors, and booms. He was flashing a gap-toothed grin as he chatted to a heavily made-up Paul Newman, while technicians circled around taking meter readings. Robert Redford, off in one corner, was quietly rehearsing the lightning-fast draw of the Sundance Kid.

Three cameras had been set up, two on the floor and one on the balcony. There was a buzz of excitement that told me the cameras were about to roll, so I stayed quiet while Redford-as-Sundance crouched in the doorway, then fanned his gun to shoot off his opponent's gun belt and send his weapon clattering across the wooden boards.

When Hill called "Cut," I picked up the promised stills—of Katherine Ross as well as Newman and Redford—and elbowed my way through a hubbub of Paradox women who'd turned up to audition as extras. I recognized Mabel Jeffries, a new mother for the third time who handed out Bibles in Jessie's church. She'd swapped her customary knee-length skirt and round-necked sweater for a décolleté dress of black lace trimmed at the hem with red frills.

"Another brothel scene," she said as I passed her. "But it pays for diapers."

I glanced around for Dottie, as she rarely missed a cattle call, but I was in no mood to linger or to talk, so I snaked my way through the froth of petticoats to my car, bounced over the railroad tracks at the end of Front, and headed into Paradox.

The town center was clogged with Butch Cassidy film crews, but I was able to park on Fifth and thread my way through the crowds to Jackson and the *Gazette* building on Main. The junction box outside still had a "Re-elect Dale Parker" poster plastered onto its front, but the stern face of the sheriff had now been embellished by crudely inked eyelashes and a pair of devilish horns that topped off his Stetson. A rival poster for Jay Lambert was pasted nearby, but it was half obscured by a bigger one for Mayor Carter ("Prosperity for Paradox") Williams.

Tuck was in his office, red ink smeared around his mouth where he'd been chewing the wrong end of his editing pen. His clothes were a quarrel of orange, reds, and green, again belying the inside of his head, which I knew was neat as a military barracks.

"A good newsman is not the one who gets the right answers," he'd told me when I joined the paper. "It's the one who asks the right questions."

"I called the warden at Draper," I told him. "The Indian killed someone there, not in Paradox, but in Draper. Which is likely why there's no report on file here. More than that, the warden says the Indian killed in self-defense. An inmate who came at him with a knife. But that's not the way it was presented in court, where the prosecution made him out to be the stone-cold killer the sheriff says he is. The Indian got a bad deal, Tuck. He was railroaded. He's been in jail thirteen years—since August of '55—and he's been a model prisoner all that time. He wouldn't have been on the mesa fixing culverts if he wasn't."

Tuck grunted, and bit into an oatmeal cookie from a jar he kept on his desk. I plonked the stills next to the jar, knowing he would see them there.

"I also called his old army base at Fort Ord," I said. "Did you know he fought in Korea? The sergeant there told me he won a DSC, the second highest honor this country can bestow."

Tuck tilted his head. "Are you saying he killed waging *our* war in Korea, and we pinned a medal on his chest; but when he killed fighting *his* war in prison, we locked him away for life?"

"Without parole," I said. "And that's exactly what I'm saying."

"That sound fair to you, Corin?"

I shook my head.

He reached for another cookie. "That's good work," he said. "But where does it get us?"

"Take a look at the arrest report," I told him, and shoved my copy across his desk. "The one for reckless driving. There's more here I don't understand. The report's got Lowell Smith's name on it—his Anglo name—but it was first written up as a John Doe. But then the John Doe was crossed out and Lowell Smith's name put in its place."

"I saw that," Tuck said.

"It also says the Indian was driving a Nash. A studio car," I said.

"I saw that too."

"That's not all," I told him, and jabbed a finger at the row of boxes at the top of the report. "This started out as an *incident* report. You can see the tick mark in this box here. But that, too, has been scrubbed out, and a new tick put in the next box over. Turning it into an *arrest* report."

"So what's going on here?"

Again I shook my head as he dipped a hand into the cookie jar.

"What concerns *me*," he said, after a moment of silent chewing, "is this charge of reckless driving. In a studio car, no less. I just don't get it. It's the charge the sheriff made stick, but our friend Dale could have gone for something a lot stronger than that. So why didn't he? Sheriff won't tell us—he won't say diddly to me—but the mayor might. We need to see him, Corin. Because the real question here is not about the Indian and what he was or wasn't charged with. The real question we should be asking is who's the John Doe—and what was *he* charged with?"

He looked at his watch.

"Come on," he said, and struggled into his jacket. "We might just have time to get something in the next edition."

CHAPTER THIRTY-NINE

Tuck wasn't the fittest of people, but I struggled to keep pace as he pounded along the sidewalk, slowing only when our path was blocked by the many bevies of movie people.

"Tuck," I said, "slow down. You'll give yourself a heart attack."

He paused long enough to take a breath and swipe a forearm across his brow, then started off again at the same brisk pace. I was three inches taller than he was, with most of my height in my legs, but I was still forced to move at a trot.

He bounded up the stone steps of City Hall and bulldozed into the mayor's outer office, startling Phyllis Olsen, Carter William's secretary, who sat bolt upright, hands frozen above the keys of her Underwood. Her wing-shaped glasses looked as shocked as she did, as if they might take flight and flutter around the room.

Tuck didn't break stride.

"Carter in?" he said.

"You can't go in there," Phyllis told him. "Mayor Carter's on the phone. It's election time, you know. He's a very busy man."

Tuck barged open the door to the mayor's inner office and I followed him in.

Carter's eyes widened. "Call you back," he said into the phone, then slammed it down. "Vernon, what's all this about?" he said, rising to his feet.

Phyllis had followed us into the office. "I said you were busy…" she began.

Tuck ignored her. "We need to talk," he said to the mayor. "We've a deadline looming, which means I'm in a hurry."

Carter made a show of buttoning his jacket, trying to maintain control.

"You've no right barging in like this," he said.

"We've every right," Tuck told him. "The *Gazette* speaks for the people of this town every bit as much as you do."

He waved the arrest report under the mayor's nose before he slapped it onto his desk.

"Take a look at that."

Carter glanced at it. "Sheriff's business," he said, and edged the report back toward us.

"Maybe so," Tuck said. "But this report claims an Indian—this Lowell Smith the sheriff's trying to capture—was arrested for reckless driving. This was back in 1955, Carter. I was forty-seven years old in 1955. Just bought myself a Chevy Two-Ten with Powerglide automatic and a neat little seat adjuster that let me wiggle my backside to get settled in behind the wheel. Only the second car I ever owned. Yet here we have an Indian—an *Indian*—joyriding around town in a studio car, no less. A Nash, the report says. Owned by Universal when they were here to make *Taza*. Does that seem likely to you? Because I don't buy it. You needed clout to get yourself a studio car—you still do—and that's something no Indian has ever had, especially not in 1955."

"All right, Phyllis," Carter said, shooing his secretary out with a flick of his hand.

"No studio would *lend* an Indian a car," Tuck went on. "Which means if he was driving it, he must have stolen it. Grand theft auto gets you a lot more jail time than reckless driving, so why didn't Dale charge him with that? He'd shot and killed a couple of Indians, and for a lot less reason too. I don't think he'd have held back with *this* particular Indian out of the kindness of his heart, do you?"

"It's still Sheriff's business," Carter said.

"Except," Tuck said, "the report was originally written up as a John Doe. Before it became a Lowell Smith. And you and I both know what that means, Carter. You were covering for someone. Like that time Dennis Hopper got caught snorting coke, or when Jack Nicholson knocked out a guy's teeth at the Double-D. They both got busted, but a John Doe on their arrest reports kept their names out of the papers. You came up with that idea, you made that happen, so I'm guessing your fingerprints are all over this report too. Who were you protecting, Carter? Who's the John Doe here?"

I'd never seen Tuck this pushy. His every gesture, every word, was played for effect. And it seemed to be working. The mayor sat down, fiddled with the cap of his fountain pen, and looked up at Tuck.

"You're shooting from the hip," he said. "With no clue of your target."

"You want me on the inside shooting out? Or on the outside shooting in?"

"You don't know what you're talking about. Or what you're getting into."

"I know there's a loose end here, Carter, and I hate loose ends. I figure we'll give it a tug and see how it unravels. That's what our readers would expect. Readers who in a few short weeks are going to be voters."

"It's old news, Vernon. Thirteen years old. No one's going to care now."

"The Indian makes it current. He's on the run, so he's news *now*."

The door of his office opened a crack and Phyllis poked her head in. "Your meeting, Mr. Mayor—in five minutes?"

"Hold them off," he told her and waved her out again.

He gripped the scrolled arms of his chair and rocked back and forth. His jaw twitched and when he leaned forward to steeple his fingers, he pushed them together so hard his nails blushed purple. The wall behind him was covered with cherrywood framed photos of John Wayne, Clint Eastwood, Rod Steiger, Barbara Stanwyck, and Jean Simmons. In every one, a beaming Carter Williams was present, often with Posie and sometimes with Jelly. I could read a few of the inscriptions. "Sincere thanks." "Ever in your debt." "Utah rocks." "Love and kisses." "Let's smooch again next year."

He took a deep breath, let it out again as a sigh.

"The studios trust us," he said. "They know we can keep a lid on things. That's one of the reasons they keep coming back. They know we're discreet."

Tuck said nothing, stared him down.

"You won't be able to print what I tell you," Carter said.

"I'll be the judge of that."

"You'd be sued for every cent you've got. No more *Gazette*, Vernon."

"My risk," Tuck said.

He pulled up a chair and gestured for me to do the same.

"It was Wayne Coleman," Carter told us. "He was the trigger that started the ball rolling."

CHAPTER FORTY

Wayne Coleman

In 1955, on the day Yiska Begay stepped off a Greyhound bus in the center of Paradox, twenty-five-year-old Wayne Coleman was patrolling the back streets of town following his usual route. He'd picked up his cruiser from the lot behind the sheriff's office—a four-door Mercury "shoebox" with a red bubble on the roof, a windshield cut in two by a thick divider, hooded headlamps, soggy springs, and gray faux-leather seats that had been cracked by the heat and weight of too many backsides. A heavy chrome spotlight was anchored near the driver's side mirror, which Wayne could adjust by reaching through his open window.

He was working the evening shift that day—from six in the evening until two o'clock the following morning. He drove east on Adams, south on Seventh, west on Tyler, north on Fourth. Then, at a few minutes past seven o'clock, he stopped by the Burger Chief next to the DreamKatcher Motel and picked up the house special—a Sooper Dooper Burger 'n Bun with a side order of onion rings to go—along with a bottle of Coke that he poured into a Dixie cup half filled with ice. He'd eaten a mess of burritos for lunch that day—beef with chili and cheese and refried beans—but he couldn't always eat Mex. His stomach couldn't take it.

Back behind the wheel, he bit into the burger and savored the mix of grease, ketchup, and relish as well as the soothing effect of the carbs in the soft white bun. Wayne liked his food, and for the most part it liked him. But it was still a puzzle to him why his arms and legs remained pallid spindles while his belly continued to swell.

He chomped on the burger and slurped the Coke until the straw sounded the death rattle that said the cup was empty except for ice. He licked ketchup and relish off his fingers, popped the last onion ring into his mouth, then crumpled the burger wrappings into a ball and tossed them into the footwell beside him. He fired up the engine and headed out of town, following the cutoff that would take him to Eldorado. Dale had ordered him to make the movie set part of his nightly patrol, because Universal wanted it sealed at the end of every day to protect their cameras, arc lights, reflectors, booms, stands, microphones, cables—and who knew what else—that the shooting of *Taza* demanded.

He puttered along in no particular hurry. The cruiser surfed the raised ruts of the road in a jarring motion that did not sit well with the fizz and bubble of his Coca-Cola and the oleaginous mess of burger and rings. Each lurch produced the kind of burp Wayne's new wife would never have allowed at home. He flipped on the radio to pick up KBEZ and hummed along with some of the hits. Eddie Fisher, Doris Day, Patti Page. He particularly liked Rosemary Clooney's "This Ole House" with its catchy chorus. *Ain't a-gonna need this house no longer; Ain't a-gonna need this house no more.*

By the time he reached Eldorado, a canopy of stars shone above, dulled only by a gibbous moon. He bumped over the railroad tracks at the end of Front Street. Kids liked to jump on the potash wagons there when the train rumbled through town from the Burr Creek mine, then leap off a hundred yards farther on when the engine picked up speed again. Kids were always doing dumb things like that. They'd sneak into the Silver Dollar saloon and drink from the bottles of fake whiskey, or they'd haul off the genuine sacks of grain that were stacked on the boardwalk outside the general store. A few had been known to climb onto the gallows near Boot Hill, where Danny Schaeffer had nearly hanged himself when he swung his feet clear of the ground; and sometimes older boys raced their factory Fords and Chevy trucks up and down the main drag.

He rolled down his window and smelled the sap in the freshly cut pine the carpenters had used to construct most of the new buildings.

The fake town still amazed him, the way it had sprung out of the desert like a flower after rain. He didn't know how Mayor Carter had brought the project off, but he'd heard stories of the big dollars Universal was throwing around. Most of the money went to Hollywood stars who earned more in a week than Wayne would see in a lifetime of writing tickets, but much of it wound up in local businesses and the pockets of local people. What was it the mayor liked to say? *Hollywood takes only pictures and leaves only money.*

Wayne drove the length of Front Street, past the shells of the buildings—the apothecary, funeral parlor, barber's shop—then slowed to a stop, his brake lights flaring. He made a wide U-turn and headed back the way he had come, peering into the deep-throated alleyways on both sides of the street. Back at the railroad tracks, he looped around the blacksmith's forge and bumped over the tamped-down desert strip that paralleled the main street before he pulled to a stop at the rear of the Silver Dollar saloon. He turned off the engine, doused his headlights, and stared up at the backs of the stepped facades of the fake buildings visible now in silhouette. He used the key of his cruiser to pick at a trace of ketchup on the front of his uniform before he clambered out to lean his elbows on the roof and take in the cool night air. No one around. Peaceful and quiet as a ghost town. Just the way he liked it.

Wayne knew the *Taza* movie had something to do with Injuns—Apaches, he thought—and the struggle between Geronimo and...that other one. On the tip of his tongue, it was. Began with C, he was sure of it.

He sauntered along the desert strip, then ducked into the alley between the hotel and the fakery of the barber's shop with its red and white striped pole.

"Cochise," he said out loud, giving himself a slap on the thigh. "Geronimo and Cochise, that was it. I knew I'd get it."

He walked the alleyways as Dale had instructed—up one, down the next—until he reached the edge of town, where it petered into the desert; then he returned to his cruiser and sat in the back, where there was more room to spread out.

Next thing he knew, the moon had shifted until it was way to his left. Must have been asleep, he thought.

He climbed out of the cruiser, yawned and stretched, then padded along the desert strip to the livery stables, where he relieved himself.

A strange shape caught his eye. Blocking the alleyway between the forge and the stables.

He frowned. He was sure it hadn't been there before. He started toward it, figuring it might be a piece of equipment—a dolly perhaps or a camera left on its stand. But as he drew closer, the shape morphed into something more familiar.

A car. Square and solid.

A Nash, he decided. A Nash wagon.

He dropped into a crouch as he approached it from the rear, then stopped short when a match flared inside the Nash and two cigarettes glowed like fireflies in the dark. He crept forward again, still in his crouch, until he saw two heads haloed by the glow of the dashboard light. The tinny sound of music floated toward him, followed a few moments later by a couple of cigarettes that curved in graceful arcs on either side before they landed in the dirt in showers of sparks.

The two heads in the car came together. Then one of the heads disappeared, the smaller one in the driver's seat—it had to be the woman's—while the other—the man's head in the passenger seat—tipped back against the headrest.

Wayne smiled. A courting couple. Time to give them a fright.

He unclipped his baton and stepped forward on the driver's side. Rapped hard on the roof of the car. Three times in quick succession. A confusion of limbs thrashed inside the Nash, accompanied by a deep-voiced shout of surprise. The man's head in the passenger seat snapped toward him, while the woman's head whipped round with a look of horror on its face.

Which brought a look of horror to Wayne's face too.

Because the woman wasn't a woman, but another man. Baby-smooth cheeks, a thick shock of hair, and heavy-lidded eyes.

"Lord Almighty," Wayne gasped. He took a step back and reached for his gun. "Out of the car," he shouted. "The both of you. Get out *now*!"

But the driver—the man who should have been a woman—fired up the engine, slammed the Nash into gear, and took off, the back end fishtailing wildly as the rear wheels spat out a spray of desert dirt.

CHAPTER FORTY-ONE

Corin Dunbar

"So Wayne Coleman sprints back to his cruiser and gives chase," the mayor told us. "The Nash he's after has no headlights. Either the driver forgot to put them on, or he was too panicked by Wayne hammering on the roof. Wayne's a little more on the ball. He flicks on his high beams, hits the siren, and goes after the Nash. He's a long way back, but there's only one road to take if you're heading into Paradox—"

"Wait a minute," Tuck cut in. He leaned forward in his chair beside me. "Are you saying there were two *men* in the Nash?"

"That's exactly what I'm saying. A couple of queers. Wayne's not happy about that. This town may play host to a snoot full of actors and other liberal Hollywood types, but we're still a pretty conservative bunch. And remember, this was back in '55. Before sex had been invented. We don't take kindly to perverts now, and we sure as hell didn't then. You taking this down, Corin?" he said to me.

I nodded.

"I said you can't use it."

Tuck ignored him. "So what happened next?"

Carter took another deep breath, folded his hands on his desk. "Wayne catches up with the Nash at the edge of town," he said. "Here in Paradox. He sees it turn onto First. It races along, doesn't even slow when it takes the corner at Grant, but runs the one light we have. The light slows Wayne some, but he swings onto Fourth and then onto Center. It's late, so no other cars around—no one on the streets—but Wayne loses the Nash. Until he hears a screech of brakes and an almighty crash. When he turns left onto Main, he sees the driver's lost control of the Nash and has slammed it head first into the side of Jelly's car."

"His Caddy?" Tuck said.

Carter nodded. "The very same. Jelly's convertible with the bumper bullets and wraparound windshield. The car Eldorado's named for. It's parked where it always is—outside the Juniper Lodge, nose to the curb with its rear end sticking out. But now it's crumpled worse than an empty can of Schlitz. The hood of the Nash is buckled too, but the two queers inside are unhurt. The driver kicks open his door and makes a run for it, hightails it into the night. Wayne doesn't give chase, but pulls out his gun, waiting for the passenger to appear. Which he does. 'Hands high, mister,' Wayne shouts. But the guy isn't going anywhere. He looks at Wayne over the roof of the Nash and says calm as can be, 'Sorry about the mess, Officer, but I'll see to it that all damages are covered.'"

Carter stopped and looked across his desk at Tuck, who was leaning forward as far as his stomach would allow.

"And this is your John Doe?" Tuck asked.

"Yep," Carter said. "Our very first one."

CHAPTER FORTY-TWO

Wayne Coleman

Wayne Coleman hustled his prisoner into the backseat of his cruiser, away from the few gawkers who'd tipped out of the Juniper Lodge at the sound of the crash. He considered cuffing the man, but his prisoner offered no resistance. He lounged against the faux leather of the backseat and courteously asked if he might smoke. And Wayne, confused by the civility of the request, said, "Yes, go ahead," as if the two of them were strangers swapping pleasantries rather than a rattled cop holding a suspect for a lewd and criminal act.

The Juniper's night porter ("It was Luke Sims," Carter said, "before Dale gave him a badge") had heard the crash and joined the gawkers. Wayne told him to keep the rubberneckers away from the tangled cars in case of explosion, as he could hear something *plip-plipping* onto the tarmac and thought he could smell oil or maybe gasoline.

He then drove his prisoner to the sheriff's office and called Dale Parker at home.

"You'll never guess who I got here in the office," he said, his heart pumping.

"You're right, Wayne. I won't guess."

"I hope you're sat down, Sheriff."

"Wayne, some of us got beds to go to, and you just got me out of mine."

"It's just that—well, I don't know how to put this."

"Will you quit scratching your ass and get to the point?"

In slow, halting sentences, Wayne told Dale what he had seen in Eldorado.

"Two men in a lip-lock," he said. "I chased them into town, Sheriff. Where they crashed into Jelly's Caddy outside the Lodge."

"So where are they now?" Dale asked.

"I lost one. But I got the other. He's right here in your office." Wayne craned his neck to peer in through the open doorway, saw his prisoner sitting, legs crossed, in the customer chair, quietly smoking. "You'd never guess who it is, Sheriff," he said.

"Will you quit playing games, Wayne?"

"It's Rock Hudson," Wayne said, his heart once again racing.

Dale was quiet for a moment.

"Are you toying with me, Wayne," he said. "Because if you are…"

"No way, Sheriff. You know me better than that. I'm telling you straight."

"No, Wayne, what you're telling me is Rock Hudson's a perv. Hollywood's number one ladies' man. You're telling me he's queer."

"That *is* what I'm telling you," Wayne said. "So what do I do with him? I mean, I can't take him into the desert and beat some decency into him, can I? Not like I oughta."

Dale was silent another long moment.

"Keep him there, Wayne," he said. "And do nothing 'til I get there. You're good at that."

CHAPTER FORTY-THREE

Corin Dunbar

"I couldn't believe it," Carter told us. "I mean, Rock *Hudson*? The guy's six-four, six-five. And built too. Like a truck."

"I don't think size is a factor here," Tuck said.

"Maybe not, but Rock Hudson's up there with John Wayne. Gary Cooper. Gregory Peck. He's a *man's* man. I saw him in *Tobruk,* where he single-handed won the war. And he's been Doris Day's love interest in I don't know how many films." He shook his head. "Straight as an arrow on the big screen. But in real life? Bent worse'n a paperclip."

"So what did Dale do?" Tuck prodded.

"Sodomy's a crime, and you can bet Dale doesn't like queers. He wanted to charge the guy. Throw him into jail and toss away the key. But charging Rock Hudson? Even Dale can see there's got to be repercussions. He lets Hudson make a phone call. To his agent. A man by the name of Henry Willson. He's handled situations like this before, bailed Rock out of trouble any number of times by keeping mention of his proclivity out of the press. Willson phones the studio—that's Universal—and half an hour later the studio calls me. This is right after I've just hung up on Dale. 'Don't even *think* of charging Rock Hudson,' they tell me. One hint of scandal, even a tiny *whiff*, and they'll pull *Taza* out of Eldorado, and never—and I do mean *never*—make another movie here again." He drew a hand across his throat. "We'd be dead in the water. They'd shut us down, even before we'd got ourselves properly going."

"So Dale didn't charge him?"

The mayor shook his head. "We let Mr. Hudson go. Free as a bird. No hint of scandal. Just like the studio wanted."

"But that didn't end it."

Carter shook his head. "There was still the small matter of the crash," he said. "Dale's got a couple of wrecked cars sitting on Main Street, the studio's Nash and Jelly's Caddy. He tells Wayne to write up an incident report covering the crash, nothing else. No mention of Rock Hudson, and no word on what happened in Eldorado. Wayne writes up the report as a John Doe like he's told. He puts in the what, where, and when of the crash, but leaves out the why. Plus, there's no description of the driver—height, weight, age, that kind of thing—because, of course, Wayne doesn't know who the driver is. So those boxes are left blank.

"We thought we had it covered. The gawkers in the Juniper hadn't seen Rock Hudson. Luke Sims was a wrinkle. He'd seen Hudson in the back of Wayne's cruiser, but he didn't know the man was a perv. To keep him sweet, I persuaded Dale to offer him work as a deputy—better pay, better hours, better benefits. Wayne was on board, willing to do what Dale told him. And Lick Gardner—he was editor of the *Gazette* at the time—agreed to keep the crash out of the paper in return for an exclusive interview with Rock that the studio set up. The whole mess was swept away out of sight, as good as never happened. The studio was happy. We were happy. *Everyone* was happy."

"So what went wrong?"

"Leland Jellicoe," Carter said. "He went wrong. He was madder than hell when he found out his beloved Caddy had to be scrapped. He wanted blood, someone to blame, someone to crucify. He wouldn't let it go."

"You didn't tell him?"

"About Rock Hudson?" Carter shook his head. "We had to draw the line somewhere, and we drew it at Jelly. He was spending most of his time in Hollywood, and I was pretty sure he would talk."

"So what did you do?"

"We did what the studios do whenever they need to protect a star. We got ourselves a stand-in."

CHAPTER FORTY-FOUR

Dale Parker

Sheriff Dale Parker learned of the problem with Leland Jellicoe the following morning while he sat in his office, gently swiveling in his chair. His feet were up on his desk as he leaned back and sipped a cup of Folger's coffee his secretary had brought him. Erma always whisked the spoon around in the mug until she was sure every last granule had dissolved, which drove Dale nuts as he was forced to listen to an endless *clink, clink, clink* of spoon against china. But he let her do it because making coffee was women's work.

He'd been up most of the night and felt tired as well as frustrated. He'd wanted to book Rock Hudson, but he knew the studios wouldn't let him. He knew, too, that they could play rough. When Carter Williams had come back from one of his trips to Hollywood, he'd told Dale how Clark Gable had once killed a woman when drunk-driving; but the studio—MGM—had paid off the victim's family, bribed the district attorney, and even persuaded a low-ranking MGM executive to take the blame in Gable's place.

"There's no telling what those people will do," the mayor had said. "They're a law unto themselves."

Dale leaned back in his chair just shy of the tipping point and crossed his feet at the ankles, one metal-tipped alligator boot resting on the other. He squinted past them through the open door of his office to where he could see the Injun in his cell. The Injun had been locked up overnight and was now eating a Spartan breakfast of rice and beans that Erma had handed him through the bars. The Injun sat ramrod straight on the edge of his bunk and slowly spooned the mess of food into his mouth. He must have known Dale was watching, but he kept his gaze fixed on his bowl.

Dale had drained the last of his coffee when his phone rang.

"We got a problem," the mayor told him. "I can't give Leland the name of the driver like he wants, because for one I don't know who it is. And for two Rock Hudson's name would then be sure to leak. Which is exactly what we don't want."

Dale shifted his backside so he was looking at the Injun through the gunsight V of his alligator boots.

"I've got an idea," he said. "That might be just what you need."

CHAPTER FORTY-FIVE

Corin Dunbar

"You mean you *framed* the Indian?" I blurted out.

Tuck put a restraining hand on my arm. Something else he'd taught me: Don't interrupt a source when he's in full flow of a story.

Carter spread his hands. "What else could we do? We had no choice."

He stood abruptly and pushed back his chair so it rolled away behind him; then he strode to one of the tall windows overlooking Main and stared out.

He turned to face us.

"You remember what this town was like back then, Vernon. There was no work. No jobs. Businesses were closing. Ranches were struggling. Those were drought years, remember? Barely enough rain to baptize a baby. But that first year—the year the studios arrived—it was like the coming of spring. The whole town filled up. Brimming over with actors, directors, producers, makeup gals, camera crews... And every single one of them paid good money to rent our rooms, eat in our restaurants, drink in our bars. There wasn't a soul in Paradox who wasn't making money out of the movies. And it was good money too, whether they were hiring out cattle and horses, or working as extras, scouts, drivers, carpenters, painters, wranglers, guards. Paradox came *alive*, Vernon. For the first time, the town was suffused with...*hope*."

He strode toward us, arms spread.

"But it didn't just *happen*. No fairy godmother woke up one day and decided to smile down on us. I pushed this town out on a limb.

Further out than maybe I should have. Issued bonds, went into debt—all so we could build Eldorado. Universal was only the second studio to come here, and *Taza* was the first of their movies. If it had pulled out, we'd have been left high and dry, stranded with a fake town no one wanted and a mountain of debt we couldn't dig out from under." He clasped his hands together as if in prayer. "We were on the hook," he said. "We'd have been ruined. *All* of us, Vernon. The whole town."

"The Indian was a veteran," Tuck said. "He fought for his country. For *our* country."

Carter retreated behind the bulk of his desk.

"Maybe so," he said. "But Rock Hudson was a major star. It wasn't just Universal that had money sunk in him; half of Hollywood was riding on his coattails. Some actors might have ridden a scandal out. Like Robert Mitchum when he was busted for marijuana. But Errol Flynn crashed and burned over that rape charge, remember? He *never* recovered. What do you think the reaction would have been if it came out that Rock Hudson was a *faggot*?" He shook his head. "I couldn't let it happen, I just couldn't. The studios would never have forgiven me."

"The Indian won a DSC. A Distinguished Service Cross. For putting his life on the line."

Carter slumped into his chair. "You think I don't know that?"

"And *you* sent him to jail."

"It was meant to be for a couple of months. Nothing more. What would that have meant to an Injun? A roof over his head and three meals a day, all at taxpayer expense. It'd have been a vacation. You know what those people are like. Going to jail's a rite of passage for them. Like us going to college. They all do it sooner or later. I didn't know he'd kill someone in Draper. And I didn't know he'd get life. I couldn't see that, I'm not clairvoyant."

"It was self-defense," I said, butting in again. "The Indian killed in self-defense."

"Well, he's out now, isn't he?" Carter said, and suddenly stood again. "Dale thinks he's after revenge. And maybe he is. It was Dale who doctored *this*," he said, flipping his hand at the arrest report on his desk. "It was Dale who ticked the boxes. And *he* put Lowell Smith's name in place of the John Doe. To me it was just paperwork. We didn't need it at the trial. It was never meant to see the light of day. And it never would have done if this Lowell Smith—or whatever his name is—hadn't gone and escaped."

"You sent an innocent man to *jail*," Tuck said. "You can't weasel your way out of that."

"He was collateral damage," Carter said. "Wrong place, wrong time. I can't be blamed for that, can I?"

He thrust his head forward, his fists clenched at his sides. Tuck's cheeks were blotched red and Carter's were too. They stared each other down, until Carter broke away and marched again to the window.

"Take a look outside," he said. "Go on, get off your fat backside and tell me what you see. You see people on the sidewalks. People in the streets. They're in the restaurants. In the bars. They're crowding out the Juniper. The Double-D. You see stores, Vernon, busting at the seams. You see a town that's got *life*. A future. You're looking at money out there. Three out of every four dollars that gets spent in this town comes from the studios. That money doesn't grow on trees, and it doesn't come out of the ground. That's *Hollywood* money, Vernon. So yes, I may have done the Injun wrong. But I did right by my people. I did my job. I did what I'm paid to do. *I—saved—this—town.*"

CHAPTER FORTY-SIX

"The mayor's right," Tuck said as we pounded along Main back to the newspaper's office. "We can't print a word about Rock Hudson. First, it would ruin his career for no particular benefit to anyone other than those people who thrive on salacious gossip and sensationalism. Second, we'd be sued—successfully, I have to say, as we've no proof of his supposed homosexuality—which means we'd lose the paper and I for one would be out of a job. And third, it would do a lot of damage to the town, even now, if the studios pulled out—which they might, given Rock Hudson's continuing high standing in the industry."

"You mean you're just going to let this *go*?"

"I didn't say that," Tuck snapped back, stung by my accusation. "I said we couldn't write about Rock Hudson. But we might be able to do something for the Indian. Sometimes," he said, "I'm ashamed of our institutions and the authorities we rely on to keep us straight and honest. We pride ourselves on having the best democracy in the world and a rule of law that gives every man a fair and equal crack at justice. But the plain fact is, money talks. Or rather, it swears. And when it does, it bends the law in favor of the rich. And the powerful. It always has and it always will. Never trust those in authority, Corin, that's my advice. We need to put a check on them, and sometimes newspapers are the only way to do that. They help give disenfranchised citizens a voice."

He marched on, his pace increasing along with his indignation.

"We railroad too many people through our courts," he said, "and no one raises so much as a peep—just as long as it's someone else, someone poorer, someone blacker, someone different. We've been cheating Indians ever since *our* ancestors landed on *their* shores. Broken every single one of the treaties we signed, going right back to that tribe in Delaware we tricked into helping us fight the British. Well, you can't say we're inconsistent; you have to give us credit for that. Indians are way overdue for justice in my opinion. So no, I'm not about to give up on this. I'm just not sure the best way to get the story into print."

He dodged around a clutch of people blocking the sidewalk, and through the crush I caught a glimpse of the flowing chestnut hair and huge brown eyes of Katherine Ross. Tuck must have seen her too.

"You get those stills I wanted?" he asked me.

"On your desk," I told him. "By the cookie jar."

He grunted in response, blew a kiss at Dale's defaced poster on the junction box, and lumbered up the *Gazette's* steps ahead of me.

At the top, he stopped and turned around so abruptly I smacked into him.

"Corin," he said. "Forgive me. I forgot to ask. How's Ark?"

Tuck was one of the few who genuinely cared, but I was still surprised by this sudden show of interest.

"Some days are better than others," I told him vaguely.

He took my elbow and guided me back down the steps.

"Then go home, Corin. I meant what I said yesterday. Take all the time you need. We can manage fine without you, crucial though you may think you are to the paper's survival. Come on," he urged, "I'll walk you to your car. Where are you parked?"

Back on Main Street, he stopped again, forcing me to stop with him.

"There's something I've been meaning to say to you, Corin. It might just be me, an old newspaperman sticking my big nose into matters that don't concern me, so if you want to bite it off, go right ahead. Messing in other people's affairs is a habit of mine and not always a good one."

"What's on your mind, Tuck?"

He looked down at the sidewalk, scuffed at the ground with his shoe. This wasn't like him. Words were his currency, the tools he deployed to earn a living. He was always able to pluck the right one out of the air. But now his words were caught in the back of his throat as if he didn't like their taste.

He took a moment to draw breath. "I care about you, Corin," he said. "I've watched you grow from the scared kid you were when Jessie took you in to an able young woman with a mind of her own." This, too, wasn't like Tuck. He wasn't given to declarations, least of all ones of affection. He'd always said he was better with facts than feelings—one reason, I'd long concluded, he'd never found a wife.

"What I'm trying to say, Corin, is you're going to have to let Ark go."

I shook my head. "What are you saying, Tuck?"

He looked me in the eye. "What happened to Ark wasn't your fault, and you can't think it was. We live in a world that's full of doubt and uncertainty. We have to make decisions when we don't have anything like enough information. We can't foresee what's going to happen. If I've learned one thing in life, it's this—a little nugget of wisdom. If you're not making mistakes, you're doing something wrong. Which is a fancy way of saying that mistakes are inevitable. Because *not* making mistakes is in *itself* a mistake. It means you're not living life to the full, you're not taking chances. You've locked yourself in a room, afraid to come out. You took a chance with Ark. It took *courage* to do that. To hitch your wagon to another human being. Same thing with buying Connie's bull. That took courage too. Those weren't mistakes, Corin. And they shouldn't be a cause for regret."

I opened my mouth to speak, but he raised his hand like a cop.

"No, wait," he said. "Indulge an old man who has your interests at heart." He pulled a handkerchief out of his pocket and dabbed at his forehead. "I have to say this, Corin. You'll want a family one day. Kids...a boy...a girl... " He let his voice trail off. "None of my business, is it?"

"No," I said, sounding harsher than intended, "it's not."

He looked away, toward the pack of people still thronging around Katherine Ross, then back at me.

"Something else that's not my business," he said. "I know you've been trying to decide about Ark, what you should do, what *he* should do. The fact is, and I'll come right out and say this, the best move you can make now is to send him back to the Severill."

"Not an option," I said.

"Think about it, Corin. He'd get better care, have some company—"

"I know all the reasons."

"—maybe a physio who could help improve his condition."

"You've been talking to Jessie, haven't you?"

He paused. "We do have lunch from time to time. You know that."

I shook my head again.

"I know you hate the place, Corin."

"Ark does too. I'm not sending him back. I made him a promise."

"Jessie's worried," Tuck told me. "And not just about the ranch. She's concerned about you too."

"She tell you to say that?"

He didn't answer. Not directly.

"You can't let Ark die," he said, taking both my hands in his. "I know he's thinking along those lines. But you can't do it. You can't help him. Jessie's got her own ideas about Hell and how you could spend an eternity there. That's her way of thinking, not mine. But helping someone to die is a crime, pure and simple. We're not talking right and wrong here, Corin. We're talking the law. Dress it up any way you want, put a smear of lipstick on it, if that's what you fancy. But assisting a suicide is tantamount to murder, with no ifs, buts, or maybes. That's the way the law sees it, and that's the way the courts judge it.

"We've got ourselves a sheriff in town who's happy to push the law to its limits and then some. He likes to lock people up, and is happy to see them light up in an electric chair. Dale's not a man you want to cross, Corin, especially after you said no to his boy. At best, you'd be swapping the prison Ark's in now for a *real* prison all of your own. You're a smart woman, Corin. I'm sure you'll figure it out. But don't rush into something you can't undo. And don't give in to Ark simply because he's a man. Not all men know what they're doing. Sometimes it's best to ignore them."

"You finished?" I said.

"I guess I have. I've said my piece."

"Well, thanks, Tuck," I said, colder than I meant. "I'll bear all that in mind."

And I turned and walked away.

Doc Mullins had warned me that Ark might sleep after a seizure, and that's how I found him when I arrived back at the bunkhouse. Dominga told me he'd spent the better part of the day like that, lost in a deep slumber.

When he finally awoke, I sat by his bed and read him a race-for-the-moon article in *Time* magazine that recounted various "firsts"—first humans to launch from Kennedy, first humans to witness an Earthrise, first humans scheduled to set foot on the moon. At six o'clock, I made him tea, then left him alone again with Dominga so she could give him a sponge bath.

On the front porch, I sat in my usual chair and sipped an Earl Grey (a favorite of Ark's). I had no intention of listening to Tuck, however wise his advice might be. I leaned forward and rested my chin in my hands, rocking on my seesaw of doubt. A movement caught my eye and I looked up to see a red-tailed hawk circle the sky, its wings spread wide to catch the thermals. Suddenly, it clamped its wings flat to its body and dropped into a dive, swooping low, claws outstretched, as it pounced onto something on the ground. A flurry of movement, a swirl of dust, and the hawk rose again with the limp body of a lizard locked in the vise of its talons.

I sat there a long time, and when it began to grow dark, I wandered over to the corrals as I often did when I needed to think. I relished the quiet, broken only by the snickers of the horses as they heard me approach. I looked toward the ranch house, a cardboard cutout against the fall of the night, and recalled the lives that had passed there—the hopes, the dreams, and ambitions. I petted Walnut, then made my way to the barn, but was stopped by a dry rustle that came from the bushes. I bent down to arm myself with a rock, ready to scare away a raccoon or coyote. The rustle came again, louder this time, and a buck deer bounded past me in a panic of high-kicking hooves.

I turned back toward the bunkhouse and the light that beamed out of the kitchen. I wasn't ready to go inside, so I sat on the steps of the porch and watched the stars come out. The start of a new day for Ark, when dusk became his dawn. I'd been there less than minute when I sensed a movement, black against black, on the edge of the darkness.

I called out, "Anyone there?"

Feeling foolish, talking into the empty night.

The air stirred and a shadow moved, and my heart jumped a warning notch. Not an animal. Not this time. It was too close to the bunkhouse.

I stood and moved up the steps as an apparition emerged from the gloom, the whites of its eyes bright.

It was the Indian. Yiska Begay.

PART FIVE

CHAPTER FORTY-SEVEN

Corin Dunbar

Yiska's eyes burned red with exhaustion, and the blood on his face had dried into crusty veins that patterned his skin like the war paint of his ancestors. His jet-black hair, sweat-slicked off his forehead, hung in matted strands to his shoulders; while his shirt, tattered when I'd seen him before, was shredded. He looked every bit as wild and feral as when I'd found him crouched in the tamarisk.

But he had a name now. An Indian name. Yiska Begay. And he'd ceased to be the heartless murderer I'd thought him to be and instead become a man twice crossed by a system that was meant to protect him, same as it had always protected me.

We stared at each other, neither of us moving. To him, I must have appeared a wacky white woman, entirely unpredictable. But also, perhaps, his haven of last resort.

"You're bleeding," I said.

There was no aggression in his face. Nor any fear.

"You must need water," I said, and fetched a glass from the kitchen, along with a bowl and a clean washcloth and the bottle of antiseptic we kept under the sink. He stayed in the shadows by the porch, half cloaked in the night. I beckoned him toward the pump by the barn and watched as he stripped off the remnants of his shirt. Water coursed down his neck and across his back as he washed away the dirt and grime in a delta of muddy streams. I pulsed the rod to keep the water flowing, and he sluiced it over his shoulders and chest. The muscles in his arms worked and rippled when he reached around to scrub his back and then his stomach, iron-flat and taut. The sight of his body provoked another memory of Ark, naked and lusting, that sent a rush of desire running through me like the one I'd suppressed with Cal.

I scurried back to the bunkhouse to cover my confusion. Ark was again asleep, turned on his side away from me, so I quietly sifted through the wardrobe for his largest shirt—a loose-fitting one—along with a pair of sandals I knew would be too small for Yiska, but might offer protection for the damaged soles of his feet.

Back at the pump, I helped him struggle into the shirt—tight across his chest and under his arms—then dabbed his feet with the antiseptic. He inhaled sharply as it found its way into the mess of cuts and abrasions that gaped raw-red against his dark skin.

I tore the washcloth in half and used the pieces to bandage his feet. He jammed on Ark's sandals, and winced when he stood to test his weight.

He eyed me warily.

"Why are you helping me?" he said.

I shrugged, not knowing how to marshal the kaleidoscope of thoughts and emotions that had filled my head and sent me tearing after him the minute I'd heard about his escape. Always shifting, always changing, they fractured along new fault lines every time I managed to pin one down. How could I explain the craziness that had stirred inside me when I saw the rat bite on Ark's leg and the wave of hysteria that had overwhelmed me when I'd been faced by the truth that I could neither keep Ark safely on the ranch, nor break my promise and send him back to the Severill? How could I explain to Yiska the threat to Jessie's ranch and the seesaw of indecision that was tearing me apart? That I'd gone after him because I thought he might help give Ark the resolution he wanted.

"My husband," I said. "He had an accident—" as if that were an answer—"and now he wants to die." Yiska said nothing, and his silence released a tension within me. "I don't want him to die. I want him to live. Here. With me. So we can have a life together, no matter what kind of life it turns out to be. But Ark wants to leave, to continue a journey he thinks will take him back to the stars. I'm not sure I can hold onto him. Or whether I should even try. I want to do what's best for him, but what is that? The doctor says he'll never recover, but no one can be certain of that, can they? And even if he doesn't get better, that's not to say his life is over."

I blurted out the words as if Yiska were a lifelong friend, there for me to confide in, and once started, I couldn't stop. At some point, I helped him hobble around to the front porch, where we'd be out of Jessie's line of sight from the ranch house, and settled him into a chair.

And I kept on talking.

I told him about the bull. The accident. The weeks and months that Ark spent in the hospital and then the Severill. I told him about Ark's belief that death was not an end but the start of a new adventure. I'm sure I didn't make much sense, but I felt an overwhelming need to unburden myself, and Yiska was willing to listen. More than that, he seemed to understand.

As we sat on the porch together, bathed in the silver patina of a rising moon, I told him everything. Because he was a stranger from a different world, a different life. And because he didn't judge me.

I fetched him more water and a plate of food that Dominga had prepared for Ark. He spooned it down in seconds, and when he'd finished I told him I knew that he'd been framed for a crime he didn't commit, that he'd been given a sentence of life without parole for a murder that was really self-defense.

"Are you bitter?" I asked at one point.

He shook his head. "Bitterness destroys you."

"Sheriff thinks you're out for revenge."

"I want to go home to the Nation, that's all."

When the night air chilled me to a shiver, we moved indoors to the kitchen. I served him another plate of food and as he sat at the table, dressed in Ark's wrangler shirt, I was pulled back to the long evenings Ark and I had spent there together, planning our future, laying out our mutual dreams. A choke of emotion rose in my throat and I had to turn away.

I was heating water for coffee when the phone rang, making me jump. It was Jessie, calling from the ranch house to ask if she could borrow some lard.

"I'll be right over," she said.

I felt a sudden rise of panic. "No, no," I said. "I'll bring it to you."

I checked again on Ark to find him breathing long and slow, still asleep. I told Yiska to stay where he was, and then I left.

It took longer than expected for me to deliver the lard, as Jessie was eager to talk. It was late, too late to start baking, but Jessie wanted to quiz me about Ark. And my "intentions," as she called them. I parried every approach and told her Ark was alone, so I needed to get back.

When I returned to the bunkhouse, my heart again skipped a beat; the kitchen was empty. But then I heard the murmur of voices coming from the bedroom, Ark's upbeat and alert, and Yiska's much deeper, coming in short, staccato-like bursts.

"Corin," Ark said, when I pushed open the bedroom door. "Come on in and join us."

He lay on his back, wide awake under a blanket, his head and shoulders propped up on a stack of pillows. Yiska leaned against the wall, arms folded across his broad chest, outside the circle of light thrown by Ark's bedside lamp.

"I've been getting acquainted with your new friend," Ark said.

I looked across at Yiska. He shrugged as if to say, *his description, not mine.*

"He's been telling me his story," Ark told me. "How he ended up in our house. And I have to say, it's quite a remarkable tale."

I frowned inwardly, wondering what Yiska might have said. I'd never told Ark about him, or about the part I'd played in his escape.

I looked at Yiska again. His shadow danced and shrank on the wall behind him as he stepped forward into the light.

"I told him you've been helping me," he said.

I nodded as if I knew what he meant. I didn't want to spoil the mood. Ark seemed buoyant, brimming with an energy that had been missing since his latest seizure.

He lifted his head.

"I have to admit," he said, "that I was a little surprised when Yiska here strolled into my room, and thought for a moment I must be having a drug-induced dream." He reached for the trapeze and pulley above his bed and strained to lever himself higher on his pillows. "Once I knew he was real, and not an apparition, I offered him a bite to eat. But he tells me you've already taken care of that."

"I have," I said, and the three of us fell silent. They looked at me as if I was intruding.

"You must be hungry too," I said, treading carefully.

When he nodded, I returned to the kitchen, where I again could hear the buzz of their conversation. I set a bowl of soup on a tray and carried it through to him. Yiska had moved to the chair by the bed, kicked off Ark's sandals, and sat with his legs out straight. He scraped the chair to one side as I placed the tray on the bedside table and bent to help Ark sit up. As I struggled to move him, Yiska lightly touched me on my arm, then reached under Ark's shoulders and in one effortless motion lifted him into a sitting position. Ark had always been slim with only a sliver of fat padding his frame, but since the accident he'd grown so frail you could see his bones sharp-jutted at his shoulders, elbows, and wrists. I stuffed a wad of pillows behind his back and again left the two of them together.

After half an hour scrubbing pots and stowing leftovers in the fridge, I cracked open the bedroom door to find them still deep in conversation. Yiska leaned toward the bed, hands clasped, elbows on knees; while Ark had rolled onto one side so he and Yiska could talk face-to-face. They stuttered into silence when they saw me, as if I'd caught them hatching a plot.

"Yiska's been telling me the Navajo believe that the Milky Way joins Heaven and Earth," Ark said, a measure of triumph in his voice. "The stars in our galaxy mark the route that everyone takes after they die. So you see? I'm not crazy. And I'm not alone. Yiska gives the stars different names, but we see the same ones, and we know they link us to an afterlife. The Navajo have no word for death, but call it—"

"*Adin*," Yiska said. "Which means 'no longer available.' It's a better description, because we're still somewhere. We don't just disappear."

I looked from one to the other. Yiska seemed to have fanned a flame in Ark that I'd recently failed to do. I opened my mouth to speak but was stopped in my tracks by the sound of a car. It swung around the side of the bunkhouse and came to a stop at the rear.

The three of us froze.

CHAPTER FORTY-EIGHT

I waited for Yiska to glide to the window, smooth as a skater on his bandaged feet. He wrenched the rusty clasp to one side, jammed the heels of his hands under the frame, and pushed it up. It didn't budge. He rattled it hard enough to dislodge the dust and grit that glued it together, squeaked it open, and punched out the screen. He shoved his head and shoulders over the sill and slithered into the darkness.

"This is exciting," Ark said. "I haven't had this many visitors in a long time. Nor so many surprises."

I ducked into the kitchen in time to see a shadowy figure flit past the window as someone climbed the steps onto the back porch. The hinges on the screen door squeaked, and there was a cursory knock, before the kitchen door swung open.

"Hell—*ooh*—oo!"

"Dottie!" I said, closing my eyes in relief. "What are you doing here? I mean, I'm glad to see you, but—"

"I know, it's been too long," she said. "And it's late. But I had to tell you my news."

She used a foot to shut the door behind her, then moved to the table, pulling off a pair of kidskin gloves as well as a chiffon scarf that covered her hair. This was a different Dottie from the one I was used to. Gone were the killer heels, replaced by a pair of plain black pumps with just the stub of a block heel. And when she slipped off her coat, her usually bared thighs were demurely covered by a knee-length skirt, dark blue and straight. Her breasts, always her most advertised feature, were as deflated as post-party balloons, cowering inside a loose-fitting blouse that was fastened at the neck by a pussy-cat bow.

"I can't stay," she said, plonking herself down in a chair. "Well, only a moment. But I came to tell you I'm leaving—leaving Paradox."

"For where?" I said. "Why?"

Dottie had never been farther than Blanding, except for one brief trip with her father to visit an aunt in Salt Lake City.

I joined her at the table. She leaned forward and grasped my arm.

"For Hollywood, of course. Where else would a girl go?" She smiled happily and sat back, the better to enjoy my reaction.

"But how—?"

"I've been hired!" she said, and threw her arms wide. "I've got a part! Not in a movie, but in a pilot. For a TV show called *The Brady Bunch*. It's about a large family with a potful of kids, far more than they can handle. It's a sitcom, meant to make you feel good about families in general and yours in particular even if you could murder every last one of them. I play a schoolteacher who helps out when one of the kids needs coaching or is flunking out."

"Dottie! That's fantastic!"

"Isn't it just?" And she bowed her head like a diva accepting applause.

"But a *schoolteacher*?"

"I know. A serious case of miscasting. But that's show business for you. Always pretending to be someone you're not. I met the producer in the Double-D. He saw me when I was in my waitress uniform. I was late for work that day, so I wasn't all dolled up with the boobs and the lipstick and the hair—and he liked my look! I had to audition, and I can tell you I've never been so scared in my life. I borrowed some of my mom's clothes to look as frumpy and dowdy as I could—well, I was playing a teacher, wasn't I?—and it worked! I don't think I've ever been so surprised when he offered me the part. Or so happy. It's my ticket out of here, Corin. It's my first step on the ladder."

"That's terrific news," I said, and meant it. "You've earned it, Dottie. I'll miss you, but it's what you've always wanted."

"I know. Thank you. It hasn't sunk in. I cannot *believe* I'm leaving." She planted a hand over her breasts. "I have to be demure, so the leading ladies go back in their box. I'm a schoolmarm now. I need to behave."

"Dottie, I'm thrilled."

"It's a dream come true," she said. "Better than in the movies." She stopped and reached across the table. "But here I am, prattling on about me, and I haven't asked about you. How is *he*?" she said, with a tilt of her head toward the bedroom.

"Ark? He's fine."

"Can I see him?"

I hesitated, thinking back to the last time she'd visited. "He's sleeping," I said.

Her face slackened, showing her relief. "Well, tell him I said 'hi.'"

"I will."

She was quiet a moment and as her expression changed again I caught a glimpse of my life through her eyes. Trapped in Paradox and doomed to a life of servitude, tethered to someone most people viewed as little better than a corpse.

A dead end all round.

"I'm sorry I haven't visited much," she said.

I squeezed her hand as she had done mine. "It's okay, Dottie. Really. We're fine." I stood up, suddenly keen for her to leave. "Ark'll be sorry he missed you."

She took the hint and slipped on her coat and gloves.

"I'll be watching for your name in lights," I told her, and gave her a hug. "I hope it works out just the way you've wanted."

"I'll send you a postcard. With a picture of the Hollywood sign."

I watched her walk to her car; then as she drove away, I flashed the porch light on and off as a sign to Yiska that he could return. A few minutes later, he limped into the kitchen and sank onto the chair Dottie had just vacated. I refilled the kettle and set it on the stove for another pot of coffee, and as it rattled its way to a boil with an ear-piercing whistle, the back door suddenly flew open and Dottie reappeared.

"Sorry, but I forgot—"

She stopped, mid-sentence and mid-scream. Yiska jumped out of his chair to send it crashing to the floor behind him. He took a step back.

"What's *he* doing here?" Dottie said, one hand pressed to her face.

I grabbed her by the arm and hustled her outside.

"Is that who I think it is?" she said.

I nodded.

"The runaway Injun? But he's a *murderer*, Corin."

I shook my head. "No. He's not. He's here helping me. With Ark."

"*Helping* you? The whole county's looking for him. They've got roadblocks up—"

"I know."

"—because he's a killer, they said so on the radio."

"I know. But it's...complicated," I said, unwilling to tell her more. I grabbed her by the shoulders and shook her to get her full attention. "You have to promise me, Dottie. You have to promise you won't say a word."

"But—"

"No, Dottie. Please. Just promise. Promise you won't tell a soul."

"Are you sure you're *safe*?"

"I'm sure. Ark and me, we're both safe. But I need you to promise."

"But why?" she said. "What's he *doing* here?"

"Just promise me," I said, shaking her again.

She nodded uncertainly.

"Say it," I said.

"I promise."

"Not a soul?"

"Not a soul."

"Good. Now why'd you come back?"

"I forgot my scarf. I think I left it—"

"Okay. Stay here," I said.

I rushed in to fetch it.

"You need to trust me, Dottie," I told her when I came out onto the porch again. "Will you do that?"

"You're sure you know what you're doing?"

"I'm sure," I said, with more confidence than I felt. "Just remember your promise, okay?"

"Okay."

I gave her another hug. A goodbye hug, but also one I hoped would cement our agreement.

I hurried her to her car, and this time I watched her drive all the way to the valley road. Only when her brake lights flared and she turned and headed toward Paradox did I go back into the kitchen.

CHAPTER FORTY-NINE

Dottie DeVine
(née Dorothy Wittering)

When Dottie left the ranch that night, it was close to ten o'clock. A cool, cloudless night showcased a sky glittering with stars. She drove through the roadblock—now manned by a listless Luke Sims—then slowed again at Balanced Rock as she tossed up between the valley road to Paradox or the cutoff that went through Eldorado. Either route would take her to the Buena Vista Mobile Home Park, where she'd been born and where she still lived with her abandoned mother in a single-width metal box of a trailer.

Dottie's real home, however, was a gated residence on Mulholland Drive with a circular driveway, lap pool, private movie theater, and an eagle's-eye view of the fairyland lights of Hollywood. She knew this home inside out because for the past ten years, her purse had held its picture, ripped from a copy of *Silver Screen Magazine*. She'd pored over it so often the folds of the picture were cracked, and the edges had grown torn and tattered; but each night before she slept she would smooth it out and trace the curve of the driveway with her finger, mapping the route she would one day take from the pool to the bathhouse and then to the bevy of rooms that made up the master suite.

Dottie's childhood in the mobile home park had not been easy. Her father, Edgar Wittering, had been a mining engineer who'd found work designing underground tunnels and shafts for the Crestview Uranium Mine near Moab. In 1940, the second year of the mine's operation, the main shaft collapsed, killing thirty workers. Edgar was blamed, blacklisted by his industry, and forced to sell his six-room clapboard house in Moab and move to the rented Buena Vista trailer in Paradox. No one could say why—perhaps because of the shame he felt over his inability to provide for his family—but soon after the move, Edgar began to dress as a woman, wearing mail-order blouses, skirts, and lacy underwear that he'd parade around in like a runway model.

When his mail-order bills became too large, his wife, Hazel—a nervy woman, thin as a whippet—was forced to buy Edgar's dresses at the Fashion First Emporium on Main, and then spend long hours letting out seams, dropping hemlines, and sewing on hooks and eyes to make the clothes fit. Each time Edgar slipped into a dress, Hazel would spit out her disgust and contempt along with a string of obscenities, and say if he really wanted to sabotage their marriage, why didn't he cheat with another woman like a *real* man would do? At least then she'd be able to scratch out the eyes of her rival.

In spite of his liking for women's clothing, Edgar still wanted sex with his wife, so it was through the paper-thin walls of the trailer that Dottie learned physical encounters of this kind were not enjoyed by both parties—not if the sound of Hazel sobbing was anything to go by. Sex was the price a woman paid for keeping a man at her side, food on the table, and a roof over her head. As Dottie grew older, she became hardened to life in the pressure-cooker trailer. Edgar never dressed as a woman outside the home. He knew, if he did, he'd be beaten, arrested, or shot—or possibly all three. But on numerous occasions, Dottie was forced to sit beside him at dinner after he'd slipped on a blue-and-white gingham sundress or a silken wisp of a petticoat worn over stockings and a frilly garter belt. Once, when she was about twelve years old, he sat her in the glossy lap of his nightgown, slipped a shoulder strap down over the bulge of his bicep, and forced her to suckle on one of his nipples.

Dottie's retreat into fantasy started then. As a teenager, she'd lie on her bunk and gaze out through her porthole of a window at a world that existed only in her head. That world greatly expanded when she discovered the Paradox drive-in and the transporting delights of movies. She'd sneak under the drive-in's fence, crouch in the shadow of an unsuspecting couple's car, and fall hopelessly under the thrall of film. She could not believe her luck when the fake movie town of Eldorado rose from the desert and the Hollywood studios began to arrive. *Right here in Paradox!* Dottie knew it was a sign that she was destined for stardom.

Like her father, she began to dress up, but *her* masquerade was a meaningful tryout for the movie-star role she was sure she'd one day play for real. She dyed her hair blonde, slathered on lipstick, and glued on black sweeping lashes. She padded her bras and endlessly practiced the up-from-under look that had her peek out from lowered eyelids, sexy and inviting. She learned to slip a cigarette suggestively into her mouth; to rest her chin on the butt of one hand and nibble at the tip of a pinkie; to strike a pose with her head back while flashing a smile; and to wrap her arms around her shoulders and coyly tilt her head in a move that not only deepened her cleavage, but also made her appear vulnerable and weak and in need of male protection.

She knew the town folk laughed when she sashayed around in her movie-star guise. And while she sometimes attracted catcalls and come-ons from Paradox men, she frequently drew glares and abuse from the Paradox women who said she put out, that she slept around. "That girl's seen more ceilings than a can of Valspar paint" was one of the kinder comments she was meant to overhear.

Dottie ignored them and persevered. Her desire to break into the movies was constantly thwarted, but not once did she think of letting her dream die. And now, at long last, she was about to prove the doubters wrong. With a part to play and a contract signed, Dottie was on her way. To the home that had always been hers, that gated residence on Mulholland Drive.

At Balanced Rock, she swung right to take the cutoff through Eldorado. For old time's sake. A chance to have one last look at the place before she left Paradox forever.

The set was deserted when she pulled to a stop outside the Silver Dollar saloon, the scene of so many of her failed auditions. She smiled at the eyes reflected in her rearview mirror.

"So long, dull past," she said. "Hello, bright future."

She blew herself a kiss, squeaked open her car door, and climbed the three steps onto the boardwalk. On tiptoe, she looked over the top of the batwing doors of the saloon to see the looming shapes of cameras and a boom, left there after the day's filming. Just the sight of them sent shivers of expectation coursing through her. *Damn the scoffers*, she thought. *A girl's dreams really can come true.*

She pushed at the doors to set them swinging, then stepped inside, almost tripping over a clapperboard on the floor. *Butch Cassidy and the Sundance Kid, Scene 6, Take 4.* She snaked through the gaming tables, light from the moon showing her the way, and ducked behind the bar, recalling the bottles of fake whiskey she used to sip when she played here as a child.

It would be champagne from now on.

She stepped in front of the long mirror, the one set in a carved mahogany frame that Jelly had reportedly brought in from Chicago, and was plumping her hair when she was startled by a voice.

"Hey, Dottie!"

She froze. She'd thought she was alone. The voice came from outside, so she padded back to the batwing doors and peeked over the top into the street. Two men slouched against the hood of her car. She felt a momentary rush of fear, but relaxed when she saw one of the men was in uniform. She walked down the steps of the boardwalk, and became further relieved when she recognized Russ Preston, a wrangler, part-time mechanic, and now, apparently, an overnight security guard in Eldorado. She'd known him for years. The other man was familiar—moon-faced and stocky, he wore a plaid shirt tucked into Levi's, and oiled leather boots—but she couldn't recall his name. Both men, she immediately noticed, stank of liquor.

"This here's my baby brother," Russ said, clapping the moon-faced man on the shoulder. "He's been dying to meet you. Ain't that right, Harvey? Been having wet dreams about you, even before his balls dropped. You used to tease him some. Me too, I reckon. One time when we were digging graves on Boot Hill?" He waved loosely toward the funeral home farther along the street. "Lie on the back of a hearse, you would, catching rays in your red frilly bra. But I guess you don't remember, huh?"

Harvey Preston laughed. "Well, *I* remember," he said. "And *he* does too," jerking his head at a third man who emerged from the alley next to the saloon, buttoning the fly of his jeans.

"Where'd the little lady come from?" the third man said. He was a big-bellied redhead, a few years older than the other two.

"Just dropped by to keep us company," Russ told him. "Didn't you, Dottie?"

"Well, we're mighty glad to see you," Redhead said, "because we were getting bored here by ourselves." He pulled a quarter bottle of whiskey out of his back pocket, took a swig, then passed it to Harvey. "We was just saying not much action around here and then—whadda you know—you show up."

Russ said, "Quit sucking on that bottle like it's your girlfriend's tit, Harvey, and offer the lady a drink."

"I'll pass," Dottie said.

"Aw, come on, Dottie. Don't be like that. Take a drink with us, won't you?"

"She doesn't mix with the local boys," Harvey said. "She only puts it about for the Hollywood crowd, everyone knows that."

"That right, Dottie?" Russ asked.

She pulled her car keys out of her coat and made for the driver's door; but Harvey levered himself off the hood to block her way.

"Russ here says you like to party," Harvey said. "We like to party too. Don't we, fellas?" He winked at Dottie and cupped one hand over his groin.

"Get outta my way," she said, shoving him hard with both hands. Harvey had fifty pounds on her and didn't budge an inch.

"C'mon, take a drink with us, why don't you? Won't do you any harm. Might even loosen you up some."

Dottie glared at him a moment, then softened her expression. "Okay," she said.

"Well, that's better."

She jerked the bottle out of his hand and flung it into the night.

"Aw, man, you ought'n to have done that," Russ said. "We were just enjoying a little drink and being social. And then you go and do a thing like that."

The red-haired man behind her moved quickly to grab her by the shoulders. When she spun around, he tried to kiss her. She kneed him in the crotch, but he held her tight and twisted her arm into a lock.

"Keep still, damn you," he said, and again tried to clamp his mouth onto hers so she nearly choked on the mix of breath, tobacco, and whiskey.

She broke free, but other hands held her and forced her back against her car. Someone pinned her arms and ripped at her coat, and she felt cold night air on her breasts as another hand tore at her skirt and groped between her thighs.

"I tried to fight them off," she told Dale later that night. "But there were *three* of them, Sheriff. I couldn't hold them *all* off. They were just too strong."

"You saying they raped you?" Dale asked.

"Yes," Dottie said, in a suddenly small voice. "They did."

After the attack, she'd wrapped her coat around herself and scrambled into her car. She stopped once to throw up by the side of the road, then drove straight to the sheriff's office, where Wayne Coleman—the deputy on duty—called Dale, who came in right away, bringing Cal with him.

Now Dale sat with his feet up, his hat tipped to the back of his head, and his gun belt flung across his desk. He wore his full sheriff's uniform, neat as if on parade, his badge a shining star.

"That's a pretty serious charge, Dottie," he said. "You sure about this?"

"Of *course* I'm sure," her voice rising again. "You think I could make a *mistake*? They threw me over the hood of my car. Held me down and ripped at my clothes..."

She sat slumped in the chair opposite Dale, facing a framed photograph that hung on the wall behind him. "Lyndon B. Johnson," the caption read. "America's 36th President."

"And this was Harvey Preston you say? And some redhead guy you didn't know?"

Dottie nodded.

"But not *Russ* Preston, he didn't touch you."

She shook her head.

"So just the two of them had some time with you."

"They didn't have *time* with me, Sheriff. They *raped* me. How often I have to say it?"

Dale raised his hands. "Now, take it easy, Dottie. I'm just trying to figure out what happened here. Who did what to who."

"You think *I* don't know?"

"I'm sure you do. But I just need a moment so's I can put it together."

He plucked at his lower lip and scratched behind one ear. Cal stood in the corner by the door that led to the backyard lot. He was kitted out in his uniform too, but his shoulders were hunched and he was stooped low, hands in pockets, as if he didn't want to be there. That afternoon, he'd had another row with his father when Dale cornered him in the front office and bawled him out in front of Wayne and—worse still—Erma Belnap. A woman, and only the office help. And all on account of his failure to catch the Injun and put him back behind bars.

"He's a dumb savage," Dale had said. "How hard can it be to git him? I need him back in Draper before the warden runs out of patience and calls in the state troopers. I don't want *them* stomping around the valley. Makes me look bad, like I can't get the job done. And that's not something I want to put in front of the voters, not this close to the election."

"I know the Preston brothers," Dale now said to Dottie. "They're Wilmer's boys. A good man, he is. And a good shot. How come they were out there in Eldorado?"

"Russ was in uniform," Dottie mumbled. "He works there as a security guard."

"And the other two?"

She looked up. "I don't know, Sheriff. I just know what they *did*. They were drunk. They had whiskey."

"That redhead's got to be Marv Pratt. Don't you reckon, Cal?"

Cal lifted his shoulders in reply, took a long pull on a Lucky Strike.

"His dad's in the Legion," Dale said.

Dottie shifted again in her chair. The pussycat bow that had fastened her blouse straggled from her neck like a spent party-streamer. She'd re-fastened the two buttons that were left on her blouse and tucked what remained of the material into her skirt, which was now split along one seam and twisted around so its zip ran like a scar up her belly. Her stockings were gone, and so, too, were her panties. Smudges of mascara circled her eyes—black as a panda's—and tears that she still couldn't restrain formed salty runnels down her cheeks. She clutched her coat around her, tight as a hug.

Dale let his feet drop to the floor.

"Well, I'll go talk to them," he said. "See what the Preston boys have to say. Cal, you take care of Dottie here. And Dottie, you might want to freshen up a little, get rid of that guck on your face and...well, whatever else you need to do."

CHAPTER FIFTY

Two hours passed before the sheriff returned. During his absence, Dottie had dragged herself into the washroom, where she stared numbly at the pale and puffy mask that looked back at her from the mirror. She used dampened toilet tissue to wipe the smears off her face and to swab between her legs. Then she pulled her coat tight again and went back to wait in the sheriff's office.

Dale dropped into his chair and swung his feet onto his desk.

"Okay," he said. "I talked to them, the Preston boys. Then I drove by the Pratts and had a word with Marv. He don't deny that he was there and neither do the Prestons. So we're all on the same page so far. Russ was in Eldorado in his capacity as a security guard, just like you say, Dottie. And the other two, they were there to keep him company. That's what they tell me, and I've no reason to doubt them.

"They say they had a bottle with them, so we're all agreed on that too. But then we get what you might call a discrepancy. They say you turned up, Dottie, unexpected. But the activity that went on after you showed, well, they say *that* was con-sens-ual. The way they tell it, you had a drink with them, maybe more'n you should have, and then you put out for them. All three of them say that. They say you... accommodated them. Not all the boys, mind. Just Marv and Harvey. Russ stayed out of the action 'cause he was working and didn't think it right on company time. But the other two, they admit they took turns with you. But they claim you were eager for it and wanted to take them on."

"They're liars, Sheriff. They *raped* me," tears again welling in her eyes.

"So you keep saying. But they tell a different story here."

"Well, of course they would. They're not going to come out and *admit* it, are they?"

"Maybe not. But there's three of them, Dottie. All singing from the same hymn sheet. And there's just you telling me different."

Dottie squeezed her eyes shut. When she opened them again, she spoke in a small injured voice.

"They raped me, Sheriff. That's all I can say. They held me down and...and...raped me."

Dale nodded, leaned back, and clasped his hands behind his head.

"Get her a Kleenex, will you, Cal? And some water too. Oh, and fetch me a coffee while you're at it. Hot. Make it hot. It's gonna be a long night and I'm gonna need something to keep me upright and ticking.

"What we got here, Dottie," he said, "is a clear case of he-said, she-said with me in the middle. I got no way to know which of you is telling the truth. You gotta see things from my side of the fence. I can tell you're pretty beat up, but that can happen if you take on two at once, especially if you been drinking."

"I wasn't drinking, Sheriff," she said, in the same small voice.

Dale shrugged and used his shirt cuff to polish the badge on his chest. "I'm not saying you were, Dottie. But you do have a way of living in a world the rest of us don't always see. I'm just saying there's not a whole bunch I can do here. You got one story, and these boys have another, and I'm caught piggy-in-the-middle with nothing to push me one way or the other."

"I'm telling the truth."

"And I'm not saying different. But those boys are pretty solid too. They tell me you came by looking for fun and you found it. Maybe a little more'n you bargained for, but that's what they're telling me."

"Don't I have the right to say no?"

"Course you do, Dottie. But if every man took no to *mean* no, well, no one'd ever get laid and the human race would come to a standstill." He tipped forward to rest his hands flat on his desk. "The problem I got here, Dottie, is the law doesn't recognize the crime of rape. Not in this state. It's *forcible* rape, that's what the law books say is wrong. Now, I know you're all mussed up with your clothes awry and such, but I don't see cuts. I don't see bruises. You got some dirt marks on you, on your legs and maybe round your backside there, but I'd expect that if you done what these boys say you done."

"It was three against one. But I struggled, Sheriff. I fought back best I could."

"That could be. But there are other factors to consider here. Russ could lose his job for one. I know you say he didn't...didn't do what the other two did, but he admits to drinking, having a bottle, and passing it round."

"You just going to let them walk away free?"

"I didn't say that," Dale told her quickly, as she collapsed into sobs. "I'll do my job exactly the way I'm supposed to. I'll take statements from each of the boys, and from you too. But to make a charge stick? I need evidence. Hard evidence. And that's not something I've got. Not unless you want me to take a peek up under that skirt of yours and see if I can find any signs of forcible entry."

He leaned back in his chair again. "Fact is, Dottie, you've been parading around town these past few years all dolled up with your chest stuck out, sending an invitation that any man would be happy to take you up on. You done that as long as I can remember, so it's not surprising if a few of the boys didn't pick up on it and act accordingly. The only thing that surprises me is it didn't happen sooner. So what I suggest is, you let me handle the investigation and you take yourself home, have a hot shower, get yourself cleaned up, then off to bed and see how you feel in the morning.

"In the meantime, Dottie—and I hope you don't take this the wrong way—but my advice would be to keep your knees together. In my experience, no girl ever got herself in trouble doing just that. Works every time, believe you me."

CHAPTER FIFTY-ONE

Corin Dunbar

The morning after Dottie's visit, I left the ranch early. Luke Sims was manning the roadblock, and just as Wayne had done, he waved me through with barely a glance. On Main Street, I was forced to move at a crawl as the center of Paradox was again awash with production cars, pickups, and grip trucks. The Butch Cassidy crew was marshalling resources for an outdoor shoot at the head of the valley, and that one scene required a myriad of booms, cranes, dollies, and cameras, as well as an hysteria of shouted commands.

I parked on Third and ducked into the Well-Heeled Shoe Store, where I bought a pair of size ten boots, the first I saw. They were high-ankled and round-toed with black leather laces and thick military soles that were made for walking. Not the best choice for injured feet, but better than the improvised bandages and too-small sandals that Yiska was struggling with.

I tossed the boot box onto the passenger seat, then drove down Pierce to avoid the chaos on Main. As I turned onto Fourth, a police car swung in behind me, and when it filled my rearview mirror, I saw Cal hunched over the wheel. I kept an even speed until he flashed his lights and sounded a *whoop-whoop-whoop* with his siren to make me pull over. I watched in my mirror as he climbed out of his cruiser, settled his Stetson, and started toward me. His eyes were blacked out by aviator sunglasses, and he affected the swagger-walk I'd once admired but now found annoying. He was dressed for business in his tan shirt with the Blade County Sheriff shoulder patches, cream tie, and brown pants. Around his waist was a heavy gun belt with night-stick and flashlight, as well as a pair of handcuffs that winked and glinted in the sunlight. In his gun hand, he carried a manila envelope that he thwapped against his thigh as he walked.

I cranked my window fully open.

"What's the problem, Cal?" I made no effort to keep the testiness out of my voice.

"No problem, Corin."

He removed his sunglasses and I saw his green eyes slide over the interior of the Plymouth, pause at the boot box, then come to rest on me.

"You stop me just for a chat?" I asked him.

"Didn't mean to get your back up," he said. "But there's a small business matter we need to attend to." He looked away, fiddled with his hat again, and ran a finger round the inside of his collar.

"So what is it, Cal?"

He slapped the envelope against the palm of one hand. "Got to give you this. You won't like it, Corin. But it's for the best. You'll see."

He backed up a step as I opened it.

The contents didn't make sense at first.

"What is this, Cal?"

"Called a commitment order, Corin. Sworn out before Judge Ryland."

I stared at the blur of close-typed words. "So translate it for me. What's it trying to say?"

"It's about your husband—"

"I can see that. I can see Ark's name."

"He's being committed—"

"Committed?"

"To the Severill. He's a health risk, Corin. A danger to himself. And to others."

"Bull*shit*!" I said, and flung open the car door, forcing him to take another big step back. I scrambled out to face him. "What in hell are you talking about?" I thrust my chin up at him. "A danger? How can someone like Ark be a *danger*? He's confined to his bed!"

"Now, I don't want to fight, Corin—"

"You've got no right—"

"I've got every right. More'n that, an obligation. I'm just doing my job here. On account of what Doc Mullins's been telling me."

"Which is *what* exactly?"

"That your husband got bit by a rat—"

"He shouldn't be telling you that."

"But it's true, isn't it? Your husband, helpless as a newborn, gets some rat come crawling out of the woodwork to take a bite out of his leg. You can't deny that, Corin, and you can't deny that's a health risk."

"You want to send him away for *that*?" I shook my head. "No way."

"He needs taking care of, Corin. Everyone knows that. And he's not getting it at your ranch."

"You think he'll find it at the Severill?" I could feel my body shaking. My voice too. "No one would visit him; he'd be abandoned. No one would even know he was there."

"It's for the best, Corin."

"So you keep saying."

"And not just for him. For you too. You need to get on with your life, and he's holding you back. He doesn't belong here, Corin. Not in Paradox. Not in this *country*." He moved in closer and tried to grip my shoulders, but I batted him away.

"I don't want a fight," he told me again. "But Ark's got to be committed. Judge says so. Your husband needs protection, and not just from rat bites. There's talk of suicide, is what I hear. With Jessie saying you might be thinking of helping him on his way."

I took a deep breath, let it out slow. Tried a count to ten, but made it only to three.

"Jessie? What has she been saying?"

"I'm just looking out for you, best I can. Jessie is too."

"You want him gone, don't you? You want him out of the way. You couldn't care less about Ark *or* where he goes. You just want him gone." My hands were clenched at my sides, and I could feel my heart thumping heavy against my ribs.

"It's *you* I'm looking out for, Corin. I told you that."

"And I can't look out for myself?"

"Not right now, you can't. You need someone to do your thinking for you. You shouldn't be working at the *Gazette*, running yourself ragged with some half-assed job. You should be home. At the ranch. Raising a family. Living a life. Not caught in the trap you're in with not even sense enough to see it."

"I've plenty of sense, Cal," I said. "For starters, I got rid of you."

He started to say something, but I climbed into the Plymouth, slammed the door in his face, and drove off, peppering him with a salvo of grit.

I'd reached the corner of Main before I cooled off enough to start thinking again, but it still took the blast of a horn from a grip truck to jolt me back to life. I swung a U-turn and drove to Jay Lambert's building on Fifth, where I double-parked outside Mason's Drug. I stormed into the lawyer's office just as he was getting off the phone and slammed the commitment order onto his desk.

"Get me out of that," I said, and stood back, hands on hips, feeling my cheeks burning.

"And good to see you too, Corin," he said. "Why don't you sit yourself down and let me see what we've got here."

Jay reached for his glasses, huffed on the lenses, and wiped each one meticulously with a cloth, then hooked the wire temples behind his ears and settled the frames onto the bridge of his nose.

"This is a Civil Involuntary Commitment Order," he said.

"I know that!" I all but shouted. "I need you to make it go away!"

He peered at me over the top of his glasses with a lawyerly affectation I hadn't seen him adopt before. True to form, he was dressed in a three-piece dark suit brightened by a tie daubed with a geometric art-deco design.

"Let me call the courthouse," he said. "Have a word with Judge Ryland."

I paced back and forth, arms folded across my chest, as I listened to one side of a conversation that was mostly questions, interspersed with grunts and the occasional "uh-huh" from Jay.

"What?" I said, when he hung up.

"Well, it's legal. And it's binding too. It was signed by Cal in his capacity as a law officer, and it was co-signed by your aunt Jessie in her capacity as a relative."

"Aunt *Jessie* signed it?"

"She didn't tell you?"

I shook my head and took another angry turn around his office before I stopped and faced him again.

"How can I fight it?" I said.

"You can't. Cal's given you three days to get Ark committed. If not, then he'll enforce this."

"I need to stop him."

Jay leaned back in his chair. "I'm a lawyer," he said. "I'd love to take your money. It's what we lawyers do. But if you fight this—or defy it—you'll wind up with a hefty bill from me and even more trouble than you're in now. I can try for a stay. But I can't get you a revocation."

"Cal can't come onto the ranch, barge into our home, and take Ark *away*. Can he?"

Jay spread his hands. "He can if he's armed with this order. He's the law. The state. The government. We're only as free as the government allows us to be and sometimes not even then. You know," he said, after watching me pace around his office some more, "this order could have an upside to it. You ever stop to consider that?"

I shook my head, still seething.

"If Ark goes to the Severill," Jay said, "the insurance company will pick up the tab, I told you that. It'll have no choice. Jessie won't have to sell the ranch, so you'd be saving her from that particular brand of grief. And you won't have to work at the *Gazette*. You'd be free to get on with your life again."

"That's what Cal said."

"And he could be right." Jay paused, waiting for me to respond. When I stayed tight-lipped and silent, he went on. "You know, Cal Parker wasn't the only one who was disappointed when you fell for Ark. You could have had your pick of most any man in town. You still can, Corin. You never realized that, did you? That was always a big part of your appeal. As your lawyer—and, I hope, your friend—my counsel is to see this order for what it is. A silver lining. A chance for you to do right by Ark and to move on to a better future for yourself. It's worth considering, Corin. Because frankly, I don't see you have any other choice."

I stopped pacing and turned on him. "There's always another choice," I said.

I dropped a dime into the pay phone in the doorway of Mason's Drug and called Tuck to tell him I wouldn't be coming in that day.

"You okay?" he said. "You sound like you're phoning from the other end of the country."

"A lot on my mind," I told him.

"You're not sick, are you?" I heard the ding of a spoon against the side of a cup. One sugar, two sugars, three.

"I'm fine, Tuck. Really."

A woman with pompadour hair and pancake makeup rapped on the window outside.

"People waiting," I told Tuck. "I gotta go."

"Well, if you're sure you're okay..."

"I'm sure," I said, and hung up.

But I wasn't sure. Not until I climbed behind the wheel of the Plymouth again. I'd left the car in the sun and inside it burned hot as a furnace. I cranked open the side windows and sat with my forehead pressed against the steering wheel. Sweat trickled down my face like tears and I knew my hands would shake if I didn't keep them locked tight around the wheel in fists. It seemed everyone had an opinion, and they were all agreed.

But I knew I was the one who had to decide. And then act.

It wasn't the court order that forced the issue. Nor the risk of Jessie losing the ranch. These were real problems. But I saw them as practical problems open to rational solutions. I may not have known what those solutions would be, but I was confident I'd be able to find them.

What pushed me over the edge was something Cal had said. That I needed someone to do my thinking for me. That made me madder than I cared to admit. Yet wasn't I saying the same thing to Ark? Denying his right to choose. Taking away his independence, and saying, "Leave it to me. I know best."

I thought of Gene and the way he'd sent me away. I'd been a child then, at an age when we don't expect to have control over our lives, but I still resented the way I'd not been given *any* say. Ark felt the same, when his parents shipped him off to England. I thought of Rose Watson and the Friedan book she'd lent me, how it helped me see that as a girl, as a woman, I could sweep aside the limitations that others tried to impose on me. And I thought of Yiska and how he'd been locked away because he was an "Injun." Not deserving of any rights. Ark may have been crippled by his accident, but that hadn't turned him into a child. His body was damaged, but his mind was intact. He was still his own man, still in his prime, as Doc Mullins kept reminding me.

I knew what I had to do. I'd made the decision the day I went to fetch Yiska. I just hadn't acknowledged that fact or accepted the finality of what it meant. I had to give Ark what he wanted and set him free. I had no right to control his future just because I had the power. It was *his* life, *his* story—and *his* right to determine when and how it should end.

CHAPTER FIFTY-TWO

Cal Parker

Across town, Cal Parker sat slouched behind the wheel of his cruiser outside the candy-cane awning of the ice-cream parlor on Grant and sucked on a strawberry-banana shake. His mind should have been on the Injun and the best way to catch him; but the better part of his thinking was tuned to the commitment order he'd handed Corin, and to the shoebox he'd seen on the passenger seat of her car.

The box had been labeled "COMBAT BOOTS."

Which was strange.

She must have bought them for Ark; there was no one else in her life.

But why would she buy combat boots for a man who couldn't walk?

CHAPTER FIFTY-THREE

Corin Dunbar

"I don't know how to do it," I told Ark.

I felt lightheaded with a strange energy fueled by purpose and newfound sense of direction. I could see Ark felt the same. His cheeks were flushed, no longer a parchment white; and he seemed buoyed by a vigor I knew I would need to draw on.

"*He* knows," Ark said, inclining his head toward Yiska.

When I'd left the bunkhouse that morning, Ark had been alone, propped up in bed on a phalanx of pillows as he listened to the radio I'd brought through from the kitchen. KBEZ had dispensed with its Top Twenty countdown to broadcast news of the Apollo space race and the launch of an orbital mission the following day. When I returned to the bunkhouse a little after noon, he was still propped on pillows, but Yiska was with him. He'd slept on the floor of a room once used by itinerant wranglers, but now he sat in the reading chair next to Ark's bed, dressed in a fresh shirt (another of Ark's) and a pair of Levi's (also Ark's) that were pinched at the waist and rolled up at the cuffs.

"We've worked everything out," Ark said.

I looked at him for an explanation, but it was Yiska who supplied the answer. He dipped into a pocket of his jeans and pulled out a swatch of blue chambray that he must have ripped from his prison shirt and then tied into a pouch secured at the neck with a length of bindweed. He unwound the bindweed and spilled about twenty or thirty round, tan-colored seeds into his palm.

"Moonflower," he said, and held out his hand to show me. "I collected them yesterday. In the desert."

I shook my head, not understanding.

"We use moonflower roots to treat our wounds," he said. "And if we have pain in our muscles, we brew the leaves into a tea. But these seeds are toxic. They can kill. They act fast and there's no pain. They send you to sleep. But you never wake up."

I poked at the seeds. They looked harmless as counting beans.

"How many does it take?" I asked.

"Eight, ten. We've more than enough. But Ark cannot die here. Not in this house. His *chindi* would remain and bring you bad luck. Bad for you and bad for him. Bad, too, for the spirit that is trying to leave him."

He tipped the seeds back into his pouch and secured it with the bindweed. "Is there somewhere he can be taken?" he said. "Somewhere with meaning?"

My eyes locked on Ark's and a mist of tears blinkered my vision as I shifted my gaze to our canyon photo by his bedside. It seemed an eon since we'd posed for it. A moment of joy and elation, frozen in time, which proved how happy we'd been, but also mocked our present by showing how far we had fallen.

"Yes," I said. "There is."

"Then we should go there tomorrow," Yiska said.

That evening, Yiska lifted Ark, limp as a rag doll, and carried him on to the front porch. I settled him into a chair, packed him upright with cushions, and wrapped him warmly in the tree-of-life blanket Jessie had given us for our wedding. A cool breeze blew, a reminder that winter would soon be settling in, but Ark welcomed the fresh air moving against his skin.

We sat side by side and looked at the stars. All five thousand, speckling the sky and carving out the sweep of the Milky Way.

"That one's mine," Ark said, and pointed me toward a spangled star just to the left of Vega, now high in the sky. "And that can be yours," indicating another nearby. "Unless," he added, "you'd prefer to pick one yourself."

"I'll let you choose," I told him.

"Then all we need is a shooting star. To serve as an omen. A good one. You know you'll always be able to look up and see me, don't you?" he said. "I'll be up there, waiting. But there's no need for you to hurry."

"Are you really sure about this?" I asked him.

He reached a hand out from under his blanket. "I've never been *more* sure."

"When we first married," I said, "I pictured us on the porch like this, growing old together and gazing up at the stars. We've had so little time."

"And it's not over. Because it's time that'll bring us together again."

I leaned toward him to rest my head on his shoulder. Yiska had left us alone, but we heard him moving about in the kitchen.

"You realize," Ark said, "that Cal could have kept him from prison?"

I lifted my head.

"The night he was supposed to be driving that car," Ark said. "A deputy came in to the cell block and saw Yiska there. He could have supplied an alibi, said Yiska was locked up so couldn't have been tooling around town in a car."

"That was Cal?"

"Tall, blond hair, green eyes? Yiska described him."

"That's Cal," I said.

"You have to help him," Ark said. "Not just me. You have to help Yiska too. Help him be free."

"I will."

"Promise?"

"Promise," I said.

It was a commitment I'd already made to myself.

❖

I woke the following morning to find sunlight streaming warmth through the bedroom window. I'd crawled in beside Ark and placed a hand on his chest to feel the thud of his heart. I lay still, watching him sleep and searing into my brain every line and curve and nuance of his face. It scared me to think if I reached out like this tomorrow, there'd be no one there. I felt a loneliness creep over me like ice settling on winter water.

I dragged myself out of bed, pulled on some clothes, and joined Yiska in the kitchen.

"We need to make him ready," he said.

I filled a bowl with warm water and fetched our softest towels and two sponges from the bathroom. Then I stroked Ark's cheek to rouse him.

Together, Yiska and I washed his chest, then his back, brushing lightly over his body and the road map of veins that threaded close under his skin. I ached to see his limbs so wasted and the milky whiteness of his feet, idle so long they were free of any scratch, blister, or blemish. Ark kept his eyes closed. He'd always hated the invasion of privacy that came with washing, dressing, and tending to his bodily needs; but when I massaged oil into his chest, his eyes flicked open and he flashed a smile. I took my time, aware that every touch could be my last.

We helped him into a clean white shirt and the black pants he'd worn on our wedding day, although they swaddled him in folds of excess cloth. I combed his hair away from his forehead and saw again the rush of color that had come to his cheeks.

"How do I look?" he said. "Am I ready for my close-up?"

Yiska lifted him up, one arm under his shoulders, the other beneath his knees, and carried him out to the Dodge. I looked for signs of doubt, a flicker of second thoughts, but his spirit was alive and strong as ever. I wedged him into his seat to protect him from bumps and jolts, and wrapped him again in our tree-of-life blanket. Then I climbed in beside him.

Yiska put the Dodge into gear.

"Ready?" he said.

"Ready," Ark told him, and held my hand in both of his.

CHAPTER FIFTY-FOUR

Jessie Dunbar

At noon that day, Jessie Dunbar eased herself onto a red leather banquette at the Double-D for an early lunch with Tuck. The occasion was one of the "dates," as he liked to call them (much to her annoyance), which always prompted him to rummage through his closet for clothes he hoped would match (today's ensemble of checked shirt and checked tie threatened to give her a migraine). By the look of his razor burn, he'd also shaved more closely than needed, and then stung his jowls with a powerful slap of Old Spice that promised to overwhelm the aroma of food.

"I'm worried about Corin," he said as he bit into a BLT he'd ordered with double bacon and two extra squirts of mayonnaise.

"You're not the only one."

"She phoned me yesterday to say she wasn't coming into work, and she sounded...distracted. Not her usual self."

"That could have been my fault. I signed a court order with Cal Parker and he'd just served it. To get Ark committed."

"To the Severill?"

Jessie nodded.

"You think that's wise?" Tuck asked. "I mean the court order."

"I think it's necessary."

"How did Corin react?"

"She hasn't. Yet. I've been keeping out of her way."

"You didn't see her this morning?"

Jessie shook her head.

"She didn't come in today," Tuck said. "Nor did she phone."

Jessie frowned.

"There's nothing going on, is there?" Tuck asked.

Jessie put down her fork.

"I think I'd better get back," she said.

She arrived at the ranch a few minutes past two o'clock. Most problems in life, she thought, could be left in the hands of God. But sometimes those hands needed guidance. The court order was meant to settle Ark's future once and for all, save the ranch, and put an end to the dangerous ideas that Corin entertained. Jessie still quailed at the thought of the fight the order was sure to provoke, but she was certain it marked the best way forward. Not just for Corin, but for Ark too. Suicide was a crime. One that God would never forgive.

She drove straight to the bunkhouse, found the Plymouth there, parked in its usual spot. But the Dodge had gone. She clumped up the steps of the back porch and rattled the screen door to announce her arrival, then stepped into the kitchen, breathing hard.

"Corin? You there?"

When there was no answer, she strode to the door of the bedroom, rapped once, and swung it open. No sign of Ark. He should have been there, in bed where he always was. She looked around. Nothing out of place. A jug of water, with motes of dust idling on its surface, stood on the bedside table, alongside an empty tumbler and an amber-brown bottle of pills. Behind the pills stood a stick-legged lamp and the framed photograph of Corin and Ark in their petroglyph canyon. And tucked into the frame of the photograph was a plain white envelope.

Jessie marched over and picked it up. The envelope was sealed but not addressed. She hesitated only a moment before she tore it open. There were two sheets of paper inside. She spread one of them out.

My Darling Corin,

We've talked so much in recent weeks that I feel we've said everything it's possible for two people in love to say. But I need to thank you one last time for creating—and sharing—the best days of my life. You made my time here more golden than I ever thought possible. I hate to leave, but I hate, too, to stay and be a burden. Remember, the decision is mine, so there's no need for guilt. I'm going because I am sure that one day we'll be together again. But as I told you last night, don't rush your time here on Earth. Not when we have an eternity in the stars. I know you will bring others great happiness just as you did to me. You have that gift, which you must share in the same generous way you shared it with me.

All my love, always,

Ark

Jessie quickly unfolded the other sheet of paper.

To whom it may concern:

I, Noah (Ark) Stevenson, am of sound mind and judgment, although sadly not of sound body. I have decided to end my current existence as I prefer the opportunities of death to the imprisonment of life. My beloved wife, Corin, has played no part in my decision; indeed, she has rigorously opposed it. I have planned my suicide carefully and intend to carry it out entirely on my own. I have persuaded Corin to take me to a place that is dear to us both, but she has no knowledge of what I plan to do there. I apologize to anyone I have hurt or inconvenienced, but now I am just going outside—and may be some time.

Ark Stevenson

Jessie stood transfixed. She skimmed the notes again; then as if suddenly shocked into life, she fled from the bunkhouse, pausing only to grab the rifle stowed in the rack behind the kitchen door.

CHAPTER FIFTY-FIVE

Corin Dunbar

I let Yiska drive so I could support Ark and keep him warm. We passed Tuck's cabin and snaked through the curves of the wash to stop at the house-sized boulder and pool of water that marked the entrance to our canyon. Yiska carried Ark up and over the bench of rock and nestled him among the sun-warmed boulders. Well over a year had passed since Ark and I had been there, but our canyon had withstood the onslaughts of flashfloods and drought. The sheer rock walls painted in sunset colors towered as high as I remembered, and the pokes of green where plants dared to grow through the desert sands looked as vibrant as ever. The Three Wise Men had shed a few of their branches, but the water-pocket pool where we'd cooled our beers still cupped a puddle from a thundery shower.

I cushioned Ark with the pillows I'd brought and wrapped him again in the blanket. Yiska built a pair of rocky armrests to wedge him better into his seat.

"My very own throne," Ark said. "Better than royalty."

We'd positioned him facing west so he could see the chorus line of petroglyph dancers as well as the rays of his exploding star. I felt in a daze, as if my mind were veiled in mist, but Yiska moved smoothly and with purpose. To the right of Ark's throne, he built a marbled-rock firepit; then using the Barlow knife I kept in the Dodge, he cut tinder-dry stalks from the sagebrush that grew in clumps all around us and bound them into bundles like the switches of a witch's broom. A dusky scent filled the air, bringing back the many times

Ark and I had hiked through the desert, running stems of sagebrush through our hands as we went.

I helped Yiska crisscross the switches inside the firepit, one on top of another, then hunted for a flatish stone that we balanced on stubs of rock to make a table. Beside this crude altar, Yiska placed a canteen of water brought from the truck. He reached into his pocket and pulled out the blue chambray pouch containing the moonflower seeds, untied the bindweed at its neck, and scattered a few of the seeds onto the altar, spreading them out with his hand.

"Move closer together," he told us.

I shuffled sideways to sit by the altar next to Ark, who held himself upright, a rapt observer of the preparations being made in his honor. My heart ached to see the sharp jut of his shoulders poking through his light cotton shirt, and the curves of his cheekbones showing as shadows under a skin that was blanched again to the ghostly pallor of the dead. But his eyes still sparkled with life. Dark and shiny as obsidian, they flicked from Yiska to the firepit to the petroglyphs and then to me. He was like a camera, recording every detail of the scene.

Yiska knelt by the firepit and lit the stems of sagebrush to a fiery crackle that unnerved a desert hare to break cover and dash to the other side of the canyon. He tamed the flames to a smolder so the smoke wisped and coiled like a genie from a bottle, while a canyon bluebird flitted from rock to rock and the sun slid lower in the sky.

"The smoke must cover you both," Yiska said as it shrouded us in a gossamer cloak. "It will draw out bad experiences from the past and purify you both in body and mind. It will also let Ark contact the spirits and assure his immortality."

I reached over and squeezed Ark's hand. His fingers felt as cold as winter. Already a void was opening between us as I sensed him slipping away. A ship leaving harbor.

"I'm ready," he said. "It's time." He seemed calm, but there was a spark of excitement in his voice.

"You must give him the seeds," Yiska told me. "They need to come from someone he loves."

Ark smiled gently as he inhaled the sweet aroma of the sagebrush smoke. I looked up to follow his gaze and saw a pair of raptors circling in the thermals above us.

I let go of his hand to pick up the seeds, and an overwhelming sense of loss came crashing down on me hard as a rock fall.

Ark sensed me weakening.

"Kneel in front of me," he said. "I want your face to be the last image I see, the one I'll carry with me on my journey."

"I can't do it," I said.

He took both my hands in his, looked me in the eyes. "You promised," he said. "And we never break our promises."

I counted out five seeds.

"You must also give him water," Yiska said. "Then after he takes the seeds, we should not talk."

The canyon walls blurred like a heat haze and my hands started to shake. Tears welled in my eyes and suddenly I was wracked by heaving sobs as the full horror of what I was about to do swept over me with the force of a tsunami.

"I can't," I said again, shaking my head and sobbing.

"Please, Corin," Ark said.

I felt the warmth of Yiska's hands on my shoulders.

"Let him go," he said. "You must."

I told myself again that I was doing this for Ark. It was part of my punishment for the role I'd played in the accident. I picked up one of the seeds and held it to his lips. As he leaned forward to take it, I saw hope in his eyes that I knew would be missing from mine. I placed the seed on his tongue, gave him a sip of water. Our eyes locked. There was no hesitation, no doubt, just a grateful acceptance.

He held back a moment longer, then swallowed.

"Another," he said.

I fed him a second seed.

Then a third.

As I picked up the fourth seed, a shot rang out. A rifle shot that boomed and exploded around the bowl of the canyon and resonated off the rocks. It echoed back and fed on itself until it reached a crescendo that filled my mind with uproar and confusion. For a moment, Ark stayed stiffly upright. Then he crumpled over and a trickle of blood seeped from a wound in the side of his head.

I was stunned by the gunshot, so deafened that the world moved in silence around me. Dimly, I saw Jessie stride toward us, her rifle trained on Ark, ready to fire again. She shouted something to Yiska, who had turned to face her, and he backed away, arms raised. I tended to Ark, wiping away the small dribble of blood that oozed from his head. He was still conscious, hit only by a shard of sandstone that Jessie's shot had chipped from the rock behind him.

"Get away from him!" Jessie shouted, loud enough to overcome the roar in my ears. She stomped toward me and used her foot to knock me sideways. "Go on! Move!" she said, and kicked out at me again.

I half rose and staggered back, but she grasped her rifle—stock in one hand, barrel in the other—and bunted me hard like a cop controlling a crowd.

"Leave him be!" she said. "You hear?"

Over her shoulder I saw Yiska drop into a crouch beside Ark. He picked up one of the seeds from the altar. Held it to Ark's lips as I had done.

Ark dipped his head, his tongue flicked out, and he took the seed into his mouth. Yiska fed him another. And another.

Four, five...

Ark turned to look at me as I moved away, drawing Jessie with me.

"Thank you," he said, mouthing the words. "Thank you for everything."

I held him as before, supporting his body and resting his head against my shoulder as he slowly drifted away. I don't know if he dreamed, but at one point he jerked suddenly as if locked in an internal struggle.

"Ark," I said. "It's me."

I don't think he heard. But his hand inched toward me, and I wrapped my arms around him. Felt the poke of his ribs as they rose and fell with each labored breath. I stroked the graying skin of his face and traced the jutting outline of his cheekbones. That seemed to settle him, but his breathing suddenly quickened.

He drew several deep breaths, followed by one so drawn out that it yielded to a quiet sigh of surrender.

I waited for him to breathe in again.

But he never did.

Jessie had Yiska pinned against the canyon wall, holding him at gunpoint until I haltingly explained that he was a friend, not a threat. Then I moved away, huddled by the water-pocket pool as the two of them tended to Ark's body.

They wrapped him in the tree-of-life blanket and carried him to the shelf of rock under the petroglyphs—the chorus line of dancers and Ark's exploding star. They worked in silence, burying him under a mound of rocks that were marbled with orange and green and streaks of silver.

When Yiska placed the final stone, he circled the grave, using a switch of sage to brush the soil clean of footprints.

Jessie said a prayer for Ark and me, but we left no marker. There was no need. Ark wasn't there. He'd already moved on.

I knew I couldn't go back to the bunkhouse, so I asked Yiska to drive us to Tuck's cabin, the three of us wedged into the front seat of Jessie's pickup, her arm around me, my head slumped against her shoulder. I was certain I'd never sleep that night, but at some point I must have collapsed, as the next I knew it was morning and I was lying in Tuck's bed, the familiar smell of coffee fooling me into thinking it was just another day.

I raised myself up, but hit by a sudden panic, I sank back empty and drained. I knew Ark had thought he was a burden, but I had to believe he'd moved on for himself and not for me. I drew comfort from the last look on his face and that final "thank you" he'd mouthed in farewell.

CHAPTER FIFTY-SIX

Dottie DeVine
(née Dorothy Wittering)

Dottie had spent a sleepless night lying in her bunk of her single-wide trailer. When she closed her eyes, it was only to spool through her mind the fantasy image of her home on Mulholland Drive with its circular drive and sea-blue lap pool. A vision so real, she could smell the jasmine and eucalyptus of the Hollywood Hills and taste the champagne bubbles of success as they fizzed and popped on her tongue. It was a dream that now was within reach. But also one in peril.

A clause in her new contract—the morals clause, the "keep your panties on" clause, it was called—kept running through her head, read so often, she could recite it by heart. "If the conduct of the undersigned is in any way detrimental to the Studio and/or undermines and/or devalues the integrity and/or the performance of the assigned character and/or the production... then this agreement will be terminated forthwith..."

...terminated forthwith...

She'd worked too hard, waited too long. She could not let her chance slip away. There was nothing in Paradox to keep her, especially after the rape. But if it ever came out that she'd willingly had sex with two men (while a third looked on), then the morals clause would kick in and her new contract would be...

...terminated forthwith...

She opened her eyes to pick out the dark silhouette of her suitcase, packed and ready to go, and the new dress she'd bought at the Fashion First Emporium on Main. It hung from a hook on the back of her door.

Something had died in her, because of the rape. But dammit, she thought, the men who'd killed Dorothy Wittering had not laid a finger on Dottie DeVine.

CHAPTER FIFTY-SEVEN

Corin Dunbar

That same morning, I was sitting head in hands on the rickety bench in front of Tuck's cabin, memories of my life with Ark running amok in my head. The door beside me opened and Jessie came out.

"Here. Drink this," she said, and handed me a steaming mug of coffee.

She sat next to me in the sunshine and sipped a coffee of her own. Two mule deer and a fawn browsed a few feet away on the rubber rabbit brush that had sprouted around the cabin. It was quiet enough to hear them munching. Not even as much as a whisper of breeze.

"I'm sorry, Corin," Jessie said simply. "For everything."

I leaned my body against her, and she put an arm around my shoulders.

"The commitment order," she said, "was meant to *save* Ark's life, not to end it. I'd never have signed it if I'd thought it would push things so far."

"It wasn't the order," I told her. "It was Ark. And me." I straightened up again and the two mule deer jerked their heads in alarm. Their ears swiveled toward us before they both stotted away.

"Did you really intend to shoot him?" I asked.

"Oh, yes. I did my best. But my shooting eye's not what it used to be. And there was a lot of smoke. From that fire you lit."

She took another sip of her coffee.

"I couldn't let you kill him," she said. "You'd have gone to Hell. For an eternity."

"But if *you'd* killed him, you'd have gone to Hell in my place."

"Maybe," she said.

"No 'maybe' if it's what you believe."

"Well, God might have been busy elsewhere. He does have other people to keep an eye on, you know."

"But that's not what you think, is it?"

"Killing Ark would have made no difference. Not in my case. I'm headed that way already, so one more black mark wouldn't have tipped the scales." She paused, but I could see she wasn't finished. I waited for her to continue.

"There's something I've long wanted to tell you," she said, "but I never found the right moment. And then...well, too many years went by and it became harder and harder, and I guess I got scared. Afraid of what you would think."

"What are you saying, Jessie?"

She glanced sideways at me, tried out a smile, then drew in two quick breaths.

"I was never one to tiptoe round the mountain, was I? So I guess I'll come right out and say it."

"Say what, Jessie? You're beginning to frighten me."

"It's about Gene," she said, and paused again, staring off into the distance.

"What about him?"

"He's not your father."

"Not my father? What are you talking about?"

"He's not your father," she said again. "And Grace wasn't your mother."

I shook my head, not understanding.

"Times were different back then, Corin."

"Back when?"

"You remember," she said, after another long pause, "that first time I took you into your canyon? I showed you some initials. A.K.W. That's Aiden Kimball Winward. A bit of a mouthful, but he came here to make movies. Soon after Pearl Harbor. Not the Westerns that

Hollywood churns out now. But wartime movies that spelled out reasons for fighting. Propaganda, designed to show young men—and some women too, I suppose—why they had to sign up and go to war for Uncle Sam. Clark Gable appeared in one. Jimmy Stewart too. And so did John Wayne. Aiden was a director who worked for the Office of War Information. We went to that canyon a lot. Just the two of us. It was *our* special place too, Corin. Aiden Kimball Winward," she said, as if making an introduction. "He was your father."

It took me a moment to think this through.

"Are you telling me you're my *mother*?"

She nodded once.

"You were conceived there. In that canyon. Right where Aiden carved his initials."

I sank back against the cabin wall.

"It wasn't possible," she said, "for a woman to have a child outside wedlock. Not in those days. I'd have been called a slut, a tramp, a whore. I could've put up with that, taken the sticks and stones hurled my way—maybe thought I deserved them. But the stigma didn't just fall on the mother. It fell on the child too. The *innocent* child.

"You'd have been a pariah, Corin, same as me. Labeled a bastard. People—good people, Christian people, normal everyday people— would have shunned you, talked about you behind your back. They'd have stopped their kids from playing with you, their sons from marrying you, so it'd have been a burden you'd have carried all your life. People thinking you were inferior until you began to think it too. I couldn't let that happen."

She arched her back and craned up at the sky.

"When Aiden left to enlist, I was pregnant with you. I didn't know and nor did he. He was a fine young man, Corin. He'd have made a stir in Hollywood, if he'd been given his chance. But he was killed fighting the Japanese over some island—Manus Island, it was called—in a battle no one remembers today. But I remember him. I remember his vitality, his beauty. I thought I loved him, and maybe I did. But we were both so young, it could have been a physical attraction I was meant to deny. Memories play such tricks," she said, "but he's stayed perfect for me all these years, the way people do when they die young. You have his eyes, Corin. And the same thick, dark, wavy hair."

She reached for my hand as tears welled in her eyes.

"My parents—your grandparents—sent me away and insisted I put you up for adoption. They were ashamed of me. I thought of running away, but then Gene and Grace found they couldn't have children, so I agreed to let them have you. I didn't want to, but everyone said it was for the best, that Gene and Grace *deserved* a child, as if somehow I did not. Handing you over—a warm scrap of a thing, pink-faced and bawling—that was the hardest thing I've ever done. You were wrapped in a blanket with a rabbit on it I'd embroidered myself."

She wiped a sleeve across her cheeks.

"I told myself you were still in the family, that I'd be able to watch you grow. But when Grace died, I saw my chance. Gene wanted to keep you—*insisted* he keep you—but you'd never been formally adopted; it was just an arrangement we'd come to. I threatened to take him to court, to fight him all the way. Which is when he gave in and agreed to let you go. It broke his heart. Yours too, for a while. But I knew what I'd lost, and I wanted you back."

She looked down at the ground, scuffed the dirt with her foot.

"I tried to tell you—once when you asked if I would adopt you, and again at your wedding. But that was *your* day, not mine, and I didn't want to spoil it. Weddings are about hope for the future, not mistakes from the past, so in the end I said nothing. Gene wanted to write, but I told him if he did, I'd burn his letters. So you see, Corin, I'm already a sinner, several times over. It doesn't matter what I do now. I'm already headed for Hell."

It was too much for me to take in. My father wasn't my father, but a set of initials carved into a rock; and my mother wasn't my mother, but the woman I'd always been told was my aunt. With Ark gone and now this, my world had spun off its axis, the building blocks toppled, my story erased like chalk from a blackboard. For one giddy moment,

I felt I might disappear, as if there was no real "me," only a flickering illusion of the kind Hollywood loved to create.

I left Jessie on the bench and circled behind the cabin, weaving a mindless route, then came back to Earth when I heard the throaty grind of an engine. Yiska had hiked into the canyon to fetch the Dodge, and now it bounced and jolted toward me. He pulled to a stop, but before he could kill the engine, I shooed him into the passenger seat and climbed in behind the wheel.

"We need to leave," I said.

CHAPTER FIFTY-EIGHT

Cal Parker

Cal Parker pulled his cruiser into the lot behind the Sheriff's office and settled behind his desk. He was glad to have the place to himself. Dale was out campaigning, Wayne Coleman was manning the roadblock, Luke Sims was off duty, and Erma Belnap was visiting her aged mother, who'd slipped on her porch and snapped a hip. Cal rinsed out his NRA mug and made himself a coffee, added cream and two heaped sugars, and then lit a Lucky Strike. As he blew out a careful smoke ring, the iron-barred door at the front of the office grated open and Dottie pushed her way in weighed down by her new suitcase.

"Sheriff's out," Cal told her.

"Not him I came to see," she said, and set her suitcase down. "It's you I want to talk to."

Cal waited as she rolled Wayne's chair up to his desk and sat facing him. Not the wannabe movie star today, he thought. But nor was she the tearful victim he'd seen last night. This Dottie was different again. Ramrod straight, dry-eyed and controlled, with a determination he could see in the set of her jaw.

"Erma coming in?" she asked.

He shook his head. "Just me on my lonesome."

He attempted a smile.

It wasn't returned.

"I'm sorry about what happened," he said.

She ignored his apology, took a moment to smooth the front of her skirt. She was dressed today in sober gray, her feet slipped into a pair of old-maid shoes. Her knees were pressed chastely together, so Cal wondered if she'd taken Dale's advice—or did an attack like the one she'd suffered do this to a woman?

"What's on your mind?" he said.

She fiddled again with her skirt and yanked down the hem.

"Did you write up a report? About what happened?"

Cal nodded. "Dale did."

"What did it say?"

"Just what you told us."

"That I was raped?"

Cal nodded again and tapped ash into a saucer on his desk.

"And what about the Preston brothers? And that Marv Pratt? You write up reports for them?"

"Dale took their statements too."

"And what did *they* say?"

"What they told us. That they had...that they had sex with you, Dottie. Well, the two of them did, anyways."

"So it wasn't rape?"

"Not in their telling."

"But that's not true."

"I'm not saying it is, Dottie. I'm willing to believe you."

"But not enough to do anything about it."

Cal drew on his cigarette. "It's what the witnesses said, Dottie. I can't mess with that. And nor can the sheriff."

"So case closed." Her voice flat.

"That's up to Dale. But he does say the investigation's pretty much over, if that's what you're driving at. Everyone agrees what happened. It's just a question of were you willing."

"What happens to the reports now?" she asked.

"They get filed."

"Here?"

Cal pointed with his thumb over his shoulder. "In Dale's office. Erma's got a system."

"And they stay there?"

"Until we ship them to City Hall. They've got storage there that we don't have."

"And who can see them at City Hall?"

"Well, with the investigation done, they get filed—"

"But who can *see* them?" Dottie pressed. "Secretaries? Clerks? Lawyers?"

"Well, sure—"

"Journalists too?"

"I guess. Anyone, really. If they know where to look. Or what to ask for."

Dottie fell silent. She'd been sitting bolt upright, but now she stood, moved to the side of Cal's desk, and hooked a foot around the metal can he kept there for trash. She scraped it toward her, dumped the contents onto the floor, then banged it upright on to his desk.

"Now, Dottie—"

"Burn them," she said.

"I can't do that, Dottie. You know that."

She rattled the can at him. "Put the reports in here and burn them."

"Dale would skin me alive."

"Burn them, Cal. I don't want anyone seeing them. Not now. Not ever."

"Dottie, I'm sorry what happened to you, really I am. But there's nothing I can do."

She stared levelly at him, long enough to make him squirm.

"This Injun you're looking for," she said. "Suppose I was to tell you where he's been hiding and where you're likely to find him."

Cal hustled out to his cruiser, strapping on his gun belt as he went. He flipped on his siren long enough to cut a swathe through the congestion of traffic and headed out of town, taking the cutoff through Eldorado, deserted now with filming wrapped for the day. His mind churned. From what Dottie had said, the Injun had been hiding out at

Jessie's ranch with Corin's full knowledge. The clues had been there if only he'd put them together. But they didn't answer the question: *why*? Why was Corin sheltering him?

Something to do with "helping Ark," Dottie had said. Cal didn't know what that meant, but a scramble of thoughts were fumbling for traction in his brain. When Jessie had cosigned the commitment order, she'd hinted that Ark might be suicidal—an attitude Cal could well understand. He'd have swallowed his gun and pulled the trigger if he'd been busted up as badly as Ark. She'd hinted, too, that Corin might be planning to give him a hand.

Cal wasn't sure he believed everything Dottie had told him, although to seal the deal he *had* burned the reports. But if the Injun really was at the ranch, Cal planned to bring him in. To show Dale he could get the job done.

He flipped his siren on again to force a cattle truck out of the way, but as he sped past, his mind lingered on something else Dottie had said. He'd never understood why she hadn't been able to snag a single part in a movie, but had always assumed—with her dyed hair and pumped-up boobs—that she'd mastered the art of the casting couch.

But before the rape, Dottie had told him, she had been a virgin. Or as she had delicately put it: she had still been intact.

CHAPTER FIFTY-NINE

Corin Dunbar

I pulled the Dodge to a stop next to the Plymouth and told Yiska to stay put, then ran into the bunkhouse for a hunk of bread and a canteen of water that I thrust into his hands like a parting gift.

We needed to switch cars.

"Get in the back," I said, tipping forward the front seat of the Plymouth. "On the floor. I'll cover you with a rug."

As Yiska bent to fold himself in, we both heard the soft scrunch of tires as a police cruiser nosed around the side of the bunkhouse. It slid to a halt, Cal at the wheel.

I didn't move. Yiska did, but only to straighten up, the bread and water clutched in his hands.

Cal eased open his driver's door and stepped a cautious boot out, gun drawn. He moved toward us like a cat stalking prey, then angled off to one side so he could draw a better line on Yiska.

He tilted his head at the bunkhouse but kept his attention locked on us.

"He still in there?"

"Ark?" I shook my head.

"Where is he?"

"In the Severill. Isn't that what you wanted?"

"And Jessie?"

"Not here either."

Cal licked his lips. "I'm taking the Injun in," he said, his arms out straight, sighting along the barrel of his gun.

I moved to stand between them.

"Stay out of this, Corin."

"I'm taking him to the Nation," I said. "It's where he was headed all those years ago."

"The hell you are."

"It's where he belongs."

"I'm warning you, Corin. Back away!"

"Get in the car," I told Yiska, and gave him a one-handed push to set him in motion.

Cal stayed in his shooting stance as I took slow, deliberate steps toward him. His knees were flexed, his gun in both hands, but now pointed at me.

"You could have kept him out of prison," I said. "You could have spoken up. Said he wasn't driving the car that night."

"You're in my line of fire."

He crabbed sideways so he had sight of Yiska again, but I matched him move for move. A couple of dancers.

"You could have said something, Cal. You could have said he was locked in your cells that night. You *saw* him there."

"I'm not fooling here, Corin."

"He was innocent, Cal. And you knew it."

"He killed a man."

"In self-defense. In prison. Where he didn't belong. Where he wouldn't have been if you had only spoken up."

"He's a killer on the run," Cal said, with an upward flick of his gun at Yiska. "That's all I know. And I'm taking him in. Now move outta my way before you get yourself hurt."

"What are you going to do, Cal?" I took several more careful steps toward him until his gun was all but nudging my ribs. "You going to shoot me? You going to shoot us both?"

"I got a job to do, Corin, and I'm gonna do it. So move. Now!"

Dark patches of sweat sopped the armpits of his shirt, and a sourness I could smell rose off him.

"Get in the car," I told Yiska again, still looking at Cal, but speaking over my shoulder.

This time, he obeyed. I heard the clump of the front seat as it snapped back into position, then the slam of a car door.

"You're breaking the law, Corin," Cal said. "Like it seems you been doing a lot of these past few days. Could get yourself into a heap of trouble over that. And now you want to do this?"

"I'm taking him home. Where he deserves to be."

Cal shook his head. "I can't let that happen."

"Then you do what you have to do," I said, and turned my back on him, feeling the twitch of a target between my shoulder blades as I stepped toward the Plymouth.

"I'll shoot out the tires," Cal said. "Put a hole in the Injun too. Right between the eyes."

I whirled round to face him. "You should have *said* something," I yelled. "You should have spoken *out*!"

"I didn't have a choice."

"Of *course* you had a choice. There's always a choice."

"It's not that simple."

"It *is* that simple. You couldn't stand up to your daddy. That's the naked truth of it."

"I was eighteen. New on the job."

"Eighteen," I said, and moved back toward him. "Old enough to be a *man*."

Our eyes locked and his gun wavered. I turned again and stalked to the Plymouth, climbed in, and started the engine, then swung the car in a tight circle. As I headed down the track and onto the road to Paradox, I caught sight of him in the rearview mirror, his gun gripped in both hands, but now pointed down by his feet.

"Damn you," I heard him yell. "Damn you, Corin! DAMN YOU ALL TO HELL!"

And I saw the kick and dance of dust as he fired a volley into the ground.

❖

More than the usual flow of pickups and trucks was heading into town, a sure sign of early morning filming at the head of the valley. But I still wasn't prepared for the stop-start pace at which we inched forward. I soon saw the reason. A state trooper who'd parked his cruiser by the side of the road; and another who'd pulled his vehicle onto the shoulder a hundred yards farther on. State troopers didn't belong in the Waterpocket Valley. Or anywhere else in Blade County. This was Sheriff Dale Parker's turf, and he didn't take kindly to outsiders horning in.

"Troopers on the road," I warned Yiska, still on the floor in the back of the car. "Stay down and keep out of sight."

I craned my neck to see what else was holding us up. There was no sign of Wayne Coleman at the roadblock. Nor of Luke Sims. Only a clutch of troopers and a red-and-white striped barrier that hadn't been there before. It stretched across the full width of the road. As each vehicle approached the barrier, it was swarmed by troopers who crawled like ants over every inch. Doors were opened, trunks flipped, backseats searched. No way I'd be waved through as I'd been hoping. The troopers even snooped under the bellies of the larger transports as if they expected Yiska to somehow be clinging there. My instinct was to turn tail and flee, but a three-point turn now was sure to attract the wrong kind of attention, and anyway I was boxed in by a flatbed in front and a high-sided grip truck behind.

The minutes ticked by. A trickle of sweat ran down my back. I leaned forward to unstick my blouse from the seat and saw, in my off-side wing mirror, a sheriff's cruiser closing in fast from behind. No siren, but the cherry light on its roof spun around and flashed. It veered onto the soft shoulder to undertake the long line of stalled traffic and sent up a fountain of dust before it skidded to a stop by the red-and-white barrier. Cal climbed out, adjusted his gun belt, and spoke to one of the troopers, who pointed in my direction.

I cowered in my seat as the trooper started toward me, a meaty guy with heavy strides that scuffed up eddies of dust. He wore a shiny peaked cap and a poker face, and his mouth was set in a straight line. His eyes, shielded by dark glasses, looked black as sockets in a skull.

The cool of his shadow blocked out the sun as he bent down to rap a knuckle on my half-open window.

I wound it down two more turns.

He touched his hat. "Ma'am," he said.

I looked up at him.

"Deputy there says you need to get into town in a hurry. Got a sick husband you need to visit."

I nodded dumbly.

He peered over my shoulder, saw the shovel and coil of rope I kept in the back, then turned again to me. He did not look under the blanket that covered Yiska on the floor.

He tipped his hat a second time.

"Why don't you pull out of line and swing on through?" he said. "We got blocks on all the roads—right across the county—so you'll be stopped again for sure. But at least we can get you on your way from here."

He stepped back and signaled to a trooper by the barrier. I steered the Plymouth to the far side of the road, then drove toward the barrier as it was slowly raised. I did not look at Cal, but as I swept past I caught a glimpse of him, stony-faced beside his cruiser.

Just shy of Balanced Rock, I pulled off the road to let Yiska clamber into the seat beside me. He took a long pull of water from the canteen I'd given him.

"You heard?" I said.

He nodded and took a bite of bread.

"We'll never get through," I told him. "Not all the way to the Nation. Not if they've got other barriers up."

"I'll take my chances on foot."

I looked around at the barren flats. A few clumps of saltbush that wouldn't give cover to a desert hare.

We sat in silence a moment. A silence that was ripped apart by the piercing screech of an air whistle.

"Sit tight," I said, and slipped the Plymouth into gear. "Could be there's another way."

❖

I raised a storm of dust as I raced the Plymouth along the road to Eldorado. The whistle sounded again, louder this time. And closer. I told Yiska the potash train could take him as far as Blanding, a long way from the Nation, but at least he'd be outside the phalanx of troopers who ringed Paradox like a noose.

I pressed my foot hard to the floor and tested every nut and bolt of the Plymouth until I was sure it would fly apart. When the ragged roofline of Eldorado showed against the horizon, I slewed the car off the tamped dirt of the road and bounced across the open desert, swerving only to avoid the cacti and stubs of brittle bush that poked up out of the soil. The steering wheel danced and jiggled in my hands, and loose grit drifted the Plymouth into a skid. I figured I'd rejoin the cutoff and drive down Front to the railroad tracks at the end to intercept the train there.

But Front was blocked by two low loaders with cameras mounted on their cargo beds. They were drawn up nose-to-tail, both with entrails of wires that snaked over the ground and onto the boardwalks either side of the street. I slithered to a stop and yelled to Yiska that he'd have to run, I couldn't take him further. There was only time to exchange the lightest of touches and then he was gone.

He'd reached the batwing doors of the Silver Dollar when a movement caught my eye. A police cruiser had pulled up by the railroad tracks, "Blade County Sheriff" emblazoned on its side. Its door opened and Dale Parker climbed out. He lowered the brim of his hat against the sun and leaned back against the hood. I wasn't the only one to think the train might offer a way of escape. Yiska must have seen him too, for he flattened himself against the wall of the saloon, hidden in shadow.

I slid out of the Plymouth and felt a tremor, strong as an aftershock, under my feet. The potash train thundered into view, its engine puffing billows of steam. Its wheels squeaked, pistons churned, a bell clanged, and once again its whistle screeched. It slowed as it came into town, bunching up its long line of hopper cars, and rumbled past Dale and his cruiser, shaking the earth around him. It clanked and clattered across Front, its whistle sounding again and its steel wheels grinding along the rails until it made them hum. Then it began to gather speed as it shuddered out of town and headed again for the desert. I watched it grow smaller as it disappeared into the distance, trailing cotton balls of steam. Then once again there was silence.

I waited for Yiska to make his way back to the Plymouth. Dale couldn't see him, not with the sun full in his face and Yiska still in shadow.

Yiska pushed himself off his wall. Took a deliberate step to the edge of the boardwalk and into the light.

Dale tensed and straightened. His right hand twitched and moved to his gun, and I knew at once what Yiska planned. The moonflower seeds he'd gathered in the desert had been for him. He was just like Ark, trapped in a prison that was not of his making, facing a life sentence he didn't deserve. And now he was taking the same way out. Suicide.

By cop.

Dale turned toward Yiska and squinted into the sun. His gun hand twitched again. But as Yiska took a second step farther into the light, the batwing doors of the saloon blew open behind him and out stepped an Indian. A Navajo.

Dale dropped into a crouch as another Indian appeared. And another and another. Until there were a dozen or so, maybe as many as twenty, swarming out of the saloon and over the boardwalk, spilling into the street.

The Butch Cassidy audition Tuck had told me about. To replace the tracker who'd broken his leg.

Yiska didn't move as the other Indians flowed past him like a river coursing around a rock. They pushed and shoved and jostled against him, and still he didn't budge. But then one of them elbowed him into life and he moved off with the others, blending in. He crossed the street with them and climbed on board a battered school bus that had been parked the other side of the street. Through its smeared and dusty windows I saw him pass along the aisle and sink into a seat near the back.

Two security guards followed the Navajos out of the Silver Dollar and marched in tandem to a production car parked next to the bus. They climbed in, and as the bus choked and stuttered into life, they pulled their car in front of it. Dale eased up and his hand moved away from his holster. He slid into his cruiser and swung into position at the rear of the bus. A double escort—one at the front and one at the back—to get a busload of Indians past the cordon of troopers.

As the bus bounced over the railroad tracks and turned onto the road for Paradox, a dusty sticker plastered on its rear bumper caught my eye. Fringed in yellow with a feather headdress adorning an Indian chief's profile, it read, NAVAJO NATION OR BUST.

CHAPTER SIXTY

L ate the next day—our second wedding anniversary—I slid the tarp off Ark's Olds 88 and with Felipe's help coaxed its engine from its first coughs of refusal into a choking roar. The car hadn't been driven for more than a year, but I'd never had the heart to sell it as that would have been to discard part of Ark.

I drove to the top of Dolores Mesa, arriving in time to catch the wildfire of a crimson sunset scorching the sky. I parked and walked to the spot where Ark had set up his telescope the night of his star party and placed my feet where I figured his had been, just as he had mirrored his hand to the ancient petroglyphs on our canyon wall. I settled onto a bench of sandstone and watched the dying sun dull the rocky outcrops around me from red to gray to coal-black silhouettes.

I waited as Saturn appeared, then watched Mars rise. By then I could easily pick out Polaris by following the pointer stars of the Big Dipper, just as Ark had shown me. I could also see Vega and the two nearby stars Ark had said were ours. I waited for more stars to show— the celestial lamplighter making his rounds, as Ark had once said— and when the sky was aglow with the energy of all five thousand, I built a small rock altar like the one we'd made for Ark in our canyon. I lit a lily-scented candle, carefully sheltering it from the wind so its flame grew and for a time enlivened the dark.

I stayed on the mesa all night—long after the flame had sputtered and flickered and the breeze had carried away the last of its scent. I hugged my knees against the cold and watched the sky rotate above me until a sliver of light threaded across the eastern horizon and I felt the stirrings of a new day.

The following year, on July 20, I sat with Jessie in the kitchen of the ranch house. I'd moved back into my old room with the plumped-up pillows and the red-and-green quilt that had been hand-stitched by one of Jessie's friends from church. The pinewood floor still shone just as it had when I first arrived in Paradox, and the two square windows were hung with the same cream drapes patterned with flowers. Segos.

The Utah state flower.

Jessie and I had been up since dawn, because the fifteen head of cattle we'd shipped in that day needed to be watered, fed, and settled in to their pens. Also, I was still working at the *Gazette*. I could have quit as we now had enough money coming in, but Tuck had promoted me to features writer and I was keen to stay on and see how far my talents could take me.

At eight o'clock that evening, we pulled up our chairs at the kitchen table with a pot of Earl Grey between us and a plate of cookies Jessie had taken hot from the oven. Her new TV was against the wall, resting on a butcher block her father—my grandfather—had made.

We waited for the set to warm up, keen to see the culmination of the dream Kennedy had kindled near the start of the decade, now being beamed live into millions of households around the world.

A shaky black-and-white image showed a tiny part of a scarred surface. Then came a shape the commentator said was a footpad of the lander. After what seemed an age, the clumpy boot of a space-suit loomed into the frame, and at four minutes before nine o'clock Paradox time, Neil Armstrong's voice, reedy with static, announced that he was taking one small step for a man, but a giant leap for mankind.

The first man on the moon.

Except Ark Stevenson had beaten him to it.

Or so I like to believe.

PLEASE POST A REVIEW

If you enjoyed this book, and we hope you did, can we ask you to post a review on Amazon and/or Goodreads? Your opinion matters, and a star-rating with a few words of recommendation would help other readers – and us – by making the book stand out from the crowd. Thank you.

Richard Starks
Miriam Murcutt

ACKNOWLEDGMENTS

We would like to thank the people who shared their memories of working with the Hollywood Studios in Utah. Their participation greatly contributed to the story we wanted to write. Among them: Karl Tangren, rancher, cowboy, and horse wrangler, who worked for the Studios as a driver and extra and managed the horses rented by the Studios when they were filming in Moab; the late John Hagner, founder of the Hollywood Stuntman Hall of Fame, former stuntman and double for Hollywood stars; Lin Ottinger, owner of the Dinosaur Man and Rock Shop in Moab, who worked as an extra, driver, and location scout.

Thanks, too, to the men and women who fascinated us with tales of the lives they lived on Utah cattle ranches: Shirley Stewart, Mary Engleman, and Inalyn Young Meador, all members of the Daughters of Utah Pioneers, Moab; Cricket Green, rancher and owner of Land and Water Searches; and the late "D.L." David Lester Taylor and his wife, Colleen, former ranchers from Castle Valley, Utah.

Thanks to Robert Kirby, author, columnist, and historian for Utah Law Enforcement Memorial, for providing historical data and photographs of Utah police officers and vehicles of the 1960s; and to John Timothy Halter of the 1949–1953 Ford Mercury Association, Columbus, Ohio, for the much-needed specifications on the vehicles used as police patrol cars in the 1950s and 1960s.

We'd also like to acknowledge as a source the excellent book *When Hollywood Came to Town—The History of Moviemaking in Utah* by James D'Arc, former curator of the BYU Motion Picture Archive, the BYU Film Music Archive, and of the Arts and Communications Archive of the L. Tom Perry Special Collections at Brigham Young University. We also drew on the paper "Native American Demographic and Tribal Survival into the Twenty-first Century" by Russell Thornton; and the book *Code Talker* by Chester Nez.

For access to its oral history archives (and leads to other historical resources), we are indebted to The American West Center, University of Utah, Salt Lake City. We'd also like to thank The Moab Film and Western Heritage Museum, Red Cliffs Ranch (formerly White's Ranch), Moab, for its informative exhibition on the history of filmmaking in the area. And we much appreciated the time taken by Bega Metzner, director of the Moab to Monument Valley Film Commission, to give us an overview of filming around Moab now and in decades past.

Finally, we would like to thank Chris Fortunato (our former literary agent, now retired) for his helpful assessment of an early draft manuscript, as well as Editor Dana Isaacson, whose astute but gently delivered critique of a later draft resulted in a much more compelling and (we hope) readable book.

Richard Starks
Miriam Murcutt

ABOUT THE AUTHORS

R ICHARD STARKS is an award-winning journalist, former investigative reporter, editor and publisher, and now a full-time author. He has written nine other books, both fiction and non-fiction, in genres that include crime, horror, travel, true-life adventure and economics. He has also written for business and consumer magazines as well as for television. His books have been published in six languages. Born in England, he now lives in Boulder, Colorado, and is an avid traveler to the more remote regions of the world, as well as a frequent mountain hiker and runner.

M IRIAM MURCUTT is a former journalist and editor turned marketing executive with wide experience in the publishing industry. She has an MA in English Literature and now works full-time as a writer. She has researched and written four other books, all narrative non-fiction, which have been published in seven countries. Born in England, she lives in Boulder, Colorado, where she is a student of Spanish and a volunteer interviewer for a Carnegie Library oral history archive.

Both authors are long-standing members of the Authors Guild. You can visit them at www.starksmurcutt.com

AUTHOR CONTACTS
email: starksmurcutt@msn.com
website: www.starksmurcutt.com
facebook.com/@starksmurcutt
twitter.com/@StarksMurcutt

The authors love to talk to book clubs and are happy to draft discussion questions for any that would like to schedule a Skype, Zoom, or Face-Time meeting. Please email your interest to starksmurcutt@msn.com.

Made in the USA
Las Vegas, NV
25 March 2024

87737766R00184